CAN

Susan Morbach rec... tape. It was the coa... minded her of porno... college once, horribly lit, grainy, so coarse, so ugly, so unreal.

It was real for her now. Her daughter Kimberly. On screen. The gun in her hand. The falling bodies. The silence of it all. Like someone dying in outer space. It couldn't be real.

But it was very real for Susan Morbach, a mother seeing her nightmare come true . . . for Patrick Paige, a cop more involved with this case than a pro should be . . . and for Kimberly, the star of a video that gave only a hint of her X-rated role and was only a preview of unspeakable things to come. . . .

BACKFIRE

ERIC SAUTER

BACKFIRE

AN ONYX BOOK

ONYX
Published by the Penguin Group
Penguin Books USA Inc., 375 Hudson Street,
New York, New York 10014, U.S.A.
Penguin Books Ltd, 27 Wrights Lane,
London W8 5TZ, England
Penguin Books Australia Ltd, Ringwood,
Victoria, Australia
Penguin Books Canada Ltd, 10 Alcorn Avenue,
Toronto, Ontario, Canada M4V 3B2
Penguin Books (N.Z.) Ltd, 182–190 Wairau Road,
Auckland 10, New Zealand

Penguin Books Ltd, Registered Offices:
Harmondsworth, Middlesex, England

Published by Onyx, an imprint of Dutton Signet, a division of Penguin
Books USA Inc. Previously published in a Dutton edition.

First Onyx Printing, November, 1993
10 9 8 7 6 5 4 3 2 1

 REGISTERED TRADEMARK—MARCA REGISTRADA

Printed in the United States of America

PUBLISHER'S NOTE
This is a work of fiction. Names, characters, places, and incidents either are the
product of the author's imagination or are used fictitiously, and any resemblance to
actual persons, living or dead, events, or locales is entirely coincidental.

For Aaron, who just arrived.

AUTHOR'S NOTE

I want to thank John O'Riordan for his help in portraying certain police procedures. If it's right, he's responsible; if it's wrong, I am. Various other aspects of the city including geography, streets and landmarks, have been altered to suit the story.

1

They buried Tom Ferris in the rain.

Patrick Paige looked down at the mourners from the hillside as they stood around the grave, uncomfortable in the chilly downpour. Most held umbrellas, holding back the rain as they clustered around three sides of the ceremonial tent. At the outer edge of the crowd, he saw the grim blue mass of police uniforms; to one side, the honor guard wearing white gloves, hats covered in plastic rain bonnets, rifles held at rest. Beneath the overcast skies, their brass buttons looked as dull as sand. Only their rifles, catching the wet glimmer of the rain, seemed to shine.

Next came friends and relatives, huddled together beneath the tent, a somber mass of blacks and grays. The green tarp, heavy with rain, sagged under the weight and sent streams of water splashing down on the backs of the mourners standing just outside.

The mayor did not attend. He was busy fighting the budget, or so he said. The deputy mayor was there, plus a handful of local politicians, city council members, a state representative or two, looking just as uncomfortable as the rest of them.

At the center of it all, Paige could see the flag-draped coffin, and the hands of the priest as they moved above it; the priest was the only person, at least in Paige's mind, who did not seem out of place. Tom didn't believe, but he'd have wanted the priest there just the same. He would have thought of it as covering his bets.

Paige wondered what Tom's girlfriend thought of it all.

He saw her standing next to the priest, wearing a gray suit, her shoulders still hunched up against the rain even under the tent. She glanced in his direction, a slow somnambulant turn, as if she'd heard a distant sound and was merely curious. He realized she wasn't looking at him, but at something just beyond the edge of the crowd.

A yellow backhoe, mud-splattered, the driver smoking a cigarette, waiting to get out of the rain. That was how they did it these days, Paige thought. Nobody used shovels anymore except to clean up around the edges. How could he have forgotten that?

The rain slackened, the honor guard raised their rifles into the air, and the noise, like a sudden crack of thunder, close and dangerous, drifted away into the mist. From below the cemetery—a wide wedge of rock and trees that sloped to a promontory overlooking the River Drive—Paige heard the blast of a car horn.

The sound of the horn seemed to startle the mourners into movement. They hurried away in clumps, making their way through the field of stones, leaving Marion alone with her grief. She held the flag, folded into a thick neat triangle, in her hands. He'd forgotten about the flag, too. When a cop died, they always gave the widow the flag. It seemed shameful to him somehow, embarrassing, like winning a door prize that you didn't really want.

The sky opened up again. Paige waited until most of

the mourners were in their cars and pulling out, headlights shimmering through the heavy rain as they drove away. Then he walked down to say good-bye.

Marion spoke to him, quietly and without surprise, as he entered the sanctuary of the tent.

"They told me you were leaving the force," she said. "You know what I think about that, don't you?"

"No," Paige said. He stood next to her but kept his eyes on the large silver-white coffin. Up close, it looked immense, almost grotesque, as if someone had made a mistake somewhere and sent the wrong size. He tried to remember his wife's coffin and it all came back to him quickly. Hers was exactly the same size. It seemed to swallow her up.

He raised his eyes and saw that Marion was watching him.

"I think it's a good way to kill yourself, Pat," she said.

Paige shook his head to say no, he hadn't done anything like that. Hadn't left the force. Hadn't thought about killing himself. Hadn't done much of anything. Ate. Slept. Watched the play-offs on television. Let the telephone ring and ring and ring. Sorry. Nobody home.

"I've been home for a few days," he said. "That's all."

"You didn't come to see him."

"Marion," he said gently.

"I know, I know," she answered him. "You still didn't come to see him. Maybe that was a good thing. Everybody else came. People I didn't even know *knew* Tommy, they came." She stopped, caught her breath. "You're the only one who didn't come, Pat."

"Would it have made a difference?" he asked.

She turned on him now, whirled around at the end of the grave, one foot sliding awkwardly on the muddy ground, but she stayed upright, the stiffness of her shoulders acting as ballast, holding her to her true course.

"Maybe," she said. One hand fell away from the flag and she pointed at the coffin. "I want you to tell me why he had to die, Pat," she said. "That might help. Can you do that? Can you tell me why he had to die like *that?*"

He had no answer for her. He had asked the same question when his wife was killed and hadn't found one either. People died. In ways you could never imagine. That was the hardest part, the one fact you had to learn to live with, knowing that you never could.

"Did you think they wouldn't let me see him?" Marion said, her voice shaking. "Did you think I wouldn't find out what happened?"

She began to cry. The sound held him in place, held him as stiffly as Marion was holding herself. Stupidly, almost blindly, he looked at his hands. He had no place to put his hands.

He reached for Marion's arm, to help her finally, to lead her away. So that he could follow.

Marion shoved the flag into his hands. Hard. He caught it before it fell to the ground.

"Here, Pat," she said, "you take it." She looked all around, at the sky, at the rain, at the muddy earth beneath her feet, before finally settling on his face. She pushed the flag again, struck at it with her fingers, just to make sure.

"You *keep* it," she said. "What do they expect me to do with a goddamn flag now?"

Paige held the bundle close, sheltering it like a child, and watched her go, the color of her suit merging with the rain and the gravestones until his eyes could no longer tell them apart.

The realization came to him, swift and clear. Everyone he knew was gone. Despite everything he had done to stop it, they had slipped through his grasp and fallen away.

I need to get back to the job, he thought, I need a new

case. Today, tomorrow, soon. He was certain Tom Ferris would have understood.

After the paperwork went through, Paige transferred from Major Crimes to Homicide, and got what he was looking for.

Small consolation, perhaps, but better than a flag.

2

A month before the robbery, Bobby Radcliff went to buy a mask. He took the Ben Franklin over to New Jersey and drove out route 70 to Cherry Hill. There was a place called the Costumery, just past the racetrack, in one of the strip shopping centers that lined the highway. He'd found it in the yellow pages and disliked the name immediately. It sounded like a frozen yogurt place or something, like the owners were ashamed of what they were selling and were trying to make it sound better than it was.

There was a costume shop on Walnut Street in Center City, but that was too close to home. The only other one he knew about was all the way up in Burlington, and he was smart enough to stay away from there, though he wouldn't have minded the drive. He liked driving.

Bobby had a '75 Camaro painted felt green with a flat black primer hood. He had customized the car himself, taking out the backseats and everything else he could think of to keep the weight down. He changed the oil every month and did the tune-ups himself. He wouldn't own a new car because they all had emission controls on them that added about thirty pounds to the car, and besides, they were computerized and you couldn't take them apart unless you were an aeronautical engineer. The Camaro was a *real* car. It had points, plugs and a carburetor, and a rebuilt 389 V-8 that he had pulled from a '68 GTO, replacing the transmission and drivetrain himself.

He wanted a Jack Nicholson mask. He'd thought about it for a while and decided that was the one. With a lot of teeth, that killer grin. Not the way Nicholson looked in *Chinatown*, although that wouldn't have been too bad. He sometimes did imitations of the scene where the little guy cut Nicholson's nose in half, working on the accent until he got it just right. You know what happens to nosy little kittycats? Maybe he'd try it out on the job just to see if anybody got it.

Then he thought, no, he wouldn't talk at all, not a word. That would be even scarier. Nothing but those big white teeth and a gun.

He wanted a mask that showed Nicholson's face the way it was in *The Shining*, peeking through the bathroom door, hair plastered all over his face, ax blade gleaming. Heeeere's Bobby!

He drove around the circle where route 130 cut into 70, making sure he took it slow, didn't cut anybody off or cause any problems because that would not be smart at all. A few miles later, he spotted the name on the sign in front of the shopping center and pulled into the lot. It was a Wednesday afternoon, mid-July, the parking lot filled with suburban shoppers, women in shorts and halter tops, all driving BMWs and Coupe de Villes, big Jersey canoes. The women seemed to float through the waves of heat coming off the hot asphalt.

He locked the car and walked into the costume shop. It was a small place, long and narrow, glass booths squeezed in on both sides and filled with dozens of different moustaches and beards and glues. Both walls were covered with masks strung up on white pegboard. Others dangled on wires directly overhead, row after row of decapitated monsters.

Most of them were full head masks made from heavy latex, the kind that you pulled down right over your skull.

There were three other people in the shop, two kids and an older man who was probably their grandfather. The kids were looking at ghoul masks and making spooky noises at one another. The man talked over their heads to the owner, a chunky guy with glasses and a haircut that looked like something off one of his own masks.

Bobby Radcliff moved closer, smiled politely and got the owner's attention.

"Be with you in a second," he said and Bobby smiled politely again and waited.

"Can I help you?" the owner asked, coming over to him.

"Yeah," Bobby said. "I want a Jack Nicholson mask."

The owner shook his head.

"Sorry, we don't have him. They don't make them."

"They don't make them?"

"That's right. But we've got lots of others, Schwarzenegger, Stallone—you know, Rocky—Freddy Krueger, King Kong."

They didn't have Jack Nicholson? He couldn't believe it. Why would anybody *not* make a Jack Nicholson mask?

"You sure about that?"

"Positive," the owner said. "I asked."

"Yeah? What'd they say?"

"No market." The owner swiveled around. "I got the Joker. That's close."

Close. Except the Joker had green hair and looked like a jerk.

"Goddamn," Bobby said. "What's your biggest

seller?'' He kept his voice low, staring down into his own reflection in the glass.

"That's easy,'' the owner said and reached behind the counter. He laid a pair of masks on the glass top. "Ninja Turtles. They're back-ordered from last February. These are the last two I've got.''

Bobby didn't know whether to punch the guy or throw up. He stared at the green molded features and tried to imagine what he'd look like and shook his head. A definite no. He glanced up at the wall behind the owner and scanned the faces. Half of them he didn't even recognize. Then he came to one at the end of the top row and pointed to it.

"Give me Elvis,'' he said.

"Face or full head?''

"Full.'' It would hide his hair.

He couldn't have Jack Nicholson, what the hell did it matter?

Back at the apartment he tried it on, checked his look in the bathroom mirror and wondered what Cross would say about it.

Cross would say it looked interesting. That was what Cross said about everything.

Hell, yes, it was interesting, Bobby thought. That wasn't even half of it. Before he was through, it was going to be just about the most goddamn interesting thing around.

A month later, the two kids were waiting for him by the entrance to the High Speed Line just like they said they would. Bobby thought they might back out in the end, but there they were, eager and ready to go.

The kids were his idea, strictly his own, the best one he'd ever had, a true original. He walked over to them casually, the way he always did, carrying his size easily and confidently. He had a thin waist and broad shoulders and worked out with free weights in the apartment, not too much but enough. His hair was the color of dust and hung down over his forehead. He kept it cut just above his clear blue eyes. It gave him a boyish look, made him appear younger than he was, and that didn't hurt. People, he had observed, constantly underestimated him.

He came closer to the kids. The fourteen-year-old nodded his head in recognition. He was trying to look tough, Bobby decided, trying to be more than what he was, which was a skinny street kid who was scared to death. Which was all right with him. He wanted them scared. They'd do what he told them.

The fourteen-year-old's name was Tim Cochran. Bobby knew his uncle, an ex-biker named Wayne. Bobby bought dope from him occasionally, even though Wayne charged seriously outrageous prices. He always had dope, and that made up for the fact that he was a major scumbag. The other kid, slightly younger, wanted Bobby to call him Rap. Bobby had to laugh, a white kid with flaky blond hair, not much bigger than a flyswatter, with eyes like a pair of cracked marbles stuck in his weird little doughboy face who wanted to be called Rap.

He first saw the two kids shoplifting a drugstore on Chestnut Street and caught up with them while they were drinking sodas in Reading Terminal Market.

"If I was a cop," he'd said sitting down, "you guys'd be on your knees in some alley." Rap started to get up but Bobby grabbed his arm and pulled him back. Tim stayed glued to his chair, out of fear or stupidity, Bobby couldn't decide which. "You do nice work, Tim," he said. "Uncle Wayne know you're into this kind of shit?" Tim didn't say a word. Smart kid. Bobby patted his cheek. "I got a better idea. You interested?"

They were. The rest was all a question of stringing them along and Bobby was good at that. He'd been doing it for years to everybody he met including Cross. Especially Cross.

Bobby stood next to Tim while the noise of the Speed Line whined and clattered all around them.

"You all set?" Bobby asked him. Tim was wearing jeans and a black T-shirt and high-top athletic shoes. The laces dangled around his ankles.

"Sure," Tim said and stuck his thumbs in the pockets of his jeans and cocked his hips.

Oh Lord, Bobby thought, too many James Dean movies. Then he realized the kid probably didn't even know James Dean, probably thought he was some jock on MTV.

"You remember what you're supposed to do when you get inside?" Bobby asked both of them.

"Yeah," Tim said. "We run around the store, drive everybody nuts."

"Then?"

Tim nodded. "Then we freeze 'em."

"Right," Bobby said.

"When do we get the guns?" Rap asked.

Bobby shook his head. "I told you, when we get there."

"Far out," Rap said.

Bobby pointed to the train platform.

"In you go then." The two kids started for the train.

"Hey, Tim," Bobby called.

Tim stopped and turned around.

"Tie your shoes. I don't want you falling all over yourself."

"Sure," Tim said, a little uncertain how he was supposed to react. "I'll do it on the train."

"You'll do it now. That way I know you can follow orders."

"Sure," Tim said. "No problem." He knelt down and laced up his shoes while Rap stood next to him looking nervous.

Bobby noticed that Rap wore Hush Puppies. They

looked old and decrepit, like they'd been left out in the rain once too often.

The two kids scampered into the station. Bobby followed at a distance. He carried a large briefcase. Inside the briefcase were the guns, a pillowcase, his mask, and a cheap sport coat and matching clip-on tie that he'd bought at one of the discount malls. He waited while they boarded the train.

They're all right, he thought. They're going to do fine.

But then again, maybe not.

The plan was simple. They would ride the High Speed Line to Camden—on separate trains, of course. There was a car waiting for him in a garage near the downtown station. Bobby'd stolen it a week before, a white Duster that was a supreme piece of shit but wouldn't attract any attention.

Once he got the car, he'd pick the kids up a few blocks north at a designated corner and drive to the liquor store, a place called Louis Liquors on the edge of the ghetto. Camden was all ghetto, but this was one of the better run-down neighborhoods. At least he wouldn't get shot on the street by some lowlife asshole trying to rob *him*.

He'd drop the kids off a block from the store, park the car and wait a few minutes before going in while the kids did their stuff. That was Bobby's idea, one he kept thinking he ought to get some kind of award for, if they gave out awards for most original armed robbery of the year.

The kids would go into the store and start galloping around, maybe break a few bottles, and just generally raise all kinds of uncontrollable hell. Bobby told them they had to keep it up for at least a minute before they got caught. He figured by that time every employee in the store and probably a few customers would be chasing them around the aisles.

"Now here's the thing," Bobby had told them. "When you get caught, I want you in the back of the store, right next to the beer coolers. Not in the middle, not in front, but in the back. As far away from the register as you can get. Understand?''

Because when they got caught, the two kids, Tim and Rap, these little fucking kids, were going to take out the guns they had hidden in their shirts and just plain terrorize the shit out of everybody.

While that was going on, Bobby would waltz in and clean out the register. After that, a quick ride through scenic Camden, bury the car somewhere, the two kids hop the Speed Line back and he'd follow along later, dressed in a sport coat and tie and carrying the briefcase and looking like a used-appliance salesmen.

Then a short meeting that night on the piers to pay off the junior G-men and he'd be home free and clear. Who was going to remember some guy wearing a mask while they were being held hostage by a couple of kids pointing Smith & Wessons down their throats?

Bobby still had a few nagging thoughts about the kids. Not much, a little tug at the back of his mind, enough to set him on edge. What if they get scared? What if they fuck up?

What if they get caught?

Not smart, Bobby thought as he boarded the train and settled in for the short ride to Camden, not smart at all.

The whole thing rolled out ahead of him like a movie, and he saw it all through the camera's eye, a tight shot on the world in front of him.

The kids were long gone by the time he got off the train and found the Duster. He pumped the accelerator a couple of times and the car turned right over. He pulled out of the garage.

''Running very smooth,'' Bobby said, bopping a sharp little rhythm around the steering wheel with his hands.

The kids were waiting on the right corner. They

hopped in the back, and Bobby pulled away, taking his time. He opened the attaché case and took out the two guns and handed them to Tim and Rap over his shoulder. He watched them in the rearview mirror.

Rap held the gun up and stared at it like it was the answer to his dreams. Bobby reached back over the seat and pushed it down.

"We don't advertise," he said. "Put 'em away." They stuck them in the top of their pants and pulled their shirts down over them. He tilted the mirror and looked. It wasn't too obvious. Like they had dicks the size of small tree stumps, peeking right up over their belt buckles.

The guns weren't loaded. He didn't want them blowing some poor joker away by accident. The kids didn't know that and were too hyped to notice.

Except maybe Tim. He kept staring at Bobby like he wanted to ask a question but wasn't sure whether he should or not.

"Any questions?" Bobby asked. Neither one of them spoke.

"Good." He turned around and went back to watching the streets as the car rolled through Camden.

Bobby stopped a block from the liquor store and let the kids go the rest of the way on their own. He had his mask out and held it in his lap, squeezing it hard. The mask made a kind of squishy sound, like somebody smacking their lips together. The kids opened the front door and went inside. Bobby looked at his watch.

It was the middle of the afternoon, almost three, and there weren't that many people on the street. Bobby had watched the place off and on for the past month and knew that the next big rush wouldn't come until close to five. It varied a little. Sometimes it was more like six before people started pouring in. But at three o'clock the store was practically dead.

One minute to go. He stuck his fist inside the mask

and held it up in front of his face. He dropped it quickly and counted off the seconds. Forty. Thirty. Twenty. Ten. He slipped the Elvis mask over his face. He held the gun against his leg, feeling the weight, enjoying it.

"Time to go to work," he said and got out of the car.

The kids had finished their run when Bobby went through the front door. He could see them standing in the rear of the store, right by the beer cooler like he told them. A handful of people, maybe five, maybe six, huddled together in front of them, hands raised, eyes wide with fright and surprise. A radio played in the background, a funky little rap ditty to keep the customers happy.

Bobby looked up at the video camera that panned the front of the room and tried to make sure it caught his good side.

He turned immediately to the left, toward the woman at the cash register. She saw him coming and started to reach beneath the counter.

"Freeze," Bobby yelled and raised the gun, keeping it level with her face. The woman stopped in mid-motion.

"Hands up." He turned toward the back of the store. "Everybody down in back! On the floor! Now!" The people dropped all at once. It was like a cartoon, Bobby thought. If he told them to get up and dance around, they'd probably hop all over themselves trying to get in step.

A thought whistled through his mind. I could just shoot them. Kids first, then the rest. Just blow them all away. No witnesses, no crime. Goddamn.

He spun around on the woman and tossed the pillow-case at her. She was young, in her mid-twenties, about his age. Neat cornrows across the top of her head, hanging in a beaded fringe down the back of her neck. She looked scared.

"Fill it up," he said.

"There isn't much," she said.

He moved in closer, watched her jump, and shoved

the pillowcase across the counter, feeling the urge to put a bullet right down the middle of those neat little cornrows.

"Shut up and fill it!"

The woman popped the register open and started shoveling bills into the case.

Somebody in back started crying.

"Shut up back there," he yelled and saw Tim jump at the sound of his voice. The crying stopped.

The woman finished filling the pillowcase and dropped it on the counter.

"Thank you," Bobby said and grabbed for it.

Then something extraordinary happened.

A black man popped up behind one of the back rows. Bobby saw it all in a flash. The man was wearing a tricolor skullcap and a dirty green army jacket. He had his hands raised straight over his head, fingers clutching at the air.

"Don't shoot, don't shoot," he yelled.

Bobby snapped his arm out and fired.

The man threw himself to the floor. Bottles exploded, glass and liquor spraying in a wide plume across the aisle. Before he fell, Bobby saw the man clutch at his chest. He aimed lower and pumped off another shot, glass flying everywhere now. It filled the air with a fine sparkling mist. The man stayed down.

Bobby was already in motion.

"Move, move!" he yelled.

In the back, people were screaming, scrambling for a place to hide. The two kids stood in dumb surprise, their backs to the cooler, not moving, just staring at the shattered bottles, paralyzed by the sound of the shooting.

"Now!" Bobby yelled. They ran toward him down the center aisle, Tim in front, Rap following close behind. Bobby watched them come, framing the shot in his mind. Bam! Tim goes down, flies backward through the air as if pulled by a rope. Bam! Rap bursts like a pricked balloon, blood pours down the front of the cooler.

They hurried past him, racing out the front door. Bobby ran after them, thinking as he burst onto the street that there was absolutely no excuse in the world for missing a perfect shot like that one.

"Jesus Christ!" Tim was saying, "Jesus Christ!" He was huddled down in the backseat, scrunched up beside Rap, knees tucked tight against his chest, Rap not saying a word, the skin on his face turning yellow-white, the exact color of sour milk.

"Shut up!" Bobby yelled and started the car. He pulled out into the street and took the first corner too fast, the tires squealing on the hot pavement. He ripped his mask off and stuffed it between his legs next to the gun.

"Take it easy," he said to Tim. "Don't do anything stupid." His voice was calm, soothing, talking the kid down, making sure everything was under control.

"Don't do anything stupid?" Tim cried. "You shot that guy!"

"I did what had to be done," Bobby said.

"Oh yeah?"

"Yeah. It went okay."

Tim said nothing but his face had lost some of its panic. He was getting used to it now, Bobby thought, feeling better about the whole thing, probably imagining himself doing the shooting. Bobby pulled off on one of the streets and stopped the car.

"Okay, toss 'em over."

The kids dumped their guns on the front seat and scrambled out of the car. They stood there waiting for him to say something to them, give them a pat on the back for doing what they were told. They both looked scared, especially Tim. He was too smart *not* to be scared, Bobby thought.

"Nice work," Bobby said. "I told you it'd be interesting."

They wanted more from him. He had no more to give.

"Go on," he said. "See you tonight."

The two kids hesitated, looked at each other, and ran for the train.

Bobby took the sport coat out of the attaché case and slipped it on. He snapped the tie into place and adjusted it in the mirror, combing his hair with his fingers.

When he was finished, he left the keys in the car, figuring that in Camden it would last two, maybe three hours max before somebody got the bright idea to steal it, and walked to the Speed Line.

On the train back to Philadelphia, Bobby stared out the window at the cars as they passed on the bridge, saw the people in them as so much background noise in his life and the starring role he had picked out for himself. They had no idea what it was really all about, none of them. They were extras, just tagging along for the ride.

It was chilly down by the river at night. The air was dank, clammy, almost liquid, thick with the smell of dead fish and rotting wood. It was like sitting on the river bottom, waiting in the darkness inside the abandoned pier on the south end of Delaware Avenue.

Bobby sat on a pallet and waited. The light from the power station on the other side of the short, narrow channel barely reached him. It drifted across the water through the open doors of the building and spread around him in a faint gossamer haze.

He heard footsteps in the distance, hard and distinct, the sound bouncing between the rusted steel walls and the wide concrete floor. Then a cry, cut off suddenly. One of them must have tripped, he thought and stood up. Time for the big payoff.

The money from the robbery wasn't as much as he'd wanted but it wasn't too bad either, thirty-two hundred dollars and some change.

The kids were to get two hundred dollars apiece. The

cash, in tens and twenties, was stuffed in two separate envelopes. When he was counting it out, Bobby decided he ought to put in an extra fifty as a bonus. Why the hell not?

The kids stepped into the circle of filmy light, two little black shadows. Bobby was disappointed that he couldn't see their faces. He made a pretense of checking his watch.

"Right on time," he said. "Very prompt."

"You got our money?" It was Tim who spoke, standing slightly back and to the side of the other one.

"Of course," Bobby said. He handed over the envelopes, stretching to reach Tim.

"There's something extra for you in there," he said.

"How much extra?" Tim asked.

Bobby laughed. The kid never lost a beat.

"Fifty bucks."

Tim opened his envelope and leafed through the money.

"Two minutes' work," Bobby said. "I figure you made about a hundred twenty-five a minute."

"You made more," Tim said and stuffed the envelope in the back of his jeans.

"That's right, I did." He thought the kid might have something else to say, but Tim was silent, moving back toward the building, getting lost in the shadows.

Bobby fingered the gun in the pocket of the jacket, thumb rolling back and forth over the handle.

He looked down at Rap.

"You interested in any more work?"

Rap turned to Tim.

"I don't think so," Tim said.

"Too exciting for you?"

"Just not interested," Tim said.

Bobby put his hand on Rap's shoulder, a fatherly touch.

"You aren't thinking of doing anything stupid?"

"No." He wouldn't look at Bobby. Instead he kept his eyes down, staring at the envelope full of money in his hands.

"You sure?"

This time Rap looked up.

"We don't squeal."

Bobby smiled. "Okay."

"Let's go," Tim said.

Rap began walking away.

Bobby took out the gun, holding it next to his leg so neither of the kids would see it until the last second.

"Hey, kid," Bobby said in a soft voice. He imagined his words drifting out toward the edge of the light, fluttering on iridescent wings. Rap stopped and turned around. "I think you're right."

Bobby Radcliff shot Rap in the center of his chest. The kid went down in a flash of light. Just like somebody jerked him with a string, Bobby thought. He straightened his arm and moved it to the right, as Tim ran like crazy along the inside of the building.

It was awfully hard to see, nothing but darkness and murky shadows out beyond the light.

One of the shadows moved.

Bobby tracked it, fired once, twice. The shadow kept moving. He saw Tim break through one of the doors.

Bobby ran after him. When he got to the door, he crept along the outside of the building, the lights of the power station sparkling in the water, brightening up the landscape. But he didn't see Tim. He hurried along, moving fast toward the front of the building, listening for the sound of Tim's footsteps.

He couldn't hear a thing. He stopped. In the distance, he saw the two small buildings right next to the chain link fence that separated the pier from the service road. To the right, a pair of abandoned containers stacked on one another. To the left, another narrow channel and beyond that, two more abandoned piers. He listened again. Nothing. The kid had vanished.

Had he slipped into the water? Had he gone all the way around to the other buildings? Was he hiding somewhere right in front of him? Was he hiding behind the containers?

Where did the little fucker go?

Bobby heard something move and swung the gun around, arm steady. It was nothing, a rat crawling through the piles of trash that lined the front of the fence. He kept walking, taking his time, staring hard into the darkness. The shadows seemed to move with every step he took, but it was only his eyes playing tricks on him.

Bobby calculated he had only a few minutes before he'd have to leave. Gunshots attracted attention, even down there.

If I was a little kid where the hell would I be?

The question drew a blank. The problem was, Bobby thought, he never really was a little kid, not like these two. Not like anybody.

He decided it was time to go. Before he did that, though, he had something to do.

Rap was lying on the concrete right where he'd fallen. Bobby took the Polaroid from his jacket pocket and looked through the lens, checked the flash and snapped the picture. For an instant, everything went white. The camera whirred once and the picture slid into his hand. He put it in his shirt pocket. He folded up the camera and reached down for the money. The envelope was torn on one corner and sticky with blood.

Bobby wiped the envelope on his pants and stuck it in with the picture. Blood never bothered him. But he did wonder how much it bothered Jacob Cross. Might be interesting to find out someday.

———

From the top of the stack of containers, Tim watched the car drive away. He lay flat on the rusted metal, trying to keep as low as possible, trying, really, to burrow deep down into it, so deep that no one would ever find him. He stayed like that for another five minutes before he risked climbing down to look for Rap.

He found him right where Bobby had shot him, just a bloody little rag with a big dark stain running all over the front of his white T-shirt, spilling onto the concrete around the body. It looked like he was lying in the middle of a mud puddle. Tim stared down and couldn't believe what he was looking at.

But he didn't cry. He had learned a long time ago not to do that. Don't cry. Don't whine. Be tough. Take it like a man.

He ran from the building toward Delaware Avenue, heading . . . where? Home? Home was out.

That left nowhere. He was on his own. Bobby was going to come looking for him and he was on his own. He reached the road and ran across, racing up the street, a moving target under the cool phosphorescent lights. He turned right and ran up another street lined with storage yards filled with piles of machinery behind tall chain link fences topped with razor wire.

His pants felt wet, and for a moment he thought he might have been shot. Then he looked down and realized he'd pissed all over himself. Out of fear and terror. Just like a girl. He slowed down, stumbling along beside the fence, trying to brush the stain from his pants. It wouldn't go away. No matter what he did, no matter how hard he tried, it just wouldn't go away.

That was when he started to cry.

3

Paige kicked at the concrete and lit another cigarette, his seventh of the morning. The sun was already hot, the inside of the building stifling, and he could smell the river and the rot that swept through the open doors. That was why he was on his seventh cigarette and it was only nine o'clock. He'd started smoking again, going on two months now, and even though he hated the whole idea, he couldn't bring himself to quit. It was, he decided, the only really tangible benefit of joining Homicide. Everybody in Homicide smoked except the captain. Captain Glover didn't smoke and nobody smoked in his office.

When Paige requested his transfer, Glover asked to see him. Paige sat in the extra chair in Glover's office, a small cubicle in the middle of the wide grungy room that was Homicide, and watched while the captain read through his file.

"I was a little surprised to get this," Glover said and shut the file, tossing it on his desk.

"Why's that?"

"Because I like teamwork," Glover said. "Teamwork

is what gets arrests." He nodded at the file. "You've been on your own a long time."

"Maybe I need a change."

Glover picked up the file and weighed it in his hand as though he could judge Paige's credibility from what was inside.

"I knew Tom Ferris pretty good," Glover said. "It was a damn shame what happened to him."

"Yes, it was."

Glover waited. Paige shifted his weight in the chair but didn't say anything more.

"I don't need another hero around here," Glover said.

"That's not what I'm after."

Glover considered it. "No," he said. "I didn't think so." The captain looked at his calendar and flipped a few pages. Then he pushed the file across the desk.

"Give this to one of the commissioner's elves," he said. "You start next Monday, first shift."

Paige picked up the file and started to leave. The smell of cigarette smoke mixed with the tart odor of floor cleaner hit him when he opened the door.

"Pat," Glover said behind him. "Just in case you were wondering. About Grant. I'd have killed the son of a bitch, too."

Paige was assigned to Five Squad, the department team charged with handling unsolved or difficult murders. There were ten men in the squad, including a sergeant and a lieutenant, and shift time didn't count. They worked until the job was done. Now it was a little after nine in the morning and he was on the job, standing in the middle of a numberless pier, a rattrap built of corrugated steel, the faded blue marine paint scarred with rust, smoking his seventh cigarette of the day and looking down at the dead body of a kid with a hole in his chest.

Paige had seen dead bodies before. He'd just never seen one that looked quite so small and tragic. The kid lay on the dirty concrete with his arms out at his sides and his feet stuck neatly together. The way kids make angels in the snow, Paige thought.

He had trouble looking at the body, seeing things he didn't want to see. He tried to imagine them written out in standard police prose, words that were dull but precise, passed from hand to hand, filed away in cabinets, lost in the shuffle; he could not. He felt assaulted by the details right in front of his eyes.

The concrete around the body was dark and caked with blood. The tip of one finger had been chewed by some animal, probably a rat, and a stub of bone stuck out, the end smeared with pale tissue. There were more bite marks on his arms and face.

And there were flies. Winter, summer, spring or fall, it didn't seem to matter. There were always flies. They covered his face and crawled up into his hair. It was light blond, like the color of straw. Paige forced himself to watch. He felt the first small spurt of anger, like dry heat beneath his skin. He wanted to keep the vision clear in his mind.

I'm going to get this guy.

Paige waited while a pathologist from the medical examiner's office went over the body, probing the chest wound. The surgical gloves made his hands appear waxy and yellow, unnatural things. Dead hands digging into dead bodies, he thought.

Jack Rudolph, another Five Squad detective, came over to him. Jack was younger than Paige by a few years and wore his hair short and dressed like a teller. Rudolph had shot and killed two robbery suspects the year before. They'd bumped him along civil service, made him a detective and moved him to Homicide. Paige wasn't sure it was a good idea but that was how things got done.

"Lieutenant thinks it's drug-related," Rudolph said.

"He does? Why?"

Rudolph shrugged. "They found a joint in the kid's pocket."

The lieutenant, Paige thought, had an extremely limited imagination.

"When did they start shooting white kids for holding a joint?"

"Who knows?" Rudolph said.

"Any ID?"

"Not yet."

Which meant not ever, probably. Kids that got themselves shot didn't carry identification. They didn't carry Boy Scout badges and secret decoder rings, either. They had joints in their pockets and holes in their chests. They ended up in the dirt.

Paige crushed the cigarette out on the sole of his shoe and slipped the remains in his pocket.

"He wants you to look around, check out the front."

"On my way," Paige said. He'd been thinking of doing that from the moment he arrived.

As he walked through the building, Paige began going over what they knew. A couple driving home from a party along Delaware Avenue had reported hearing what they thought were gunshots at around two o'clock in the morning. The man was an army veteran and was certain they were gunshots but was vague about where the shots might have come from. Near the river was all he said.

A patrol car made a quick tour of the area but found nothing. When the sun came up, they went back, found the chain cut on the fence gate and went in on foot. That's when they found the kid.

That was all they had.

Paige stopped at the corner of the building and watched as several detectives went over the ground, examining it for anything that remotely resembled evidence, placing each item carefully in a paper bag, each bag numbered with the particular section the detective was covering.

Paige tried to put himself in the mind of the dead kid. What was he doing down by the piers in the first place? It seemed unlikely that he was just out for a stroll, although Paige wasn't prepared to dismiss that possibility entirely. Was the kid hiding from someone?

Maybe. Running from down near South Street maybe, where the streets were filled with hundreds of kids just like him. But it was an awful long way to run, and why hide here? Why not South Street? Or Lombard? Or any of a dozen other places. Why here? Another question followed immediately. What if the kid was meeting someone here?

He thought about what the lieutenant had said. Maybe it was drugs after all.

But he couldn't help thinking it had to be something more than that. Why come all the way down here to buy dope? The kid could have done that right on South Street and nobody would even blink; they'd smile and think about other things and walk right on by. You could buy drugs on South Street without even breathing hard.

Then why come all the way down to the piers?

Unless someone brought him down there.

To do what?

To shoot him.

If that was the case, then what did the kid know that made him worth shooting?

Paige's vision seemed to cloud up. The question brought him all the way back to his original starting point. What was the kid doing down at the piers in the first place? He had no answers and the questions had worn him out. Give me something to look for, Paige thought, give me something I can put my hands around.

He thought again of the kid's body, the smallness of it, its perfect stillness, and felt another burst of anger.

Paige lifted his head and saw the buildings by the fence and the nearby stack of abandoned containers. I'll start with them, he thought.

He missed the scrape on the side of the container the first time he went over it. It slipped by him, lost in the rust and dented metal and the exposed slivers of broken plywood. Paige saw it finally, on the top of the bottom container, a long tapering scuffmark that looked like it was made by someone in a hurry, their foot scraping the edge as they scrambled up the side.

Paige found a handhold and hauled himself up. He was eye-level with the mark. The rust had been knocked away and there was a thin line of dirt along the edge. He followed the line of the scuffmark and found another one halfway up the side of the second container, the same size as the first.

The kid went up here, Paige thought. When he reached the top of the second container, he found what he was looking for, the place where the kid had stayed to watch the front of the building, waiting for whoever had shot him. The top of the container was covered in dirt and grime, and he could see the outline of the kid's body.

He stared at it for a minute, seeing the point where the kid's shoes had cut a line in the dirt and where his arms and head had been. He must have seen them drive up, Paige thought, and then waited until they went behind the building before climbing down. That was how the kid did it, Paige thought.

But the more he stared at it, the more he began to realize that something wasn't right. It took him a few more minutes to figure out what it was.

It was the size of the marks. They were bigger than the dead kid's body by almost a foot. He knelt down closer, measuring off the distance with his eyes. Maybe the kid had moved, wiggled around a bit to get into place. Paige looked again. No. The line that the kid's feet had made was perfectly straight, like he'd been dropped from the sky. Paige saw where his arms had been, where he had laid his head. No movement there, either.

Maybe the dead kid hadn't been up here at all.

Paige climbed down from the containers and walked back to the body. The pathologist was finishing up and they were getting ready to take the kid away. A portable gurney lay flat on the concrete next to him, body bag on top, open, waiting.

Two detectives lifted the kid up and set him on the gurney. It looked easy, Paige thought. Like picking up a sparrow. The kid was very thin. His bloody T-shirt clung to his chest, and Paige could see the outline of his rib cage sticking through.

The pathologist peeled off his gloves and stuck them in his bag. Paige followed him back to his car. Paige knew him but couldn't recall his name. He thought it started with a D—Debbs, Downs, something like that.

Diver, Paige remembered.

"I hate doing kids," Diver said quietly. Paige wasn't sure whether the pathologist was talking to him or to himself, venting a common emotion. Nobody liked doing kids.

"How tall was he?" Paige asked.

Diver spoke in a strange monotone, so quiet it was almost a whisper. "About four foot six, give or take half an inch. I'll get a better measurement later. Why?"

"Just wanted to know. They find the slug?"

Diver nodded. "Looks like a thirty-two." The pathologist shrugged and opened the car door. The inside of his car was a mess. Papers, crumpled up fast-food bags, half a candy bar that had melted on top of the dash, oozing chocolate and peanuts. It looks just like my car, Paige thought.

"Can I use your tape?" Paige asked.

"I got two more to do this morning."

Paige waited.

Diver sighed and reached into his coat pocket. "Keep it," he said. "I've got a spare around here somewhere."

Diver got into the car and braced his hands on the wheel, his arms straight out as though he were trying to keep himself from crashing into something. A jet swept low overhead, on its descent to the airport. Diver waited until it passed to speak.

"I keep thinking it can't get any worse," he said in that same quiet voice, the pitch of the words rising at the end and making it sound like a question, familiar and disturbing. "But it always does."

He drove away without saying good-bye. Paige looked at the measuring tape in his hand. It was small and cheaply made, not much bigger than a fifty-cent piece. The case was broken and Diver hadn't bothered to fix it. Like so many things, Paige thought, easy to lose, easy to replace. Another throwaway.

He went to measure the marks on the top of the container.

His first guess had been right. The marks on the top of the container measured a little over five and a half feet. Unless the dead kid had shrunk, he'd never been up there.

Then who?

It might have been the shooter but Paige didn't think so. Why would the shooter hide? He had the gun. If the kid had been shot in the back, ambushed, Paige might have thought differently. But the shot had come from the front, probably from a few feet away.

No. It wasn't the shooter.

It was another kid.

The idea struck him immediately as the right one. Two kids come to the meeting. One kid hangs back. The first kid goes down and the other one takes off. The shooter comes after him. The kid picks the nearest place to hide and climbs up here. The shooter looks for him but not too long because he can't be sure who else might have heard the shots. The shooter leaves. The kid takes off, running for his life.

The shooter was going to be looking for him. That meant that Paige had to find him first.

If he could.

Paige didn't have to wait that long to find out why the first kid got shot. It was all over the evening news. He was eating a roast pork sandwich in a bar on Front Street a few blocks from his house and they were showing videotapes of a liquor store robbery in Camden that had happened the day before.

Paige hardly ever saw the news at home but the food was bad enough that he started watching it in the bar. They ran the videotape five minutes into the broadcast. The first segment showed a pair of kids running through the store, grown-ups chasing after them as they tore up and down the aisles. The videotape made the actions look choppy, cartoon figures galloping stiff-legged through a distortion in time.

Paige saw the face of the dead kid as he zipped past the camera. The other kid followed right after him, taller, a little more graceful and with a giddy smile on his face. Paige tried to memorize his face but he went by too fast.

The next segment showed a man in a mask bursting into the store. He carried a gun and looked like Elvis. The guy in the Elvis mask stopped before the camera and turned his head to the side, giving the camera a perfect profile. Paige thought it was a strange thing to do. He wanted to see it again but the segment changed.

This time it showed another man rising up from the middle of one of the aisles, his hands held high in the air. In one quick motion, Elvis spun around and shot him. Bottles of liquor exploded. The man in the aisle grabbed his chest and started to go down. Elvis pumped off another shot and more bottles exploded. The man in the aisle disappeared and the tape ended.

The newscaster turned to his partner and said, "Amazing footage, Diane."

"Wow," Diane said grimly.

That was one way of putting it.

The newscaster went on to point out that the shooter had missed the man in the aisle. The man had been hit by a large piece of flying glass. That's why he'd grabbed his chest. The guy was lucky.

Not like the kid at the pier.

Paige paid for his sandwich and drove back to police headquarters, known locally as the Roundhouse because it was round—more or less. Paige had seen pictures of it taken from a helicopter. From that angle, it looked like a pair of amoebas mating.

The men of Five Squad were watching the tape on a small portable television that someone had rigged with a battered VCR. It was set up on one of the empty desks in the middle of the room. The other desks were piled with boxes of photos and stacks of paper, an oasis of debris at the heart of the department.

Paige didn't know if the video equipment belonged to the department or not. Probably not. They hadn't had new equipment for what seemed like decades. The city was in debt. Taxes were going up. Crime was going up. The budget couldn't handle it. People brought in their own stuff when they needed it.

Jack Rudolph nodded his head at Paige.

"Camden's sending over a tape," Rudolph said. "We got this off the news. You believe it?"

"We get any calls?" Sometimes people called in when they saw a suspect's face on television. Not often but it happened. Paige wasn't counting on it happening this time.

"It was just on," Rudolph said.

"So nobody called."

"Not yet." Rudolph was an optimist.

One of the men, a black detective named Jerome Teets, said, "Run that one more time. I want to see Elvis again."

They ran the tape again and Paige watched Elvis enter the liquor store, stop and turn his profile to the camera. It struck him then. The guy's posing. He wanted the camera to pick up his best side. Jesus. Maybe the guy's a frustrated actor.

Paige watched the rest of the tape, saw the guy pump off two shots and run from the store. The guy didn't hesitate, Paige thought. He'd had practice. Maybe he wasn't an actor.

"So where do we go from here?" Rudolph asked after the tape was over.

"We talk to Camden, then we go get this mother-fucker," Teets said. "I'm staking my claim. Elvis is mine."

No, Paige thought, he's mine.

4

The room seemed cold to her suddenly and the chill settled into her bones. I must be getting old, she thought, and closed her arms around herself and rubbed them with her hands.

Her husband interrupted his speech. It was always a speech, wasn't it? Even if he was just ordering dinner, somehow it always turned into a speech. He had that gift.

"What's the matter with you?" he asked her.

"I was cold," Susan Morbach said.

Her husband, State Senator James Morbach, Jim to his colleagues and constituents, gave her an irritated look and went back to his speech and his audience of one.

Their daughter. Kimberly Anne Morbach. Sixteen years old, straight brown hair, worn long, pretty face—prettier than I was at that age, Susan thought. I had to learn how to be attractive. So many lessons over the years. Her daughter tried to look everywhere in the room but at her father and found no escape. When he was speaking, Jim Morbach commanded attention. He used his voice like a club, beating down every distraction. He had that gift.

Kimberly managed to look bored, then defiant, then

scared, the flat line of her mouth drooping down slightly. Kimberly kept her hands behind her back, fingers digging into the palm of one hand. Jim probably didn't notice. Susan did. Her daughter was scared but still trying to be brave. Susan admired the effort, the way she stood up for herself.

I wasn't that brave at her age. But I was scared. Terrified was a better word. Of what? Of everything. Every move she made, every word she uttered, every possible mistake that might occur appeared before her like a knife, ready to cut her down.

Not anymore. State senators' wives didn't get scared, particularly the wives of state senators who were being thought of as the next candidate for the U.S. Congress. One more good election to the State House and the rest of it would be a walk. There was nobody else to do it, everyone agreed. And what would she be if they went to Washington? What would she be, the wife of a freshman representative, out there in the big wide wonderful world of national politics, no matter how attractive or poised or smart?

Scared.

It was the answer that had given her the chills. She looked at Kimberly and had the urge to wrap her arms around her daughter, to huddle with her for warmth, to take shelter there as much as to give it.

Her husband held a piece of paper in his hand, a letter from the school describing his daughter's latest behavior blitz. She had called one of her summer school teachers a Nazi pig. Not without some justification, Susan thought. She knew the teacher, and the woman was both a pig and a bully. The teacher had been picking on one of the girls in class—a sweet but unremarkable student named Alice —and Kimberly had told the woman to lay off. The teacher told her to be quiet. Kimberly called her a Nazi pig—a *fat* Nazi pig, to be precise.

Her husband snapped the letter sharply in the air with each phrase.

44   E r i c   S a u t e r

"Just what the hell were you thinking about?"
Snap went the letter.
"Answer me."
Snap.
Crackle, pop, Susan thought.
"I thought we straightened this out the last time."
"She deserved it," Kimberly said stubbornly. "She always picks on Alice because she knows she won't fight back. The woman's a pig."
Susan had to keep herself from smiling.
"That's enough!" her husband shouted and began waving the paper back and forth in front of him like a flag.
"But Daddy," Kimberly began. He cut her off.
"I don't care, Kimberly," he said. He held out his hand as if he were measuring the height of the air. "This isn't the first time. I've got a stack of complaints about your behavior this high. Talking back, skipping, disrupting class. I'm sick and tired of it and it's going to stop. Do you understand me?"
Now we were getting to it, Susan thought. She felt sorry for Kimberly. Didn't she know it was an election year? Didn't she know what they could do to him? Didn't she know how it looked, his daughter rattling the status quo at one of the best private girls' schools in the city?
The slightest infraction, the tiniest misstep, and State Senator Jim Morbach, a leader in the statehouse, a sure-shot candidate for the U.S. Congress, Big Jim Morbach would end up as one more men's room joke in Harrisburg. Too bad about Big Jim, too bad about the election. If it hadn't been for his daughter, why he might have really gone places.
Susan heard herself thinking in her husband's voice and cut it off.
"Don't you care about what happens to this family?" Jim said. "Don't you give a damn about anything but yourself?"

Kimberly's eyes grew larger, turning into big frightened circles. The tears would come now. She felt them in her own eyes and held them back. She wanted to say something, tell her husband that Kimberly truly didn't understand. *Ambition* was a word she didn't know. Its siren call hadn't reached her ears.

"Why do you do this?" he asked, his voice suddenly serious and ever so reasonable. "Is there something I don't know about?" He paused dramatically. "Is it drugs? Are you taking drugs now?"

Kimberly began to tremble, the words cutting into her, breaking her down. Susan could feel the hurt.

"No."

"Are you drinking?"

"No!" Kimberly said forcefully. "God, what do you think I am?"

Jim Morbach put on his stern face. He used the same expression when he got to the end of every speech. You could set your clock by that look. Time to wrap it up. Time to drop the big one.

"What I think, young lady, is that you've gotten into trouble for the last time."

Kimberly's face seemed to contract, shrinking in on itself. When it cracked from the strain, the words and tears came pouring out.

"All they do is lie to us!" Kimberly shouted. "They're the ones who don't care! They don't want us to learn, all they want to do is make sure we behave ourselves." The last few words were drenched in contempt. "They sit around the teachers' lounge and complain about what horrible little shits we are. They really get off on that."

Jim snapped the letter in his daughter's face.

"That's enough!" he shouted. "Now you listen to me. This is going to stop. Do you understand? You are going to behave yourself and you're going to start right now!

"As of now," Jim said, "no more cars, no more dates, no more parties. You're going to stay in, study, and that's it." He rattled off her punishment on his fingers. It's like he's talking to a constituent, Susan thought, delineating the merits of the latest transportation bill.

Kimberly stood her ground. Not that it would do her any good, Susan thought.

"Why is it always me?" she cried. "Why do I always get the blame?"

"Because you're the one who's always in trouble!" he yelled back. "Now go to your room. This discussion is over."

"Daddy!"

"Now!"

"I hate you!" Kimberly screamed.

Her husband took one step closer to his daughter, hand starting to move upward as though he meant to hit her. That was when Susan finally stepped between them. She took Kimberly by the arm, felt her move to shake her off, and held on tight.

"Come on," she said and turned her daughter toward the stairs.

"I'll take care of this," she said to her husband.

"It's about time," he said and stormed away.

Fuck you, you Nazi pig. The words were on her lips before she even knew it. She bit them off and swallowed hard.

Not the first time, she thought.

There were no more first times for anything anymore.

Kimberly threw herself on her bed and curled against the headboard, her face turned away from her mother. Susan sat beside her, crossed her legs, and folded her hands over one knee. Picture-perfect. She looked at herself. I've been to too many fundraisers. She unclenched her hands and rested them on the bed. One hand sought out her

BACKFIRE 47

daughter's leg. She put her hand there, gave it a squeeze. Kimberly didn't move. Susan removed her hand.

"Kimberly," she said and couldn't think of what to say. She did not have the gift. She tried again.

"It's hard," she said and stopped once more. Why can't I just say it?

Kimberly turned around, her eyes red and swollen.

"How would you know?" she said. "How would you know anything?"

Susan felt her heart breaking, little pieces of it falling away like stones down the side of some immense mountain. The stones fell, the mountain remained.

"Because I live with him, too," Susan said quietly. "I've lived with him longer than you have."

"I hate him," Kimberly said.

"I hate him, too, sometimes," Susan answered and watched for Kimberly's reaction. The words had their desired effect. She looked surprised. Had they had this conversation before? Susan doubted it.

"You do?"

"Yes, I do. I didn't like him very much tonight, either."

Kimberly shifted on the bed. "I'll say."

"Nobody's perfect, Kimberly. Not you, not me, not your father. And we don't always do what's right. We try but we don't always succeed." Susan moved in closer, putting her hand back on her daughter's leg. "You have to learn to live with what you have. I know it's not easy. Sometimes it's the hardest thing in the world. But that's all there is." Susan paused. "I love you. You know that. Your father loves you, too."

"No, he doesn't. He loves politics. That's all he cares about."

"That's not true," Susan said and realized she was lying to her daughter. Or at least hedging on the truth.

Not the first time for that, either.

"He loves you," she went on, carrying the lie as best she could. "It's just that this election is very important to him. If he does well, it means a chance to go to Washington. You can help him. He needs your help."

"He wants me to wear one of his stupid hats to school. God. Can you see me in one of those things? I'd rather die."

Susan laughed, and to her surprise, Kimberly laughed with her.

"They are kind of stupid, aren't they?"

"You wear one."

Yes, Susan thought, I wear a stupid hat.

Her daughter suddenly turned serious. She was as changeable as the weather. One minute crying, the next minute so obstinate you wanted to stuff her in a meat locker.

"Why do you do all those things?" Kimberly asked.

It's the price I pay to have the power. That was the truth, the mountain that would not move. I like having influence, I like being listened to, I like what being his wife allows me to do.

"Because I want to help him," Susan lied. The lies were piling up, weighing down on her. She knew the weight by heart.

"But why do I have to?"

"Because you're his daughter. I don't have any other answer for you. That's the way things are."

Kimberly closed her eyes. "Did he really mean what he said?"

"About what?"

"About the parties and stuff."

"Why don't we just leave things alone for a while. You stay out of trouble for a while and I'll see what I can do. Okay?"

"How long is a while?"

"For *a while*."

"You mean I can't do anything?"

"Kimberly," Susan said, letting just enough sternness seep into her voice to make her point. "I read the letter. You can't just walk away from this. You're going to have to learn to control yourself. Give it some time. Give yourself some time. Think about what you're doing."

Give us all some time and maybe things will change. Now, she thought, I'm even lying to myself.

"You can talk to me if you want to. You know that."

"No," Kimberly said, her voice sounding distant and defeated. "I'll do what he wants. I won't make any more trouble. But Mrs. Wilson is a pig. The biggest."

"I know she is." Kimberly looked surprised again. "Don't you think I know that? But you can't keep on defying her. You know why?"

Kimberly shook her head.

"Because you're the one who's going to get in trouble if you do. Not Mrs. Wilson. Not even Alice."

"But you should see what she does, the things she says to her."

"I can imagine. But Alice is going to have to learn to defend herself. That's not your job. Your job is to get a good education so that someday you can change things the way you want them to be. I wish I could make it easier for you but I can't."

Kimberly sighed. "I know."

"So you'll stay out of trouble? At least for a while."

"You mean until the election's over?"

"Yes, that's what I mean."

"That's almost three whole months!"

"I know how long it is."

"All right," Kimberly said at last. It was a reluctant admission.

"Thank you," Susan said. She held out her arms. Kimberly hugged her for a few seconds and then broke away. Susan wanted more, wanted to hold her daughter close for the rest of her life but knew that wasn't possible. Like so many other things. She walked to the door.

"Mom?" Kimberly said.

"Yes."

"Did you ever get into trouble?"

"A little. About average." She wanted to give her daughter something, a small gift to let her know she was on her side. "I wasn't as brave as you are. Sometimes I wish I had been."

The last was a private thought that somehow got loose. Kimberly hardly seemed to notice.

"What did you want to be? When you got older, I mean, before you met Daddy and everything."

And everything, Susan thought. So much to cover with one small word.

"I wanted to be a dancer. A ballerina." Her answer caught her off guard. Another one that had gotten loose somehow. She hadn't thought about it for long time and now it was right there in front of her. That had been her fantasy, the dream of a frightened little girl.

Kimberly looked puzzled.

"Why didn't you do it?"

"I don't know," Susan said. Her words seemed empty and vague, a gloss over what her life had become. She heard them for the very first time and didn't care for the way they sounded.

"I bet you could've been good," Kimberly said.

"I might have been."

She really didn't know.

Not the truth, not a lie.

But enough of both to still hurt.

It was well past midnight when Kimberly Morbach climbed out of bed. She was fully dressed. She moved quickly, taking a few clothes from her dresser and a handful of things from the bathroom, some deodorant, makeup, a small box of tampons, and put them in her backpack. When she was done, she moved quietly down the stairs to the kitchen and then to the laundry room and the back door. Her bike was there, hung on a rack in the hall.

She took it down carefully, opened the door and pushed it onto the porch. She checked her money again, counting out the twenties in her hand. A little over two hundred dollars, enough to get her going.

Kimberly walked her bike through the backyard and down the drive to the road. The house, on one of the better streets in Chestnut Hill, was dark, practically invisible behind the trees. The darkness was a good thing, she thought. That way she couldn't see it and if she couldn't see it, she wouldn't miss it.

From there she could ride into Center City. It would take an hour or so but it wasn't so bad. She'd done it before, ridden down to South Street to hang out, gone down there to be free of her father and his demands. It was the only thing she could think of to do now.

Nobody listened. Nobody understood. Nobody cared.

Maybe her mother did. But so what? Her mother was still trapped in the house, still caught in his lies. She wasn't going to let that happen to her.

Kimberly got on her bike and pedaled away, gliding through the nighttime alone. She was free.

Timothy Cochran was free, too, trying to fall asleep on the garbage-strewn pavement behind a dumpster in back of a small grocery store on Bainbridge, a dozen blocks from the river, using a box filled with black rotted lettuce as a pillow. The smell kept him tormented and awake—the way the waxy sides of the box stuck to his face, tugged at his cheek every time he moved, the sticky sound it made when he tried to pull away, the feeling in his guts like something was grabbing at him, trying to jam his intestines up into his throat. His teeth chattered in the heat. He smelled like piss and garbage. He'd never been so frightened in his life.

He'd spent the day running from one hiding place to another, never staying more than an hour or so in each place. The money from the robbery was still stuffed in the pocket of his jeans, but he was too scared to spend it. What if the police knew about him? What if they were looking for him, too?

For some reason, he kept thinking of the liquor store, the way Bobby had shot the guy. Like it was nothing. The same way he'd shot Rap. He saw the guy in the liquor store go down and then he saw Rap flying through the air. The two merged into a single image, just like in the movies. Except this wasn't like the movies at all.

A car stopped in front of the alley, and Tim curled up in a tight little ball and pushed himself further into the darkness. The car gunned its engine and took off. He started to cry again and bit down hard on his cheek to make it stop. He was going to get through this, no matter what, he was going to make it through.

But how?

Every sound made him jump, every shadow made him tremble with fear. An hour earlier, a rat had come scuttling down the alley to the dumpster, and he was so scared at first, not knowing what it was, that when he saw it, he was too afraid to chase it away. The rat made a leisurely inspection of the pavement, caught a whiff of him, and scurried off. A few minutes later, a solitary drunk relieved himself on the wall near the end of the alley, whistling out of tune in the dark.

Cars went by, laughter and music faded in and out of his hearing like some bizarre new language, half-heard, half-imagined, garbage cans rattled, dogs roamed through the streets, swift black shadows cast up under yellow streetlights, enormous creatures that made him shut his eyes tight in terror. He wanted to die, he wanted to scream, he wanted to tear at the stinking awful clothes that he wore.

He wanted to go home.

His uncle would take the belt to him again. He'd use the buckle end, the way he always did. Tim could feel the snap of pain, the way it would rip across the back of his legs. His uncle never liked to use his fists. He liked the belt, the one he had picked up in New Mexico, big square buckle, the piece of turquoise in the center chipped in one corner, stubby little stones laid out like an arrowhead around it, their sharp edges cutting into him as the belt came down, the sound of the leather like the hissing of a snake as it flew through the air.

He wanted to go home. He wanted to take everything back, make it all different for once. He wanted to crawl into his bed and never come out.

He couldn't go home. He couldn't go anywhere.

He had to hide. Bobby was coming to kill him and he had to hide. Here. There. In places filled with garbage and rats.

The tears came again and this time he didn't have the strength to stop them. The words came with them, a whispered prayer that shuddered in the dark, keeping time with the fearful beating of his heart.

Please God save me.

5

Bobby was up early, doing his regular morning workout and watching the tape of the robbery on the television. He kept his weight bench in the living room, and he was flat on his back, hoisting a set of dumbbells up from the floor to a point directly over the center of his chest. He exhaled with each lift, holding them up until his arms started to shake and then letting them down with a thud.

The noise added something to the tape, a weird counterpoint to the action on the screen.

Whoosh . . . boom! The kids went through the front door.

Whoosh . . . boom! He made his entrance. Whoosh . . . boom! He blew the guy away. It looked pretty good on the tape, but not so good in real life.

The newspeople had the scoop. He had missed the guy completely. The bullets hadn't even come close.

The tape stopped. Bobby pumped the weights a few more times and dropped them to the floor. He rested on the bench and breathed through his mouth, cooling down. Then he shut off the VCR and took a shower. He would start looking for the kid right after breakfast.

Bobby ate at a twenty-four-hour diner on South Street, a block or two from the river. He had heard that mob guys ate there but he hadn't seen anybody who looked like they were in the mob. Just some young couples who acted like they'd just rolled out of bed. The women smiled romantically and the men looked smug. Bobby decided they were cheapskates with little bitty dicks. He ate his breakfast and ignored them all.

The phone had rung while he was in the shower that morning. He had ignored that, too. It was probably Jacob Cross checking in on the hired help. Eventually it stopped ringing. Bobby took a mouthful of water and spit it at the curtain.

"When I get around to it," he said.

The first time they met, Bobby was trying to rip Cross off and not having any luck. He was out on the Main Line, looking into the study through the French doors and getting ready to bust out one of the panes with a brick he'd torn out of the patio. It was two o'clock in the afternoon. The door was outlined in alarm tape, a little silver strip that ran around the edges with a connector at the top. He had two pieces of wire, each about three feet long, and a roll of electrical tape in his pocket. He would bust the pane, tape a pair of wires onto the main connector on the frame, and then attach the other ends to the connection on the door. That way he'd have plenty of room and wouldn't break the circuit when he went inside.

Cross walked into the study. It was pretty funny when he thought about it now. Cross stood there staring at him. Not frightened. Curious. As if he was trying to make up his mind what Bobby was doing there. Bobby thought it was pretty obvious. He was the one with the brick in his hand.

They stared at each other for a few minutes while

Bobby made up his mind to use the brick if Cross made a grab for him. Cross was tall but didn't look that strong.

He was wearing a pair of khaki pants, Docksiders, and a navy blue short-sleeve knit shirt. He looked like a college freshman but his hair was gray, almost silver, and receding near the temples. Bobby thought he was a stockbroker.

Cross told him to come inside. Bobby heard the words and thought, This guy is completely nuts. Or he had a gun. Maybe shooting somebody was just the thing he needed to put a little extra zip in his step.

"It's open," Cross said.

"Fuck you," Bobby said and took off.

Cross called to him as he ran across the backyard.

"I wrote down the license number of your car," he said. "I doubt if you'd get more than a few blocks."

Bobby slowed up. He still had the brick in his hand. He could still whack him. If it came to that. Bobby turned around and saw Cross standing at the edge of the patio, arms folded casually across his chest, smiling patiently, and Bobby realized it wasn't going to come to that at all.

When he was inside, Cross asked if he wanted something to drink.

"Ice tea, soda?"

"You got a beer?"

"Heineken?"

"Whatever," Bobby said.

The study was filled with books, floor to ceiling shelves on two sides, a heavy wooden desk angled so that it looked out on the patio, a smaller table right behind it with a fax machine and a computer, burgundy leather couch set against the opposite wall and a pair of matching chairs right in front of the desk, big oriental rug on the floor. And pictures. A lot of pictures.

Bobby got up and looked at them. There was Cross with three other guys on a big cabin cruiser, holding up the ass end of a marlin; on the golf course, wearing a white golfer's brim, squinting into the sun; dressed in a tuxedo, standing in a crowd of good-looking men and women while a chandelier dangled overhead; on the tennis court, in front of City Hall, on the steps of the Capitol. Cross got around.

Some of the pictures had inscriptions on them. The tennis picture was one: "To JC, Great Game, Great Election." Bobby finally recognized one of the men in the picture, a U.S. senator. Then he started to recognize other people. They were all politicians, some from the state, a few from New Jersey, a couple of federal judges he remembered reading about in *Time* magazine.

Cross came back with the beer.

"These all friends of yours?" Bobby asked, taking the bottle from him.

"In a manner of speaking."

"What manner is that?"

"I help them, they help me. Isn't that what friends are for?"

"You give them money," Bobby said.

"Sometimes. It depends. Sometimes they just need my advice."

"They pay you for that, right?"

"Of course."

"A lot of money?"

"If the advice warrants it, yes, a lot of money."

"Nice work."

"It has its moments. Why don't you sit down?"

"Sure," Bobby said and rested his hip on the edge of the desk. Just in case Cross had a gun in one of the drawers. But Bobby seriously doubted that. He seemed totally at ease, like this sort of thing happened to him every day.

There was something else, too. Cross wanted him for something. What it was, Bobby couldn't imagine. He took a sip of the beer, looked at the pictures again and then at Cross.

"So, what sort of advice have you got for me?"

"Well," Jacob Cross said thoughtfully, "I suppose you could put down the brick."

Bobby spent the morning looking for Tim around South Street but didn't find him. The failure was beginning to irritate him. Where was he? Where in the whole goddamn city could the kid be hiding?

He thought about going to see Tim's uncle but decided against it. His uncle wouldn't know and probably wouldn't give a shit, either. It was another lesson learned on his way up. Know who you're dealing with. Tim's uncle was a prick and Bobby'd had his fill of pricks lately.

Maybe Tim wasn't even around. It was a possibility, but he'd keep looking for him anyway. If Tim was gone, he was gone, and it would only cost him a couple more days to find that out. He had the time. Maybe something interesting would turn up while he was looking.

That first afternoon with Cross had been interesting. Bobby finished one beer and had another. He settled into the leather couch and answered questions. It was like a job interview, although he hadn't had many of those. He felt like he ought to be wearing a suit and tie, nice pair of wingtips. Have his resumé handy just in case.

"Have you ever been arrested?" Cross asked.

"When I was sixteen," Bobby said. "I got caught trying to sell a car full of clothes."

"They were stolen?"

Bobby didn't even dignify that one with an answer. It was a case of good luck, bad luck. The good luck came when he was cruising the loading docks at one of the malls and found one wide open and nobody around. There were half a dozen pallets filled with boxes of T-shirts and swimming trunks. It took him about ten minutes to load his car.

Then came the bad luck. It was summertime, so he drove out to the Shore—Wildwood—and set up shop on a back street a few blocks from the ocean. He sold the shirts for ten bucks and the trunks for twenty; if you bought two pair, you got them both for thirty. For a while, it seemed like half the kids in Wildwood were waiting in line. He was thinking this might become a regular gig.

One of the kids turned out to be an undercover cop who was looking for drugs. He bought a T-shirt and two pairs of trunks. Twenty minutes later, four squad cars descended on the parking lot and Bobby was in handcuffs, his face squashed up against the hood of his car while the cops laughed at him and checked to see if he had a gun stuck in his underwear. They did a terrific job. His nuts ached for two days afterward.

They busted him for possession of stolen goods and, just to be pricks, for not having a retail permit, but they didn't have enough evidence to get him on burglary charges. He told them he bought the clothes from some guy in a blue pickup with out-of-state plates. He was still a juvenile and that was his one saving grace. The judge let him off with probation and a stern warning. Bobby got the message.

Don't sell stolen clothes to undercover cops in Wildwood.

"What did you do after that?" Cross asked.

"I went into burglary," Bobby said. "The hours were better."

"What about your parents?"

"What about them?"

"Didn't they object to your choice of careers?"

"They weren't around."

"Where were they?"

"Florida, I think. Maybe it was Texas. Who knows?"

"Do you know where they are now?"

"No," Bobby said. Then, smiling sweetly, he added, "Maybe they're dead."

Bobby found a fence, a Russian émigré who owned a jewelry shop but did most of his business in the backroom melting down stolen gold jewelry. The Russian had been a criminal in the Soviet Union. When he got to the United States, he soon realized he was as close to heaven as he was ever going to get.

In the Soviet Union they put you in a labor camp for stealing or they took you into a cell and broke your hands. In America, they didn't put you in a labor camp. Instead, they gave you something called plea bargaining where, if you pleaded guilty to a crime you *didn't* commit, they let you off for the one you *did*. The Russian loved it. Bobby stole for him for a while, got bored, and moved on.

"Did you finish school?"

"Yeah," Bobby said. "Went to college, too."

Cross looked like Bobby had hit him with the brick.

"I beg your pardon?"

He had dropped out of high school in the ninth grade, but when his probation officer told him he could make it up—and cut his probation short—Bobby signed on. He went to night classes, which was fine with him because he got to sleep late in the day, and worked as a burglar in the afternoons. When he got his diploma, his probation officer was so tickled he asked Bobby if he was interested in college. Bobby said he didn't have any money for college. His probation officer told him not to worry, there was money available. So he enrolled in a junior college in the suburbs.

It was great. He went to class—they turned out to be dumber than his high school classes—and spent part of his evenings ripping off cars from the parking lot and selling them to a chop shop in the Northeast.

When he wasn't in class or stealing cars, he dated suburban girls who bought their clothes at Saks and thought that their twats were made out of stained glass. They didn't fuck on the first date or even the third but a quick blow job in the front seat was a perfectly acceptable alternative.

He took a lot of film classes because they were the easiest. All you had to do was watch movies and then write what you thought of them. The film professor used a lot of strange words—*mise-en-scène, montage,* and *auteur*—and said that most American movies, especially the Westerns which Bobby liked, were nothing but reactionary racist propaganda. Bobby thought the professor was a complete sack of shit, so Bobby took what he said, threw it right back at him and got along fine.

The professor helped Bobby with the movie he had to make for class, a fifteen-minute epic about a teenager who gets framed by the police for a crime he didn't commit. When he tries to tell a newspaper reporter about it, the police hang him in his cell. In a neat twist, the reporter, instead of investigating the crime, writes it up the way the cops tell it, as a jail suicide. Bobby played the teenager. The professor loved it. He gave him an A for the course.

College life, Bobby decided, was just like dealing with his probation officer.

6

Paige ate two blueberry bagels and drank a cup of coffee for breakfast at a stand-up counter near the corner of Fourth and South. It was a little after eight and South Street was deserted, except for a few refugees left over from the night before. Two of them were sitting on a stoop next to the theater right across the street from him.

They were teenagers, both male, both white, one maybe eighteen, the other a little less, dressed alike, black jeans, paratrooper boots and T-shirts, hair so short they looked like new army recruits, smoking cigarettes, staring at him through the dim morning haze with sullen eyes. One of them wore an earring, a jagged bolt of metal lightning that reached down to the top of his shoulder. His knuckles were badly scraped. Even from across the street Paige could see the scabs.

What the hell ever happened to hippies? Paige thought. He finished the bagel, bought two cups of coffee, some more bagels, and carried them across the street.

"Here," he said, handing over the bags. "You look like you could use something to eat."

"I ate," the one with the earring said.

His friend was already biting into one of the bagels. He glanced over at the one with the earring but kept eating.

"Thanks, man," he mumbled between bites.

"No problem. I'm looking for a couple of kids. Maybe you can help me."

"What'd they do," the one with the earring said, "piss on your hood?"

"I just want to talk to them."

"You a cop?"

No, Paige thought, I'm Binky the Clown.

"Yeah, I'm a cop."

"I don't like cops."

"I don't like cops myself," Paige said. "But it looks like I'm stuck with the job."

The one with the earring opened his mouth wide and laughed. He had a small black swastika tattooed on the inside of his lower lip.

"I know everybody on this fucking street," he said. "If they're here, I know 'em."

Paige gave him a description of the dead kid. If they hung out together on the street, maybe he'd get a lead on the one who was still alive.

The teenager with the earring helped himself to a cup of coffee while Paige talked, nodding his head like he'd heard it all somewhere before.

"Yeah, yeah," he said, "I know 'em. A couple little shoplifters. None of the stores will let 'em in the front door."

"You know their names?"

"Nobody's got names down here, man," he said. He poked his friend in the ribs. "I don't even know who this asshole is. What'd you say your name was?"

"Asshole," his friend said.

"See what I mean?"

"You know where they hang out?"

"Any place they can." He reached into the bag, pulled out a bagel, examined it and dropped it on the sidewalk. He pressed down with the toe of his boot, smiling up at Paige while he crushed it into the concrete. "Bagels suck."

Paige shrugged and started walking toward Third. There was a convenience store that was already open. He'd start with that and keep going until he found somebody who could give him a name.

By noon Paige had found four different shopkeepers who knew the kids but didn't know their names, either. The owner of a T-shirt shop said he thought they lived somewhere nearby but wasn't sure. He had no real reason to think that. It was just a guess. Paige felt like he'd been chasing his guesses all morning, around and around in one big pointless circle. All it did was make him hungry. He ate a cheesesteak for lunch and drove to the Roundhouse.

Jack Rudolph was sitting at his desk writing a note.

"I just called you," he said.

Paige reached for the note. It said, "I just called you—" Find something that works, Paige thought.

"We got a name," Rudolph said. "Somebody saw the tape on the news and called in, said they thought one of them looked like a kid from the neighborhood." Rudolph took a small notebook from his pocket and flipped through the pages. "The name is Dubowski, first name William."

"What's the address?"

"Kensington, right off Aramingo."

A nice part of town, Paige thought. Working class gone to seed. Crime was considered a good job opportunity in Kensington, especially burglary. The standing joke in Major Crimes was that they liked to steal so much because they were really mutants, brain-damaged from all the chemical plants along the river. A lot of black and Hispanic families had moved into the neighborhood recently and shaken everything up. Street fights were an everyday occurrence. An all-around great place to grow up.

"Did she tell the kid's parents?"

"I told her we'd handle it."

"Good," Paige said. "You call the parents?"

"Not yet."

"Don't. Let's just go."

Rudolph followed Paige down to the parking lot.

"You know," he said, "you ought to get an answering machine or something. That way you won't miss anything."

Paige's answering machine was in the spare bedroom on the third floor, the place where he stored all the things he had no more use for in his life. He had put a lot of things in that spare room. It was like a part of his brain that no longer functioned; it made him feel comfortable, just knowing he didn't have to think about it anymore.

"I haven't missed too much so far," Paige said.

"One of these days you might. You never know."

Paige knew. But you couldn't explain that to an optimist.

The house was about what he expected, a tiny redbrick rowhouse on a narrow street filled with tiny redbrick rowhouses. Trash cans left on the street marked off parking spaces, like the territorial droppings of some steroid-crazed bear.

The sidewalks were tilted and cracked, the earth settling under the weight of too many years of cramped living. People sat on their stoops, air conditioners going full blast in the upstairs rooms, while downstairs the front doors remained wide open to keep an ear to the street. Comfort and suspicion, like unspeaking guests, crowded together in the houses, mingled in their dark and narrow hallways. Through the doorways, Paige could hear the sound of the television sets tuned in to a game show, canned laughter settling over the sidewalk like another layer of dust, thick enough to leave tracks.

It dawned on him as he approached the house that he'd

never before had to tell anybody that their son had been murdered.

Rudolph knocked. Paige waited, hands clasped together just below his waist, rocking slightly on his heels—the standard cop stance.

The face of a middle-aged woman peered out through the screen. She seemed to be bent down, as if she were crawling from the mouth of a cave. Paige caught the smell of cigarette smoke and hairspray.

Rudolph already had his shield out.

"Mrs. Dubowski?"

"Yes?" the woman said in a tentative voice.

"Can we come in? We'd like to talk to you."

"What for?"

"It's about your son," Paige said.

The woman straightened up, one fist buried in the thickness of her hip. Her mouth was a small pinched hole.

"What the hell has he done now?"

"Can we come in?"

"Sure, sure," she said and opened the door for them.

The woman wore a pair of green slacks and a shapeless flowered blouse—the slacks too tight, the blouse too big. She looked like a top ready to fall over at any second. She walked ahead of them, grabbing a pack of cigarettes off the bottom of the stairs, sticking one in her mouth, lighting it as she led them into the living room. The room was like a rainy day—the washed-out colors of the furniture, the air growing cloudy with cigarette smoke. The television was on and people were applauding. An empty feeling settled over Paige and he felt lost in the dreariness.

Rudolph sat on the couch. Paige remained standing. The woman flopped down in a recliner next to the television and tapped her cigarette against the ashtray resting on the arm of the chair.

"Goddamn kid," she muttered. Her voice was raw

and unpleasant. "What kind of shit has he gotten into now?"

Paige took a step toward her. The move was so sudden and deliberate that the woman reared back in the chair as though she expected him to hit her. It surprised even him. He had wanted to hit her; the urge had been that strong.

"Do you have a picture of your son?" he asked.

"What for?"

Rudolph looked at Paige. He shook his head.

"Can we see the picture, Mrs. Dubowski?"

"Sure, sure," she said. "I got one in my purse. Pretty recent. Last year or so."

The woman went into the back of the house. When she returned, she was holding a picture in her fingers. She gave it to Paige. The photograph was smeared with cigarette ash.

The face of the dead boy looked up at him. He stared at the camera with an anxious smile. Trying hard to please.

He handed the picture to Jack Rudolph.

"So what's the big secret here?" Mrs. Dubowski asked. She was standing by the chair, stubby fingers fidgeting with the seam of her slacks. "What'd he do, rob a bank?"

"Your son is dead," Paige said. "He was killed two nights ago."

The woman dropped into the chair and sat very still, a column of cigarette smoke drifting up in front of her face like a veil. She looked around the room as though she were searching for something, anything that would make his words go away. Her eyes settled on the television.

Paige walked over and turned it off.

She put out her cigarette and looked up at him. She wasn't crying. She only seemed confused.

"Mrs. Dubowski," he said quietly, "we need to ask you some questions."

"Killed? You said he was killed? How?"

"Someone shot him," Jack Rudolph said.

"Who shot him? Who shot my boy?"

"We don't know," Rudolph said.

"Do you have any idea what your son was doing two nights ago?" Paige asked.

"No." She shook her head in amazement. "I never know what he does. He comes and goes whenever he wants to. Never minds, never listens, stays out all hours, getting into trouble. Goddamn kid, I told him something would happen if he didn't watch it—"

Her words caught up with her and she began to cry. The flesh on her face seemed to fall all at once; it was like watching an avalanche rolling down a hill, destroying everything. Paige reached out to take her hand and she let him.

Eventually she stopped sobbing.

"Would your husband know where he was?"

"George? I don't know. Maybe. He works at the shipyards. He's been awfully busy lately. You can ask him."

Jack Rudolph made a small notation in his notebook. Paige couldn't remember him taking it out. He had also taken out some pictures they'd had made from the videotape.

"Mrs. Dubowski," Rudolph said, "could you look at these pictures and see if you recognize any of the other people in them?" He gave them to her and she held them up.

"What is this?" she asked.

"Your son was involved in an armed robbery," Paige said. "These are pictures of it."

"A robbery?"

"Yes. Do you recognize the other boy, Mrs. Dubowski?" He pointed to the face in the picture. It had been blown up from the videotape and the image was grainy and slightly distorted as though it had been taken underwater.

Mrs. Dubowski stared at the face.

"That's Timmy Cochran," she said.

"Who?" Rudolph asked.

"Timmy Cochran. He's a friend of Billy's. I used to see him all the time."

"When was the last time?" Rudolph asked.

"Oh Lord, I don't remember. A year ago, maybe. He stopped coming around."

"Do you know his address?"

"He lives right here in the neighborhood," she said. "With his uncle. His parents went away someplace. I don't know where. Is he dead, too?"

"No," Paige said. "We're trying to find him."

"Should I call?"

"No," Paige said. "We'll take care of it. Maybe you should phone your husband and tell him to come home now."

Mrs. Dubowski looked stricken.

"I don't think they'll let him just leave the job, not in the middle of the day like that."

"I think they will," Paige said and helped her out of the chair.

While she was making the call, Paige got a phone book and looked up Timmy Cochran's address. There was a listing for a Wayne Cochran three blocks over. Another street just like this one, Paige thought.

"You want to stay here and talk to him?" he asked Rudolph. "Maybe the husband knows something."

"I'll go through his room, see if he left anything." Rudolph shook his head. "I hope the old man knows where he is."

"Ask him," Paige said.

Mrs. Dubowski stopped him at the front door. "George said he'll be here as soon as he can."

"Good. It would be very helpful if you let the other detective take a look at Billy's room."

"He won't mess it up?"

"No. He'll be very careful. We're trying to find out

what happened to your son. He may have left a note or something in his room that might help us.''

Mrs. Dubowski looked more confused than ever.

''Maybe he should wait until George gets home,'' she said.

''That's fine.''

He opened the door. The heat and humidity hit him all at once.

''Those pictures,'' Mrs. Dubowski said to him. ''I didn't tell you.''

''You didn't tell me what?''

''I saw them on the news the other night.''

Paige avoided asking the next question. She answered it anyway.

''I didn't even recognize him. Neither one.''

''It's hard to recognize people on television, especially with something like that.''

She looked at him in horrified amazement.

''I turned it off in the middle of it,'' she said. ''I thought they must have been somebody else's kids.''

Paige walked to Timmy Cochran's house. It was almost an exact replica of the Dubowskis', only this one was covered with green asphalt shingling instead of brick and there were white metal awnings over the downstairs windows. A battered blue Plymouth was parked directly in front. Paige looked in the window. The backseat was filled with tools: hammers, saws, a large box of nails, two pails, and a bucket of drywall compound. A sheet of plastic had been laid down under the tools to protect the upholstery. It didn't seem to have helped much.

Out of habit, Paige bent down and put his hand on the exhaust pipe. The metal was cold. The car hadn't been driven for a while.

Paige had his shield out before he reached the front door.

He expected the worst.

The man who answered was probably close to his own age, Paige thought, but with a fat puffy face that made him look much older. The lines around his mouth and eyes, crooked furrows in the thick folds of skin on his cheeks, curved down to meet what was left of the point of his chin. He wore a white T-shirt with the sleeves ripped off, a pair of jeans and black boots.

There was a red skull tattooed on his right biceps. The skull rested on a bed of flames. Below the skull was the word OUTLAW and a date, 1973.

He came to the door in a wheelchair.

"Wayne Cochran?"

Cochran glanced at his shield without expression.

"Yeah?"

"My name is Paige. I'm looking for Tim. Is he here?"

"Haven't seen him. What do you want him for?"

"When did you last see him?"

"I don't remember. He ain't around."

Paige put his shield away. "Then I'll talk to you instead," Paige said. "Inside."

Cochran took a few seconds to make up his mind but finally spun the wheelchair around. Paige followed him into the kitchen. The house smelled like marijuana, the sweet stench gone slightly stale in the heat. Cochran smoked dope and was an ex-badass. He was a liar by definition. What else was he?

The biker opened the refrigerator and took out a bottle of Miller. There were two empty bottles on the kitchen table. Cochran twisted off the cap and took a long drink.

"So what about him?" Cochran asked.

"He was involved in an armed robbery two days ago in Camden. There was another boy with him. The other boy was murdered."

Cochran lowered the bottle of beer.

"Son of a bitch."

Cochran settled back into the wheelchair, a slow glacial movement that seemed to stretch out for hours. His surprise was genuine—and somehow false at the same time. He's trying to figure out just how much trouble he's in, Paige thought. Cochran took another drink.

"We'd like to find him."

Cochran stared across the top of the bottle.

"Good luck. He ain't here."

"Has he been here in the last two days?"

"How the hell would I know?"

"He lives here, doesn't he?"

Cochran sat up.

"I don't keep him on a leash. He does what he wants."

"When did you see him last?"

"I don't know. Last week, maybe. He was here on Saturday, him and his little buddy."

"Billy Dubowski."

Cochran nodded. "That's him." At least Paige knew where Billy had gotten his dope. Cochran took another drink, the glimmer of an idea forming in his eyes. "He the one that got popped?"

"Yes." Paige marvelled at the word. *Popped.* It sounded so harmless, like the title of a cartoon: *Billy Dubowski Gets Popped.*

"What about his parents?"

"They split."

"Recently?"

"Last year," Cochran said. "Day before Christmas."

"Where are they now?"

"Who the hell knows? Colorado, I guess. They said they were going to send for him when they got settled. Guess they ain't got settled yet."

"So they left you the house and the kid?"

Cochran shrugged.

"Do they ever call or write? Send you money?"

Cochran shook his head. "Are you kidding?"

"Then how do you pay for it?"

Cochran grinned. "Disability."

"Where's Tim go to school?"

"Fergussey. When he goes."

"You have any idea where he might be?"

"I told you. I don't keep him on a leash."

Paige took the pictures out and handed them to Cochran.

"Recognize anybody?"

"Tim. Billy." He squinted at the picture. "Elvis."

Paige took the pictures back.

"Can I look at his room?"

Cochran thought about that for a minute. It was mostly for effect.

"Go ahead. You won't find nothing." He waved his hand in the direction of the hall. "Up the stairs, last one on the left."

Cochran hadn't lied to him about that. There was nothing in Tim's room. There was a single poster on the wall beside his bed, a rock group that came charging out of the middle of a fog bank carrying several lingerie-clad women with them. The poster was torn in several places and patched with tape. The tape was brown with age. In the closet he found a pile of dirty clothes and a stack of old *Penthouse* magazines. Other than that, the place was stripped clean. The kid didn't live here, Paige thought. No kid lived here.

Cochran had gone through the kid's room and cleaned it out. Paige was almost sure of that. But what had he taken? What was he hiding? He went to the top of the stairs. He could hear Cochran in the kitchen, cracking open another bottle of beer, banging it on the table to make sure Paige knew he was still alive, the chair wheels squeaking on the linoleum. Paige slipped back down the hall to take a look at the other rooms.

Cochran didn't hide things very well. On a closet shelf

in one room, Paige found a grocery bag full of dope. Cochran had a little bit of everything: Baggies of marijuana, a couple dozen crack vials, even some blotter acid with the logo of the Grateful Dead stamped across them, a few bottles of pills. He lifted the grocery bag off the shelf. It was a little too heavy. The bottom of the bag sagged in the middle.

The gun was buried beneath the baggies. Paige pushed the dope away and looked inside. A .44 automatic, silver gray. He took it out. Nice. Anybody who sold dope these days probably needed a gun like that.

Paige examined it. The .44 had been cleaned but not recently. And it hadn't been fired. In any case, it certainly wasn't the shooter's gun; if it had been, Billy Dubowski wouldn't have had a chest. He dropped the gun in the bag and rummaged around some more. He pulled out a money roll, held together with a rubber band, and gave it a quick count. Close to four thousand dollars. He sat down on the bed.

There was something wrong here. It was so obvious he hadn't even seen it.

Why would a man in a wheelchair keep his dope on the second floor?

The back door slammed.

"Ah shit," Paige said and took off down the stairs, taking the grocery bag with him.

Cochran was having a lot of trouble getting over the fence that ran around the small backyard. He had one leg hooked over the top and was trying to pull the rest of his body up with it.

He looked over his shoulder at Paige and struggled some more. Finally he gave up and collapsed on the ground.

"Nice try, Wayne," Paige said.

"Fuck you," Cochran said and lunged at him, going for his knees. Paige stepped to the left and swung the grocery bag up as the biker went by. The bag hit Cochran square in the forehead and tore open. Cochran sprawled on the ground, both hands clamped over his face.

Paige collected the dope and the money and stuffed it into what was left of the bag. He dropped the gun in his coat pocket. It felt like he was carrying an anvil.

"Terrific move," Paige said. Cochran touched his forehead and winced. "That must hurt like hell. Getting smacked with your own gun and everything."

"You don't have a warrant," Cochran said. "Whatever you found, you got no warrant."

"What law school did you go to?"

Paige sat him up in the middle of the yard and handcuffed him.

"You got no right to be here," Cochran said. "This is private property." He was a little drunk, Paige realized. The words seemed to dribble out of the side of his mouth.

"You do any time, Wayne?" Paige asked. It was a casual question, like asking about the weather, but he was pretty sure of the answer.

"Yeah," he said. "So what?"

"Dope?"

Cochran looked at the bag and nodded.

"Is that how you're paying for the house?"

"You fuckers are all the same," Cochran said and started to work his mouth around to say something else. "I want a lawyer."

Another prince.

"Shut up," Paige told him.

"You can't tell me to shut up in my own place."

"You're right, I'm being a prick." Paige lifted Cochran to his feet and pushed him into the house. He stopped in the kitchen, kicked the wheelchair out of the way, and took the cuffs off one hand.

"You try anything, I'll break your nose."

Cochran shrugged. Paige ran one of the cuffs through

the refrigerator door and slipped it back on Cochran's wrist. If he tries to run, Paige thought, the refrigerator will fall on him. Probably kill him. Paige decided he liked the idea. He sat down in the wheelchair and lit a cigarette.

"Let's try this one more time," he said. "Where's Tim?"

"I got nothing to say."

"But you ought to," Paige said. "Might be in your best interest."

"I didn't tell him to knock over no liquor store."

"No?"

"What are you, nuts?"

"A little," Paige said. He picked up an empty beer bottle and tossed it in the air.

"Oh man," Cochran said. "You think I'm scared of a fucking beer bottle? You don't know shit."

Paige lowered the bottle but kept it in his hand. He prodded the bag with it.

"You pull any liquor store jobs lately?"

"I told you, I don't do liquor stores."

"Know anybody who does?"

Cochran grinned.

"I guess not," Paige said. "You just sell dope and treat your nephew like shit."

"Fuck you."

Paige emptied the grocery bag on the table.

"Billy Dubowski had a joint on him when he died. Did he get it from you?"

Cochran laughed. "Little prick probably stole it. The kid was a born thief."

Unlike you, Paige thought. You probably had to go to night school.

"Nice dope," Paige said.

"You still don't have a warrant."

"I got a surprise for you. I don't need a warrant."

Paige spread the roll of money out on the table. That

got Cochran's attention. "All I need is Tim. The joker who shot his friend is out there looking for him. I want him alive."

"Hey, he's all yours. I got no use for him." He kept looking at the cash.

"That's a lot of money, Wayne."

Cochran shrugged.

Paige thought about what would happen if he busted Cochran. The public defender's office would step in immediately and Cochran would be out in about four and a half minutes. No warrant, illegal search, no case. He wouldn't get to keep his dope, however. He'd probably lose the money, too.

The only thing Paige had going for him was the fact that Cochran gave him permission to search Tim's room. The DA could make the argument that at that point Cochran's permission to search—coupled with an acknowledgment of the ongoing homicide investigation—was open-ended. A judge might rule in their favor. It would be a thin argument and the DA might not want to try it. On the other hand, he could talk to Kate Evans and she might go along with it. Maybe they could work a deal.

The biker stood there, leaning back on the refrigerator, seemingly unaffected by it all. Whatever anger Paige had felt earlier was gone, replaced by a feeling of sheer exhaustion. What could he do to this guy that would make any difference whatsoever?

The most he could hope for would be to give him a hard time for a few hours. Maybe Cochran had an outstanding warrant or two lying around someplace. Maybe they'd find something in the house to tie him to the robbery. Maybe pigs would fly.

"Where'd you get the gun?"

"I bought that gun legal."

"Where?"

"Florida."

Right, Paige thought. In Florida you could buy a cruise missile if you had the money. The stupidity of gun laws never failed to amaze him.

"Ballistics can take a look at it." Paige smiled. "Maybe you shot somebody else with it."

"I never shot anybody."

"Of course you didn't," Paige said. There was a phone on the kitchen wall. Paige called for a squad car. Cochran looked bored.

"You know Tim was on television," Paige said after he hung up. "They showed a tape of the robbery on the news."

Cochran grinned again. "I don't watch the news, too many niggers on it." The bruise on his forehead was red and swollen to about the size of a quarter.

Not nearly enough, Paige thought. I should have hit the son of a bitch with the bottle when I had the chance.

Rudolph was waiting in the car when Paige got back.

"Find anything?" he asked.

"A bag of dope and a big gun."

Rudolph looked at him.

"His uncle sells dope. That's where the Dubowski kid got the joint. What'd you get?"

"Nothing," Rudolph said. "He keeps a gun?"

"He's insecure."

"What if he decided to branch out?"

Paige shook his head. "He doesn't have the brains."

Timothy Cochran watched the police put his uncle in the patrol car. He was hiding behind a parked car a few yards down on the other side of the street, crouched next to the bumper so he could look out along the side and get a perfect view of the front door without being seen.

A detective stood on the front porch and watched the patrol car drive off. Tim waited until the detective walked to the corner and disappeared and then waited an extra few minutes just to be sure.

He started to get up, then dropped back down. What if there was another cop around someplace? What if they had the house under surveillance? Tim's mind went into a panic, thinking of all the things that would happen to him if the cops got hold of him. The robbery, Rap's death. It didn't matter that he was fourteen years old, not when somebody died. They weren't screwing around anymore, they fried kids his age for that stuff.

He sat frozen against the wheel well, his knees right up next to his chin. His heart was pounding and his hands were sticky with sweat.

What was he going to do?

He tried to think. What if he went around to the other side and made his way through the backyards? That way they wouldn't see him from the street. But what if there was a cop already inside the house?

Rap had said that cops were stupid but what the hell did Rap know? Rap was dead.

What if Bobby was somewhere around here, waiting for him?

He hugged his knees closer, trying to keep his fear under control. It was no use. The danger was everywhere. He glanced quickly at the house again and at his uncle's car, and then at the others on the street.

Bobby might be sitting in one them right now, just waiting for him to make a move.

His terror took control. He got to his feet and stayed low, scrambling along the parked cars. Any minute he expected to hear a door opening and see Bobby running down the sidewalk to catch him. He hurried along, the fear like a dead weight riding on his back. When he got to the end of the block, he broke into a run, so scared that he couldn't even look around to see if anyone was really chasing him.

It didn't matter. In his mind, he could already hear the footsteps. Even in the daylight, they reminded him of the sound of gunshots in the dark.

7

One of the first jobs Bobby did for Jacob Cross was on a neighbor. Cross didn't call it a job—it was more of a private joke, he said, just between friends.

The friends in this case were Al and Cheryl Silverman. An old story. Cheryl, a good-looking woman in her late twenties, had been a secretary in Silverman's accounting firm. Silverman divorced his wife of thirty years, married Cheryl, built a new house and started acting like he'd just discovered the true meaning of life.

Bobby could see the house from Cross's living room, a big modern palace made of pinkish brick that was set back from the road on a wide sloping hill dotted with pine trees. There was a black Mercedes and a little Japanese convertible parked in the driveway. Cross gave him a new Sony videocam, a diagram of the house and a key, and told him what he wanted done.

Cross wanted him to take some home movies.

The morning he slipped into the house, Bobby noticed that the black Mercedes was gone. He hid in one of the closets in the master suite, an enormous room with a bathroom at one end, big king-sized bed with a canopy in the middle and a sitting area with a couch and matching chairs at the other, directly in front of the closets. The door of one of the closets was slightly askew, leaving a crack on one side just big enough for the camera lens. Bobby adjusted the lens. The couch came into sharp focus.

Cheryl walked out of the bathroom, naked, her head wrapped in a white towel. She bent over the bed and toweled off her hair. It was blond and fashionably short. She turned toward the closets. Definitely not a natural blonde. Good tan except on her ass and around the small black triangle of pubic hair. She ran her fingers through her pubic hair, straightening it out. Excellent grooming habits.

Bobby looked through the camera and zoomed in close. Nice tits, no sag at all, no tan lines either. Probably went topless in the backyard. He thought if he looked close, he might find a few thin white surgery scars. A little help never hurt.

She returned to the bathroom and came out carrying a tube of K-Y Jelly. Then she lay down on the couch right in front of him, squirted a big glob of lubricant on her fingers, and started playing with herself.

Bobby turned the camera on. A few minutes later, the front door opened and somebody came galloping up the stairs.

Daddy's home, Bobby thought.

But unless Daddy was about twenty years old and wearing a pair of cutoff jeans and a Gatorade T-shirt, it probably wasn't Al Silverman.

She didn't even wait for him to undress. She undid his zipper, pulled out his cock, and starting sucking on him while he stood next to the couch, knees buckling slightly as her head bobbed up and down. He kept his hands on both sides of her face and his eyes closed while she worked her tongue all over him.

Bobby thought his own head was going to explode.

Finally, he had to look away and just listen. It wasn't any better. By the time he put his eye to the camera again, they were on the couch. She had her legs spread wide, head buried in the corner, hands holding on tight to the back of her knees while the kid slammed into her with pistonlike precision.

Bobby found himself staring at her face, her look of greedy determination, straining hard to meet each thrust. She didn't give a shit about the kid. The kid didn't exist at all except as some sort of device.

They finished quickly, rested for a few minutes and then started up again, this time on the bed. Bobby adjusted the camera angle and settled down into the darkness on the floor of the closet, listening to her moans and thinking about her face and all the secrets that it held.

When he handed over the videotape, Cross smiled.

"Now it starts to get interesting," he said.

He was right. Even Bobby had to admit that.

It was a lot simpler the second time around. Bobby went into the house in the middle of the night and made his way to the family room that looked out over the pool and the grove of red maples that blocked off the back of the house from the rest of the neighborhood. He switched on the television, put the tape in the VCR, adjusted the picture and turned the volume up high enough to wake a corpse. Then he slipped into the bathroom down the hall and waited.

He didn't have to wait long. Silverman arrived first, feet stomping on the stairs, coming to an abrupt halt in front of the television, round face trapped in the glare of the screen. Silverman was a little on the beefy side, hair going gray, fading past his temples. He squinted at the screen and then started yelling.

"Cheryl! Get down here!"

Cheryl appeared momentarily. She was dressed in a

shimmering white nightgown and stared at the television in disgust.

"What the hell is this?" Silverman demanded. He grabbed her by the arm and dragged her over to the television, stuck a finger right on the screen where his wife's lovely blond head was riding up and down on the kid's dick, and screamed, "What the hell is this shit!"

"Can't you figure it out on your own, Al?" she said and reached over to turn it off. She didn't make it.

Wrong move, Bobby thought, definitely the wrong move. He could see what was coming next, knew exactly what was about to happen.

Silverman let go of her arm and grabbed a handful of hair, pulling her head down so that she was bent halfway over. She fought him, screaming, raking his arm with her fingernails and swinging wildly at him. One of her punches caught him in the stomach and he grunted in pain.

He drove his fist into the middle of her face. She fell over, legs collapsing beneath her. He dragged her back up and punched her again, a short overhanded blow that bounced off the side of her face and slid down her cheek.

"You fucking whore!" he screamed. "You fucking two-bit whore." He tore the nightgown off her shoulders and punched her again when she tried to pull away. She screamed but the words got lost.

He pushed her face against the television screen, rubbing it back and forth.

"You like it?! You like what he's doing to you?!"

Bobby watched it all, letting the images roll over him, dissecting each one, camera angles, focus, the way the images seemed to dance across Cheryl's busted face, the single strand of fabric that still hung across the top of her body, torn and splattered with blood, the bloodstains going from red to pitch-black in the television's crazy light. Bobby stored the images away, an endless reel he could play again anytime he wanted.

The doorbell rang.

Even with the noise from the television, the bell sounded clear and bright. It seemed to wake Silverman up. He looked at his wife's broken face and let her go, a gesture of pure disgust. She fell at his feet and began to crawl toward the couch.

He turned down the television and listened. The doorbell chimed again. In his mind, Bobby thought of it as the touch of a magic wand.

"Oh, Jesus," Silverman said and ran out of the room. Cheryl continued her slow crawl to the couch. Bobby heard Cross's voice and followed its passage through the house.

Cross turned on the lights and Cheryl Silverman screamed.

"Turn them off, turn them off!"

Cross waited just enough to take in the scene in its entirety. The blood on the television screen, the torn nightgown, the woman on the couch, hiding her face from the light. Waited a little too long, Bobby thought, right past the buzzer into overtime. He was enjoying it, getting into the blood and the pain, trying to act nonchalant, but even from a distance, Bobby could see the fever in his eyes.

Interesting, Bobby thought.

Cross turned out the lights.

"My God, Al," he said, "what happened here?"

"He beat me up!" Cheryl screamed at him. "That's what happened. The bastard beat me up."

"You fucking whore," Silverman said and went for her. She pushed herself along the couch to get away from him.

"That's enough, Al," Cross said and grabbed his arm.

Al pointed at the television. "You tell her that," he said. Then, to Bobby's surprise, Al Silverman broke down and cried like a baby. Cross gently maneuvered him to a chair and sat him down, patting his shoulder lightly.

The doorbell rang.

"What the hell?" Al said.

"Let me go check," Cross said. He came back a few seconds later.

"It's the police."

"Oh God," Al said, his voice pleading. "I can't believe this is happening. You gotta take care of them for me, Jacob. I can't get involved with the police."

"Let 'em in," Cheryl said suddenly. "Let the whole goddamn neighborhood in. I want everybody to see what he did to me." She wiped the blood and tears away with the back of her hand and winced. "I hope you like jail, you fat, miserable cocksucker, because that's where I'm going to send you."

Cross waited a moment, then said reasonably, "I could do that, Cheryl, but then they'd have to see what you did as well. Is that what you really want? Have something like that get around?" Cheryl sunk into silence that seemed to last for hours. Finally, she waved him away.

Cross took care of the police. When he returned, Al shook his hand.

"I owe you for this," Al said. "You just let me know, anything you want, you just let me know."

"Oh," Cross said smoothly, "let's not worry about that right now." He reached over and turned off the television. "But I think we've seen enough of this, don't you?"

Taking care of the police wasn't a big problem for Cross. He had called them in the first place.

Of course, Al wouldn't know that, Bobby thought, not even while Cross was squeezing him for whatever he wanted—money, information, leverage; or maybe just a personal IOU that would sit there unused until the exact moment it was needed most.

Cross had his secrets, Bobby had his. He'd already made copies of the tape for himself.

A month later, after Bobby had made sure Cross

would be gone for the day, he pulled into Al's driveway and parked next to the convertible. He walked to the front door and rang the bell.

Cheryl answered it. Her face had pretty much healed, the bruises around her nose and eyes had faded to a sour yellow, and she had a pair of shiny new white teeth to replace the ones her husband had knocked loose. She was wearing shorts and a little white T-shirt that left her stomach bare.

Bobby tapped the door frame with the tape.

"Hi, there," he said.

Cheryl glared at him.

"Is this some kind of sick joke? Why don't you tell Al to cram it up his ass."

"Do I look like a joke to you?"

"You look like somebody with a lot of bad ideas. If you think I'm paying for that, you're dreaming."

"If I wanted money I wouldn't come to see you," he said. "Al's the one with the loot."

Bobby pushed his way past her, stepping into the hallway. He moved up close, running the tape up and down her bare arm, watching the goose bumps rise and fall.

"Shit," she said wearily and closed the door. She leaned against it, arms crossed, and looked him up and down. "You're a real treat, you know that. You want to tell me how you got the tape? I thought we had the only one."

Bobby threw the tape up in the air, caught it, and then tossed it to her.

"It's a gift. Keep it. I made some more copies."

"Some?" she said, and laughed. "And if I don't do what you want, you'll what, send the rest to the health club? Maybe my mom? Is that the deal?"

"Are you like this at Christmas, too?"

"Last Christmas I was in Miami, spoonfeeding Al's crazy old man. He craps all over himself and tries to feel me up. He thinks I'm his wife. I don't know which is worse.''

Bobby grinned. "I've been to Miami."

"I bet you have," Cheryl said. "You're a real sport. What have you got in mind?"

Bobby pointed toward the stairs.

"That's what I thought," Cheryl said. She waved her hand to move him along. "Let's get going, hotshot. I've got an appointment in an hour."

Bobby laughed. He was enjoying himself, not at all what he expected, but still having a very good time. He followed her up the stairs, watching her ass shake underneath the thin shorts.

"You got a great ass," he said.

"Lucky for you," Cheryl said, looking over her shoulder. "If my brains were as good as my ass, I wouldn't be in this mess in the first place."

She undressed, took a towel from the bathroom and laid it down on the bed, folding it in two to protect the spread. She was already wet when he slipped into her. He didn't have to do a thing.

Through it all, Cheryl tried to avoid looking at him, but he held her face with one hand and never let his eyes leave hers. He wasn't sure what he was looking for but didn't find it anyway. She did the rest on automatic pilot, tickling his ass with her fingertips, looking slightly amused when he came, squeezing his nuts to get it all. Neat, sweet and very professional. Bobby had to admire her for that.

When they were finished, she wiped herself off with the towel and dropped it on the floor.

"Just so you know," she said. "This is it. No instant replays. No return engagements. You can send that tape to the goddamn networks for all I care."

"What about Al?"

"What about him?" She marched over to her dresser and took out a shiny new gun from the top drawer, holding the gun up so he could get a good look at it. "I took it once. If that bastard lays a hand on me again, I'm going to blow his fat ass all the way back to New Jersey."

He got dressed first and watched her put on her clothes.

"You know," she said, "you never did tell me where you got the tape."

"I made it."

She shook her head. "That's what I thought. Did Al put you up to it?"

Bobby shrugged.

She looked at him curiously, as though she were deciding just how much she really wanted to know.

"Never mind," she said finally. "I'm not sure I give a shit anymore. It's too much trouble."

When they left, she dropped the gun in her purse.

"You carry that thing around with you?"

"Just to the shooting range," Cheryl said. "Practice makes perfect. You ought to keep that in mind—you and whoever you work for."

Bobby laughed all the way out the door.

At his apartment, Bobby ran the tape again, watching her face on the screen and thinking about the way she had looked at him from the bed. He tried to merge the faces together, looking for the connecting thread that ran between them. He couldn't. Instead, he discovered something different, an incident from his past that he had all but forgotten.

It was right after he had made his class film. He found himself driving through his professor's neighborhood and stopped in front of the house. The professor was gone, out of town for some film festival. He had taken Bobby's film with him, hoping to get it into competition.

Bobby broke into the house and began to wander around, moving between the rooms in a kind of daze. He had the feeling he could get lost in there, staggering through a darkness of his own making.

When he found the professor's film library, he had no idea what he was going to do. Only his hands seemed to know.

He took down all the films, dozens of reels that the professor kept in an air-conditioned vault in his study. The vault was lit with dull red light to protect the fragile reels. Bobby carried the film cannisters out one at a time, opened them up and dumped them in the middle of the floor. When he had emptied them all, he stirred the strands of film around with his hand, the celluloid cracking between his fingers.

He went out to the garage and found a can of gasoline. He poured the liquid into the pile and watched while the strands of film slowly melted together. He left the gas can in the middle of the pile of ruined film and drove home.

A week later, he returned to class. The professor handed his film to him without a word, staring down at him for several minutes, as though he didn't quite know what to say. In the end, he said nothing.

Bobby saw himself in the professor's eyes, not really caring what he saw in them, only that he was there. As it turned out, he got an A for the course and not much else.

Bobby took a break from his search for Jim to see a movie, the two-forty show at the Ritz, a dollar off the ticket price. He found a seat near the rear of the theater, on the aisle, like he always did.

The movie was part of a Truffaut revival. Bobby had only seen one Truffaut film in his life, *Jules and Jim*, and he had liked it. He liked the ending especially, when they drove the car off the bridge. This one was called *Day for Night*. It was supposed to be about movie-making and Bobby figured he might learn something.

The theater was virtually empty. There couldn't have

been more than a dozen other people in the theater, mostly couples, one or two singles.

Bobby preferred it that way. There was nobody around to interrupt the movie. Sometimes he went alone to the afternoon matinees at one of the mall theaters. No one went to those shows, and most of the time he'd have the place all to himself.

A young girl, long brown hair, a knapsack slung over one arm, was walking up the aisle. She kept her head down when she walked. Bobby thought she looked a little lost, like she didn't know where she was going. He smiled at her when she went past.

"How're you doin'?" he said.

The girl raised her head and smiled back. Her smile was faint, almost invisible. Bobby liked her smile. There was a whole world of possibilities in that smile.

The lights dimmed and the movie started. The girl returned to her seat a few minutes later, sliding in under the flickering light like she was looking for a place to hide.

The movie wasn't all in subtitles. Some of it was in English. Which was good. He didn't like subtitles. Plus there were a couple of sex scenes, and you didn't need subtitles for that. Bobby didn't learn much that he hadn't known before except the part about shooting night scenes in the daytime. They used a special kind of filter that made it look like it was dark. Not really, but close enough. He thought about some other films he'd seen and realized that most of them were shot the same way. The problem was, when they did it, you could still see the shadows from the sun.

He was distracted by the girl and had a little trouble concentrating on the film. His eyes kept straying to her, sitting by herself in the third row, scrunched down low so that only the top of her head was visible. Hoping to disappear, Bobby thought. He tried to imagine what she was like, where she was from, what her story was, but he kept getting his thoughts mixed up with what was on the screen.

It was just like reading subtitles.

When the movie ended, Bobby stayed in his seat. The girl was one of the last to leave, waiting until the rest of the people filed out before making her way to the exit. Bobby fell in behind her.

When they were outside, he came up beside her. She was digging in her backpack for something.

"How'd you like the movie?" he asked.

The girl looked at him suspiciously.

"It was okay," she said. Her eyes darted around, everywhere but to his face. It made her seem like she was getting ready to run away.

"But not as good as *Jules and Jim*," he said quietly.

"No." She looked surprised. "You liked *Jules and Jim?*"

"One of my favorites."

"Really? What about *The 400 Blows?*"

Bobby made an edgy motion with his hand. He hadn't seen the movie but had read about it someplace.

"I know what you mean," the girl said.

They stopped talking for a minute. He wanted to be alone with the girl, get to know her a little bit before he made his decision.

"What are you doing now?"

The girl was suspicious again. A normal, healthy reaction, Bobby decided. She shouldered her backpack, straightening out the straps.

"I was going to meet some people for dinner," she said.

"Mind if I tag along?"

"I don't know."

"Come on," he said. "I don't bite."

She hesitated for a moment, then said, "I guess it'll be all right."

"Terrific," he said and held out his hand. "My name is Bobby."

"Kimberly," she said and took his hand. Her skin was warm, a little moist. He held on longer than was absolutely necessary just to see what would happen. She didn't let go.

"Kimberly what?" he asked.

"Just Kimberly."

"Nice to meet you, Just Kimberly."

She laughed a little and took her hand away.

"Kimberly."

Perfect, Bobby thought.

Of course, there were no friends. She said they must have gotten lost somewhere and Bobby went along with the lie. They ate at a small place off Second. Kimberly picked the restaurant. Bobby had never been there before and liked everything about it except the waiter. When he ordered wine with dinner he mispronounced the name of the vineyard and the waiter corrected him, sounding the name out phonetically so that Bobby would understand.

"What a jerk," Kimberly said when he left.

Bobby pretended that it didn't matter.

When the waiter brought the bottle to the table, he only set down one glass.

"She's underage," the waiter said.

It pissed him off but he let it go.

"God," Kimberly said after the waiter took their order. "I drink wine all the time at home. I don't see what the big deal is."

"Me neither," Bobby said and pushed his glass over to her plate. "It's a stupid law."

She took a small sip and shuddered. "That's good," she said. She wiped her mouth with the end of her finger. It was a delicate motion, almost childlike, a wonderful movie moment.

"Are you laughing at me?"

"No," he said. "I was just thinking how pretty you are."

"Get out of here."

"That's exactly what I was thinking."

"I don't like my hair," Kimberly said. "It's too long."

"No," Bobby said firmly. "It's great just the way it is."

Kimberly rolled a strand between her fingers.

"Maybe you're right," she said. "I was going to get it cut but I couldn't make up my mind. Maybe I'll just leave it."

The waiter brought their salads. He acted like he wanted to say something but Bobby gave him a hard look and he left.

"Did you really like *Jules and Jim?* Or were you just saying that?"

"I've seen it three times."

Kimberly played with her salad. "What about the ending?" She was fishing, trying to confirm what he said.

"The lovers drive off a bridge together," Bobby said. He let his fork trail into the air, the kind of romantic gesture he'd seen actors make. "The perfect ending."

Kimberly smiled, nothing held back at all.

"I just love that movie," she said.

Bobby picked up his wineglass.

"Here's to the movies."

They stayed for dessert, a piece of strawberry pie for him, a chocolate hazelnut torte for Kimberly. He paid for dinner. Kimberly tried to pay for her half but he refused. He'd finished most of the bottle of wine and took the rest of it with him. He had the urge to crack the waiter with it, one quick shot up along his ear just to teach him some manners, but what would be the point?

He didn't want to scare the girl. Not yet.

They walked down South Street to the river and leaned

on the thick metal railings watching the people going up
the gangplank into a three-masted schooner that was docked
alongside Penn's Landing and had been converted into a
restaurant.

"Did you ever eat there?"

"No," Bobby said. "Should I try it?"

"Don't bother," Kimberly said.

"You been there a lot?"

"Lots of times," she said and changed the subject.

Two thoughts jumped into Bobby's mind. Her family
had money. You had to have money to go to a place like
that.

And two, much more important, Kimberly was a runaway. Every time she came close to talking about her family, she skipped right over it. Stiffened right up, shoulders
locked into place, mouth set in a small unhappy line.

Trouble with the family unit, Bobby thought. Happens
every day. People churned them out, watched them grow
up, and then they didn't know what the hell to do with
them. Everybody got fucked. People had more luck with
their pets than they did with their kids.

Kimberly looked unhappy and scared.

"I think I better split," Kimberly said.

Bobby folded his arms across his chest.

"What's your hurry?"

"I've got to meet my friends," she said and swallowed her words.

He took her hand, rubbing his thumb across her
knuckles.

"You don't have to lie to me, Kimberly," he said. "If
you want to split, split. But you don't have to make up
anything. I don't own you."

Kimberly bit down on her front lip, uncertain of what
to do next.

"You got a place to stay tonight?"

She shook her head.

"You could go home."

"No."

Firm. Very definite. Home was out.

"Come on," he said. "You can sleep on my couch."
He took her hand and started to pull her away.

She hesitated but didn't let go.

"I don't know," she said.

"What's the matter? You think I'm going to try
something?"

"Well, yeah," she said. "Maybe."

"What kind of a guy do you think I am?"

"I don't know."

"Listen, if you got a problem with it, you don't have
to come. It's as simple as that. I don't force anybody to do
what they don't want."

"I don't know."

It was a very delicate moment. One false move and
she'd be out of his grasp. He squeezed her hand and gave
her his best smile.

"Look," he said, "we'll go to my place. If you don't
like it, you can leave. No pressure. You decide. Okay?"

"Okay," she said. "But if I want to leave?"

"You leave."

"Okay. I've got to get my bike first."

They picked up her bike from the rack in front of the
theater and held hands all the way to the apartment. He
carried it up the stairs for her.

Kimberly stopped at the front door. She had a puzzled
look on her face.

"What do you do?"

"Do?"

"I mean work. Don't you have a job?"

"I'm self-employed," Bobby said.

"You don't sell dope or anything?"

"No. I'm a collector. I collect things from people."

"You mean like trash?"

"No. Like money."

Kimberly didn't understand.

"When people don't pay their bills on time, I find out whether they've really got the money to pay them. Sometimes they don't. But sometimes they do and they just don't want to pay. You know, they want the stuff for free. In that case, I take it back. Cars, televisions, stuff like that."

"Isn't that a little weird, taking things from people?"

"A little. I don't work that much anyway."

"That's great," Kimberly Morbach said. "Then you can do whatever you want to."

Bobby held the door for her.

"Always have."

8

Paige went to see Kate Evans at the DA's office on Thirteenth Street. He went late and didn't call and was absolutely certain he would find her at her desk. Kate had no other life beyond the cubicle she occupied on the fourth floor, at least none that Paige had ever discovered.

She was sitting at her desk, a pile of trial folders on her left, an ashtray filled to overflowing on her right. A cigarette smoldered in the ashtray and smoke hung in a dirty yellow haze above her head.

Paige rapped on the wall.

"Hello," he said.

"Hello yourself."

"How are you?"

"Is that a trick question?"

Paige laughed and pulled a chair up next to her. Kate crushed out the smoldering cigarette and lit another one.

"Did you hear the news? Brickman's going to Washington. The duplicitous little shit. He should do well there, don't you think?"

Brickman was Harvey Brickman; head of the DA's

white-collar crime task force and the departmental whiz du jour.

"Didn't take him long."

"One year, three months, two whole days. I can't wait to read his resignation letter. The word is he's going for the JFK mystique—ask not what you can do for your country, ask what your country can do for you. What the hell ever happened to public service?" She took a long drag and blew smoke over Paige's head. "I think Stalin had the right idea. He had all the lawyers shot."

She smiled sweetly. "And what can I do for you, Pat?"

He lit a cigarette. Their smoke mingled together. It must be love, Paige thought.

"I need help keeping somebody in jail."

"That's a nice thought. What'd he do?"

"Dope, maybe assault. Maybe knowledge of a homicide."

Kate listened thoughtfully and plucked a phantom piece of tobacco from her tongue. "That's too many maybes, Pat. Is there a warrant in here someplace?"

"Not exactly."

"Why don't you tell me the whole story and don't leave anything out."

Paige told her. Twice. The first time she listened without interruption. The second time she asked questions.

"He gave you permission to search the boy's room?"

"Yes."

"And you went in the other room?"

"Yes."

"Why?"

"I thought it was a good idea."

"Well, it wasn't. The court doesn't like good ideas, they like probable cause. You know that."

"I thought he might be hiding something about Tim. I still think he is."

Kate shook her head. "Sorry. That won't hold up. The dope won't hold up, either. The assault might. Then again the judge might say you've been a bad Scout and take away your merit badge. How soon can you find the boy?"

"I haven't the faintest idea."

"You booked him at the Roundhouse?"

Paige nodded.

"Well," Kate said, "I suppose we could take him on a station tour. Has he got a lawyer?"

"Probably."

"Then we'll ship him out to someplace interesting for the evening. Back to Kensington. At the very least, we can lose him for a couple days. Is the boy in real danger?"

"His friend's dead. He will be, too, if I don't find him."

"I can try for a material witness ruling. It's a homicide. Maybe his lawyer's a jerk. That's the best I can do. If you find anything that'll help, call me."

"Thanks, Kate."

He stood up and put the chair back against the file cabinet.

"Pat?" she said. Then shook her head. "Never mind."

"What?"

"I'm glad you're back." She laughed. "Listen to me. I sound like my mother."

"Don't you like your mother?"

"No, I don't like my mother. Everybody else does. What the hell, they never had to live with her."

Paige ate dinner at Arby's and spent the rest of the night parked in front of Tim Cochran's house, watching and waiting and going home in the morning with nothing.

Glover called him into his office the next afternoon. There were two other people crowded into the cubicle. Glover sat uncomfortably in his chair, hands on top of the desk, looking like a man who'd already left for the day.

A woman sat in front of his desk, somewhere between thirty-five and forty, short brown hair, hands folded primly in her lap, a red-and-green silk scarf draped carefully over one shoulder of her beige suit. There was an expensive-looking briefcase beside the chair. She seemed a little over-dressed for a meeting with the cops. In fact, she looked like somebody who had been overdressed most of her life, not spoiled so much as conditioned.

Next to her stood a gray-haired man in a blue blazer, gray slacks, a blue oxford cloth shirt and a blue-and-white paisley tie. He wore penny loafers. There was a certain arrogance about him, a sense of privilege, like a child who's been given too many toys and now thinks he deserves them all. Paige decided it was his face. It belonged on somebody else's body. He looked familiar, but Paige couldn't figure out why or how.

"Why don't we bring Detective Paige up to speed on this thing," Glover said. He nodded at the woman. The man in the blazer leaned down to whisper something but the woman shook her head. She seemed mildly annoyed at him. Maybe it was his penny loafers.

"It's all right," she said and looked at Paige. "My daughter is missing. She's been gone for two days. We don't know where she is or if she's in trouble. We don't believe she is, but we'd like some help finding her."

"Who is she?" Paige asked.

The woman raised her eyebrows.

"Kimberly Morbach. Her father is Senator James Morbach. I'm Susan Morbach. Her mother."

Paige looked at the man.

"Who are you?"

"I'm a friend of the family," he said and glanced at Glover. The captain looked right through him.

"Where's the senator?"

"He's in the middle of a re-election campaign," Susan Morbach said quietly.

"Oh," Paige said.

"The point," the man said, "is that we'd like your help. No press, no publicity. The senator doesn't want this to turn into a political thing."

"I can see where that might be a real problem for him," Paige replied. "Being a politician."

"Do you?"

"Captain," Paige said, "can I talk to you for a minute?"

Glover seemed relieved just to get out of his office. He followed Paige out through the small wooden gate and the worn-out benches and into the hall. They stood together by the drinking fountain.

"What the hell is this?"

"I'm in a kind of a bind here," Glover said.

"That means I'm screwed, right?"

"You think I've got a choice? Somebody calls the mayor, the mayor calls the commissioner, the commissioner calls the commander, and the commander tells me what to do. And I do it."

"This is serious bullshit."

"They just want some help."

"Tell them to hire a detective."

Glover laughed. "They just did. They asked for you. Make it easy on yourself. You're already looking for one kid. Check around for another one. Hand out a few pictures, ask a few questions. Nobody's expecting miracles here."

"She is," Paige said. "Who's the guy?"

"His name is Cross. Some kind of advisor. He showed up with her."

Paige thought about the man's face again.

"Never mind," Paige said. "I know who he is."

"Yeah?"

"He's the one who called the mayor."

The man in the blazer was gone. Probably in leaning on the commander, Paige thought, using his phone to give the mayor a call. Susan Morbach was alone in the office, the briefcase propped open on her knees. She smiled at Paige, a smile so warm and generous, with just the right touch of awkwardness to it, that he suspected she might have pulled it from her briefcase along with the manila envelope she held out for him.

"I brought some pictures," she said.

Inside were half a dozen photographs. The best was a black-and-white school picture, a close-up of the girl's face. To his surprise, Kimberly Morbach looked completely normal—a girl who had dates and liked horses and hung out at the mall with her friends.

"Were you expecting something else?" Susan said. The smile was still in place, but there were little stress lines around her mouth and he could see the dark skin peeking through the makeup around her eyes.

"She doesn't look like a runaway," he said.

"What exactly do they look like?"

The last one I saw had a hole in his chest, Paige thought but kept his mouth shut.

"I could use some extra copies of this one if you've got them. Also anything you can tell me about where she might go or who she might stay with."

Susan Morbach collected the pictures.

"I'll send over some copies tomorrow," she said. "As for where she might go, I don't know. I talked to the school and several of her friends. They don't know where she is, either. I don't think they were lying."

"Has she done this before?"

"No."

"Then why did she do it now?"

Susan thought about it for a moment.

"Two nights ago, she had an argument with her father."

"What about?"

"There was some trouble at school. She called one of

her teachers a pig. Frankly, I think she was right but that doesn't make it any better. That was the night she ran away.''

"Any calls?"

Susan shook her head.

"She have money?"

"Probably. She didn't take her wallet. I don't know why. But she took her credit cards." Susan held up her hand. "I've already contacted them. They said it would take at least a day to trace one of her cards—if she uses it.''

"Drugs?"

Susan Morbach shook her head.

"You sure?"

"Yes, I'm sure."

"She drink?"

"No," she said. "You sound like my husband."

"I hope not," Paige said. Susan smiled. Paige thought she was going to laugh out loud. It took her a lot of work not to.

"I'm in the middle of a homicide right now," he said. "But I'll do what I can. I may not be able to do anything."

"I understand. The boy who was killed. I read about it in the paper." Susan reached out her hand as if to touch him, then pulled it back. Her awkwardness was genuine this time.

"Kimberly's a good girl," she said quietly. "She knows what's right and what's wrong. I just want to see her come home safe."

She handed him a business card. "I have an office on Walnut. Please call me there if you find out anything."

Paige read the card. It said, PHILADELPHIA RESOURCES, INC. Susan Morbach was the executive director.

"It's nonprofit," she said. "We're middlemen. We try to bring people with money and resources together with people who don't have either.''

"Having any luck?"

"Sometimes."

Paige walked her to the elevator.

"Why did you pick me for this?"

"My husband was given your name. He said you came highly recommended."

"I'm surprised he even knows I exist."

"Maybe you're better known than you think."

"If I was, he would have been here himself."

Susan frowned, as if she thought he was being dense on purpose.

"My husband has other priorities," she said. "He's a politician. That makes him more of a movie star than a father, don't you think?"

"What's that make you and Kimberly?"

"Extras," Susan Morbach said. "Just like you."

When Paige returned to his desk, he found a pale beige business card stuck on top of his phone. He looked at it for a few seconds before picking it up.

The printing on the card was clean and crisp.

JACOB CROSS, ATTORNEY-AT-LAW. No phone. No address.

Paige turned the card over. Cross had written him a note.

"I knew your father," the note said. "Let's have lunch."

Paige understood Susan Morbach's position completely. His own father had been a politician.

9

A week after meeting Kimberly Morbach, Bobby Radcliff realized he was starting to run low on drugs. Not running out, exactly, but definitely cutting into his supply.

By then, it didn't matter that much. Kimberly Morbach was in the ozone most of the time anyway.

She sat curled up at the end of the sofa and stared at the television set. While she watched, her mouth would drift open in a slow languid motion and close again as if pulled by an invisible string. It reminded Bobby of a fish dying on a dock. She moved occasionally, sometimes to change the channel, sometimes to stagger off to the bathroom. If she remembered. When she spoke to him, it was usually to ask if he could make the walls stop melting.

That first night, Bobby had played his movie for her. She cried when it was over, telling him through the tears how she thought it was so sad and so beautiful.

"It's just a movie," Bobby had said.

"No," she told him, "it's more than that. It's true."

She wanted to see it again, and pointed out things on the screen: the way the cops were always seen towering over him, making him appear smaller than he really was; the way the reporter never wrote down anything he said; the way the shadows emphasized his solitude.

Bobby wanted to tell her those were all accidents. Nobody planned them, they just happened that way—the way he found her, for instance. But he didn't want to spoil the moment for her.

Now she sat there, her jaw moving slowly up and down, all on its own, watching a soap opera. In the middle of the scene, she changed the channel. To the weather channel. She didn't seem to notice the difference. This is your brain, Bobby thought. This is your brain on drugs. With a side order of bacon.

That first night had been the hardest. She'd had enough strength to fight him then. It was fun for a while, but he finally got tired of it and slapped her hard enough to knock her halfway across the room. She wouldn't stay down. When she tried to get away, he clipped her one along the back of her neck and she stayed down after that.

He tied her up, wrapping a fifty-foot piece of cord around her legs, pulling them up close to her chest and tying her hands behind her back and the other end of the rope to her ankles. That way, if she tried to move, she'd end up flat on her face or her back. Either way, she wasn't going anyplace.

Just before he wrapped her mouth with duct tape, she managed to say something.

"Please don't kill me," she whispered.

"So young and so morbid," Bobby said and pulled the tape around her head a couple times and dumped her in his bedroom closet, where he could keep an eye on her.

Then he got the needle ready.

The first shot was a combination of blotter acid and methamphetamine. He cooked half a dozen fifteen-milligram Desoxyn tablets in a small saucepan on the stove and watched the little yellow tablets bleach white in the boiling water. He waited for the water to cool and dropped in two hits of the blotter acid and let them soak. He had a make-shift hypodermic—a needle taped onto the end of an eyedropper—and filtered the liquid into it through a cotton ball.

"Good veins," he told her and slid the needle into her arm. He flagged a little blood into the needle and shot her up.

The effect, as Bobby remembered it, was like going from zero to sixty in no time at all.

She stiffened and threw her head back suddenly, eyes rolling into the white. He could hear her teeth grind, an involuntary reaction to the speed. She couldn't speak; she was too wired to speak. Instead, she just sat there shaking as the rush of chemicals spurted through her system. He loosened the duct tape around her mouth, giving her a little more room to breathe.

It was also a precaution. She might start to vomit, and with the tape on, she could choke to death. There was also the chance she might go into shock but he doubted it. He kept a bowl of cold water and a washcloth nearby just in case. Her eyes bulged, round and moist like a frog's.

"Shit's a real bitch, isn't it?" he said.

He kept her in the closet for the first four days, keeping the hits of acid and speed fairly regular. He would sit with her occasionally, scrunching down on the other side of the closet just to keep her company. She didn't seem to recognize him. Occasionally, she screamed, her voice howling through the tape, sounding like it was coming from another room, another universe.

On the fifth day, he took her out of the closet and shot her full of phenobarbital and let her sleep, although it took a few hours for her to finally settle down.

Kimberly still knew how to eat, but as a precaution, in case she forgot, Bobby gave her some of his vitamin tablets. She didn't fight him on it. As for food, she liked chicken noodle soup and canned ravioli, even though most of it ended up on her lap. She ate peanut butter sandwiches like a hound, licking the peanut butter off the bread and leaving the discarded pieces on the couch.

When she started to panic a little that evening, Bobby hit her with a short dose of acid and speed. She took it like a trouper. No more shakes. No more screams. She just closed her eyes and swayed back and forth. He thought she looked like Stevie Wonder when she did it. Except that Little Stevie probably hadn't pissed in his pants lately.

Now she sat there, a dark stain spreading down the side of one leg, staring at him with a terrified expression on her face. The stain moved further down her leg and spread to the couch.

"I bet if I put you in a snowsuit," Bobby said, "you'd swell up just like a sponge."

Kimberly started to cry.

"I didn't mean to," she said. "I forgot."

"You think that makes it okay?"

Kimberly took hold of his hand and rubbed it against her cheek. "Please," she whispered.

Bobby put his arm around her. She moved closer to him but kept hold of his hand, rubbing it across her cheek. He reached down to her breast, squeezing it softly. She didn't respond. He started to get up.

Kimberly held on tight to his hand. She smelled of urine and sweat and her hair hung straight down across her shoulders, dirty and lifeless. Bobby patted her cheek.

"You need a bath."

At first, she was afraid to get into the bathtub. Bobby had to coax her to get into it. After that, she sat still while Bobby washed her, working the lather around her breasts and between her legs. He shampooed her hair and the suds ran down her face into her eyes.

"It hurts," she said.

"Keep your eyes closed," he told her. She did what

she was told and he brushed some of the shampoo away.

He rinsed her off and pulled her out of the tub. She was small enough that he could lift her up without any effort, almost like a child. He toweled her off and stood back to watch while she shivered in the harsh white light of the bathroom, arms pressed tight against her sides, not bothering to cover herself: a tiny little girl with fist-sized breasts and pale brown tufts of pubic hair. The light playing off the whiteness of the tiles seemed to shrink her down, making her look even smaller and more helpless.

It reminded him of the kid lying dead on the concrete.

Bobby closed the lid on the toilet and told her to sit down on it. She complied instantly, sitting very prim, knees pressed together, hands cupped firmly over each one.

He pushed her hands away.

"Open your legs," he said.

Kimberly blinked back tears.

"Open them," he said. She moved them apart slightly. Bobby put his hand between her knees and pushed her legs all the way open, casually playing with her pubic hair, then moving his fingers lower.

"You know how to use that?" he asked.

Kimberly acted as if she hadn't heard him. He moved his fingers some more. Her mouth opened slightly.

"Do you?"

"Yes," she whispered.

He took his hand away and patted her cheek. "Why didn't you say so in the first place?"

Bobby walked her down the hall to his bedroom and turned on the light. There were piles of clothes on the bed and the floor. He swept them out of the way. She got on the bed without being told.

"What I want you to do," he said, "is keep your eyes open. Okay?" Kimberly did what he asked. He took off his pants and kicked them into the pile with the rest of his clothes. Going to have to do some laundry one of these days, he thought.

He leaned over her, pressing down with his weight, and kissed the side of her face. She closed her eyes, squeezing them so tight that the only thing he could see was a thin line of puffy red flesh wet with tears.

"Open your eyes," he said. "I want to see them."

"Please," she said, looking at him at last. "Don't hurt me."

Bobby smiled.

"This is something very special, just between us."

He watched her eyes, seeing the pupil expanded in a dark moist circle, swallowing light and tears.

"Peekaboo," Bobby said and pushed himself into her.

Kimberly didn't say anything when he put her back in the closet. Instead, she was very cooperative, almost helpful. But he put the tape on her, just to be sure.

She started to cry again.

"A word to the wise," Bobby told her. "Lighten up. If you're a really good girl, maybe we'll do something later. A little shopping. Would you like that?"

Kimberly managed to nod.

Bobby closed the door. Then he collected the guns and the mask and got the needle ready again.

In the darkness of her cell—that was how she thought of it, the place he sent her when she was bad—she tried to hold certain thoughts in her mind: the face of her mother, the way her bed felt when she snuggled down into it, the scent of the lavender sachet that she kept in her bathroom. Her thoughts scattered and ran, broken pieces of a past she was no longer sure was her own.

When she closed her eyes, she saw flashes of bright crimson flame. When she opened them, the walls moved. At other times, she felt as if her face was swathed in cobwebs, and when she tried to shake them off, her mind did a lazy rollover as though she were rotating in space somewhere.

At odd moments, the fear would rise up inside her, a dark shadow that hung on every sound and movement, perceived or imagined. When it came, she could only shut her eyes tight and pray for it to go away. It never really did; it seemed as much a part of her now as the depressions that roared in behind the fear and left her weak and helpless. When that happened, the man would carry her to the couch and try to feed her.

She had no interest in food but let him try because that was what he wanted. It ran down her face and dripped into her lap and she watched with a strange fascination as though it were happening to someone else.

If she dropped her chin, she could touch the rope that he had used to tie her up. The surface of the rope felt like the scales of a snake and the chemical taste of the tape that covered her mouth stuck to her tongue. She could smell the man's skin, a slightly astringent smell, high and wild, feel his touch, lose herself in the empty glow of his eyes. That was why he wanted hers open.

The sensations flew at her from out of the darkness and then disappeared. She had no control over them, no more than she had over the wind or the man himself. What was his name? She couldn't remember. Where had he come from? Nowhere. It seemed he was always there. Before he had been her father; now he had another name, one that he kept hidden from her.

If she was bad, he punished her. If she was good, she got to sit on the couch and watch television. He had told her that. Now she was back in the closet but she didn't know why. Maybe it was because she had got the couch wet. Maybe it was something else.

When she found out his name, she would find out what she'd done wrong and never do it again. Not ever.

Her jaws ached from grinding her teeth and her skin

felt cold and sticky from sweat. The man had left her legs untied and they no longer hurt as much. Except that there was an occasional spasm, like little electric shocks running through them. Her right foot was numb. Her arms felt heavy and there was a growing pain in her chest when she breathed.

She coughed up phlegm behind the tape, felt it lodge on the edge of her tongue and swallowed it.

She pushed the pain deep down inside of her where it didn't matter. If she tried real hard, she could forget about it entirely, pretend it wasn't there. Like everything else.

She had some memory of who she had been but it was overshadowed by who she was now. Her mother couldn't find her. No one could find her.

And her father didn't care.

Kimberly Morbach didn't need anything but the man who held her captive.

She felt her bladder release again, a small trickle that spread out across her bottom and down the back of her legs. Tears welled up in her eyes again, ran down her cheek and under the tape. She could taste the salt.

She wasn't going to do this anymore.

She wasn't going to be bad anymore.

She would do whatever he told her to do.

10

How many hamburgers could one man eat and still survive?

Paige counted the crumpled-up wrappers on his front seat. Twenty-seven so far this week. His car looked like a landfill, little balls of paper scattered everywhere and streaks of dried ketchup across the vinyl where he had made a halfhearted attempt to wipe it up. He took a drink from a half-empty cup of coffee and immediately spit it out into the street.

Paige looked inside. A cigarette butt floated lazily in the day-old coffee, surrounded by a grimy slick of ashes and tobacco. He dumped the rest of it out the window and lit another cigarette to kill the evil taste in his mouth.

It had not been a good week.

They had let Wayne Cochran go. After playing hide-and-seek with his attorney—a soft-spoken man in a plaid suit who had turned out to be a lot smarter than he looked—the judge told Kate Evans better luck next time and cut the ex-biker loose with a warning. If his nephew showed up and Cochran didn't produce him, the judge was going to take it personally.

Wayne lost his gun, his dope and his money. His attorney said he would appeal. Fat chance.

Paige spent the rest of his time looking for Tim, returning to South Street again and again and finding nothing each time. The same was true for Kimberly Morbach. Nobody had seen either one of them and nobody cared.

Except Susan Morbach.

After two days of no luck, he stopped by her office on Walnut Street. It was half a block from Broad on the second floor of an old building recently redone in ersatz art deco, which meant some new carpeting in the lobby, a fresh coat of paint on anything that didn't move, and fake brass wall sconces every four feet. They added a fake name—the Winslow Arms—and probably tripled the rent.

They missed the elevator, though. It rattled and hummed and took half a minute to go one floor.

The elevator opened directly into the offices of Philadelphia Resources, Inc. There was a small reception room—salmon-and-white with black leather chairs, lots of plants and *National Geographic* magazines and a four-color brochure filled with group photographs of various city folk, all of them looking deprived but spunky.

Give it a rest, Paige thought. He hated cheap cynicism and hated it even worse when he found himself falling into it. He reached for a cigarette and stopped when the receptionist tapped a small sign on her desk with a pen. THANK YOU FOR NOT SMOKING, it said. As if to compensate, she gave him a warm smile and Paige felt suddenly out of place, as if he'd turned a corner somewhere and found himself in a world where everything he had learned no longer applied. It happened infrequently but enough that it made him wonder.

What had he missed?

Would it matter if he knew?

Susan Morbach appeared, standing in a hallway. He walked toward her, wondering if he asked her these questions, whether she'd have an answer for him. She struck him as a woman who knew about all different kinds of rules and what they meant. When he got closer, he changed his mind about asking her.

Susan Morbach looked like hell.

"Have you found her?" she asked.

Paige thought he might lie to her, tell her that he had a lead or that someone had seen her and he was following it up, but that wasn't true, wasn't part of his rules, and when it came down to it, they were the only ones he knew well enough to follow.

"No," he said and the dark circles of her eyes seemed to grow darker as though they were filling up with blood, draining her heart and leaving her skin even paler than before. He took hold of her elbow but she brushed his hand away.

"Jesus Christ," she snapped, "I can stand on my own two feet." Then, more softly, "I'm sorry. I don't mean to bite your head off. Come back to my office."

Her office was the same color as the rest of the office except the pictures on the wall were of her husband and daughter. In only one, Paige noticed, did the two of them appear together. It was probably just a coincidence.

Susan slumped in her chair. Paige saw a map of the city spread out on the desk in front of her, with various sections outlined in red. The outlined sections started with Center City and worked their way out from there in a lop-sided spiral.

"I've been doing my own searching," she said. "I haven't found her either."

"It's only been a few days."

She put her finger on the map, punching the paper.

"You may not think so," she said, "but I know what it's like out there. She could be dead in two hours, let alone two days." She looked away from him, out her window to the rooftop on the other side of the building and took a deep breath. "I don't know what else to do."

"What's your husband think?"

"My husband doesn't worry about things until they're right on top of him. He thinks she'll be home any second now, tired, scared, begging his forgiveness. When he's done yelling at her, he'll ship her off to a boarding school in New Hampshire where he won't have to think about her anymore."

She seemed to remember he was there. "Do you smoke?"

Paige nodded.

"Give me one, please."

It was an oddly gracious request, and Paige shook one out of his pack for her.

"I haven't smoked in ten years," she said. "It's not so bad when you borrow them, is it?"

"Worse," he said.

She laughed and dug around in her desk drawer. "Do you always tell the truth?" She made it sound like a question of personal hygiene.

"Not always." He handed some matches to her.

"So it's just for me?"

The question, as he understood it, was—did his attitude have anything to do with her husband? No. If it did, he wouldn't even be there.

"You deserve it. At least I think you do."

"Do you have many friends, detective?"

"Not that many."

"I just wondered," she said and lit the cigarette, took a short drag and held it away from her. Then she dropped it in a coffee cup on the desk. It made a sizzling sound as it died. "God, what an awful taste. I don't know why I started smoking in the first place."

She shook her head. "I'm sorry. I'm babbling."

"You don't have to apologize."

"No," she said. "I suppose I don't." She picked up the map and shook it. "This is all I've been able to do. I go from the map to the street and back again. I don't sleep. I hardly eat." She dropped the map on the desk. "I never thought I'd have to do this."

"Have you checked the hotels?"

"No."

"What about the airlines? The bus station?"

Susan shook her head.

"Those are all places you should be checking. I don't have the time for it."

She wrote a note for herself on a yellow legal pad.

"All right, I'll start this afternoon. Anything else?"

"Use the phone. It's easier than walking and it'll save you some time."

"Safer, too."

"Yes."

It dawned on him that he had just opened a door. Susan followed him inside.

"Are you telling me that I shouldn't be looking for her?"

"No. But you shouldn't be out on the streets by yourself. Especially at night. It's not safe. You know that."

"Do you think she's in danger?"

"She could be. I don't know."

"Do you think she might be dead?"

The word stopped both of them cold.

"No." It was a lie but not much of one. She could be alive, she could be dead, she could be anywhere in the world. It did no good to speculate. Speculation made you crazy.

"But you think it's a possibility?"

"Not right now."

"I wish you'd stop talking like a cop and just answer my question. Do you think she's been killed?"

"I don't know."

"There's a terrific answer," Susan said bitterly.

He tried once more—an explanation, of sorts.

"I gave her description to the medical examiner's office and told them to call me if they get a body. They haven't called. So until they do, stop thinking about it. It won't help."

"Nothing helps."

"That's not true. Maybe she's sitting in the Holiday Inn right now watching television. She might even want to come home. All you have to do is let her know. But you're not doing that."

"I don't know what else to do."

"For one thing, you could stop treating it like a political problem."

"My husband—"

"Your husband isn't even involved. He sends somebody like Jacob Cross around to deal with the mess."

"It isn't like that."

"It's exactly like that. You know it, I know it. Jacob Cross knows it. The only one who's been left out is Kimberly."

She let her hands play out along the edge of the desk.

"You make us all sound like monsters."

"You're not," Paige said, putting the emphasis on the *you*. He wasn't sure about the senator. He might make the grade.

He was surprised to find Susan Morbach smiling at him. What bothered him, he decided, was that he liked it.

"I can see why you don't have a lot of friends."

"I wonder about it myself sometimes."

"That makes you different from almost everyone I know."

"I doubt that."

She began to straighten her desk, folding the map up carefully, arranging papers in neat square piles, brushing her hair back with her fingers, regaining some composure in the process.

"If you think I'm going about this wrong," she said when she finished, "then tell me what I should do."

"What you should have done in the first place. Get the police involved—officially. Talk to the media. Let them look for her. Stop pretending that you can do it alone."

"Will you still help?"

"As much as I can."

Paige was going to say don't count on me but didn't. He couldn't decide whether he was lying again or just learning to be polite. Either way, it didn't feel very good.

"I want my daughter back," Susan Morbach said. "I'll do whatever I have to do. Nothing else matters."

Susan Morbach called him a few hours later. The conversation was short. She had spoken to Jacob Cross and it was decided that his suggestions were premature and overly alarmist. They were certain Kimberly would turn up very soon. She whispered, "I'm sorry," just before she hung up.

Now Paige sat alone in his car and thought about Jacob Cross and tried to put his dislike for him on some kind of scale that might make the whole thing palatable, and then he was thinking about his father, and he realized he had confused the two of them, and his hatred, so far away and so diffuse, came to rest somewhere closer to home.

He dropped it and put his mind on his work.

Where was Tim Cochran? And where was Kimberly Morbach?

He had another thought, more disconcerting than the others because it had come out of nowhere.

Where was Susan Morbach?

11

Kimberly Morbach sat in the front seat of the car, floating along in a white oval of light, a dense, formless cloud that held her in place. Without it she thought she would drift away. Bobby's hand snaked through the cloud and covered her own. It felt warm and elastic, the flesh as thick as rubber. She held it tight, one more anchor in an anchorless world.

"You really like that shit?" Bobby said. Kimberly didn't respond. She heard him, he was sure of that, but she was too blown away to answer, noodling along in her own little acid bath, watching the walls breathe. Bobby had been into acid once but didn't do it anymore. All that psychedelic crap gave him the shakes. He did speed, he did coke, he smoked an occasional joint. He could walk on water if he had to.

Bobby gave her breast a squeeze and walked his fingers across her chest to the other one. He believed the right one was smaller.

"Now why do you suppose that is?" he asked. "Maybe it's just God's way of saying fuck you, nobody's perfect."

Kimberly coughed, a short hacking gasp that sounded like someone tearing a piece of cardboard in half.

"We'll have to pick you up some medicine," Bobby said. "Be a real bummer if you croaked."

Kimberly heard the word and crouched lower in the seat. It was so very clear in her mind. If I stay in the cloud, she thought, death won't ever find me.

Bobby thought he'd do it in the city this time. There was a new CVS store just off South Broad. He'd been in it twice that week and liked what he saw. Nice clean wide aisles, lots of light, and doing a steady business from all the Italian widows in South Philly. He could park in the center parking lane of Broad, and from there it would be an easy shot to I-95 or the Walt Whitman into New Jersey. Any way he looked at it, it was just about perfect.

And when it was over, he could decide what to do about the girl. As much as he hated to admit it, he liked having her around. She wasn't much trouble, and she gave him something to do between jobs. If worse came to worst, he could always drive her out to the Pine Barrens and dump her in a swamp. You could dump half of Philadelphia in the Pines and not even make a ripple. In a couple of years, she'd turn into a cranberry bush.

Maybe he'd take a drive out there just for something to do. There was an old abandoned cabin he'd found one time, back in the woods near the Batsto ironworks, and he wouldn't mind going back. He had the drugs in the car. It might be fun to spend a few days in the ozone with Kimberly. Really get to know her. The cabin had a water pump and an outhouse and a fireplace. All he'd need would be a few blankets and some food.

He stopped at a McDonald's and ate dinner in the car. Kimberly picked at her french fries, moving them around the white paper bag and spreading them out over her lap like pieces of a jigsaw puzzle.

"Don't play with your food, dear," Bobby told her. "It makes you look like an asshole."

Kimberly stuck a french fry in her mouth and chewed it slowly.

"Now take a drink of soda."

Kimberly raised the cup and sucked through the straw.

Bobby took the gun from under the seat and pressed it against the side of her mouth. He rubbed it slowly over her lips, pushing the straw out of the way. Her mouth closed over the end of the barrel and she began to suck it, nursing diligently on the cold gray metal. Bobby threw his head back and laughed. He took the gun away. Kimberly stuck another french fry in her mouth as if nothing had happened.

"You're too much. I ought to patent your ass." Kimberly kept on eating. "Hurry up, dear," he told her. "We're going on a little trip."

She didn't hear him. He finally got tired of waiting for her and grabbed the french fries and Coke and dropped them out the window.

He parked the Camaro in the center of Broad Street, right behind a white Buick, taking up two spaces so he wouldn't have to worry about getting out. It was nearly eight-thirty, the light just beginning to go, the sun dropping in an orange fireball behind the buildings. There were a few people on the street, not too many. Most of the neighborhood was still eating dinner or getting ready to go out.

Bobby checked his gun and then took out another one from under the seat, the same one he'd given to Tim Cochran. For some reason, he couldn't remember where he'd gotten it from. There were some scratchings on the barrel that looked like somebody had tried to cut their initials into the metal with a screwdriver but that didn't help him. A gun was a gun. You aimed it at somebody. The gun went bang. Somebody died. But not today.

"We're going to play cops and robbers," Bobby said to her. "Only we're going to be the robbers." He wrapped her hands around the handle of the gun and pressed them together. "What you have to do," he said, "is point this at the first son of a bitch you see. That's all. Just stick it in their face and don't move. Think you can handle that?"

Kimberly nodded. Bobby took the gun away from her, broke open the cylinder, just to make sure it was empty. "No bullets for the bimbo," he said and laughed. Make a great title for a movie. With Richard Widmark if he was about thirty years younger. The new guys didn't have a hair on Widmark. He could scare a cinderblock to death.

He closed the gun, twisting the cylinder around. Then he cocked it and gave it back to her. She took hold of the gun with two hands, just the way he'd showed her.

Bobby took her chin and turned her face toward his. He was going to tell her that if she had any ideas about making a run for it, he'd know it and he'd kill her. But her eyes were like two empty windows and her face was a blank wall. He slipped the mask over his face, tugging it down into place. She looked at him curiously, as though she suddenly understood who he really was.

He patted her cheek.

"Don't you worry, darlin'," he said, laughing at his own tattered drawl. "Tonight you're ridin' with the King."

The salesgirl behind the counter saw them come in. She looked at Bobby's face and giggled.

"Can I help you?"

Bobby laid the gun on the counter level with her stomach. She backed into the cigarette rack behind her, spilling half a dozen cartons on the floor.

"Yeah," he said. "You can take all the money from the register and put it in one of those plastic bags you got down there before I blow your silly ass all the way into next week." Bobby looked past her head, high up on the wall, and saw the store's video camera. He ran a hand over the top of his skull, preening for the lens.

Kimberly stood next to him. "Turn around and face the nice people, honey," he said, spinning her toward the back of the store. "Show them what you got." He had to raise the gun himself, straightening her arms while the salesgirl stared at him in amazement.

Kimberly looked like a store mannequin with a toy gun in her hands.

"Point it at somebody, for Christ's sake," he told her, and she swung the gun around on the first person she saw, an old woman with two bottles of hair rinse in her hands. The woman screamed.

The whole store came to a standstill. He made a quick head count, six, seven, eight in all: five men, three women, mostly older, one young guy in a black leather jacket closer to the front, standing beside an older man in a seersucker suit and a straw porkpie hat.

"We're going to keep this simple," Bobby yelled. "Bring your wallets and your purses down to me and drop 'em in this bag." He turned to the salesgirl. "Let me have another bag, honey." She was so startled by the new request that she stopped emptying the register. Her hands shook over the money and tears welled up in her eyes.

"Don't stop what you're doing," he said. "Just reach down and get me a fucking bag." She slapped a fistful on the counter.

"Let's go folks," Bobby said. "We haven't got all day." He looked back at the salesgirl. "You about done there, sweetheart?" She nodded and handed over the bag, backing into the cigarette rack again.

Kimberly pulled the trigger on the empty chambers.

Bobby heard it quite clearly, snap, snap, and turned toward the sound.

He saw it all in a blur. At first, he thought it was the young guy in the leather jacket, but it was the other guy, the one with the straw hat. He lunged at Kimberly and Bobby swung the gun around and fired without really aiming.

The slug caught the old man in the neck and spun him around. He slammed face first into a shampoo display, rolled over and lay there, fingers clutching at his throat, struggling, choking on his own blood.

The young guy moved and Bobby fired again. It hit him high on the right side, punching a neat hole in his black leather jacket, and jerked him off his feet. He sprawled across the center of the aisle, blood pouring out of him onto the brightly waxed floor.

"Son of a bitch," Bobby said.

Kimberly kept pulling the trigger, snap, snap, snap, with no expression on her face except blind fear. Casually, almost reluctantly, Bobby clubbed her with the barrel of his gun, bringing it down across the side of her head, tearing off a small piece of skin and hair. Bobby saw the bright patch of red before she began to crumble. She sat down hard, as if someone had pulled her legs out from under her, and leaned back against the counter, her eyes rolling over.

The old woman began to scream again. Bobby wanted to put a bullet in her, too. Instead, he yanked Kimberly to her feet and dragged her out of the store, holding her up when she started to fall. It was like dragging a dead animal around. Her bones had turned to rubber. He pulled her to the car, opened the door, and threw her inside.

He pulled out of the space without looking, punching the Camaro, fishtailing up Broad, through one red light, swerving behind a slow-moving taxi, through another light, not knowing and not caring if anybody was behind him.

He passed Veteran's Stadium and the Spectrum and turned right on the other side of JFK, dropping back into third, cutting across two lanes to make the ramp onto I-95.

Once he got on the expressway, he tore off the mask and threw it on the floor. He knew what he had to do. They couldn't stay in the city. In half an hour, the bridges would be blocked, maybe a little longer before the police had a decent description of the car. Then they wouldn't be able to get out at all.

He took the turnoff for the Walt Whitman, sailing down the ramp and out again into the funhouse of the wide toll plaza, the red and green flashers shining across the top of the booths, brake lights and turn signals winking at him, the whole scene covered with the sickly glow of the overheads, as though they were swimming through the same greasy yellow sea.

The exact change lanes were backed-up. Bobby eased the Camaro down and looked for the shortest line. He dug in his pocket for change and came up with a handful of bills instead. They scattered across his lap. He pulled across the plaza, zipping in behind a white furniture van with Delaware plates. When he got to the window, he handed the guy two dollars and drove off while the collector hung out of the booth, waving a fistful of change at him.

From then on, he knew the route by heart. Down to the 295 exit, then north again to route 30 and from there a straight shot south to Hammonton. After that he could wind his way through the Pines, using the county roads to get to Batsto. He slowed down, cruising along through the suburban nightmare of shopping malls and cut-rate motels. There weren't any cops on the road and nobody seemed to be chasing him. He drove until he found a liquor store and parked at the far end of the lot behind a long row of cars and with a clear exit around the back of the store.

He looked over at Kimberly. She was snuggled up against the door with her eyes closed. She appeared to be asleep. Bobby pulled her face into the light. The other side of her head was bleeding. He could see the bloodstains on the door handle, still shiny and wet. He let her go and she slumped back down on the seat.

Then he realized she no longer had the gun. He

searched all around her and couldn't find it. She must have dropped it in the store, probably right after he banged her upside the head.

"You dumb shit," he said. He sat back and thought about what he was going to do. He could dump her out right here. He could take her with him. He could drive all the way to the ocean and drop her off a dock.

So many choices. So little time. Bobby grabbed the CVS bag from the floor and pulled out a handful of bills.

He took out a hundred in twenties, and stuffed the rest of the money back in the bag. Kimberly didn't move. He locked the car and went into the liquor store, taking his own gun with him.

The store was deserted except for a young couple who stayed in the wine section. Bobby heard them arguing over which chardonnay to buy, whether the French was over-rated and which California label had the best price. Somebody ought to shoot those two just for being on the planet, he thought.

The clerk was watching a baseball game on a small color portable. Bobby picked up two bottles of vodka that were on sale, a six-pack of Coke, a carton of orange juice, two six-packs of beer, and a few bags of potato chips and nuts. The clerk put it all in an empty cardboard liquor box and rung up the total, keeping his eyes on the television all the time.

The station broke into the game for a special news bulletin. Bobby glanced at the television. The announcer's face seemed to be about the size of a postage stamp.

"One man was killed and another critically wounded tonight during a robbery of a South Philadelphia drugstore," the announcer said. "We have Brad Jenkins live at the scene. What's it like down there, Brad?"

Bobby moved down the counter to get a closer look.

"It's pretty grim, Mike. As you can see behind me,

the police have the area sealed off and they're questioning witnesses inside. From what we've been able to put together, it went down something like this.

"At around eight o'clock tonight, two people—one of them male, we believe, wearing an Elvis mask, the other one female, entered the CVS store near South Broad and Porter Street and demanded money.

"According to the police, one of the customers apparently tried to tackle the woman and was shot in the throat. He died in the store. Another man, a relative, was shot in the chest. He's been taken to Methodist Hospital next door and is undergoing surgery right now. No word on whether he's expected to live. Can you hold on a second, Mike?"

The reporter turned away and spoke with someone off camera.

"Mike, we have a tentative identification of the female assailant. She has been identified as Kimberly Morbach, the daughter of State Senator James Morbach, who's up for reelection this fall. This has not been confirmed by police as yet but we're hoping to get a confirmation any minute now. Again, I repeat, Kimberly Morbach, the daughter of State Senator James Morbach, has been tentatively identified as one of the two people involved in a robbery and shooting in South Philadelphia tonight.

"This is Brad Jenkins with Action Cam-Six in South Philly. Back to you, Mike."

Bobby looked away from the television while the clerk rang up the total.

"You want any beef jerky with that?"

"Why not?" Bobby said. He had the feeling of suddenly being plugged into the universe, with all that power right at his fingertips.

"That'll be forty-six dollars and forty-eight cents," the clerk said.

Bobby dropped three twenties on the counter.

"You got a phone in here?"

The clerk shook his head. "Next door—at the gas station."

"Let me have a couple bucks worth of quarters with the change."

Bobby carried the box out to the car and put it in the trunk. He checked Kimberly, didn't notice anything different in the way she looked—only in who she was and what that might mean. She was still a dumb shit but her daddy had turned out to be a real gem.

He punched out the number and waited while the electronic voice told him how much to deposit. He dropped in the quarters.

Jacob Cross answered on the second ring.

"Yes?"

"Hey, how're you doing, Jake?" Bobby said, thinking how much he hated Cross's voice, the way it always sounded as if Cross had something better to do than to talk to him.

"What do you want?"

What I want is your head on a fucking stick, Bobby thought. But later, after he figured out what he was going to do.

"I don't want anything," Bobby drawled. He glanced at the car. "But I've got a real interesting problem on my hands that you might want to take a look at."

Kimberly came to while they were driving through the Pine Barrens in the dark, the cold night air blowing through the open window bringing her around. She had this peculiar image stuck in her mind, a short little film clip that played over and over.

She was in the cloud and there were voices all around her but so distant she couldn't make them out. And shapes, too. They danced just beyond the edge of her vision. The cloud began to break, ripping open in front of her, and a face emerged, a frightening evil face that terrified her. She knew exactly who the face belonged to and what she had to do.

The face was death and she had to stop him before he reached her. She squeezed her hands and they made clicking sounds, and then there was a loud crash and death disappeared, wiped away by a touch of her fingers. She felt better when the face was gone.

Now if she could just stop the buzzing in her head and the nauseous feeling that swept through her every few seconds.

Bobby leaned over, and she wanted to tell him that she didn't feel very good, but it hurt too much to talk, even to open her eyes. Bobby's voice came to her out of the blackness.

"Hey, babe," he said. "How'd you like to be in the movies?"

12

Glover put Paige in charge.

"You're the point man on this," he said. "Let Brillman take care of the details."

Brillman was the Five Squad lieutenant and, along with Sergeant DiGallo, normally in charge. He was a tall man with soft features and a lazy eye. When he looked at you, his right eye rolled around in its socket like a marble in a shotglass and made it appear as though he was staring at something on the other side of the room. He could see perfectly well, but it made him look like an idiot. He said it helped during interrogation.

Brillman accepted the news with a shrug. "Now the shit can hit your fan," he said and handed Paige a cardboard box already filled to overflowing with preliminary reports. Paige carried it back to his desk, feeling like he'd just been sent to bed without his supper.

He was just going through it when Glover came by to tell him that Senator Morbach was holding a press conference in an hour and Paige was expected to be there.

"Tell him we're making progress," Glover said.

"But we're not."

It was true. Elvis was still a mystery. They had four different descriptions of the getaway car and no license number: two people said it was a green Chevy with Jersey plates; one said a blue Porsche from New York; and the other one didn't know the make but was sure it was black with Delaware plates.

They had Kimberly's gun as well. Empty. Paige stirred that one around for a while and made a mental note to check with Camden to see if any of the witnesses at the first robbery remembered if the guns the two kids had were empty. He doubted if any of them would remember that kind of detail but it was worth asking.

The information about the gun would be kept from the press and from the family.

There were a couple of stray prints besides Kimberly's on it. They were running them now. That could take days. Ballistics could take days. And nothing could turn up. They really weren't any closer to a break in the case than they were a week ago. And now they had two dead bodies instead of one. And Elvis was out running around with the senator's daughter.

Glover made a face. "So what?"

Paige got the point.

Score one for the fan.

She was desperately afraid. The fear was like a tiny needle of fire inside of her, wildly out of control. She felt it at odd points: a tremor in her fingers, a nervous tug along her jawline, the way her eyes would not stay fixed on anyone or anything.

She found herself searching the crowd for him, anxious one moment, depressed the next, wondering if he'd forgotten, or given up, or if he'd simply taken his determination to do what he thought was right and walked away.

Images of the shooting played behind her eyes, a moving curtain of grays and blacks and whites that had broken her sleep into fragments, an archipelago of terror, rage, and tears, with no island of hope among them.

She had recoiled when she saw the videotape. It was the coarseness of the pictures. They reminded her of some pornographic films she had seen in college once, horribly lit, grainy, the film spliced so badly that the actors seemed to move from one activity to another as if they'd been picked up bodily and dropped into each new scene. It wasn't so much what they were doing that bothered her but the way it looked—so coarse, so ugly, so unreal.

It was real for her now. After watching the videotape several times, she could no longer escape from it.

Her daughter. On screen. The gun in her hand. The man's hat flying off his head, sailing away as if caught by a breeze. The falling bodies. The silence of it all. Like someone dying in outer space. It couldn't be real, they made no noise. She half-expected—half-hoped—that the man would get up and retrieve his hat. But he never did. Didn't he understand it was all a horrible mistake? That this was something that could never happen? Silently the film played itself out. The man in the mask turned and clubbed Kimberly to the floor, then dragged her outside. The tape ended. And started again.

The only sound she heard came from the people with her in the small room at police headquarters, sitting around the television, leaning forward in their chairs to watch.

Her husband, distant and grim, unable—or perhaps unwilling—to speak to her. She wanted his hand on hers, some touch, some connection, that would make her feel less alone. But he kept himself apart, and as the hope of ever reaching him ebbed away, she sank further into herself, another loss, another island.

Jacob Cross, the only one not leaning forward in his chair, sat back and gazed unperturbed at the screen. Perhaps he was studying the images, searching for some way to erase their effect. Perhaps he was contemplating his own sense of failure. She doubted it. She once believed he could read the future. Her husband had believed it, too. She wondered what future he saw for them now.

On the other hand, perhaps he was just counting up the votes.

The police were unrecognizable to her. With their bland, unyielding faces, they might as well have been the ones wearing masks. They asked nothing, gave nothing, waited instead for her to speak.

When the videotape ended—for the third time? the fourth?—she spoke to them, astounded at the clarity of her own request.

"I want Detective Paige put in charge of the investigation," she said.

She caught Jacob Cross's expression. He seemed impressed, and slightly amused, as if his ability to read the future had suddenly been fully restored.

Now she was at campaign headquarters, looking over the crowd of campaign workers and television crews. She stood next to her husband while he spoke into the forest of microphones that had been taped to the makeshift podium. The campaign workers stood with their heads down and shook their heads at his words.

"This has been a tragedy for the Garelli family," he said, "and for us as well." Anthony Garelli was the dead man; his nephew—Victor—Vic for short—was still in intensive care. He might survive, he might not. No one seemed to know for sure.

"For now, all campaigning will stop," her husband said. He went on, words flying like woodchips from a well-hewn log. She heard the word *tragedy* again, and the phrases *bearing up under the strain* and *the need for understanding in the difficult days ahead*. His words began to grate, and she had the strangest urge to put her hand over his mouth to shut him up.

She did not. She kept herself straight and poised, taking her cues from television, the pictures of the political widows as they marched behind the coffins on their way to the burial site, cool, detached, saving their grief for a less public offering.

Susan Morbach saw Patrick Paige come through the double doors in the front of the room. He closed them behind him and hung back. She smiled wanly, hoping he might see her. He did.

Then the fire inside of her arced again and she felt her lips tremble and she spoke without sound, sending the words out to him with the force of her own silence behind them, the last hope she had.

Please give me my daughter back.

Paige thought she looked out of place, standing next to her husband while he gave his statement to the press and answered questions from the reporters. The camera lights made her look small and fragile, a pale, washed-out copy of herself that seemed on the verge of breaking apart.

But she held herself still and erect and didn't give in to it. Paige admired her for that. He wished he had better news for her, some sort of reward for her strength.

In person, her husband seemed the same as he was in the campaign posters that hung on the surrounding walls draped in red, white and blue crepe paper bunting—upright, responsible, on the move, in the know, a true leader. But not your everyday swell guy. Paige looked at the pictures and then at the man and decided that the senator probably wasn't going to invite him out for beer and pretzels anytime soon.

He didn't trust Jacob Cross, no more than he had trusted his own father.

The press conference ended and Paige stepped aside while the reporters and camera crews hurried out, on their way to another drama, a new tragedy somewhere else. There seemed to be an endless supply of them these days. The senator's campaign staff milled about in small somber groups beneath the bunting like refugees from some hideous accident, comparing notes and swapping survival stories. Some were in tears, others in shock, gaunt faces and sleepwalker eyes.

Paige worked his way through the crowd toward her. Despite her grief she was still an attractive woman, he thought. Or perhaps because of it—it made her more accessible, opening doors that might have been closed to him a few days ago.

Stop being so stupid, he thought.

She took his hand and held it.

"I thought you weren't coming," she said. "I was afraid—" She cut herself off. There were so many things she was afraid of now. The list could have gone on forever.

"I was reading the files," Paige said, "trying to see if we missed something."

"And?"

He shook his head.

"Detective."

The senator spoke to his back. Paige let go of Susan's hand and turned.

Unlike his wife, Jim Morbach didn't take his hand.

"I see you made it," Morbach said. He smiled at Paige but there was something else going on behind it. The senator was waiting for an opening. I'm about to get my ass reamed, Paige thought.

"I was going over the case files."

"Going over the files?" Morbach said, a note of incredulity slipping into his voice. "You need a piece of paper to tell you how to find my daughter? Why aren't you out on the streets looking for her? What the hell are you people doing?"

"I've been on the streets, Senator," Paige said.

"I know. And you haven't found a goddamn thing. This is the second time for this lunatic and he's still out there. God only knows what he's done to her by now."

Maybe he did nothing to her, Paige thought. Maybe Kimberly Morbach was pissed off enough at Daddy to hang around with a psychotic. Maybe not. But Anthony Garelli was dead and that made her a murderer. The fact that she was Morbach's daughter made her something else. What that was, Paige wasn't entirely sure. He remembered what Glover had said and opted for the bland.

"We'll find him," Paige said. "And your daughter."

Morbach grunted. "If you'd been doing your job in the first place, this wouldn't have happened."

Fuck bland.

"Maybe if you'd done yours, I wouldn't have to be here."

Morbach's eyes bulged. "What did you say?"

Jacob Cross slid between them.

"This isn't going to help," Cross said. "Perhaps if Detective Paige tells us what he *does* know, then we can all do what's best for Kimberly."

"I want to know what he meant by that," Morbach said.

Cross put one hand on his arm. "Will you excuse us for a minute?" He steered Morbach away to a neutral corner. The senator kept staring at Paige, nodding his head slowly while Cross spoke. They were joined by another man, younger than both of them, sunburned, balding and very buttoned-down.

My father might have done that, Paige thought, settled things out of earshot before they went too far. He might also have just let them go to hell in public if he thought that it might work out better that way. His father had his own peculiar brand of perversity that made him unpredictable and made everyone else afraid of him.

"We're not dealing with this very well," Susan said quietly.

"Neither am I."

"I thought—" She shook her head and tried again. "I read about you—about your wife."

She seemed embarrassed to bring it up.

"Jacob sent us some articles. I read them last night. I wanted you to know."

Now they had something else in common.

"I'd like to hear about it sometime. After this is all over. If you'll tell me. I want to know how you got through it."

But I didn't, Paige thought.

"Who's the other guy?" he asked.

"Jerry Abelson," Susan said. "He's the campaign manager."

"I thought Cross did that."

Susan shook her head.

"Managing a campaign is detail work. Jacob watches the big picture."

"Sort of like God."

"Exactly."

Cross walked the senator back, leaving Abelson behind. Morbach looked slightly calmer. Cross was smiling. We all make mistakes, he seemed to be saying, now let's kiss and make up. Before we lose it again.

"We got off to a bad start," Morbach said. "Let's see if we can do it right. Tell me what you know."

Paige explained briefly what he knew and tried not to dwell on what he didn't. They had absolutely no clue as to the identity of the man in the Elvis mask. They were trying to match the various car descriptions with Harrisburg. It was a fool's errand and Paige knew it.

The problem was Kimberly. Was she an active participant or wasn't she? Had she been kidnapped and forced into it somehow? They couldn't tell anything from the videotape. They didn't even know if she was still in the city.

Paige ran down the list. They were doing a special computer run on all known armed robbery felons. They were working their informants overtime. They were in contact with the state police in Pennsylvania and New Jersey, not to mention the Camden Police Department. They had notified the FBI. They had cops stationed at the Morbach house and at the campaign headquarters. The phones were being wired with voice-activated recorders. Right now they were treating it as a robbery/homicide, but that could change at any minute.

Paige still had his hopes pinned on Tim Cochran. All the shelters had been contacted, and every patrol car had a photograph of the boy taped to the dash. At night, on his own time, he sat in his car in front of the Cochran home, waiting for Tim to come home. He didn't.

Tim Cochran had completely disappeared, and his uncle seemed to have gone into hibernation. Paige finally managed to contact the boy's mother. She didn't have much to say. Tim hadn't called her and she had no idea where his father was except that he was supposed to be sending money to his brother to take care of Tim. She didn't have any money and wouldn't be coming back to Philadelphia. She sounded a little drunk but mostly just tired and worn-out, and Paige was glad when he got off the phone.

Except that he didn't really feel any better. He felt worse. It was like he'd been asleep for years and just woken up to find that nowadays people threw away their lives and children because they couldn't figure out a good enough reason to keep them and they didn't waste a lot of time trying. Even, it seemed, state senators.

Paige tried not to imagine Tim dead but it was getting harder all the time.

He asked Morbach some routine questions. Not because he might get an answer he could use but because he thought the senator expected it. Even while he was doing it, he wondered if he wasn't becoming part of the disease himself.

"Have you had any calls? Any letters?"

Morbach shook his head. "Just the usual cranks. Susan?"

"Nothing."

"Have you noticed anyone hanging around the campaign, anyone you've never seen before?"

Both of them shook their heads.

"I'll talk to Jerry Abelson about that and have him get back to you," Cross said.

"What will you do when you find her?" Susan asked.

"We'll do our best to make sure she isn't harmed," Paige said. That was a real doozy. He couldn't predict what would happen if they found her. If she had a gun and she tried to use it, she'd end up dead.

If she wasn't dead already.

"You'll keep us informed?"

"Yes," Paige said.

"Every day?" Susan asked.

"Yes, every day. Maybe we should set up a time for me to call. Would evenings be the best? Say around seven?"

"Evenings are fine," Morbach said. He pulled Susan toward him, wrapping his arm around her shoulder and drawing her near. Paige couldn't get used to seeing them as a couple. Was it just his imagination or was Susan uncomfortable with the idea, too?

Stop being so goddamn stupid, he thought.

"We want our daughter back," Morbach said. "We'll do anything we can to help—anything. Just let us know."

They shook hands. Morbach huddled with Cross again and Paige caught a few brief seconds of their conversation before Susan walked him to the front door.

"Was that okay?" Morbach asked.

"Just fine," Cross said, and motioned for Abelson.

Paige's car was double-parked on Germantown Avenue, just down from the campaign headquarters. Susan stopped him at the front door.

"Will you call me?"

"I said I would."

"I meant at my office. I want to know before my husband does. If I'm not there, they'll know how to reach me. Will you do that?"

"Yes. Of course."

"Thank you."

Paige left her in the doorway and walked to his car. Jacob Cross caught up with him at the curb.

"Why don't we have a cup of coffee?" Cross said.

"Okay," Paige said and wondered if the performance this time would be as good as the last.

They sat in a coffee shop across from the train station, a table by the window. Paige could see it through the glass, all done up in green and white like a Victorian pavilion.

"I'm glad we could get together," Cross said, pouring an envelope of artificial sweetener into his cup and stirring it delicately with his spoon, adding a little milk to the mix.

"I don't have any secrets. I told them everything I know."

"We all have secrets," Cross said mildly. "Some are just worth more than others." He took a small elegant sip. "That was how your father made his living."

"And how you make yours."

"Yes. Would you like some water?"

Paige shook his head.

"I would." He signaled the waitress and ordered two glasses, one for each of them.

Paige had to laugh.

"Is something funny?"

"You remind me of him. I'd tell him I wanted a bike for my birthday and he'd get me a copy of Yeats instead."

"Did you read it?"

"Yeah, I did. Every damn poem."

Cross smiled. "Then maybe he knew what he was doing."

Paige pushed his cup across the table like a battering ram, aiming straight for Cross's heart. "My father was a liar and a thief. His charm was just part of the packaging."

And I loved him in spite of it, Paige thought.

Cross kept on smiling but his face went brittle.

"Everyone was raised wrong," he said. "That's one of the nice things about growing up. You finally realize it." He pushed his cup aside. "I want to know what you think about the case. Not just what you said. What you think."

"I think we got a real problem."

"Could you be a little more specific?"

"Why?"

"Because it's important—for both of us. Especially if things go wrong. I shouldn't have to explain it."

No, Paige thought, he didn't have to explain it.

"The guy's already killed one kid. Maybe he'll decide Kimberly's worth more to him alive than dead. If he's smart. Then it's a kidnapping—on top of a homicide. It gets tricky. Is that what you wanted to know?"

Paige decided to keep Tim Cochran to himself. If Cross wanted more details, he was going to have to dig somewhere else. Hell, he probably had them already.

"Do you have any idea who he is?"

"No."

"Then you really don't know anything?"

"I know he likes to have his picture taken," Paige said. "I thought he might be an actor. Now I just think he's crazy."

"But smart."

"Yes. Smart."

There was a brief flicker of calculation in Cross's eyes, so small and fast that it might only have been a shimmer of light passing over them. It made Paige wonder again if Cross was only playing with him—if he knew the details of the case already and was only making sure he had everything covered.

"That's good to know," Cross said and looked at his watch. "I have to go." He stood up. "Are you coming?"

"I'll finish my coffee."

Cross took a dark leather wallet from his coat and dropped a couple of bills on the table.

"I met your father once," he said. "This was after he retired. It was a fundraiser or something. He was sick then, wasn't he?"

"Bad heart."

"Yes, that was it. He was still very strong, I remember, very alert. Smarter than most of the people in the room. He never changed, never gave in to it. I liked that about him."

"He never really retired. That's what killed him."

"We all die of something," Cross said. "It doesn't really matter what. That's another nice thing about growing up. We usually get to see it coming."

He stopped and leaned toward Paige, a curious look in his eyes, as if he'd just remembered the reason for their meeting.

"Be careful with Susan," he said. "She's a very vulnerable woman." His smile returned. "But I think you know that."

Paige watched him step across the street, holding his hand out slightly at his waist to stop the traffic, a man very much in control.

Paige finished his coffee. As he started to get up, he remembered a few lines of poetry from the book his father had given him. He was amazed that they had stayed with him all these years.

"He, too, has resigned his part / In the casual comedy; / He, too, has been changed in his turn, / Transformed utterly: / A terrible beauty is born."

He couldn't remember the name of the poem or even what it was about. But the words had stuck with him.

His father hadn't changed until the very end. He died

alone in a hospital bed with a small plastic copy of the Lord's Prayer, the face of Christ worn away by so much rubbing, clutched in hands that had grown too weak to do anything else.

He wondered if his father had seen it coming.

13

When Jacob Cross was twenty-one, his father took him bird hunting with a group of local politicians from Wilkes-Barre. It was, Cross remembered, his formal coming-out party. His father was an attorney, prominent enough to have done well but not prominent enough that he could afford to make enemies. The hunting trip was an annual event that his father paid for every fall to solidify his political contacts and his business for the rest of the year.

Wilkes-Barre was an insular town, stuck haphazardly on the southern end of Scranton. People went to Scranton, sometimes for business and sometimes for pleasure, but they stayed in Wilkes-Barre. The small-town feel of the city hadn't changed much over the years even with the new construction downtown in the Square and the expansion of the Owens-Illinois plant.

The rolling hills to the north—the beginning of the Appalachians—seemed to hold everyone in place. In summer they were filled with tourists and, as the years went by, more and more second homes that engulfed the little mountain towns. In winter the weekend skiers came from as far away as Philadelphia, but nobody in Wilkes-Barre ever thought about leaving.

Jacob Cross lived in a good-size house on the edge of Forty Fort across the Susquehanna River from the city where his father had an office just off the main square where the larger, more successful firms had theirs, a physical reminder that he had not quite made it to the inner circle and never would. He hadn't made it into the Dallas Country Club either. That was another reminder, and more to the point. He couldn't afford it.

His father's business with the city consisted mostly of handling service contracts. It was easy work, a few notations jotted in the margins, some halfhearted wrangling with the businesses who supplied the city over this point or that, and a lot of handshaking all around when it was over. With the tourists there was real estate work to do, plus the usual small-firm business, wills and probate and zoning board hearings. His father became known as a competent attorney, not too swift but no slouch either. He gave you no trouble was the way most people described him.

His father's name was Walter; his mother's, Elizabeth—Lizzie to her friends. Jacob's sister, several years older than he was, was named Fran. Fran, like almost everyone else in Wilkes-Barre, had stayed after high school; she married a dentist and moved to Kingston just a few miles away from the family home.

The hunting trip began early, the cars pulling into their driveway at six in the morning. His mother and his sister —drafted annually for the occasion—cooked breakfast for everyone. The men stood around the kitchen and picked at the piles of scrambled eggs and bacon and sipped coffee, sneaking whisky into their cups because, it was widely believed, Lizzie did not approve.

When breakfast was over, the caravan would head out for the day. A pickup truck filled with food and more liquor followed the cars out to the hunting ground, a wide stretch of rolling hills near one of the small lakes north and west of the city. By the time they arrived, usually around ten in the morning, a few of the men would be too drunk to do much of anything but fall asleep in their cars, but tradition demanded they at least make the effort, and they did.

They would spend the morning staggering through the trees and across the wide open fields, demanding in loud blurry voices every few minutes if it was time for lunch yet.

His father, Cross remembered, always stayed sober.

The night before the hunt, his father spoke to him briefly.

"Watch yourself tomorrow," he said. "Make some points. Might help later on." Cross knew all about later on. Later on meant law school—Columbia because it was good and cheaper than Harvard—and then back home to Wilkes-Barre and the small side room in his father's office. Cross could see it going as far as Columbia, but after that, his vision began to cloud over.

His father cleaned a pair of hunting boots while he talked, working the oil into the dark leather with a slow circular motion.

"Stick with the mayor," his father said. "Let him see what you can do."

"I've only met him once or twice."

And both times he'd been unimpressed. The mayor ran the city and the local Republican party and served on the county board of supervisors. Whatever came into Wilkes-Barre came through him. As a result, he'd grown belligerent and mean-spirited. But the voters liked him and nobody else had figured out a way to get rid of him.

"That's all right. He knows who you are."

"I'll do my best."

"That's all I expect of you, Jacob. Nothing more, nothing less."

I will be the perfect son, Cross thought.

And learn how to kiss his honor's behind.

On the way out, the mayor rode in the front seat with his father, while Jacob sat in back with the city solicitor, a tiny black-haired man named Grissom with delicate hands and eyes like an angry rat.

The mayor drank coffee from his own personalized traveling mug, which by this time contained mostly whisky. The sun rose over the mountains, light streaming through the car windows. The day was cold and the sunlight felt cold as well.

"Haven't you got any music in this car?" the mayor asked his father.

"Of course."

"Then let's hear some," the mayor said and waited while his father turned on the radio and found an easy-listening station. The mayor changed it several times and finally returned to his father's original selection.

"We need a decent radio station around here, something that plays music you can listen to without barfing." He spoke to Grissom. "Anybody up for renewal?"

Grissom leaned forward. "I don't think so. I'll check tomorrow."

"Good. Let's shake them up a little. See if they can't start playing Rosemary Cloony, something like that."

"I'll make a note," Grissom said, but Cross noticed that his hands remained firmly in his lap.

A few minutes later, Grissom spoke to him.

"Do you like to hunt, Jacob?"

"I haven't done that much of it."

"The mayor likes to hunt."

"I get a grouse every year," the mayor said. "Big one."

"Do you eat it?"

The mayor turned around. He had a high rounded forehead dotted with several subcutaneous moles. They looked like birdshot trapped beneath wax paper. Cross had the urge to touch them, roll his fingers over them just to see what it would feel like.

"Do I eat what?" He pursed his lips together when he said it, as though he were thinking about something else entirely.

"Grouse."

"Nah. I give it to my wife. Who the hell knows what she does with it."

The mayor took another sip of coffee and played with the radio some more.

"You're graduating this year," Grissom said. "Going to law school?"

"Columbia."

"Decent school. And afterward?"

Cross shrugged uncomfortably.

Grissom smiled and touched his father's shoulder.

"Didn't you go to Columbia, Walter?"

"Yes. It's a good school. In some ways I think it's better than Harvard."

Grissom thought about that for a moment. "In some ways," he said. "In others." He shrugged the opinion away and smiled even more kindly at Jacob. It was the kind of smile, Cross thought, that was universally reserved for cripples and idiots.

He was going to ask Grissom where he went to school, but for some reason—probably because he thought Grissom *had* gone to Harvard—he changed his mind. Instead, he asked the mayor.

"Where did you go to law school?"

The mayor hunched up his shoulders but remained silent.

"I didn't," he said finally. He swiveled in his seat, staring straight at Cross. "I can hire all the lawyers I need."

"That's right," Grissom said. "The mayor went to Wilkes College. A great school, right here in our own backyard."

The mayor glanced at Grissom, pursed his lips again and turned around.

"A great school," Grissom repeated. "Solid reputation. Too bad you didn't think of it, Jacob."

Cross looked at the lawyer and was surprised to find that the anger in his eyes had diminished somewhat, replaced by something very close to mirth.

By midafternoon, the mayor had not yet bagged his grouse. He marched through the fields in an angry sulk, spewing venom at anyone who came near. There was some talk—quiet talk—mostly among the drunker participants, that if the mayor didn't get his bird soon, they were going to have to buy a dead chicken, glue some feathers on it, and drop it on him from a tree.

His father stayed with the mayor, Jacob stayed with his father, and Grissom followed a few yards behind. The lawyer carried no gun and spent most of his time kicking at the ground, apparently just to see what he could turn up.

Cross hung back and waited for him.

"You don't hunt?" Cross asked him.

"I do," Grissom said. "In my fashion."

Cross carried a .16-gauge from his father's collection. Like almost everyone else, he hadn't fired a shot all day. The gun was heavy and he was bored lugging it around.

"I'm getting tired of this," he said, quietly enough so his father or the mayor wouldn't hear him.

Grissom nodded. "So's the mayor. You might do better if you went off on your own. There's too many of us. It frightens the game."

Cross took the suggestion, and when his father and the mayor were far enough ahead, he cut through a large grove of scrub oak and headed toward a new field, one that he could see through the trees.

The voices of the other men faded and he was swallowed up by the stillness. It seemed to give him more energy and he was relieved to be away by himself.

Before he reached the tree line, he heard a rustling in the undergrowth, directly behind a fallen log. He moved closer, and the rustling stopped. Cross held his breath and stepped away, moving in a wide circle so he could come at it from the side.

A blur of brown feathers burst from behind the log and sailed away to the right, gliding to a stop in the trees, a dozen yards away from the field.

Tense now, excited beyond his own imagining, Cross moved closer, watching the grouse as it huddled close to the ground, wings spread out over the dead leaves that littered the forest floor. He flicked the safety off the shotgun and carried it cross-chest so he only had to bring it up in one swift motion to fire.

The grouse ran, going to ground at the edge of the field. Cross heard his father speak, and then the mayor, bellowing in response. The bird scurried off again and Cross ran after it.

The bird broke into the open field and lifted off, surging into the sky. Cross charged the last few feet and brought the shotgun to his shoulder just as the bird swung down in a low arc over the field. He tracked it perfectly and fired. The sound of the shot exploded in his ears, followed by another somewhere to his right.

The bird fell suddenly as though it had been punched out of the air, feathers drifting through the late afternoon light long after the bird was down.

His ears were still ringing when he heard the mayor shouting.

"I got that son of a bitch! Goddamn! I got him good."

The mayor ran across the field toward the downed bird, big shoulders heaving from one side to the other like some prehistoric ox lumbering its way toward dinner.

The mayor held the bird by the neck, laughing and shaking it back and forth, when Cross approached. The mayor didn't even look at him. He was too busy waving the dead bird around, shoving it in everyone's face.

"It's mine," Cross said.

Nobody seemed to hear him, so he said it louder.

"It's mine," he shouted and this time they heard him. The other men moved away, so there was a clear open space between him and the mayor.

"Well, now," the mayor said. "I don't think so."

"You fired last. I tracked it and I shot it. It's mine."

"Maybe you shot at it but you missed."

"I didn't miss. You did."

Cross felt a hand on his arm and turned to see his father standing next to him.

"Jacob," his father said quietly, "I think the mayor's right."

"I *didn't* miss." He pointed at the mayor. "*He* missed. He's so drunk he couldn't hit his own foot." Cross looked beyond his father and saw Grissom watching him with casual interest.

The mayor dropped the grouse at his feet.

"Well, if it's yours, why don't you come and get it."

"Fine." His father tried to hold him back, but he reached for the bird anyway.

Cross didn't see the blow that knocked him down. One second he was reaching for the dead grouse and the next instant he was flat on his back and the sun seemed awfully small, a glowing white spot in the sky overhead, getting smaller every second.

When he finally found the strength to sit up, the mayor and the other men were walking back to the cars. He could hear the mayor's laughter, loud and ugly. His father knelt beside him. Grissom was there as well, holding his shotgun in one arm.

"What in God's name did you think you were doing?" his father asked.

Cross shook his head slowly and ran his fingers along

the side of his neck just below his ear. The flesh was swollen and he winced in pain.

"I thought I was taking what was mine."

His father shook his head.

"It wasn't yours," he said.

"It was. You saw it. Everyone saw it."

"No, I didn't see it. You missed." His father turned to Grissom. "You saw him miss, didn't you?"

"Unfortunately, no," Grissom said. "I didn't see anything. I was busy looking at a flower."

Cross looked around. The field was brown and barren. Grissom, he decided, couldn't have made it any clearer.

His father got to his feet, slowly, as if the time he'd spent next to his son had aged him.

"You missed, Jacob. That's all there is to it. Now let's forget about it. There'll be other times."

No, there won't. It was, he realized, the first honest adult thought he'd ever had. His father seemed to realize it, too, and moved off. Cross got to his feet and began walking. Grissom fell in beside him. He gave Cross his shotgun and hurried to catch up with the others, leaving Cross and his father to walk back by themselves, drifting across the field, a few feet apart, a distance that might as well have been infinite.

One year later, after Cross had finished his first year at Columbia, Grissom called him in New York and offered him a summer internship. Cross's father had already made plans for him to work in his office that summer, but he'd put him off, saying he might continue with classes through the summer. The last thing he wanted to do was work for his father.

"The offer comes with an apartment," Grissom said. "Not very large but it's near the Square. Nice views."

Cross accepted Grissom's offer immediately.

"Very good," Grissom said, then added, "Other times, Jacob, other times."

Cross had the feeling he was being offered something more than an internship, but what it was he couldn't imagine.

It came a few weeks before he was scheduled to return to school. Grissom had left a pile of court documents on his desk with a note asking him to make a concise summary of each for the master file.

In the middle of the pile, Cross found a two-page document that had nothing to do with any court case. He read it once, read it again, and then set the paper aside. He wanted to finish the rest of his work before going back to it.

Cross read the pages again. They were, as far as he could tell, a list of kickback payments to the mayor for the previous two years with names, dates, and amounts. When he finished, Cross knew why he'd originally set it aside.

His father's name was on the list. His amounts, Cross noted, were the smallest. Like everything else in his life, even his father's corruption had been second-rate.

Cross made a dozen copies and put the original back in the pile where he'd found it. The next morning he delivered the summaries to Grissom. The lawyer glanced over them quickly.

"Excellent, excellent," he said. "I hope you weren't bored."

"No. I found it fascinating."

"I thought you would," Grissom said. "Lawyering can be interesting. If you know what you're hunting for."

The following week, Cross drove to Harrisburg and dropped off several copies at the attorney general's office and then drove to Philadelphia and gave copies to an investigative reporter at the *Inquirer*.

Three months later, his father called him at school and asked him to come home. There was a problem, he said, his voice low and uneven. For a moment, Cross thought he had a bad connection but then realized it was only the fear in his father's voice.

"Serious?"

"I don't know."

"Can you give me some idea?"

"I thought you might be able to do that," his father said and hung up.

The police were already there when Cross arrived that night. An ambulance was there as well. For his mother. They were putting her into it on a stretcher.

She found him. His father had hung himself in the second-floor stairwell, the rope attached to a hook that he'd fastened securely to a beam over the stairs. And stepped off.

When the scandal broke, Cross's name did not appear in any of the stories. Nor was he asked to testify for the grand jury. The mayor and most of his administration were tried and convicted and sent to prison, the city solicitor being the one exception. He was appointed acting-mayor and went on later to win the office in a special election, and for two full terms after that.

When he finished law school, Cross collected his IOUs and went to work for the attorney general's office in Philadelphia and then moved into private practice.

Grissom never contacted Cross. But on graduation, he did receive an anonymous gift.

A stuffed grouse, handsomely mounted.

Cross was amused and kept it in his office for a while, then threw it out.

The dead, he decided, had gone out of fashion.

14

Susan Morbach was lost and no longer sure where she had made a wrong turn or how she might find her way back. She was near Penn, driving through the university neighborhood because Kimberly had once told her she wanted to go there when she graduated, and then suddenly she was lost in the dark run-down back streets of West Philadelphia and couldn't find her way out.

It surprised her at first. She'd spent time on these streets, and others just like them, chasing down the addresses of the people whose names appeared on the printout lists in her office, talking to women whose husbands were in prison, drug-addicted women who hated her on sight and whose children seemed to hate her even more.

But never at night and never alone. She always took an ambassador with her, usually Evelyn or Virginia, the two black women who worked on her staff. Their attitude came as a surprise, too; they were just as frightened as she was.

She had only her imagination to blame but they had experience.

She had no experience to draw on now, no one who could tell her what she was supposed to do or feel, and that lack of knowledge—that lack of *direction*—sharpened her fear. She pressed down on the gas pedal and sped through the streets unaware of where she was going, knowing only that she had to keep moving, faster and faster, in some vain attempt to outrun it.

She turned a corner, and for a brief moment the car skidded out of control, skipping over a rough cobblestone patch in the asphalt. She hit the brakes hard, and the car slid to an angry stop a few feet from a small battered station wagon. A weak sinking feeling raced through her as dozens and dozens of tiny white lights sparkled in front of her eyes.

I'm going to faint, she thought. She turned off the car, closed her eyes and waited for it to come. But nothing happened. Her heart slowed and she breathed through her mouth, sucking in lungfuls of air, and when she opened her eyes again the lights were gone and she was stopped on the side of the street and ahead of her she could see the buildings of Center City rising up, showing her the way to go.

She had never been a crier, but when she tried to start the car, her fingers slipped off the keys and she felt the tears coming again, hot and uncontrollable. It had been like that ever since her daughter had been taken. At first she was embarrassed. Now she welcomed the release. It was the only thing that seemed ultimately to help, if only for a few minutes, taking away the pain and the fear, giving her time to pull together what little strength she had to keep going.

Her husband didn't understand. He seemed to take pleasure in not understanding.

"It helps," she told him.

"It doesn't help *me*," he said.

So she had given up trying to explain. They no longer slept together. She stayed on the couch downstairs to be closer to the phone, even though there was a phone right next to their bed. She didn't sleep very much anyway and spent most of her nights dozing off to the sound of the television, waking up every now and then, then drifting back for a few fitful minutes of sleep.

She dreamed about her daughter. In that respect, her nights were no different from her days.

They were odd disjointed dreams: Kimberly as a baby, restless and cranky with croup; Kimberly clutching her first doll, a ratty hand-me-down from a neighbor; five-year-old Kimberly wearing a satin Uncle Sam suit in her husband's first campaign.

Kimberly dying slowly in some dark forgotten room.

It was that image that always brought an end to the tears, brought back her anger and strength.

She would not let that happen. No matter what, she would not allow that to take place.

Susan Morbach started the car, but instead of driving home, she drove toward Center City.

There was no point in going home. Home no longer existed. She would find a hotel instead and stay in town, close to her office, close to the police.

She thought briefly of Patrick Paige and wondered what would happen if she knocked on his door at this hour of the morning. He would let her in, of course. After that, she had no idea what would take place. Neither, she thought, would Patrick Paige.

The more she thought of it, the more she realized that she was wrong. Her own needs were becoming quite clear, growing clearer as the days and nights dragged on.

15

It was the darkness that surprised him. Driving from the brightly lit sprawl of Cherry Hill into the sudden blackness of the Pine Barrens was more of a shock than he expected. There were no streetlights and the trees were a black wall a few feet from the highway, and he drove right by the first turnoff, catching sight of the open mouth of the road as he sailed past. He was half a mile away before he even realized he had missed it.

Jacob Cross turned the car around in the middle of the two-lane road and drove back. He took his time, feeling his way through the dark. It bothered him, traveling through unknown terrain, not knowing the way—getting lost, making mistakes.

What in God's name had Bobby done?

Cross had been asking himself that ever since Bobby called to say he had Kimberly Morbach. Now he was on his way to see what Bobby had done to her. Cross was surprised he'd let her live. That was, in fact, his first question when Bobby called.

"Is she alive?"

"She's okay," Bobby had said to him, and left him to guess at the meaning of the word.

In some ways, he wished Bobby had killed her. It would have made things less difficult. Bobby might kill her anyway. If that happened, Bobby would be the only one left.

He came to a crossroads and for a moment couldn't remember whether Bobby had told him to go straight or turn left. His directions were wonderfully vague, almost a puzzle, the kind you gave to people on scavenger hunts— go to the big tree and circle around twelve paces until you see three boulders and stop. It made him angry all over again.

Cross made the left and drove a few yards until the road turned to dirt. A mile down on the right, Bobby had said, he'd see a broken-down FOR SALE sign next to a wide sandy cutout in the pines. He was supposed to drive in until he was well off the road, park the car, and wait.

Sitting there, alone, the sounds of the night animals skittering beneath the undergrowth, the sharp resin smell of the pines, the emptiness of it all, killed his anger and replaced it with fear. It crouched like a rat in the pit of his stomach, tail switching back and forth, sending shivers into his heart.

There was something else, too, something he was as unaccustomed to as the fear.

Excitement. A kind of giddy anticipation that if he had been anywhere else he would have throttled in an instant. But tonight he let it go, let the waiting heighten his senses and drive every other thought from his mind. He knew what it was, knew the reason he was enjoying it so much. It was a sweet taste on his lips and he wanted to run his tongue across them to lick up every drop.

It made him feel young again.

Bobby put his hand through the open window and grabbed Cross's shoulder.

"Spooky as hell out here, ain't it?"

Cross gave a little yelp and jumped in his seat. Bobby squeezed his shoulder hard and held him down. The only thing Cross saw was a black shadow in front of his eyes.

"Keep your pants on, Jake," Bobby said. "We still got some traveling to do."

Bobby climbed into the car and told him to drive. He led them down half a dozen narrow dirt roads, handing out directions every few minutes until Cross was thoroughly lost. Then he told Cross to pull off into the woods onto what looked like an old logging trail, two worn tracks and a high bed of weeds growing in between. The car bounced along over the ruts, headlights doing a crazy dance across the trees. Bobby looked out the window and told him to stop.

"Where are we?" Cross asked.

"The middle of goddamn nowhere," Bobby said. "You bring the equipment?"

"It's in the trunk."

"Gimme the keys."

Bobby got out and opened the trunk, stacking the video equipment—camera, tripod, portable VCR, a few tapes—alongside the car.

"You want to give me a hand back here?"

Cross went back to help. He thought Bobby was going to give him something to carry. Instead, Bobby pushed Cross face first against the car and frisked him. Cross struggled to get away, but Bobby held him down until he was through with his search.

The whole thing took his breath away and brought his anger back full force. He hated anybody to touch him, hated the very thought of it.

Cross spun around, brushing himself obsessively, trying to wipe away the feeling of Bobby's hands all over him.

"Don't ever do that to me again," he said. The words seemed to break against his teeth.

"Don't be such a putz," Bobby said, and handed him the camera and tapes. "Come on. It's still a little ways."

Cross followed, stumbling along behind him in the dark. He wished he had a gun. Not that he'd ever really used one or that it would've done him much good. But it might make Bobby think twice in the future.

Or would it? Cross knew what was wrong. Bobby thought he was in charge. The idea made him smile. Bobby could keep thinking that, of course, keep playing his games.

Right up to the point Cross told him the facts of life and took Kimberly Morbach away from him and brought her home.

There was just one thing, though. He couldn't figure out why Bobby needed the video equipment.

Cross saw the lights of the cabin through the trees. When he got closer, he saw that Bobby had put lanterns in the windows. The lights made the place seem cozy, almost inviting. It was like stumbling onto a Norman Rockwell painting in the middle of the wilderness.

"You like that?" Bobby asked.

"Very touching."

"Quaint as hell," Bobby said cheerfully as he led Cross up the overgrown path to the front door. "Here, put this on." He handed him the Elvis mask. Reluctantly, Cross slipped it over his head. It was sticky and uncomfortable but probably necessary.

Bobby laughed. It was almost a giggle.

Cross stopped. "Are you high?"

Bobby reached across and pushed open the door.

"I'm always high, Jake. That's the secret of my life. I truly don't give a shit."

The cabin was better than he expected. It was one room, water-stained walls, ruined wood floor, small and barren as a monk's cell, but it had been swept clean, the dirt piled neatly in one corner. The furniture, what little there was—a couch covered with sunbleached red fabric, a pair of old rocking chairs and a small round table—was in decent repair. A rusted potbellied stove sat at one end, a narrow metal frame bed beside it covered with some worn-out blankets.

Still it depressed him, the primitive setting, more shadow than light, the empty feeling that he had somehow reached back in time and come to a dead spot in his own history. The air was filled with a heavy musty odor, dank and oppressive, that mingled with the scent of the candles and the occasional whiff of pine that blew in through the cracked and broken windows.

There was another smell, too, one that he couldn't place. Then he realized it was urine and it was coming from Kimberly.

She sat on the couch cradling a gun in her lap. She didn't point it at anything, just held it close to her chest like a child holding a toy.

"We're still working on our potty training," Bobby said matter-of-factly. "She forgets that the bathroom's outside."

Cross stared at her through the dim light and gasped. He couldn't help himself. She looked awful.

Her face was bruised and battered and there was a patch of dried blood on one cheek. She had lost weight and her skin had shrunk to the bone. The bruises stood out, like ink smudges on dirty parchment.

Then she coughed, a slow wracking spasm that nearly doubled her over. When she straightened up, he saw her eyes, moist and hollow, two black pits in the center of her ruined face.

Cross moved closer, unwilling to touch her, hating her a little for letting this happen. The smell was worse close up. What had Bobby done to her?

Behind him, Bobby was busy setting up the video

equipment, whistling to himself while he opened the tripod and attached the camera.

"We've got to get her to a doctor," Cross said evenly, holding his anger back. He wanted to scream it.

"There's an idea," Bobby answered. "Who'd you have in mind?"

"I don't care," Cross yelled at him. "Can't you see she's in trouble?"

"I'm taking care of her," he said sharply. Then he smiled. "Besides, little bit of makeup, anybody can look good."

"Are you out of your mind? She doesn't need makeup, she needs a doctor. Look at her!"

Bobby grinned at him.

"Hell," he drawled, "I can fix that."

He stepped past Cross and took the gun from Kimberly. She looked up at him with crazy frightened eyes and screamed. It was hideous, the sound of an animal being beaten and tortured. It sang to him, high and shrill, and Cross began to lose himself in it. Bobby cocked the gun and aimed it at the top of her head.

"Just say the word, Jake, I'll blow her fucking brains out right here."

Cross reached for him but he was too far away.

Bobby's grin grew wider. He arched his eyebrows comically and pulled the trigger.

The hammer snapped shut on the empty chamber. He did it again.

"Son of a bitch," Bobby said. "I forgot the bullets."

Kimberly kept screaming, hands clenched tight in her lap. Bobby took her hands and placed the gun there. She clutched it violently, drawing it into herself.

Bobby lifted her face, turning it toward the light.

"My little girl," he said. "Don't you just want to eat her right up?"

Cross didn't respond. He kept staring at Kimberly,

seeing the marks on her face, seeing them grow and blossom, feeling some strange and frightening creature turn inside of him, terrified of what was happening yet unable to hold it back. He reached for her, watched as his fingers found her swollen cheek and traveled down along the dry rough skin of her neck.

Bobby pressed against him, his voice filled with sweetness.

"Go ahead, Jake. Give it a whirl. You can do anything you want to her."

Delicately Cross pressed his fingers against her breast. He found the nipple and worked it with his thumb and forefinger, squeezing it between them, harder and harder still until he saw Kimberly's mouth slowly open in pain.

Bobby's face was next to his, his lips at his ear, breath like fire against his skin.

"How does that feel?"

Cross couldn't find the words.

"Feels damn good, doesn't it?"

Cross knelt down in front of her, shoving her legs apart. He reached between them, the excitement racing through his body. He had never felt so free in his life. Then Bobby's hands were on his shoulders, hard and rough, pulling him back.

"But let's not get crude," Bobby said.

The filming of the ransom note took most of the night. Cross was in charge of getting her ready. Bobby gave him a bag full of cosmetics and told him to do it.

"Go for a natural look," he said and laughed.

She sat motionless as Cross applied the makeup to her face, a heavy coat of base to cover the bruises and some blusher on her cheeks for color. He put lipstick on her—dark red, the only one Bobby had bought—following the lines of her mouth carefully.

Kimberly watched him during the whole process, turning her head to gaze into his eyes. Cross thought that he saw a flicker of recognition there, that maybe she knew who he was and what was going on, but the longer he stared the more he realized it was simply an involuntary reaction, no different than if he'd struck her on the knee to make her leg jerk.

It was just like Bobby had said. He could do anything to her. He felt cool and detached, in control once again, completely at ease. The compulsion, the rage, all of it had vanished in one swift cleansing motion and what was left was so pure that he wanted to hold on to the feeling forever.

In gratitude, he kissed her on the cheek.

Bobby took one look at his makeup job and whistled.

"Hey, what ever happened to Baby Jane?"

Cross didn't get the joke.

Bobby told him he wanted to shoot the ransom note in sequence.

"That way I get final cut."

Cross had no idea what he was talking about. He sat back and watched.

Bobby started by shooting one of the chairs. He pushed it into motion and then filmed as it moved. Next he filmed the empty bed and then moved the camera to the black open grate of the stove, zooming in close.

He stuck a copy of that day's newspaper in Kimberly's hands and filmed her next, panning across the floor and up her legs to her face.

"Hi," he said. "My name is Kimberly Morbach. As you can see, I'm still alive. But unless Mom and Dad pay my friend one million dollars real soon I'm going to be dead as shit. They have two days to get the money. My friend will let them know what they have to do. P.S. I'm real sorry we had to shoot the old man."

Bobby swung the camera away from her face and focused on one of the candles, moving in for a tight shot of the flame as it flickered in the breeze.

Then, with the camera still running, he blew out the candle.

Bobby put the camera down. He rewound the tape and watched it through the viewfinder, his whole body shaking with excitement.

"Paging Mr. Oscar," he cried. "Paging Mr. Oscar."

Cross was coming down from his reverie, dreaming of what had happened with the girl, seeing her face, feeling the touch of her skin, still surprised at the suddenness of his need. He had to leave soon, and when he did, he would be back in his old life, and all of its petty charm.

"Take a look," Bobby said and handed him the camera. Cross watched the film through the viewfinder and found it a little too overdone for his taste. But it did have a kind of raw power, a vividness that worked despite the clichéd images. The police wouldn't even know what they were looking at.

"Very effective," Cross said.

"Very effective? Is that the same as interesting?"

"It means I approve."

"Approval is what I crave," Bobby said. He removed the cassette and wiped it off very carefully with his shirt. Then he handed it to Cross.

"What am I supposed to do with it?"

"Give it to the cops. Tell them you found it in your mailbox. They'll believe you."

"I'm sure they will," Cross said. He thought again of the last image on the tape. "You know they don't have a million dollars."

Bobby laughed. "Have to think big. Ask for a million, people start to take you seriously."

"What are you really thinking of?"

"Whatever I can get."

"How much is that in dollars?"

Bobby thought for a moment. "Half."

Cross shook his head. "They can probably come up

with a quarter of a million. Anything more, it would take too much time. I want this ended quickly.''

"Maybe you can float Daddy a loan," Bobby said. "Make up the difference for him."

Cross laughed. "I don't have that kind of money, Bobby."

Bobby didn't laugh. He lit a cigarette and stared at Cross through the smoke, picking idly at his lip.

"I don't think you fully appreciate my situation," Bobby said.

"I do," Cross said. "Completely. I just hope you understand mine."

"Oh yeah. I see everything as clear as day."

Cross wasn't sure. That was what had happened to him. He had gone from a stationary universe to one that changed minute by minute. He had no idea what Bobby might do. It frightened him and yet made him fearless. As though his life had started once again, accelerating at full speed from a dead stop.

"I'll do what I can about the money," Cross said.

"Then we don't have anything to worry about."

Not entirely true. When Bobby had what he wanted, what would happen to Cross? Who would give him what he wanted?

"What are you going to do?" he asked.

"Right now?"

"No, when it's over."

"I'll be in the wind," Bobby said with a faint smile.

Kimberly stirred, raised her head to look at both of them, then directly at Cross.

"Daddy?" she said.

Without thinking Cross reached out and slapped her across the face. He pulled back to strike her again, but she had already retreated into herself, rocking back and forth on the couch the way she'd been before.

Bobby grabbed his arm, hard enough that it hurt, no

longer smiling. He didn't let go, either. He spun Cross around so that they were close and Cross could see the madness in his eyes.

"You know what your problem is, Jake? You don't know how to pace yourself."

He let go and patted his shoulder and then turned him away from Kimberly with only a hint of force.

"Leave the mask," he said, and Cross did.

Bobby walked him through the woods to his car and just as he was getting inside slipped something in his pocket. Cross reached for it.

"Wait 'til you're alone," Bobby said. "Get the full effect." He shut the door. "See you real soon."

Cross listened as his footsteps faded and took out what he'd given him.

It was a photograph.

Cross turned on the overhead light and looked at it.

It was a picture of a dead boy. Cross couldn't see his face, but he had no trouble recognizing the bloody hole in the center of his chest. He turned the picture over.

On the back Bobby had written, "See how interesting it can really get?"

Tim Cochran was asleep when the rat bit him on the tip of his elbow, cutting right through the skin and hitting bone. The pain brought him awake screaming, waving his arms around wildly to get away from it. The rat squealed and darted under one of the nearby seats.

Tim clutched at his arm, feeling the blood warm between his fingers. Then he was up on his feet, yelling at the rat, chasing after it between the rows of broken chairs, running all the way up to the front doors of the empty theater until he was too weak to run anymore. He made his way back down to the makeshift bed he had made from half a dozen seat cushions and some pieces of plywood.

He'd broken into the back of the abandoned Royal

Theater on South Street one day after seeing the cop at his uncle's house, busting out a pane of glass in a storeroom window and breaking through the boards that were nailed on the inside. His hand still hurt from beating on the wood, and he thought he might have broken something.

He was hungry, too, despite the nightly forays into the streets to look for food. He found what he could in trash cans and dumpsters, pawing through the garbage for something edible. What he found was mostly bread, the wet, moldy pieces breaking apart in his hands when he picked them up. He had become less choosy as the days went on, eating things that smelled bad and tasted worse. Half the time, he threw them right back up. As a result, there was a constant grinding in his stomach that sometimes doubled him up with pain and would not go away.

He thought about using the robbery money to buy a decent meal, but it was too dangerous, too easy for either Bobby or the cops to catch him that way. So he hid during the day in the abandoned theater and spent his nights ass deep in garbage cans scrounging for food.

At night, sometimes, when he was half asleep or clutching his stomach, trying to keep the pain from tearing him apart, he thought he heard ghosts inside the theater. One night he awoke to the sound of people laughing, and it sent a shock wave through him that brought him to his feet. He heard other things, footsteps, crying, the distant, faint hum of music. Sometimes he thought he smelled popcorn cooking. The smell swirled around him like a vapor and stung his nose.

He had no idea where the sounds and smells came from—perhaps the street outside, perhaps the walls of the theater itself, the echoing spirits of some earlier time. He knew somehow that he was imagining them but it didn't matter. He could lose himself for a little while, pretend that he was watching a movie, cheering for the hero, knowing that he would win in the end. He let the dream carry him along—he had a home, a mother and father, and the world was a warm and loving place.

Except for the rats.

When he came back down, Tim knew that all he was hearing was the sound of the rats scurrying through the old building. He wasn't afraid of the ghosts but he was deathly afraid of the rats. Once or twice, when he made noises to scare them away, he heard their furious screeching. He was the intruder here. They were the rightful owners. He had no place, not even in an abandoned and forgotten theater. Tim cried easily now, breaking into tears at the thought.

It was hours after the rat had bitten him and he hurt all over. Just raising his arm was painful, sharp spines sticking into his bones. He wiped a hand across his forehead and felt the dampness of fever. Tim tried to get up and a surge of nausea swept through him. He knelt on all fours and retched. When it was over, he felt a little better and lay back down. He was so tired now that all he could think of was sleep.

Rabies. What if the rat had given him rabies?

It hit him just before he drifted off but for once the fear was too much. His mind closed around the thought and choked it out, giving him a few hours' rest, dreaming movie dreams, waiting for a hero to come and save him.

16

Paige looked for Susan.

It was the first thing on his mind as he made his way through the crowd of reporters that had gathered on the street in front of Cross's house, held back by the hastily erected police barricades and the handful of uniformed officers who stood behind them. He was accosted by microphones and cameras and shouted questions, but he pushed his way through them without answering, eyes focused on the door of the house, hoping to see her there waiting for him.

The cop behind the door pointed down the front hall. "They're in the study."

Paige noticed that the mailbox beside the door had been removed. A bright patch of clean paint showed where it had been, and the area was covered with a sheet of clear plastic that was taped to the wall.

There was chaos inside the house but of a different tenor. Voices filled the hallway, and he caught the sharp smell of cigar smoke. A pair of state police troopers stepped past him, talking rapidly to each other, giving him a brief nod of acknowledgment. Further on, he stepped over a phone company tool kit on the carpet next to a large walk-in closet. The phone man was busy patching in new lines.

They were all in the study, Captain Glover, the state police, the senator, and Jacob Cross. The senator, he thought, looked in shock. Cross, too. He sat by himself in one of the leather chairs, eyes moving rapidly over the room as if he had been suddenly brought from his bed to answer questions put to him by an invasion of strangers.

Teets and Rudolph stood next to the sliding glass windows talking to each other. Teets smoked a cigar as he spoke. Jack Rudolph nodded hello.

Only Susan was missing.

Paige's disappointment was sudden, almost breathtaking. In the next instant he wondered if something had happened to her. He started for the senator, but Glover grabbed him first, pulling him toward an older military-looking man in a crisp blue suit with salt-and-pepper hair and a trim little moustache to match. Paige had never seen him before, or the younger man in the tan suit standing next to him, so close in stature that they might have been father and son. Paige wondered if they bought their clothes together as well.

"Pat, this is Commander Jackson, and Lieutenant O'Brien."

"Stan," the man said and stuck out his hand. Paige shook it once and let go. The younger one shook his hand without speaking. You'll go far, Paige thought.

"Stan is the state police liaison on this," Glover said.

"Harrisburg?"

Jackson nodded and nodded toward the senator. "I know the family," he said quietly.

"We got a tape," Glover said. "In the mailbox."

"I saw," Paige said. "Anybody know why he dropped it here?"

"Probably because there weren't any police around," Jackson said. Paige couldn't tell whether it was a criticism or merely an observation, and decided to ignore it either way.

"When was it dropped?"

"Nobody knows. Cross says he found it when he got the mail at three-thirty this afternoon, so it could have been left the night before."

"You looked at it yet?"

Glover nodded. "Cross saw it first."

"He played it?"

"Yes," Jackson said. "Apparently, no one told him not to."

"How bad did he screw it up?"

"Not that bad," Glover said. "The crime scene people went over it and got a couple of strange partials. We're waiting for another tape player to make a copy."

"Can I look at it?"

Glover glanced at Jackson. "Let me check."

Jackson stuck his hands in his pockets and looked at Paige.

"I understand you had a rough time a few months ago."

"Rough enough," Paige said.

Jackson pretended to think about his answer. He drew his lips together, nodded several times and brushed the bottom of his chin with his fingers.

Paige knew what was going on, knew it unconsciously before they were even introduced. Jackson belonged to Morbach. Now the state police were going to be perched on his shoulder, making sure that if the investigation went wrong, he would get the blame, not them. Paige didn't like it, but there wasn't much he could do about it.

"He was your partner," Jackson said, "the officer who was killed?"

"He was my friend," Paige said.

"I'm sorry."

Paige watched Jackson's face, saw only bland indifference, and his irritation deepened.

"He was a drunk who got sloppy and made a dumb mistake," Paige said. "And you don't know a goddamn thing about it."

Jackson stiffened. O'Brien stepped forward, tense and angry.

"Now wait a minute," O'Brien said when Glover suddenly appeared between them holding the tape in his gloved hand.

"Okay," Glover said, "everybody sit down. We're going to look at it again." The tension didn't ease when they stepped apart.

The detectives moved closer to the television set while Glover put the tape in the VCR. Jackson and O'Brien stood by the senator.

The tape started and Paige tried to concentrate, but his mind was on the one person who should have been there and wasn't.

Where the hell was Susan?

The tape rolled and Paige was pulled into it.

When it was over, Jerome Teets pretty much summed up everyone's feelings.

"You believe the balls on this prick?" he said. "Sending us a goddamn *movie*?" He looked at Paige and grinned. "You might wanna call Siskel and Ebert, Pat, tell 'em we got some new talent comin' their way."

Paige asked Glover to run it again. The captain punched the rewind button and waited patiently while the machine whirred to a stop.

Paige watched it again, concentrating this time, trying to catch a glimpse of something that might identify the place. But when it was over, all he was left with was the girl.

"Anybody got an idea where this was taken?" Glover asked.

"It's too run-down to be around here," O'Brien said. "Maybe out in Montgomery or Upper Bucks."

"Too run-down?" Teets said. "When was the last time the state police were in North Philly?"

"That's what I think," O'Brien said.

"It looks like *The Waltons* to me," Jack Rudolph said.

Teets laughed. "*The Waltons*. Shit. What do you think, the fucking hillbillies grabbed her?" Everybody laughed with him.

"All right, that's enough," Glover said.

They stopped talking for a moment. Then Teets spoke again, seriously this time.

"Tell you one thing, boys and girls. The way she looks, we keep screwing around with this prick, she ain't gonna make it."

Which was the one thing everyone was thinking but nobody wanted to hear.

The senator, who had sat silently through the whole thing, left the room, followed by Jackson and O'Brien and, finally, dragging himself from his chair, Jacob Cross.

"I won't pay," Morbach said. He said it stubbornly, almost petulantly, like a schoolboy who refuses to go outside and play with the other children.

They were in the living room. Cross had closed the sliding wooden doors, sealing them off from the rest of the house. He stood with his back to the front window, the curtains drawn to keep out of the sight of the reporters camped on the front lawn. Cross could hear their voices, loud and impatient, wanting to be let in on the secret.

"Of course not," Cross said. "A million dollars is clearly out of the question."

"No," Morbach said. "I mean I won't pay—ever. I won't give them the money." His voice carried that same tone as before. But it wasn't the tone that was so alarming, it was the look on his face.

Morbach's mouth had gone rigid and he stared straight ahead as though his eyes had lost the capacity to comprehend what was right in front of him. Cross had seen that look before. It was usually reserved for anyone on staff who dared to suggest that the senator might have been on the wrong side of an issue, and it usually meant the end of the discussion and of the person. The senator went through staff the same way some people went through a bag of peanuts, one right after another.

But Cross couldn't figure out why it was happening now. Or why the senator seemed to be sweating so much or why he held his hands straight down at his sides as if standing at attention. He turned to Jackson.

"Could you excuse us a moment, Commander?"

"Certainly," Jackson said and took O'Brien by the arm. Cross opened the door and let them out.

"You didn't have to do that," the senator said. "I've known Stan a long time."

"So have I. Now could you please explain what you just said?"

"I thought it was perfectly clear. The girl in the film."

"Kimberly."

"It's not."

Cross wasn't certain he'd heard him right.

"It's not what?"

"It's not Kimberly," he said. "I know my daughter, and the girl in the film isn't Kimberly." The senator's eyes took on a bright sheen, like hard white crystals, and his upper lip quivered with emotion. "She's been behind this kidnapping scam from the start. It's obvious we're being tricked."

"Where do you think Kimberly is now?"

Senator Morbach blinked once.

"I hope she's rotting in hell."

————

There were a number of standard things to be done in any criminal investigation and Paigé had done them all. He assigned Rudolph and Teets—he couldn't resist putting them together—to the neighborhood canvas, checking to see if the neighbors had seen anybody approach the house during the last twelve to eighteen hours. Glover handled the FBI, who were supposed to be checking if a similar videotaped ransom note had ever been logged on any of their computers. They had stayed out of the investigation so far, but if things got much worse, they would invoke some obscure federal privilege and come in full strength, and then Paige could retire to Florida.

The phone trace had been set up with the phone company, the second VCR had arrived, computers were running, the wheels of justice were turning round and round in big useless circles, and Paige was busy doing what everyone else was doing. Waiting.

After twenty minutes of that, he slipped out the sliding doors of the study to smoke a cigarette in the backyard. He was standing near the edge of the patio, looking out across the yard, when he heard a noise off to one side.

A reporter and cameraman stumbled through the bushes around the corner of the house. The reporter, a young man with carefully trimmed blond hair, wore an expensive-looking gray suit. The cameraman wore jeans and a T-shirt. The cameraman threw the camera on his shoulder and aimed it at Paige.

"Back in front," Paige said.

The reporter advanced on him, microphone poised like a lance, and Paige felt like a piece of meat on the grill.

"We're in the backyard of political power broker Jacob Cross. Inside, State Senator James Morbach waits to hear news of his kidnapped daughter. Can we get a statement from the police as to what's going on inside the house right now?"

"No," Paige said.

The man gave him an angry smile but didn't drop the microphone.

"Keep it rolling."

The cameraman lowered his minicam. "Come on, Scott."

"I said keep it rolling. Don't lose it."

The cameraman shrugged and raised the camera.

"Is it true you've received a ransom note this morning?"

"Don't you people listen?" Paige said. "As soon as we've got something to announce, we'll announce it. Until that happens, I want you back in front with the rest of them."

"I don't get paid to listen," the reporter said. "I get paid for stories. Is Mrs. Morbach here?"

Paige reached for the microphone but the reporter pulled it back.

"Is it true she's moved out of her own house?"

"Jesus Christ," Paige said. "That's enough." He lunged for the microphone. The two men wrestled with it for a few seconds until Paige swung his shoulder into the reporter, knocking him backward. Then he yanked hard on the cord and snapped the plug. The cord coiled around his feet like a dead snake.

Paige rolled up the cord and handed the microphone back to him. "Enough, okay?"

"Enough my ass," the reporter said. "I'll sue you, you son of a bitch."

Paige took his arm and swung him around to the corner of the house. The cameraman kept right on filming.

"Get your hands off me!"

Paige pulled him close. He could smell the man's cologne. It was like sniffing a bowl of baked fruit.

"If you don't get back in front with the rest of them," Paige said quietly, "I'm going to wrap that cord around your neck and strangle you to death. Now move."

"You won't get away with this," the reporter said but backed off, following the cameraman around the side of the house.

"Smooth, Pat, real smooth."

Teets stood beside the sliding doors and puffed on the stub of his cigar.

"Don't you start," Paige said. He headed off across the patio to the other side of the house.

"Where you goin'?"

"For a walk."

"You plan on beatin' up any more on-air personalities while you're gone?"

"Not if I can help it."

Paige cut through the backyard, away from the reporters, and headed up the road, cursing himself for his own stupidity. He should have just walked away, gone back inside. Christ, he should have let the state police take care of it. They probably had a routine all worked out.

If Susan had been there, he thought, it wouldn't have happened. He was moving fast to get away from the house, but the thought slowed him down.

It might have happened. Might have even been worse. He might have acted like a real hero and defended her honor. That would have been very helpful. That definitely would have made the early news.

It occurred to him that he was looking for something. But what precisely? The word *love* came to mind and he cringed just thinking about it. He couldn't quite fit his mind around the word. He was no longer certain what it meant, if he ever had been. He knew he didn't have a clue when he married Connie. It was just part of his adolescent wish list: meet somebody, fall in love, get married, join the police, be a hero.

He had done it all. He'd killed Edward Grant, the burglar who had gone off the deep end and started murdering his victims. Grant had murdered Tom Ferris, cut him open with a pair of scissors, and Paige had taken his revenge. Was that what it was to be a hero?

His wife had been murdered by a burglar, too, so if it was revenge, it had come years late, too late, he realized now, to have any real meaning. When it was all over, what was most clear to him was that the years had gone by and he had wasted too many of them. He had woken up at Tom Ferris's funeral and realized that nothing had changed, least of all himself.

He'd gained one bit of wisdom, though. He knew he didn't want to be a hero anymore.

He wanted a real life and didn't have one. Susan Morbach might give him that chance. He had no idea how, only that she might help him find it somehow. Given the situation, he knew his morality was highly questionable. It was questionable given *any* situation. He understood that. But he wasn't sure it would stop him.

Paige passed close to the house just down the road. A woman stood on the front lawn, dressed in white shorts and a bright pink halter top. She had a drink in one hand and the other on her waist, sticking her hip out like she was trying to open a door with it. Paige decided it wasn't her first drink of the day. Probably not even her second. She watched him as he approached, took a long sip and called to him.

"You the Scout leader around here?"

She didn't sound drunk, Paige thought; she sounded like she was mad at something.

"No."

"Then you must be one of the Scouts." She glanced back at the house. "I had one here already today. Cute. Looked like he knew how to brush his teeth and everything."

"Jack Rudolph," Paige said.

"That's the one. Just like the reindeer."

Paige laughed.

"He didn't think it was funny," she said. "I was trying to make a pass at him and he didn't know whether to shit or go blind. What's your name?"

"Patrick Paige."

"Ah," the woman said. "I think I saw you on television."

That must mean I exist, Paige thought.

She stepped into the road and held out her hand. Paige took it.

"I'm Cheryl Silverman," she said. "Never mind the last name. I may not have it much longer." She finished her drink, letting some of the clear liquid splash down her neck. She rubbed it into her skin. Up close, she smelled like gin and bubble bath. "What the hell's going on over there?"

"Didn't Detective Rudolph tell you?"

"He wanted to know if I saw anybody creeping around Jake's house last night. That's when I made the comment about the reindeer. We didn't get too far."

"Did you?"

"Did I what?"

"See anybody?"

"Just old Jake," she said. "He's a nasty little prick, don't you think?"

"I wouldn't know."

"If you met him, you'd know. He and Al—that's my husband—they're very close. Jake farts, Al says excuse me. Very close."

Paige smiled in spite of himself.

"But you didn't see anyone?"

"Not a goddamn soul."

"Were you awake?"

"I'm awake most nights." She pulled an ice cube from the glass and sucked on it lightly, rubbing it around her mouth. "My whole life's upside down. I sleep all day and stay up all night. I've seen so many talk shows I'd like to puke.'' She waved her glass at Cross's house. "This is a real treat by comparison."

"What about your husband?"

"What about him?"

"Did he see anybody?"

"Al hasn't been around lately," she said. "Makes you wonder, doesn't it?"

"I don't know him."

"I do. You know what I wonder most? Where that prick is getting his cock sucked these days. Because it sure ain't *here*."

"Why don't you ask him?" Paige said.

Cheryl burst out laughing.

"That's good. Next time I see him I will. You want to come inside for a drink?"

"Not right now," Paige said. "I've got to get back."

If she was disappointed, she didn't show it. "Then send the other one by. Tell him I promise not to make any more reindeer jokes."

"Nice talking to you, Cheryl," Paige said.

"Oh sure. Anytime."

He was about twenty feet away when she yelled at him.

"Tell Jake Cross I got a message for him." She held up her hand, the middle finger raised straight in the air. She kept it there until Paige turned his back on her. He had the feeling she was prepared to keep it up for a long time.

Paige was in the kitchen drinking coffee when Cross found him.

"I'd like to know what you're going to do."

"Wait. Continue the investigation."

Cross paused. "I think we may have a small problem with the senator," he said. He wasn't certain how to explain it. The senator has gone completely nuts was one possibility.

"Which is?"

"He doesn't believe that's his daughter on the tape."

Paige put his coffee cup down.

"Did he say that?"

"I'm afraid so."

"Is he right?"

"No, of course not. Frankly, I don't know *what* he is at the moment. He seems to think this whole thing is something Kimberly arranged herself. The kidnapping."

"We need him to take the call when it comes," Paige said. "We need him here."

"I'm not sure I can guarantee that."

"Where's Susan?"

"He doesn't know," Cross said. "He said to ask you." He gave Paige an amused smile. "He thinks you're sleeping with his wife."

Have I been that obvious? Paige thought.

"What do you think?"

"I think," he said slowly, "that Senator Morbach is under enormous pressure and that in time he'll come to his senses."

"That sounds like a press release."

"That's usually the safest response. Have you tried her office?"

"No," Paige said and for some reason felt guilty all over again. He wanted to call, wanted it desperately, but just couldn't bring himself to pick up the phone. It was, he thought, the safest response.

"I'll call," Cross said. He disappeared into the study and returned several minutes later.

"They don't seem to know where she is either. She phoned this morning and said she was all right and that she'd call in. She hasn't."

"What about the house?"

"I tried there, too. One of your officers answered. He hasn't seen her." Cross poured himself a cup of coffee and went through an elaborate ritual of adding milk and stirring in a packet of artificial sweetener.

"Do you know where she is?" Cross asked finally.

"No. I think I know what she's doing but I don't know where. She's out looking for Kimberly."

Cross sighed. "That's what I thought."

"Are you going to tell him?"

"I don't think so. She'll show up eventually. In the meantime, it gives her something to do."

Which meant Cross couldn't control her and it kept her out of the way. Paige was impressed.

"Are you really that calculating?"

Cross smiled. "Almost always."

"Is that why you brought Jackson in from Harrisburg?"

"I don't see that it does any real harm and it makes the senator feel more secure." He sipped his cup of coffee. "You're still in charge of the investigation."

"That's nice to hear," Paige said. "I met your neighbor a few minutes ago."

"Which one?"

"Cheryl Silverman."

"Yes," Cross said. He stared into his cup, his voice exquisitely neutral.

"She likes you, too."

"Cheryl has her problems. I try to avoid them."

"It must be hard."

Cross looked up. "Why do you say that?"

"She doesn't seem like the shy type, that's all. She told me her whole life story just like that. She had a message for you, too."

Cross waited.

Paige raised the middle finger of his right hand.

Cross actually blushed.

"I didn't mean to embarrass you," Paige said, enjoying the spectacle. It was the first time he'd seen Cross caught off guard, and it made him wonder what else Cheryl Silverman knew about Jacob Cross.

"I've never liked vulgarity," Cross said.

"Then you picked a strange profession," Paige said.

Commander Jackson poked his head around the corner of the kitchen.

"Have you seen him?" he asked.

"No," Cross said. "I left him in the living room."

"He's not there anymore."

"He's someplace. Check upstairs. What's the problem?"

Jackson shook his head and disappeared.

"Maybe I should look for him," Cross said.

"How much trouble can he get into?"

"I couldn't possibly imagine." Cross set his coffee on the counter.

Paige shrugged.

"There is one thing you might help me with," Cross said. "I'm not certain how to go about it."

"Sure," Paige answered, trying hard to envision what sort of help he might be to a man like Jacob Cross.

"I want to buy a gun," Cross said, "something I can carry with me. I thought I might need some help with the permit."

"Why do you want a gun?"

"The kidnapper was here, remember. At my house. He knows who I am."

"There's a few of us he'll have to go through first."

"I'm not worried about here."

"Then stay home."

"Is that your answer?" Cross said.

"No," Paige said. "I can probably take care of it. When were you planning on buying it?"

"Tomorrow," Cross said smoothly. "What do you recommend?"

Before Paige could answer, Jackson poked his head around the corner.

"I think you'd better come with me," he said. Then he added, "The senator."

"What is it now?"

Jackson looked at Paige and then at Cross.

"He hit a reporter."

"A woman?"

"No, thank God," Jackson said, shaking his head. "A man. The reporter keeps yelling about a lawsuit. I think he's serious."

"Young guy, gray suit, blond hair?" Paige offered.

"That's the one," Jackson said suspiciously. "How did you know?"

Paige smiled at Cross. "He wants to sue me, too. Maybe we both should stay home."

17

Bobby placed the camera a few feet from the couch. Kimberly sat next to him, her head on his leg, legs curled up tight and covered with one of the ratty blankets. She looked like a waif in a silent movie, all bones and pale skin, big empty eyes staring out at the world.

Bobby spoke to the red light next to the lens. It was something he'd learned. When you were shooting a close-up, you picked something to stare at and didn't look at anything else. Because if you did, it made you look shifty and unreliable.

"My mother had a tattoo," he said. "Right on her tit." He pointed to his right breast. "Little bitty bumblebee, about the size of a dime. Didn't have any tits to speak of, just that little tattoo. She showed it to me. I must have been eleven or twelve. Said she had beestings for tits, might as well have the bee. She had another one, a chain that went around her ankle. Wasn't half as good-looking as the bee.

"After she showed it to me, I'd try to get a look at it, hang around the bathroom and shit, peek at her when she was putting on her clothes. She got on me for that, told me to quit looking at her tits. It got to be a game after a while. We'd be sitting at dinner, didn't matter who else was there, she'd look over at me, real serious, you know, like she just caught me picking my ass or something.''

Bobby pressed his eyebrows together and pushed his head forward.

'' 'You staring at my tits again, Bobby?' 'No, ma'am.' 'You sure?' 'Yes, ma'am, I'm sure.' 'Well, you saw it once today, one more time won't hurt.' Then she'd pull up her T-shirt or whatever else she was wearing and grab her tit. She'd start making buzzing sounds, waving it around. Then she'd pinch her nipple, pinch it real good, and say, 'Gotcha.' Then we'd go back to eating like nothing happened. Some guy'd be there, mouth hanging open, and she'd smile and say something like, 'Eat your french fries, honey, before they get cold.' Mom was a real comedienne.

"She liked college towns. We must have lived in a dozen of them. Texas. Michigan. Florida. We were all over the goddamn place. Settle in, stay for a few months, move on to someplace else. Never went to California. She always talked about it but we never made it there.''

He glanced down at Kimberly. "I bet you've been to California.'' Kimberly made no reply and Bobby just shook his head and laughed.

"She liked college boys, too. They'd give her whatever she wanted. Drugs. Money. Groceries. They'd trip on their own dicks just to help her out. She was older than they were—about a hundred *years* older—but it didn't show. She dressed like a hippie, long skirts, boots, all that shit. But she didn't believe in it. I don't know what she did believe in but it wasn't hippies.

"I'd find her sitting at the kitchen table in the morning, drinking coffee, smoking a joint. Rest of the house looked like a combat zone, clothes and beer bottles all over the place, but the kitchen'd be clean.

" 'You know,' she'd say, 'sometimes I think this life is just too goddamn easy.'

"First time I ever got high was at the kitchen table. Michigan. I was ten years old, I think. We smoked a joint and went to the movies. To tell you the truth, that was the best goddamn time I ever had. Some movie with Peter Sellers. Don't remember what it was about but we laughed a lot.

"She used to take me to classes with her. I swear. The big lecture halls on campus, the ones with a hundred and fifty kids in them. We'd waltz right in, Mom with her notebook and shit, take a seat in the back. She'd open the notebook and start writing in it. I'd just sit there and listen to what they had to say or look at everybody in the room and try to figure out what they thought they were doing. If it was a good lecture, we'd stay for the whole thing. If it was boring, we'd go find another one.

"One time when she went to the bathroom, I looked at what she wrote. It was one sentence: 'This guy sucks nigger dick.' That's all she wrote. I told you. My mom was a genuine comic."

Bobby stopped talking for a moment, lost in some private memory.

"I used to ask her about my old man. She didn't know. One time she'd say he was a trucker, the next time he'd be an airline pilot. My old man had more jobs than the want ads. The best one was when she said he worked for the circus.

"She said, 'You know the guys who stick their heads in the lion's mouth? That's what your father did.' I asked her what happened to him. He wasn't around, something *had* to have happened to him. 'Well,' she said. 'Dumb bastard got it bit off.' I never bothered asking her again. I figured my old man was one of those dipshit college guys she was always screwing."

Bobby laughed to himself. "We moved to Florida

when I was thirteen. That's when things started to go downhill.

"She didn't start out being a hooker. I mean, nobody starts out being a hooker. They're always something else first. But you can see it in their eyes. They're just marking time until they get to the real thing. My mom started out being a waitress, which is good training for hookers. People tell you what they want, you give it to them, and then they throw some money on the table and leave. The difference being a hooker is you don't have to clean their plates up after they're done.

"She got tired of waitressing and started dancing at a topless place outside of Orlando. That's where we were living then, some shack around the junior college. Weren't going to any classes, though.

"You ever seen a Florida shithouse? Dinky little places made out of cinderblock with a tin roof and a couple sick-looking orange trees in the backyard. They paint 'em pink and green, make you think you're living in a real house. Half the places are burned out. The rest of 'em get filled up with Mexicans and trash."

Bobby took a joint from his pocket, lit it, and sucked in a big lungful of smoke. He let it out slowly.

"They gave her a name at the bar she was dancing at," he said. "The English Muffin. That was her name. It's funny but I don't remember the name of the bar. There must have been about twenty of them, all on this one strip of highway going out of Orlando. You'd look around the parking lot, you couldn't find a new car if you tried. Looked like everybody's just come from a bondo sale."

He took a few more drags on the joint, savoring the smell. Then he crushed out the head on the leg of the couch and slipped it back into his pocket.

"They'd get these truckloads of Mexicans coming in from the fields, bunch of beaners jabbering in Spanish, jerking off their beer bottles. That was the kind of place my mom worked.

"The seats went right up to the stage. You buy a drink, plant yourself in a chair, couple minutes later you got this pussy staring you in the face. I mean, in your *face*. Guys used to do contortions trying to get at it. You ever seen anybody eat pussy off a bar? It's tough. Your fucking chin gets in the way. They had to twist their heads around and go at it sideways, tongues waggling around, trying to reach it. It's something to see.

"I used to sit backstage, listen to the girls talk. The biggest problem was the beaners didn't shave. They'd come in with three days worth of growth on their faces and just tear shit out of them. One of the girls said after a couple hours her twat was so raw, it felt like she had razor burn.

"They used to stick money up there, too. The girls'd let 'em. That was their tip. You ever see somebody with a handful of dollar bills sticking out of her cunt? It's pretty strange. The girls used to let me pull them out sometimes. They thought it was cute, this little kid playing with their pussies. I always figured if automatic teller machines looked like that, people'd *pay* to use them.

"I didn't mind it. I thought this was real life. It wasn't that much different from the colleges. People just did what they thought they had to do. I suppose what I minded was when she started bringing the customers home. Fucking beaners. It was the beaners got her on heroin.

"She called every one of them Pedro. Walk in the house with one on her arm. 'Pedro's going to be staying with us for a little while, honey.' Fucking beaner's over in the corner, grinning like he just bought himself a taco ranch. That's how she got started on smack. Mexican brown. Looked like brown sugar. *Dirty* brown sugar. She started sniffing, went right on into skin popping. The next thing I know, I'm tying her off in the bathroom, shooting it into the back of her leg. The first time I shot her up, I damn near killed her. Put it in too fast. She conked out like a dead chicken, didn't even know what was happening, big shit-eating grin on her face.

"When she came to, she looked right at me and said, 'Hey, Pedro, not so much next time.' I could have fucking killed her right there."

He looked at Kimberly. "That's how I learned to use a needle. You remember that?" Kimberly turned her head toward his voice, and he found himself staring straight down into her eyes. "Knock, knock," he said. "Anybody home?"

Bobby brought his face down close to hers.

"I tell you something. I got so good with that needle I used to shoot everybody up. That was my *chore.* You probably had to rake the leaves, hose down the Mercedes. I had to shoot up all the Pedros that came over. I figured after pulling money out of somebody's twat, shooting up spics was kind of a step *down* on the social ladder. Where do you think I went wrong?

"They started callin' me Little Doc. You know, *Leetle* Doc. 'Hey, Leetle Doc, come over here, man, and do me a good one.' The place'd be wall-to-wall Pedros. Mom'd be walking around, bare assed, begging for it. Come on, honey, give your mom another one. Used to make my skin crawl."

Bobby stopped cold, rolling his eyes up in his head like he might pass out.

"She used to suck them off in front of me. When she was up to it. The Pedros got a kick out of that, watching me watching her. I pulled a knife on one of them one time. Fucker just laughed and stuck my hand to the floor with it. Kept right on laughing while he did it, too."

Bobby held out his hand. "Still got the scar." Kimberly blinked. "You're a lousy audience, you know that?"

He reached down and pulled her up so that she was sitting next to him.

"But I took care of him. I waited until the next time he asked me to shoot him up. I cut that shit with lye and rat poison and stuck it in his arm. It's an interesting combination. The poison's what kills you but the lye just burns. Feels like you got a blowtorch in your veins it hurts so much. I was right up close to him the way I am now, looking right in that fucker's eyes. That shit hit him and he screamed just like a baby.

"But you know the great thing about it? Nobody even noticed. There were three more of them there. They were all so fucking gone, they thought it was real funny, watching Pedro roll around the floor with his guts coming out his nose."

Bobby laughed. "Hell, I thought it was pretty funny myself. So I went and did the rest of them, boom, boom, boom. Put those beaners on the ropes."

He lit the joint again and spoke to her while he was still holding his breath. His voice came out sounding like a ventriloquist's dummy.

"And then I thought, hey, what the fuck, so I did Mom up, too. Hell, I figured I was doing her a favor. Saved her the price of a ticket."

He emptied his lungs in the air overhead, watching the way the light played over the smoke.

"You see my point? Everybody gets fucked. Doesn't matter who the hell you are. You just get fucked in the end. Mom got fucked, you got fucked, and now I bet old Jake is trying to figure out a way to fuck me. Maybe he'll send the cops here, maybe he'll come himself, but he's going to try. So we'll just have to make sure we get there first."

Bobby took one more drag on the joint. He felt warm all over, like he'd just stepped outside on a bright sunny day. The smoke filled his lungs and the warm feeling spilled over into his brain, settling down heavy until he didn't feel like moving, didn't feel like doing anything except sit there and let all the shit just float away.

"You see," he said quietly, staring straight ahead at the camera, "there's always the chance you're going to lose. Always. Nobody really knows, that's the thing. But if you start to worry about it, you've already lost."

He put out the joint and looked at her. "I ain't afraid of losing. Jake is. He thinks losing is a terrible thing. And that's what's going to fuck him up in the end. Me, I don't give a shit. I'm just trying to see how far I can take it."

Bobby stood up and turned off the camera. He got a length of rope from the table and a jackknife and began tying up Kimberly's ankles. She didn't react. She rocked back and forth on the couch, lips moving in silent song.

He looped the rope around her hands and pulled it tight.

"I'm going out for a little while," he said. "Take care of a few things. Pick up a couple surprises for Jake when he comes calling. We won't have long to wait."

He picked up her feet and rolled her over on the couch, taking out the jackknife, snapping it open along his palm. Outside the sun was going down, drifting below the tree line, streaks of gold and yellow reaching up into the darkening sky.

He pressed the blade of the knife along the back of her neck, underneath her hair, and heard her gasp.

"Not long at all," he said, and started to cut.

Susan Morbach made it back to her office at eight-thirty, long after everyone had gone home. It was her favorite time, even before the kidnapping, because it gave her time not to think. She never did any work during her time alone. She did mindless things. Straightened out her desktop, drank coffee, paged through that morning's newspaper, glancing at the pictures, not really reading it.

Sometimes, she just sat there composing letters to old friends in her head, friends she hadn't seen or heard from in years. She never wrote anything important, only about shopping or what she'd seen on television—she still thought of them as "girl things"—and because they were inconsequential she never felt any sense of loss when she mentally tore them up.

Sitting at her desk now, tired and uneasy, she realized that she had been sleepwalking through most of her existence. Like some kind of dumb farm animal, she thought. She wished she could go back to those mindless times but that was over. Her marriage, her position, her role in life, all of it was gone.

All of it except Kimberly.

It occurred to her that if her daughter died, she wouldn't have the strength to start over. Would she even if Kimberly survived?

Susan looked through the papers on her desk: letters to sign, queries from the staff to answer, newspaper clippings to sort through, all signs that life still went on around her. Despite the fact that hers was over.

She glanced at the phone messages that were stacked up neatly on the corner of her desk. There were two from City Services, one from the Bureau of Prisons, one from her husband, one from Jacob Cross. The last was from her mother. She didn't need to talk to her mother again. Or the city. Or Jacob Cross. Or her husband. Or anyone.

Except for Patrick Paige. He was the only one she really wanted to talk to, but there were no message slips from Patrick Paige.

The fact that there were none meant that he had nothing to tell her, and she wouldn't drive herself crazy by calling him only to find out there was no word, no progress.

No Kimberly.

The phone rang. The sound startled her, actually made her jump in her chair. It was as if someone were reading her thoughts. She let it ring again and then picked up the receiver, punching in the line.

"Hello?"

Silence. In the background Susan thought she heard the sound of traffic going by.

"Hello?"

A cough, almost a laugh, then, "Mommy miss her little girl?"

Her whole body felt warm and light, the touch of the phone as weightless as if she were drifting on a cloud.

"Who is this?"

"Hell, I shouldn't have to tell you that."

"Where is she? Where's Kimberly?"

"Easy now. We got a long way to go before we get to that."

A wedge of hysteria pushed itself into her mind, a scream that started on the inside and began to claw its way out.

"Then what do you want?" she cried, fighting to keep her voice from tearing apart.

"I thought we ought to get to know each other," he said. Then added, "Susan."

"I'll do whatever you want," Susan said calmly. "Just tell me if she's all right."

"She's fine. A little worse for the wear, but you know how these things go."

"No," Susan said, "I don't know how these things go. I don't know how anything goes anymore."

"Then I'm going to help you. Now listen very carefully because I'd hate to repeat myself. Are you alone?"

"Yes."

Silence.

"Don't lie to me."

"I'm not. I'm alone."

"Okay. Who have you talked to today?"

"No one."

"No one?" He seemed amazed. "What about the cops?"

"No."

"Your husband?"

"I haven't," she said and stopped. What right did he have to her life? "I haven't been home in a while," she said.

"You got all kinds of problems these days, don't you?"

"You're the reason," she said.

He laughed. "I guess I am. All right, you know route seventy-three in Jersey."

"Yes. Of course."

"A few miles from the bridge, there's a sex place. Big white building with X's all over it. You know the one I'm talking about?"

"I think so."

"If you don't know, look for it. I want you to meet me there in an hour."

"An hour?"

"One hour. Just park in the lot. When you get inside, go through the peep shows all the way upstairs where the dancers are. Find a seat in one of the booths, sit there and wait for me. Order a beer or something. Pretend like you're having a good time."

He laughed again.

"All right."

"You don't call anybody before you go. You don't stop for gas. You don't stop for directions. You don't speak to anybody when you get there except to the waitress. You fuck up and I'll send your daughter back home to you in little bitty pieces. You understand?"

"Yes," Susan said. "I understand."

"Good. I want you to bring something with you. You listening?"

"Yes."

"Ten thousand dollars. In cash. Put it in an envelope and leave it in your glove compartment. Don't lock the car. Go inside, drink your beer, and wait. You understand?"

Now she was silent. She tried to keep her thoughts straight but they were moving too fast. What if he was lying? What if it was a hoax? What if, what if, what if?

"What if I can't get the money?" she said.

"I can see you're not taking this seriously," he said. "The point of all this—of the money—is to establish trust. You trust me. I trust you." He sounded genuinely disappointed, like a parent with an unruly child. Or a husband, she thought. He was patronizing her and she resented it.

"I don't believe you have my daughter," she said suddenly. "Whoever you are."

"What do you want to know about? The knapsack she was carrying? Or that nice gold American Express card you gave her? Or maybe her bike?"

Nobody knew about those things. They weren't in the papers. She felt hollow again, all her courage gone.

"Stop it," she said quietly. "I believe you."

"How about the way she cries when she gets hurt?" he said. "Let me see if I can get it right."

"That's enough," she said, pleading this time. "I believe you. I'm sorry I said it."

"Daddy!" he cried, drawing out the word, twisting it so that the sound was like a deep pain coming from inside of her.

"Stop it!" she yelled. "Stop it!"

"One hour."

The line went dead.

Susan replaced the receiver. Seconds later, she made the decision to call Patrick Paige, to tell him that she had a chance to get her daughter back. Her fingers were on the phone when it rang.

She picked it up, dreading what was on the other end.

"I know just what you're thinking," he said. "But don't be stupid. Don't call anyone, don't stop for anyone. Do exactly what I told you. Because if you don't, next time I'll send you one of her tits in a bag."

Susan put the phone back in its cradle and thought no more about phoning Patrick Paige or anyone else. She thought instead about where she could get the money.

The terrible thing, the most frightening thing of all, was that she knew exactly where to get it.

There was a back entrance to the campaign headquarters, and only four people had the key. The senator, Jerry Abelson, Jacob Cross, and herself. It opened onto a short hallway. At the other end, there was the senator's private office, and on the right, just before it, his bathroom, an old storage closet he'd had converted when he leased the space.

Susan Morbach parked her car on Germantown Avenue and walked past the headquarters on the opposite side of the street. A single police car was parked in front of the headquarters. The officer inside it gave her a look, his eyes following her for a few steps. Then he looked away. She sucked in her breath and glanced at the brightly lit windows, the patriotic bunting sagging slightly over the front door.

Jerry Abelson stood by his desk at the far side of the room. He was talking on the phone, pacing back and forth and waving his arm in the air. From a distance, it looked almost like he was dancing.

She hurried to the next corner, crossed the street, and, when she was out of sight of the police car, walked to the rear of the building. The key was already in her hand. She slipped it in the lock and opened the door.

The light was on in the hallway. She made her way quickly, opened the office door, and stepped inside, leaving the door slightly ajar. The outer door, the one leading to the rest of the building, was closed.

The safe was in the opposite corner of the room, a squat black box, slightly larger than a file cabinet, with a lopsided stack of papers on top. She knelt in front of it and twisted the knob, praying to herself that she wouldn't screw up the combination. She could hear the voices coming from the other room, none of them distinct except for Abelson's. His rose above the others, loud and anxious. She hit the last number and pressed down on the heavy metal handle.

The door swung open. Susan stopped for a moment, took a deep breath, and peered inside. The safe was divided into five separate compartments, two on the left and three smaller ones on the right. The right side contained papers and campaign documents. The left-hand compartments held a pair of metal cashboxes. She reached for the top one.

She set it on the carpet and lifted the lid. The box was filled with cash, thin packets of a thousand dollars each, held together by a narrow paper band. She plucked ten of the packets from the box and closed the lid.

"What are you doing, Susan?"

Jerry Abelson stood in the open doorway. He closed the door behind him and leaned against it, his hands clenched together behind his back.

He pushed himself off the door.

"I think you ought to put that back." He spoke quietly, almost kindly, his face locked in a flat mirthless smile. It was as if he'd caught her with a stolen candy bar in the checkout line.

Susan stood up. She held the cashbox by the handle. It seemed too light to hold as much as it did.

"Go to hell, Jerry."

"Come on," he said, holding out his hand. "Give it here. This isn't a good thing."

She stepped toward the rear door of the office.

"I need it."

"Not *that* money," he said. "You know I can't let you take it."

He was still smiling when he rushed forward suddenly, reaching for the cashbox. She dropped the money and swung the box with both hands, bringing it over her shoulder in a long arc and smashing it against the side of his face.

Abelson took one more step and then dropped to his knees, clutching his head. When he pulled his hand away, she saw the long gash on the side of his forehead open up like the thick fleshy petals of a flower. Blood streamed down his cheek and splattered on the collar of his white shirt. He sat down and stared at the blood that dripped into his open hand.

"Jesus, Susan," he said, his voice filled with surprise. "Look what you did to me."

The money lay scattered at her feet. Susan dropped the cashbox and grabbed as much of it as she could. And ran.

Except for a wire service reporter and a single remote van from one of the television stations, the media had all gone home. The altercation between the senator and the reporter had come just in time to make the evening news, and Paige watched it with the rest of the detectives in the study.

It wasn't a fight so much as it was a comedy routine. The senator made the first mistake by stepping out on the front porch. The reporter in the gray suit pushed his way through the crowd and stuck the microphone in his face about an inch from his nose. The senator slapped it away. The reporter stumbled back and then someone pushed him forward into the senator's chest. The senator got huffy and the wrestling match started. They locked arms and rolled off the porch onto the lawn before anyone could pull them apart.

From the tape, it looked like the senator was trying to

get hold of the microphone cord so he could strangle the reporter.

It was, Paige thought, a fairly common urge.

Senator Morbach had gone right home after that and had taken the state police with him.

"Senator ought to think about turnin' pro," Jerome Teets commented. "Man's got all the right moves."

Jacob Cross sat next to Paige, tapping his fingers together in his lap, acting very much like a man who wished he was someplace else.

The phone rang and everyone froze.

A few seconds later, one of the detectives stuck his head around the corner of the door and pointed at Cross.

"It's for you," the detective said. "Jerry Abelson?"

Cross took the call in the kitchen. He came back and motioned for Paige.

Teets began humming "Strangers in the Night," loud enough for everyone to hear.

Paige followed Cross into the living room and waited while he shut the doors.

"What's going on?"

"I'm not sure," Cross said. "Susan Morbach just took some money from the campaign safe."

"How much?"

"Jerry doesn't know."

Paige sat down.

"Where is she now?"

"He doesn't know that either."

"Did she say why she took it?"

Cross shook his head. "She assaulted him."

"You mean she hit him?"

"He tried to stop her and she hit him with a cashbox. He was calling from the hospital. He needed stitches. Two inches lower, he said, and he'd have lost an eye."

"What was she driving?"

"She has a black New Yorker. I don't know the license number."

"Let's find out."

Paige got up from his chair and headed for the kitchen. Cross went with him. Paige punched in the number of the senator's house.

"You talk to him," Paige said. "Tell him we need her license number. Make it sound routine."

"Yes," Cross said. "That's probably best."

Cross spoke briefly, his face clouding over. He wrote down the license number and handed it to Paige as he talked.

"That was Commander Jackson," he said when he hung up. "The senator knows. Someone already called him."

"Shit. What's he going to do?"

"Not a thing."

"That surprise you?"

"Nothing surprises me anymore," Cross said.

Paige called the Roundhouse and gave them the license number and a description of the car. He set the phone down slowly, wishing that he'd called her earlier, suddenly ashamed of his own cowardice.

"What do we do now?"

"What we've been doing all day," Paige said. "Wait."

Cross rubbed his eyes. "Then I'm going to rest for a while. In the living room. If that's all right."

"Sure," Paige said. "By the way, how much cash do they keep there?"

"We don't leave it lying around. It's in a safe."

"Okay. How much?"

"Enough. Campaigns are expensive," Cross said curtly and walked away.

Paige stood there thinking that he ought to do something—make more calls, get in his car to look for her.

But he knew it would be pointless. The only thing he could do was wait.

And worry.

He *was* worried about her. It had been so many years since he'd been worried about anyone that he'd forgotten how bad it felt.

18

It was, Susan Morbach decided, every woman's idea of hell.

When she stepped through the front door, it struck her all at once. Not that it was dirty or squalid. She had seen enough of the real thing in Philadelphia. In fact it was reasonably clean, the black rubber floor mats were swept and what looked like a fresh coat of paint on the ceiling gleamed in the dead white light of fluorescent fixtures.

The first room was filled with hundreds of videotape boxes and magazines, the light reflecting off their bright shiny covers. Several men browsed through the racks, staring at her as she made her way past the long table in the center of the room that held more videotapes, all covered with orange signs: TWO FOR $7! THREE FOR $10! She had no idea that there *were* that many dirty movies.

Susan passed through a narrow archway and into the next section. It was darker than the first and lined on both sides with video booths, white plywood boxes with cheap wooden doors. Above each door was a small light. Some of the lights were on, little red beacons marking their oc-

cupation. Next to each door was a small marquee, a photograph of what was showing inside.

Half a dozen men wandered from booth to booth,
glancing at the pictures. Some went inside, others kept wan-
dering, searching for something that struck their interest.

There was, she thought, a kind of industrial grimness
to the place, and the men who wandered through it resembled workers, gray creatures with emotionless faces driven
into motion by an unspoken force. There was no love, no
laughter, no sense that any life existed except what could
be viewed on a tiny screen in the dark privacy of the
booths.

She glanced at one of the pictures, a photograph of a
woman with her legs spread open, one hand between her
legs, the other holding an enormous penis. The caption below the picture, handwritten in block letters, read: ''She
wants 10 inches of hot cock . . . and she gets it! Great cum
shots!''

Susan thought it was one of the strangest things she
had ever seen. She followed the line of pictures to the end
of the row, each one blending into the next until they lost
all distinction. Nothing but pieces of flesh with tight deter-
mined faces, as if they were fighting to find some joy in
their joyless task. There were no human beings here, she
thought, on either side of the door.

The men stared at her and looked away, not out of
embarrassment but more out of disinterest, as if she weren't
quite up to their needs. At the end of the row of booths, a
man sat on a chair several feet off the floor, stacks of quarters on the counter in front of him. He played idly with one
stack, clicking the coins together. She heard the sound
above the music that played somewhere overhead, like the
ringing of broken bells.

Susan followed the signs to the bar, straight ahead and
up a short flight of stairs.

A slim man with a rim of dark hair sat on a stool at

the entrance to the bar, a sign demanding a five-dollar cover charge on the wall behind him. He looked at Susan, eyes traveling from her feet to her face in slow exaggerated appraisal. He kept his opinion a secret, offered no clue at all, and waved her inside.

It was dark in the bar, so dark that she had to stop for a moment to let her eyes adjust. She was afraid of stumbling, of falling down, drawing attention to herself, and it was then that she remembered why she had come to this place and what she had left behind. The phone call, the way she had swung the metal box at Abelson without hesitation—did I want to hit him? did I really want *that?* —the blood streaming down his face, the money stuffed into the glove compartment: it struck her suddenly and for a moment all of her fear came back.

Her stomach rolled over and she felt like she might fall anyway, no matter what she did, that she couldn't stop herself. She forced herself to walk, keeping her eyes focused on an empty booth along the wall a few feet in front of her and away from the stage on the other side.

She moved into the back corner of the booth, glancing around the edge at the stage where a woman with dull red hair rolled around on her back, her legs wide open, pumping her hips into the air. Susan closed her eyes and leaned against the wall.

"Can I get you something?"

Susan opened her eyes. A waitress stood at the end of the booth, a short pixie-faced girl with alien hair, the strands spiked out and stiff. She wore a black bathing suit bottom and fanned her naked breasts with an open hand while she waited.

"Can I just have a club soda?"

"You can have anything you want, but it's still going to cost you seven-fifty. You'd be better off with a beer. Same price."

"A club soda. Can you put some lemon in it, please?"

The waitress laughed. "You'll be lucky if you get it in a glass."

She's so young, not much older than Kimberly, Susan thought, and she felt an immediate tug in her throat. I'm not going to start crying, not here, not in this place. She reached into her purse and took out a ten-dollar bill.

The waitress came back and put a glass on the table.

"No lemon," she said. Susan handed her the ten.

"You want change?"

"No," Susan said. She hesitated a moment, wondering what she thought she was doing, then plunged ahead. "Do you mind my asking how old are you?"

"What do you care?"

"No reason. You look young, that's all."

"I wish I was," the waitress said with such finality that Susan let her go without saying another word.

Susan slid back into the darkness of the booth, drank her soda, and tried hard not to think about the waitress or her daughter or what a horrible place the world had become while she'd been so busy trying to save it.

She waited another ten minutes after her glass was empty before deciding to leave. She had wanted him to come to her while she was still in the bar, half expected him to materialize out of thin air in front of her eyes. That was why she kept watching the bar for him, searching the faces of the men for any hint of recognition. But instead of recognition, she received only stares, puzzled and disturbed, as though she had violated some silent code of behavior.

He isn't coming at all. The whole evening was merely an exercise in humiliation. To see if she'd perform for him. She was angry but her anger quickly turned to despair. She had come one step closer to her daughter, only to be pushed back again.

Then it hit her. What if the whole thing had been a trick from the very beginning? What if the voice on the phone hadn't been the kidnapper at all?

Then what about the money?

Susan stood up quickly, stumbling out of the booth in her rush to get back downstairs. Through the booths, past the faces of the men, smirking at her sudden escape, past the magazines and the tapes, out into the bright hothouse lights of the parking lot.

Her car was where she left it, parked beside one of the light poles, several yards from the entrance. She threw open the front door, bent across the seat and opened the glove compartment.

The money was still there. She took it out and climbed into the car, laughing at her own desperate foolishness in the rearview mirror. She could feel the tears coming again. So much effort, so much waste.

A face rose up beside hers in the mirror.

Susan started to scream. A gloved hand wrapped around her mouth and something hard and cold pressed into the side of her neck. She felt his breath, moist against her cheek.

"Aren't you a funny little thing," Bobby said, massaging her neck with the gun. "Spend all that time in the pussy palace and you come back laughing." He pulled the gun back. "I'm going to take my hand away. You scream and I'll blow your brains all over the windshield."

He removed his hand from her mouth but left it dangling across the front of her neck. So close he could reach right down and grab a sample. Mind your manners, son, he thought, and smiled behind the mask. This was more fun than beans for breakfast.

Bobby laid the gun on the backseat and reached down to take the money from her hand. He took her purse as well.

"I'm going to sit back," he said. "But I still got the gun and if you go simple on me, I'll shoot you through the seat."

He held the money up in the light.

"Is it all here?"

"No," Susan said. "I couldn't get it all."

"How much did you get?"

"Count it yourself."

Her heart was pounding and she could feel the sweat popping out of her skin. She fought to remain calm and alert. She wanted to remember everything. The taste of the plastic glove was still in her mouth. She glanced in the mirror. He was wearing the mask she'd seen on the tape.

Bobby laughed. "I guess I will." He looked at the packets. "Christ Almighty, it's bundled."

"That's the way it came."

Bobby slapped the money against his leg.

"But not from the bank, I'll bet."

Susan shook her head.

"What was that, darlin'?"

"No. Not from the bank."

"Interesting," Bobby said, and he began rummaging through her purse. His fingers found something and closed around it. "Then where'd you get it?"

Susan hesitated. "From my husband's campaign."

"He know that?"

Bobby looked at what he'd found. A loose key. A curious thing. He stuck it in his pocket and tossed the purse back over the seat.

"No."

"You mean you stole it from him?"

"Something like that."

"Something like that," Bobby said and laughed.

Susan turned her head toward him, just enough so that she could see what he was wearing. She stopped when he tapped her on the jaw with the money.

"Eyes front."

"I want my daughter."

"I want a million bucks. Think we got a basis for negotiation?"

"We don't have that kind of money."

"Who does?" Bobby said. "Why don't you make me an offer?"

Susan thought about the money in the safe.

"Three hundred fifty thousand dollars," she said.

Bobby heard the figure and thought of what Jacob Cross had said. And more important, what he didn't say. Already he was up another hundred thousand from Cross's estimate and he'd hardly even worked up a sweat.

"What do you need that kind of cash for?"

"I didn't say I had it," Susan answered. "I said I could get it."

Bobby played with the money in his hand, fanning it along his neck, just under the edge of the mask. He liked the way it felt.

"Is Kimberly all right?" She couldn't keep her voice from cracking when she asked it and gave up trying.

"She's fine," Bobby said. "I think she's got a cold."

"I want to talk to her."

"I'm sure you do." He laughed. "I want my dick to grow another inch or two, but I don't think that's going to happen either."

Her rage exploded, a red demon that took over her mind and blotted out everything else. Susan turned around and this time he let her, as if he wanted to look at her as well.

Just to see what she'd become.

"Why are you doing this!" she screamed. "Why?" It felt as if she were strangling on the words. Her throat closed around them, choking off her breath, her life, everything but her hatred.

"Just because I can." He brought the gun up and waved it in her face. "Now turn around, darlin', before I get mad."

Susan turned around, her anger becoming a weight that settled comfortably within her.

"I'll find you," she said. "If anything happens to Kimberly, I'll find you and kill you."

Bobby laid the gun on her shoulder, impressed that she didn't jump when he did it. Usually people went shit out of their minds.

"I don't doubt you for a minute. But first things first." He slid forward on the seat. "Now what I want you to do is start making arrangements for that three hundred fifty thousand. I don't care how you do it but do it quick. I'll be in touch."

"You're going to call?"

"I didn't say that. I said I'd be in touch." He rubbed the gun across her shoulder. "If you want to see your daughter, take a look at the movie I sent to Cross."

"Movie?"

"Ask him. You can watch it together. Maybe he'll even make popcorn." He took away the gun. "Now close your eyes and hold out your hand. I brought you a present."

Bobby reached down and brought up a small dark object from the floor and held it over her open palm.

Susan felt something touch her hand, feathery and soft. She opened her eyes and saw her daughter's hair spilling down in a willowy curtain, drifting through her open fingers.

"Trust," Bobby whispered to her, "is a two-way street."

He was gone but she couldn't quite remember his leaving. The door opened and closed. A few minutes later, the car seemed to sag in back and then she was alone, sitting in the front seat, clutching her daughter's hair in her lap, caressing it, the way she might have done a small frightened animal, and crying softly to herself.

She thought for a moment that she might go mad, and it was that thought, the stark realization that anything was possible now, that brought her back.

Susan looked around the parking lot but saw no one. She got out of the car, holding Kimberly's severed tresses close to her, and made her way to the entrance, glancing back at the car. The left rear tire was flat. He'd done that. She went inside the building, straight to where the man sat on his stool high above the floor.

"I need a phone."

"Around back," the man said without really looking at her.

Susan reached the phone and fumbled in her purse for change. As she did, the hair slipped from her grasp and spilled onto the floor. She fell to her knees and began scooping it up, holding it tight against her chest to keep it from falling again.

She had a vision of herself as she might have looked to anyone passing by. A mad woman on her knees clutching a handful of human hair. Is this what I've become?

She got the change from her purse and stood up. With the phone cradled against her neck, she fed the handful of coins into the slot. Then she stopped.

Where was Patrick Paige?

She remembered something that the kidnapper had said to her in the car, a movie that he had sent to Jacob Cross. Maybe that's where Paige was now. She punched in the number from memory and waited while it rang and rang and rang. She was almost ready to hang up when someone answered it.

An unfamiliar voice said, "Yes?"

"I need—" Susan started to say. She stopped and started again. "I want to speak to Detective Paige, please."

"Who is this?"

"Tell him it's Susan Morbach."

"Hold on."

She leaned her forehead against the phone, counting off the seconds.

"Susan," Paige said, "where are you?"

She tried to choke off the sobs and found she had no strength left. They rolled over her and all she could do was wait until they passed and she had her voice back again.

"Please, Pat," she said finally. "Please come and get me."

Paige found her in the parking lot. The front door of the car was open and she sat sideways in the seat, her legs over the edge, feet firmly together on the pavement.

He'd taken his gun out while he drove, kept it next to him on the seat, and he held it down at his side as he walked toward her, scanning the parking lot for anything that moved. But nothing did and he heard only the sound of the traffic moving past on the highway and the noise of his footsteps on the broken and shattered asphalt.

She saw him coming and when he got close, she held out something in her hands.

He saw the hair, rolled in a small dark circle as delicate as a bird's nest.

"Look what he did to my little girl," Susan said, the pain in her voice like nothing he had ever heard and he knelt before her and held her and let her cry, and because he could no longer stop himself, cried with her.

19

The house seemed too small for the two of them. They sat at his kitchen table, drinking coffee, Susan holding her cup with both hands, Paige pushing the handle of his with the tip of his finger, to one side and then the other, fighting the feeling of claustrophobia.

She had wanted to leave her car in the parking lot, but Paige told her no, they needed to search it. He changed the tire and she followed him back to his house. The car was now parked and locked on the street in front.

When they came inside, he felt a sense of dislocation, seeing the house through her eyes, and the easy familiarity of his surroundings turned strange. It was the loneliness of it that struck him the most. The two weeks worth of newspapers piled next to the couch that he had meant to throw out but hadn't quite worked up to yet. The dinner plate with the half-eaten piece of chicken on it, still there from two days ago. The clothes left on the stairs, the ashtrays filled to overflowing but never emptied, the row of beer cans on the countertop in the kitchen: the scattered debris of his solitary life.

He couldn't remember the last time he'd had a woman

in his house, and now that Susan was there, he felt crowded by her presence.

He fell back on his role as a cop and did the one thing cops always do before questioning—he offered to make coffee. All he had was some six-month-old instant, the brown crystals stuck together like dried mud at the bottom of the jar, and he felt embarrassed digging into it, first with a spoon and finally with a knife, trying to chop it into some useful lumps.

She remembered a great deal, some of it helpful, some of it merely puzzling. He had an accent, she said, a kind of mild southern twang that seemed to come and go.

"Did it sound like he was faking it? Could he have been from around here?"

"No," Susan said. "I don't think so. He didn't lose the accent exactly. It just came and went. Sometimes it was strong, sometimes it wasn't. He wore a mask so I couldn't hear him all that well."

"Elvis?"

She nodded.

"Did you notice anything about the way he dressed?"

"He had on a blue jacket—one of those windbreakers. I think he wore jeans but I'm not sure."

"He took the money?"

"Yes." She hesitated, not knowing whether to say anything about the campaign safe, wasn't even certain it was relevant.

Paige caught her hesitation and waited.

"He said he wanted three hundred fifty thousand dollars for Kimberly," Susan said. "He said he'd be in touch."

"Those were his words?"

"Yes. I asked him if he was going to call. He said he'd 'be in touch.' He was very specific about it." The meaning of that phrase came to her, a quick flash of his hand around her mouth, the overpowering smell of his plas-

tic gloves and the feeling of the gun against her neck, and
she felt her stomach churn. She put the cup down, held her
hands to mouth and breathed deeply.

Paige reached out across the table, but she turned him
away with a shake of her head.

"You all right?"

"I'll be fine," she told him. "Just give me a minute."
The feeling subsided gradually. "It all just came back. His
hands—on my skin." She shuddered.

"Take it easy."

"No, it's okay." She glanced at his face and saw the
concern in his eyes and smiled. "I'm all right. It's just that
he seemed so cold. I don't think he gives a damn."

"What do you mean?"

"I mean," she said, and she had to stop to think about
what she wanted to say. It was something that had been
sitting in the back of her mind, and now, as she tried to
articulate it, she had to think very carefully to get it right.
"It was fun for him. The whole thing. Sending me in there,
hiding in the car. It was like a game. I had the feeling he
was making everything up as he went along. I don't think
he really cares what happens to Kimberly or whether he
gets the money."

"Did it seem like he was acting?" He kept coming
back to that, intrigued by the possibility and trying to figure
out how it might lead him to the kidnapper.

"Yes. In a way. Like he was playing a character. Why
did you say that?"

Paige told her about the videotape, avoiding any details. He didn't want to have to tell her about the details.

"He called it a movie," she said.

He nodded in agreement, drank his coffee, kept his
eyes on the table, away from hers.

"Does she look that bad?" Susan asked quietly.

He chose his words carefully, trying hard to find a
decent balance between—between what?

"The light wasn't very good," he said finally. "It was hard to tell." He remembered the tape, the Barbie doll look of her face. "He put makeup on her."

"Why would he do something like that?" Susan asked.

Paige knew why. To cover up the bruises. You couldn't put your star on camera with her face busted up. Paige shrugged and felt like a fool doing it.

"She was hurt, wasn't she?"

"Yes."

"How bad?"

"I don't know," he said. "I couldn't tell."

"Yes, you could," Susan said. "I can see it in your eyes." She looked at her hands. "I don't know what I'll do if something happens to her. I don't think I could survive it."

"You can," Paige said, surprised at the weight of certainty behind his own words. Susan heard it as well.

"Maybe I will," she said. "But not seeing her again —not *ever* seeing her again—knowing what had happened—"

"You learn to forget that," Paige said. "You learn to remember other things."

"The good things."

"No," he said, as though realizing it for the first time. "You remember the things you took for granted. Something she wore, the way her hair smelled when she washed it, how she looked when she slept."

"Is that what you do? Remember those things?"

After what seemed like hours, he answered her.

"I try," he said.

"Tell me about your husband," Paige said. They had moved from the kitchen to the living room. Paige sat in his usual chair, the one that faced the television. Susan sat on the couch, her legs folded beneath her, skirt drawn primly over her knees.

"There isn't much to tell," she said. "I married a lawyer who turned into a politician. He was in his third year of law school at Penn and I was an undergrad. A lot of women marry lawyers."

Paige wanted to ask her if she loved him. But she kept on talking and he didn't want to interrupt.

"When we met, he didn't know what he wanted to be. He said he was thinking about joining the Peace Corps or maybe one of those storefront firms in the ghetto. It was just a gesture, one of those things that men say when they want to impress young women with their commitment to a better world. He joined Hickock and Blair the first month after he graduated."

Hickock and Blair was one of the city's largest firms and well connected politically.

"We got married right after that. Then it was like jumping checkers—work for the party, pick up a few IOUs, run for city council, run for the statehouse, go directly to Congress. Jim wants to be senator. He thinks it's his due."

"He might make it."

But he'll have to stop punching out reporters first.

"I don't care anymore," Susan said. "It's just a game." She stopped for a moment, thinking of something. "He's not that much different from the man who kidnapped Kimberly." She smiled at Paige. "And what do you want to be when you grow up, Pat?"

"I always wanted to be a cop."

"Why?"

"I don't know," Paige said but he did. It was the same reason every cop had for joining the force. He wanted to protect people, he wanted to make the world a better place, he wanted to serve. It was trite and hopelessly idealistic but that was it. For most cops, it ended abruptly the first time they had to dig through the garbage for a dead baby.

Then they realized the truth. The world didn't need protecting; it needed a muzzle and a cage and somebody to stand guard. They grew up.

"Are men always so dumb about their motives?"

"I guess," he said, and laughed. "I probably joined because I didn't want to be a politician."

"Was that because of your father?"

"Not really. It was my mother. I saw what he did to her."

"What did he do?"

Paige tried to find the right words for something he'd thought about for years but had never really said before now. It was like breaking a vow of silence, a cardinal sin. You didn't talk about your feelings. So why was he talking about them now? Because Susan was the first one to ask. His wife never asked and he wondered now if she ever really wanted to know.

"He acted as if my mother never existed," Paige said. "Whatever he did, he did for himself and nobody else."

"Where is she now?"

"Israel," Paige said. "She divorced my father when I graduated from high school and moved to Tel Aviv. She teaches school there. Kindergarten. I get letters from her all the time."

"Do you write her back?"

"When I can."

"Which is what—twice a year." There was no malice in her comment.

"More than that," Paige said. "At least three times. But I call her a lot. She has an apartment near the ocean and a boyfriend who owns a fruit stand. She's very happy where she is."

"Do you miss her?"

"Sometimes."

"But not your father?"

"No."

How could he miss him? He lived in the city and was reminded of him all the time. The city kept sliding down, choking to death on its own insularity and petty corruption. They put up new office buildings downtown while the neighborhoods died. He saw his father's hand in everything. And where he couldn't find his father, he saw his successors. Like Jacob Cross. Except now all the dealmakers lived in the suburbs and only came into town to pick up their winnings. At least his father had had the decency to live in the disaster he helped create.

So he stayed there, too. In his darker moments, he thanked his father for that. His mother wanted him to move to Israel. What could he find there that he hadn't already found here?

"Do you miss your wife?" Susan asked.

"I miss what I never had," he said, and stopped talking, letting the silence carry whatever other thoughts he might have had about it away.

Susan closed her eyes and laid her head back on the couch. The next thing she knew, Paige was standing beside her, taking the empty coffee cup from her hand.

"What?" she said, startled.

"You fell asleep," he said.

She sat up straight. He was so close now, she had the urge to hold him again. Instead, she brushed her hair back with her hands and straightened out her dress. That's when she noticed what he was carrying. A blanket and a pillow.

"I'll sleep down here," he said. "You can use my bed. I changed the sheets."

"No," she said, taking them from him, "you've done enough for one night. I'll sleep down here."

"You're sure?"

"Of course I'm sure," she said. "I've slept on couches before." A couple of days ago, in fact.

"Just so you know," he said, "you can stay here as long as you want."

"Thank you. I appreciate that."

"You decide," he said. "But no more adventures, okay?"

"Okay."

He stood there awkwardly, the first time she had seen him act that way.

"You sure you got enough blankets?"

"I'm sure. Everything's fine."

"If you need anything, you let me know. I'm right at the top of the stairs."

"I know."

"Well, good night."

"Good night, Pat," she said. "Thank you. For everything."

"No problem."

For a moment she thought he was blushing. But it was only the way the light hit his face as he turned to go upstairs.

20

Bobby Radcliff lugged the two five-gallon containers of gasoline through the woods, stopping every now and then to give his arms a rest. He would sit on one of the cans and shake out the pain. It felt like they were coming out of their sockets. The cans were heavy and the coil of rope around his neck kept threatening to drag him down. He had this vision of walking straight into the ground up to his chin, just like in a cartoon.

He felt good, though, better than he had in what?— weeks, months, years?

"I'm a man with a purpose," he said and laughed.

He picked up the cans again and walked another twenty yards before setting them down once more. What he really liked was the quiet, the whole big black emptiness out there in the woods, like there was nothing between him and the rest of the world. He could just disappear in it, fade away so completely that nobody would come looking for him and nobody would ever find him. He could strip right down to his skin and vanish.

When he was done with this, he thought, he was going to look for someplace just like this but a little more remote.

He could head up to the Northwest, stake a little claim around the Canadian border. Or down to Mexico. Or maybe make the big jump to Hawaii and go live in the jungle on one of the islands, grow himself some decent mojo and come into town once a year to pick up supplies. Maybe he'd get himself a dog.

A rottweiler would be good, big son of a bitch to keep the assholes away. But what if the dog went nuts and came after him? It happened, he read about it in the papers all the time, some poor schmuck opens the door and winds up with his dick in a doggie bag. Dog tried that on him, he'd shoot it, he knew he would. But it sure would be a big waste of money.

Better to get something smaller. Maybe one of those dogs he'd read about that laughed. That sounded better. He could sit around the campfire at night, get stoned, and the dog would laugh at his jokes.

But what if the dog didn't laugh?

What if he told jokes and the dumb mutt didn't think he was funny? Then he'd have to shoot him, too.

Maybe it'd be better all around if he just got himself a parrot.

Bobby shifted his weight against the cans, trying to get comfortable. It was the money. It made a lump in the back pockets of his jeans and he couldn't sit right. Four grand just for showing up with a handful of hair. Not enough to run away with but enough to get him thinking about more.

Because he wasn't going to pull that little shit anymore. Just the Big One. It didn't matter whether it was $100,000 or $350,000 or something in-between, it was going to be a lot more than what he had now.

And if he didn't get it, well, he still had his health.

And the girl.

He reached into his pocket and found the key he'd taken from her purse. Now what the hell was this for? It wasn't hooked to her key ring so it wasn't something she used all the time. But she kept it with her, so that meant she used it enough. There was a little tag tied to the end that he'd been puzzling over since he read it in the car.

The tag said, PRIVATE 3. Well, it was private and it was the third key. It definitely *looked* like a door key. But where was the door? He didn't think it was to their house. If it was, why would she keep it separate from the others? No, it was definitely something special and he was going to find out what.

And he wasn't going to talk to Mom again, either. Maybe he'd pay a visit to Jacob Cross before he got any hot ideas about becoming a local hero. Maybe he'd go see the senator himself, pass on some advice for his re-election campaign.

Keep 'em moving, keep 'em off balance, hit 'em where they ain't. It worked for him.

"Ah will float like a butterfly and sting like a bee," Bobby said.

He picked up the cans again. It made him feel like a coolie slogging his way through the brush but he didn't mind. That was the price you paid when you were self-employed.

The cabin door was wide open. Bobby couldn't remember if he'd closed it or not, but then he remembered he always closed it, even when he went outside to take a piss. He dropped the cans and dove into the brush beside the path and crawled fast on his hands and knees, the prickers tearing hell out of his face, but he kept moving until he was far enough away so that anyone who was waiting for him would have to play hide-and-seek to find him.

He slipped the gun from his waistband, thumbed back the hammer, and aimed it at the sliver of light coming from the open door.

"Come on, Jake," he whispered. "Come and get it."

After a few minutes, he began to feel foolish, squatting

in the undergrowth, the ground soaking through the ass of his pants, getting the four grand all wet.

"That's enough of this shit," he said and stood up, fighting the bushes to get clear. He wanted Cross to see him.

"Come on, motherfucker," he shouted. "Take your best shot."

Bobby heard a cry from the other side of the house. Kimberly.

It didn't take him long to find her. There was a smaller path behind the house, a short little squirrel run that stopped abruptly about twenty feet into the trees where a log had fallen across it. The log was rotted and slick with moss.

He heard her crying in the darkness and went back to the cabin for one of the kerosene lanterns so he could see her.

She sat with her back against the trunk, hands still tied together but her legs free. The rope hung down from her neck, and played out along the path. He picked up the end and began to roll it up. He watched her fight against it, jerking her head back each time he pulled it.

"All this time," he said with a grin. "You been foolin' me."

Kimberly screamed.

"Help me! For God's sake, help me!"

Bobby pointed the gun at her.

"God's out to lunch," he said. He moved closer, the gun aimed directly at her face.

The only problem was, she wasn't looking at the gun. She was looking at something *behind* him and pointing.

"Get him away from me!"

That son of a bitch had tricked him.

Bobby threw himself to the ground and rolled over, catching a glimpse of shadows moving near the cabin before the lantern landed on the ground next to him and went out. Then it was dark except for the single cabin window and he scooted backward on his ass until he felt the log at his back. He reached out and grabbed Kimberly around the neck, closing his hand over her mouth, keeping the gun in front of him.

"Shut up," he whispered and pulled her head to his chest.

Bobby searched the darkness but he couldn't see anything. That didn't mean Cross wasn't out there, but if he was, Bobby couldn't see him. Kimberly sobbed into his hand, and he pulled her head up so that her face was next to his.

"All right, all right," he whispered, calming her down. "Now where is he?"

"Can't you see him?"

"I can't see a damn thing. Just tell me where he is."

"He's there!" She pointed again. When he looked, there was nothing, no movement, no sound, just the darkness.

"What are you pointing at?"

"Death," Kimberly said quietly. "He's waiting for me. For both of us."

Bobby felt a spooky little finger burrow into the back of his neck. He shivered and tried to shake it off, but it wouldn't let go. It stuck right with him, digging under his skin. Kimberly buried her face in his chest, and all Bobby could do was put his arms around her and pretend to protect her.

If death is out there, he thought, I'm gonna have to get me a bigger gun.

"Hey," he said, lifting her up. "It's okay. Bobby's here. Nothing to worry about. Mr. Death comes around again, I'll blow his bony ass into the woods. Okay? You believe me?" He tried turning her face toward the cabin but she wouldn't move.

"Take a look. See? Nobody out there."

"I don't want to look."

"Hell, he's already gone. I'll show you."

Bobby pulled the lantern over, set it upright, and lit it.

"Now," he told her, "I want you to take a good look around, make sure there's nobody here, okay? We'll do it together."

They made a slow trip around the cabin. Kimberly held his arm so tight he thought she was going to break it off. When they were through, he gave a quick kiss on the cheek.

"See, I told you he was gone."

She nodded.

"But I saw him in the window."

"Yeah? What'd he look like?"

Kimberly shuddered. "Horrible."

Bobby laughed. "Sounds like the right guy."

He undid the rope from around her hands and helped her into the cottage. She stumbled to the couch and collapsed, curling up to protect herself.

"You're safe now. Give it a rest."

"You aren't going to hurt me?"

Bobby shook his head. "What makes you think I'm going to hurt you?" He had a sorrowful look on his face. "I must have been giving you the wrong impression. I'm not going to do anything. What do you think of that?"

Kimberly curled up even tighter.

"Well," he said smiling, "I'm going to do *something*. But it won't hurt you. In fact, you can help. We've got to set this place up."

It took close to an hour to get things the way he wanted. He hauled the cans of gasoline in first, putting them down by the door. Then he went through the cabin, collecting as many pots and pans as he could find.

He collected seven but had to throw out two because they were rusted through on the bottom. That left five of pretty good size, a frying pan, two old aluminum pots, and two ten-quart boilers. He put the two boilers together in front of the stove and the other pans next to the table. Then he filled them with gasoline, not really caring how much he spilled. The air in the room grew thick with fumes, and his eyes began to water.

"This'll teach me not to nigger-rig shit again, won't it?" he said. Kimberly stared at him blank-faced.

"Give me a little smile. This is funny." She was still scared but smiled weakly. "There you go, that's better."

After he filled each pan, he filled both lanterns with kerosene. He set one on top of the stove, the other on the table. Carefully he tied one end of the rope to the base of the lantern on the table, strung it across the room to the stove and tied it around the other one. He looped the rope over the beam and down to the door, pulling up the slack just enough to make it tight. But not too tight.

"All right," he said. "Come over here. Watch the rope."

Kimberly walked carefully across the room and stood next to him.

"Now stay here and don't move."

Bobby picked up the two gas cans, putting one in front of the stove and the other by the table. He lit each lantern, adjusting the flames so that they were low enough not to burn too quickly but high enough so that they wouldn't blow out.

Then he slid the gas cans in among the pans and opened each one. He tore several strips off the blanket and stuffed them into the top of each can and let them play out across the pans. His eyes were watering like crazy when he got back to the door.

He shoved Kimberly out the door, tied the end of the rope to the handle, and pulled it almost closed.

"There," he said, taking her by the arm and leading her down the path. "Mr. Death comes to call, we're gonna torch his ass like Smokey the Bear."

"Where are we going?" she said. Her voice was faint

and ragged, and before he could answer, she started cough-ing. He waited for it to end.

"We're gonna sleep in the car tonight. Just you and me underneath the stars."

They walked a little bit further. Bobby held her close to keep her from falling. She was getting weaker by the minute. When they reached the car, he opened the door and she collapsed in the back. He shoved his tool kit aside and crawled in beside her.

"Did you ever see *Butch Cassidy?*" he asked.

"I think so," she said. The fact was she was still too frightened to remember. She couldn't seem to remember anything from before. Her life was something that hap-pened a million years ago.

"Those guys stuck together right to the end when the Pedros shot them. That's how we're going to be from now on, you and me. Mi casa es su casa. You up for that?"

He waited for an answer. When he looked, he saw that she'd fallen asleep. Bobby kept talking, mostly to hear the sound of his own voice.

"You know what that means? My mom used to say that to the Pedros all the time. They come up to the front door and she give 'em a little dance and start talking Mex-ican. The Pedros liked that. They'd start grinnin' from ear to ear when they heard her talk.

"One of them told me what it meant. She thought it was something cute, you know, like 'Eat my pussy.' But she didn't know. He said it meant 'Fuck you, Yankee.' That's why they thought it was so funny when she said it."

Bobby took the half-smoked joint from his pocket and lit up. He smoked quietly for a while, blowing the smoke out through the open car window. Then he stubbed it out and put what was left back in his pocket. She shivered and moved closer, snuggling next to him for warmth. He slid down beside her and wrapped his arms around her thin body, keeping her safe. He felt good doing it, too. A little strange but good. Better than he'd felt for a long time.

"Fuck death," Bobby whispered to her. "Fuck 'em all."

It had been nearly half an hour since New Jersey State Trooper Warren Gates had heard the screams. He'd just taken a turn off the main highway, cruising through the nighttime with his window open, not thinking very much, just letting the breeze blow across his face.

Gates liked the night shift and had more or less permanently volunteered for it. Whenever anybody wanted to switch shifts, he was there, ready and able. He was by nature a night person, but that was only part of it. He liked being alone, and he felt more alone at night than any other time.

During the day, the barracks was full of people, not just the other troopers but secretaries and civilians, all of them milling around, making noise and getting in his way. But at night the place was quiet and deserted, and the highways were pretty much the same except for the drunks. Gates never minded busting drunks.

It was quiet that night, too, and Gates was cruising along when he heard what he thought was a scream. He stopped the car and tried to get a fix on it, but it was too faint and too far away. As usual, it was the trees that screwed everything up. They bounced the noise around so by the time it finally got to you, you didn't know where the hell it had come from in the first place. He got out and stood in the middle of the road, hoping he might hear another one. But there was only silence.

He was just about to get back in the car when he heard someone—a woman, he was pretty sure of that—scream for help. This time he had a good fix on the sound. It came from somewhere in front and to the left. Which wasn't that much of a help. There was nothing out there but trees and a handful of old logging trails that spiderwebbed through the woods and went nowhere.

For the next half hour, he cruised the backroads but found nothing unusual, no abandoned cars, no signs of accidents, nothing on the side of the road, and no more screams.

So Gates made a decision. He had a couple of days off. He'd come back tomorrow during the day and look around a little more, bootleg some personal time and see what he could find on his own without a whole lot of other people around to screw things up.

21

The young man behind the counter handed Jacob Cross a gun.

"This is a nine-millimeter Glock semiautomatic," the man said. He rotated the gun in a series of precise movements, giving Cross a side view, a quick glimpse of the squat black barrel. "It holds seventeen shells in a rapid-ejection clip in the handle." He flipped the gun over, popped the clip, snapped it back inside, and handed Cross the gun. It felt surprisingly light.

"The Glock fires a high-velocity bullet that travels twelve hundred and fifty feet per second and can pass through a wall," he said. "There are, of course, slower hollowpoint bullets available that flatten on impact. They are just as lethal, however. More than half of the police forces in the United States use this weapon."

The young man smiled proudly. "It's the gun of the future."

"I've never fired a gun before in my life," Cross said. He'd fired his father's shotgun, but that wasn't the same thing. Or was it?

"Most of our customers haven't," the man said. "Would you like to try it out?"

"Yes, I would," Cross said.

The man took the gun from his hand and reached behind him for a box of shells.

"Come with me," he said and pointed to a steel door at the far end of the store. "Of course, you'll have to purchase the ammunition."

"That won't be a problem," Cross said.

The young man led him downstairs to a basement shooting range.

"You're our first shooter of the day." He pointed to one of the marked-off booths. "If you'll step over to the line and put on your ear guards, please, I'll load it for you."

Cross slipped them over his head. The young man handed him the gun and motioned for him to pull back one of his ear guards.

"Stand sideways to the target," he said. "That's right. Hold your arm straight but not stiff. Sight down the barrel just like you were looking down your finger, and squeeze the trigger gently. It'll kick a little, so wait until the barrel drops before firing again." The man stepped back and put on a pair of ear guards himself. "Go ahead."

Cross pointed the gun at the black silhouette at the end of the range, aimed at the figure's chest and squeezed the trigger. The gun popped and kicked and the paper quivered. He fired twice more before looking back at the salesman and getting a nod of approval.

Cross sighted once more on the target, trying to imagine the look of amazement on Bobby Radcliff's face when he shot him, and squeezed off several more rounds. He watched the gun rise and fall, waiting until it settled back down on the target before firing again.

He kept on firing, seeing Bobby die with each shot, the body dancing across his mind in a giddy ballet of blood and bone. It was just like a movie. Maybe this is what

Bobby meant by final cut, he thought, and kept squeezing the trigger until the gun was empty and the salesman had to tap him gently on the shoulder to make him stop. Cross blinked at him as if he'd just woken up from a dream.

"Are you sure you've never done this before?" the salesman asked.

Upstairs, he asked Cross if the gun was for target shooting or protection.

"Why?"

"It makes a difference in the type of ammunition you purchase. The high-velocity is better for target. Hollow-points are recommended for home use."

Cross thought that was an interesting way to put it—home use. It made it sound like he was buying a blender.

"It's for home use," Cross said.

"Hollowpoints it is. One box ought to do—unless you'd like to practice some more?"

"No."

He wasn't planning a shoot-out. He was going to wait until Bobby turned around and then shoot him in the back of the head five or six times. Did he think he could do it just like that? Yes. With his eyes wide open. When Bobby died, all his secrets would die with him. It was an interesting way of correcting mistakes.

Then he would bring Kimberly to her parents and get on with his life. If that were possible now.

Of course it was possible. Anything was possible now.

"There's a forty-eight-hour waiting period," the salesman said. He had a form in front of him, pen poised to fill it out.

"I beg your pardon?"

His vision shriveled.

"A waiting period. We have to send out this form to the police before we can sell you a handgun. The state police get one, the sheriff and your local police department, they all get a copy. To make sure you don't have a criminal record. It's standard.''

"I'm sure it is," Cross said. "But I need the gun today."

The young man smiled politely. "I'm sorry. I don't like the paperwork either. But those are the rules." He stood there poised with the pen. "Do you still want the gun?"

"Yes," Cross said. He'd come this far.

"I'll need your driver's license please."

Cross handed the salesman his license and looked at the cabinet filled with shotguns behind the counter.

"Do I have to wait if I buy a shotgun?"

"No. Shotguns and rifles are considered sporting weapons."

"Fine. I'll take a shotgun, too. Do you have a sixteen-gauge?"

A small nod to his father.

"Of course. Pump or bolt action?"

"Pump, I think. Isn't that the easiest?"

"More or less. Did you have a particular make in mind?"

"You choose. I'll need a box of shells with it, too."

"Of course," the young man said.

The Glock came to a little over four hundred dollars; the shotgun around three hundred and seventy-five. Cross paid for them with his American Express card and left.

The young man went about his business, filling in the rest of the required form with Cross's name and the name of the store and the make and model of the gun. He separated them and looked up the name and address of the sheriff and local police where the man lived.

As he was licking the last envelope he remembered something. He'd forgotten to tell the man he had to carry the shotgun in the trunk of his car—unloaded. It was against the law to carry a loaded gun inside the car. He should probably call his house and tell him.

He thought about it for a few minutes and decided that his advice would probably be wasted. The man wanted a gun in a hurry, and it didn't seem to matter what kind. The easiest, the man had said.

The salesman had a small moment of giddy anxiety. He's going to shoot somebody, he thought. I'm going to be watching the news, and I'm going to see that man on it, and the police are going to be carrying the shotgun I just sold him. Or the Glock.

It wasn't much of a distinction, the salesman thought morbidly.

He was just being fatalistic. It went with the job. He sold guns to a lot of people—people he thought were perfectly strange—and nobody'd shot anybody, at least none that had shown up on the evening news. Not yet anyway.

Her husband wasn't there. It was a surprise and it wasn't; it hurt her and it didn't; it made her feel unsure of herself and it made her feel strong. It was a jumble of emotions so confusing that she had to put them away in a distant corner of her mind just so she could function.

Jacob Cross was there. Acting tough. Playing hardball as everyone said. She re-discovered an old feeling. She loathed him immensely. They sat together in his living room while the detectives waited for a call. She wished Paige were with her, but Cross wanted to speak to her alone, and she couldn't refuse. He was in charge of the campaign—not to mention her husband—and even though both of them seemed a million miles from her now, the election was still there, like a creature that had been mistakenly brought to life and now refused to leave.

Cross ignored her at first. He stood by the front window and looked out at the yard. There were quite a few reporters there, but the police had moved them back from the house. She had seen them when she drove up. They looked like a gang of unruly teenagers, each one clamoring for her attention, screaming out her name.

"They're bringing the FBI in," Cross said to the window. "I expect them anytime."

"Pat didn't tell me." She felt comfortable using his first name. Cross didn't like it. He turned toward her and made a face.

"*Pat* doesn't know," he said. "He will soon." He knew about the Bureau because Commander Jackson had told him. Jackson had a pipeline to everybody. That was why Cross used him. He moved across the room to the chair opposite the couch and sat down.

"What does that mean?"

"I really don't know," he said. "You might ask Pat about it. You seem to have a nice rapport established."

Why, you sanctimonious prick, she thought, and couldn't hold herself back.

"Is there a special reason you're acting like a jerk? Or are you just standing in for Jim today?"

His eyes narrowed and he pushed his head forward. When he did that, he looked absolutely reptilian.

"Let's not talk about what I'm doing," he said. "Let's not talk about that *at all*." He stuck his index finger in the air and began counting off on it. "You stole campaign money and assaulted Jerry Abelson while doing it. You endangered yourself and Kimberly. You haven't been home for two days. And you think *I'm* insulting *you?* You must be out of your mind. How long do you think we can keep all of this from getting out?"

And ruining the campaign completely, Susan thought. Just when you were getting all those *nice* sympathy votes.

"Which do you think is my worst offense, Jacob? Not sleeping with my husband or belting Jerry on the head?"

He looked at her with disgust.

"Then I'd say not sleeping at home. But then Jim

probably hasn't noticed. As for you—it's hard to tell. Your loyalties seem to be divided these days. If Kimberly dies, Jim's a shoo-in. If I screw up and get caught, you still might win but you can probably kiss the congressional seat good-bye. Tough choice.''

''You're unbelievable,'' Cross said and stood up. He returned to the window, shaking his head back and forth like a dog trying to tear a piece of meat loose from a dried-out bone.

''No,'' she said quietly. ''I just won't be badgered by you anymore. Or Jim.''

''You're lucky Jerry didn't press charges.''

''But he didn't, did he?''

''No.''

''I'll apologize to him the first chance I get. And I'm sure there'll be a nice bonus for him after the election.'' She paused. ''I told him about the money.''

''Told who?''

''The kidnapper.''

''You did what?''

''I told him we could afford to pay three hundred fifty thousand dollars for Kimberly. He accepted.''

Cross stood quite still, not quite comprehending what he'd just heard.

''That's how much is in the safe,'' Susan said. ''Unless you've spent it.''

''You don't know what you've done.''

''Yes, I do,'' she said sharply. ''I know exactly what I've done and what I'm going to do. I'm going to give him the goddamn money and get my daughter back! The rest of you can all go to hell.''

Cross had to sit down.

''That money doesn't exist,'' he said softly. He was surprised at his own fear. It came out of nowhere, a quick knife thrust into the center of his stomach.

The money in the safe was a slush fund—what was

left of it—nearly four years worth of illegal, or, at the very best, highly questionable, contributions that he had helped put together—the beginning of the congressional campaign, seed money for the future. If word of it leaked out, it wouldn't matter if Bobby had Kimberly drawn and quartered on the statehouse steps. The election would go down hard. There would be no sympathy vote at all. There would be headlines. There would be indictments. Morbach would be lucky to get a job at McDonald's. His own name would end up at the top of the list. Just like his father.

"Yes, it does," Susan said. She could read the fear in him and she went for it.

"And you told him about it?"

"I told him I could get it. I didn't tell him where."

"Did you tell Paige?"

"No," she said. "I'm not a fool."

Yes, you are, he thought, and a dangerous one. He moved very slowly, conscious of wading through treacherous waters. One wrong step and he would drown.

"Will you tell Paige?"

"Not unless I have to," she said. "I want my daughter, and I won't haggle over her like she's a rug in a bazaar. We have the money. I'm going to use it."

In the back of his mind, Cross saw the outline of a deal emerging, one that would, at least for the next few hours, freeze everything in place and give him time to clean up the mess. He swallowed his fear and returned to the chair. Sincerity was an emotion best delivered close up.

"I understand your position, Susan," he said carefully. "Just as you can understand mine. I'm sure if we work together we can solve our differences. The main thing is to get Kimberly back safe and sound."

"What do you have in mind?"

"Using that money presents a number of problems. You agree?"

"Not necessarily but I'll listen."

"Then we need to find a way to use it without putting anyone at risk more than is absolutely necessary."

"What does that mean?"

"We have to find a way to make that money legal."

"I'm not sure I understand where you're going with this."

"For obvious reasons, we can't just hand over three hundred fifty thousand dollars without showing where we got it. The FBI will want to know. So will the IRS. So will the media. We have to clean it up first."

"How are you going to do that?"

Cross relaxed. "Well," he said, "there are several ways we might approach it. I could make you a loan. You could loan it to yourselves—put up your house. We might borrow it from a third party—we just have to find the right way."

"I want it done soon," she said. "Today."

"It might take a little bit longer, Susan."

"We don't have a little bit longer, Jacob," she said. She leaned forward, holding the fingers of one hand an inch apart. "I was this close to him. I talked to him. I know what he's like. Kimberly's going to die unless we get him what he wants."

"You saw the tape," he said, digging into her vulnerability.

"Yes," she said, "I saw the tape. I want it done soon."

"I'll do the best I can," Cross said. "I'll have to speak to Jim again. To make sure he understands."

"I don't care if he understands or not. Just do it."

"Of course," Cross said. "There is one other thing you should know. He's planning a rally."

She shut her eyes and sat back. Dear God.

"What kind of a rally?"

"For Kimberly." He waited a few seconds, just

enough to let the idea sink below the surface. "He's convinced that she planned this herself. To hurt him. To hurt you. He wants to use the rally to talk to her—to convince her to come home."

"Is he out of his mind?"

"Yes, I think he is. But that doesn't necessarily mean he's wrong. Politically speaking."

"Call it off."

"I wish I could. But he's already done it. He thinks it'll help give him a big win. He may be right."

"Then I'll stop it," she said.

"I'm not sure you can," Cross said. "He put Jerry in charge."

Susan said nothing.

"He's set it up near Penn's Landing. The media's been notified. Even the networks. There'll be lots of coverage. It's going to be quite a show."

What had seemed so simple to her—get the money, pay the kidnapper, get Kimberly back—had become dangerously and irretrievably complex. It felt like she was trapped in a tar pit; each move became an agony, trapping her even more.

"You have to be there," Cross said.

She bolted from the chair.

"I will not!"

Cross took hold of her hand. He rarely touched her, but now he sensed it was the one way to keep her with him.

"You're the only one who can keep Jim under control. If you're not there, there's no telling what he might say. Or do. You have to be there. For Kimberly."

She sat down, a sudden fall, like a fortress collapsing from the weight of its own battlements.

"Why is he doing this?"

"I told you. He believes it will help him win this election. His instincts in that respect are pretty good. On the other hand, maybe he's doing it for the same reason you spent the night with Patrick Paige.'' He said it kindly. "Maybe he needs to do it to survive.''

"It's not the same thing.''

"I know that. But Jim doesn't. Have you told him about Paige?''

"Told him what? I didn't sleep with him. I went there because I had no place else to go.''

Cross nodded his understanding.

"I'm not sure Jim would appreciate the distinction.''

"Then screw Jim,'' Susan said.

A momentary lapse. He wasn't used to her vulgarity. For that matter, neither was she. She was learning, though.

"You don't mean that.''

"Yes, I do,'' she said. "We don't talk, we don't communicate—*we* don't sleep together anymore. He's gone off into some private little world of his, just like—''

Just like what? Just like he's done all our lives. When things went wrong, he cut her out as if she'd never been important to him in the first place. The revelation struck her as right. How could she have missed it all these years?

Jack and Jill went up the hill, but Jack never came down, and Jill wanted to go home.

I quit. I resign. I don't want to be here anymore.

"All right,'' she said. "I'll go. But this is it. When this rally is over, I want nothing else to do with the campaign. No more meetings or rallys or reporters. Is that understood? I'm finished with it.''

And with Jim Morbach. The decision didn't frighten or even depress her. It made her feel like a real person, one of the few times in her life that she'd ever felt that way. She wanted to hold on to that feeling for as long as she could.

Cross knew enough not to push it any further.

"That's your decision," he said. "And I respect it."

Susan laughed at him.

"You've never respected anything about me, Jacob, so for God's sake don't start now. We made a deal. You take care of the money, and I'll make sure Jim doesn't do anything stupider than he's already done. Let's keep it at that level."

He was taken aback for an instant, then found himself again.

"Fine," he said. "I'll deal with the money."

"Just make sure you do," she said and started out of the room.

He had one more question for her. Again, he was treading on dangerous ground but he had to know.

"What did he say exactly?"

"Who?"

"The kidnapper."

He had said a lot of things. She tried to remember the one thing he had told her that went to the heart of it, a kind of summary judgment of his motive and crime. She couldn't remember every word but she remembered enough.

"I asked him why. He said he did it because he could." She watched Cross for his reaction but there wasn't any. "Is that what you were looking for?"

Cross nodded. It was so perfect. It had Bobby written all over it. He could even hear him when he said it.

"Yes, that's very interesting."

Cross moved to the window again, staring out across the yard.

"It sounds like it's a game to him," he said. "I wonder if he even cares about the money."

"I think he does," she said, "I think he cares a great deal. He cut off her hair and gave it to me."

He looked at her, his face grave. She'd seen that face

before. It was the one he used when he wanted someone to believe in him.

"We'll get her back, Susan. I promise."

"Just get the money, Jacob. That's all you have to do."

No, he thought. I'll get Bobby first.

22

Trooper Gates, dressed in civilian clothes, black 101st Airborne T-shirt—DEATH FROM ABOVE—gray sweatpants and high-top athletic shoes, parked by one of the logging roads and walked into the woods. He left his service revolver locked in the trunk of his car but carried a backup pistol with him, a stubby little .32 in an ankle holster, tucked beneath his sweatpants.

The grass was still wet, even in late morning, the stalks bent under the weight, flowing toward the ground like long strands of hair. It soaked his shoes and the bottom of his pants and they stuck to his leg. He walked straight down the center of the old road, slowly and deliberately, eyes on the ground. It was the fifth one he had investigated that morning, and the first one that looked as if someone might have used it recently.

Poachers, he thought. Teenagers. Drunks. The only thing he was going to get this morning was a little exercise. He stopped for a moment and knelt down, pawing at the grass. Quite a bit of traffic back here, though. Gates saw something shiny, a shimmer of rainbow that covered the grass. He rubbed the spot with his fingers and held them to his nose.

Gasoline.

He stayed there a moment and tried to think of how it might have gotten there, but an explanation eluded him. He continued walking up the road, breathing deeply, trying to get rid of the smell of the gasoline.

He stopped when he saw the cabin, the bleached wood siding clear and distinct against the dark green of the trees.

Bobby took Kimberly with him to inspect the cabin. He was sure no one had been there during the night. He would have known it if they had. Half the county would have known it. No boom-boom, no problem.

She's calm this morning, he thought, a real peach of a girl. He practically had to lift her out of the car because she moved so slowly, stumbling along like her legs were going to give out any second. He walked with her, one arm holding her up, as they tramped through the tall grass. Neither one spoke and he liked it that way. The morning was just too damn nice to spoil it with words.

He took the gun with him—he took it everywhere now because it was smart and because she seemed to like it better when he had it with him. That scared look, the one he'd seen last night, had faded, but it was still there, ready to pop out at any moment.

Now, as he approached the cabin, he left her on the side of the old road, her head resting on the wet grass and her legs tucked up against her skinny chest.

Bobby didn't hurry, and by the time he got to the cabin path, he was moving at a crawl. Something on the ground caught his eye. It was a footprint, right in the middle of the path, the grass around it quivering slightly, trying to spring back into shape. The footprint led to others that led directly down the path to the cabin.

Bobby left the path and cut back through the woods.

He made a wide circle around the cabin, keeping well behind the trees. When he was directly behind it, he heard the sound of a window being raised.

Bobby moved forward a few feet. He expected to see Jacob Cross. Instead he saw a big guy several inches taller than he was, dressed like he'd just come from exercise class. The guy lowered the window carefully and walked around to the front of the cabin.

Now what kind of guy puts the window back like he doesn't want anybody to know he's been there?

Bobby circled back the way he came and hid behind a tree fifty feet away, where he could see the guy trying to figure out a way into the cabin without turning himself into a human torch. He was working on the hinges, picking at them with a small pocketknife.

Well, he was too smart for a tourist. Bobby was going to give him a few minutes to see how far he'd get when Kimberly dragged herself up the path in full view of the door.

They both turned at once, the guy squatting down suddenly, fumbling with the ankle of his sweatsuit, tugging at the wet material, reaching for something.

Hot damn, Bobby thought, I've seen *that* move before.

The man hesitated, just enough, trying to make up his mind whether Kimberly was going to be a problem for him.

He must have thought she was, because he yanked up his sweatpants and pulled the gun from his ankle. Bobby stepped out from behind the tree and shot him in the stomach and then a second time in the chest as he fell backward against the cabin door. He rolled over on the ground and lay still.

Jake ought to hire better killers, Bobby thought. This one was a real dork.

Bobby ambled over, picked up the gun, and went through his pockets, finding a set of car keys.

"Fuck you, Yankee."

Kimberly sat down on the path and covered her face.

Bobby was suddenly sick of her shenanigans. He pointed his gun at the body.

"You see what you made me do!" he said. "This is your fault. If you hadn't come along, this fool wouldn't be here now." He kicked the dead man's leg hard.

Kimberly started crying again.

"Stay there," he said to her. "And I mean right there."

He looked at the body again.

Jesus, what a pair of perfect assholes.

He reached inside the door and undid the rope. Then he dragged the dead guy inside, leaving a wide smear of blood on the wood floor.

He looked out a window. Kimberly was still in her spot.

One of the lamps had burned itself out completely, and the other was down to about an eighth of an inch of fuel. He refilled each one. They'd last another night and after that it didn't matter.

He thought of something else before he finished. A little present for Cross or whoever showed up next.

"I didn't know where you were," Kimberly said to him when he lifted her to her feet.

"Well, now you know. You happy?"

She wrapped her arms around him.

"I was scared."

To his amazement, his anger vanished.

"I bet you were," he said.

Bobby almost missed the guy's car, a black Ford Taurus parked off one of the logging roads. He took one look in the trunk, saw the gray-and-blue state trooper's uniform in the dry cleaner's bag and gave a low whistle.

The fool had been a cop.

He took out the uniform and held it up to himself. Wouldn't be a bad fit, he thought. A little long in the pants, though. He could always hem them.

Bobby still couldn't believe the guy was stupid enough to be out in the woods by himself. Unless he was on his own time. Which would explain why he wasn't dressed. But what was he doing out there in the first place?

Just dumb, I guess.

In the trunk, he also found the trooper's hat, service revolver, a big first-aid kit, and some blankets. He placed the uniform back in the trunk and told Kimberly to get in the car. It would be a while before anybody discovered the body, and by then he'd be back in the city. The Taurus was a popular car, and there were a lot of them. He could rip off a new set of license plates when he got back to town. And the uniform might come in handy.

Maybe Kimberly hadn't done such a bad thing after all.

He drove the Taurus to his own car and cleaned out what he needed. There wasn't much. The money. A few clothes. The tool kit. It was amazing how little he had. His life had thinned right out.

He stopped at the main road. Kimberly was scrunched down in the front seat, her head against his leg.

"I believe I owe you an apology," Bobby told her.

She smiled, so warm and so happy that Bobby didn't know what else to say. She *liked* him.

"Come on," he told her, "let's go for a ride."

23

Tim Cochran felt like he was walking through fire.

The infection caused by the rat bite burned through him. The bite itself had turned a deep angry red, and his elbow had swelled to twice its normal size. To keep the pain at bay, he kept the arm close to him when he walked. Not that it helped. His whole body ached when he moved, every muscle, every nerve, every cell. He stayed in the shadows and avoided the sun because whenever the light touched his skin, it made him feel like he was being ripped apart.

He'd lost sight of everything else. His fear—of Bobby, of the police—seemed far away, a nightmare that he had trouble remembering clearly. So he stayed in the shadows and alleyways, out of fear, out of pain, out of habit. He'd been hiding for so long, it seemed like the natural thing to do.

He had a plan. Make it to the river and follow it north until he was home.

Tim wasn't looking for a hero anymore. He was look-

ing for help, and his uncle was the only one he could think
of who might possibly give it to him.

Wayne Cochran smoked the joint down to the ash, holding
the tiny roach until it burned his fingers, and then tossed it
on the kitchen floor. With the rest of the debris. Since he'd
been released, Wayne had been on a serious binge. But now
the beer and vodka were gone and his own personal stash
had dwindled down to half an ounce of homegrown, a few
Darvons, and a small bag of crystal.

He felt bloated and sluggish and he hadn't bothered to
shave or shower since he'd gotten out of jail, but other than
that he was doing just fine. His mouth was dry, so he roused
himself out of his chair and went looking in the refrigerator
for something to drink.

Only tomato juice left. He pulled out the bottle and
shook it. There were little red lumps floating on the top of
it. He got a glass and stuck his finger across the opening,
hoping to filter them out. A couple landed in his glass anyway. Fuck it, he thought. The tomato juice congealed in his
stomach, but at least his mouth wasn't dry anymore.

He was fine for a few seconds; then his stomach
heaved. He lurched to the sink and threw up. Tomato juice
and bile splattered over the white enamel and across the
counter. He turned on the faucet, rinsed his mouth out, and
went back to the table to roll another joint for himself.

That was the secret. Once you started, you had to keep
going for as long as you could, or else your head caved in.

Cochran took a couple of tokes, felt a slow fuzzy burn
behind his eyeballs, and relaxed.

Wayne was cool, Wayne was bad, Wayne wasn't worried about all the motherfuckers who were trying to chew
his nuts off one at a time.

He had a list.

His lawyer was at the top of it. He wanted fifteen
hundred dollars by the end of the week for getting him out

of jail. If he didn't get it, he said, bad things would happen to Wayne. Like what? He'd already *been* in jail. He tried to think of what else the lawyer could do to him and it didn't seem like much. He had money and dope—at least he'd *had* money and dope before the cops took it away from him. Now he had nothing, no dope to sell and no money, just a few measly tokes. The lawyer couldn't take what he didn't have.

Besides, even if he had some dope, he couldn't sell it right now anyway. The cops would just love it if he did. They'd be on him like flies on shit. That realization led him to the second name on his list.

The cop, the miserable scumbag motherfucker who had taken his dope and his money and put him in jail in the first place. The cop deserved to die. Wayne had visions of stomping on the cop's head until it turned to jelly and then stomping on it some more. No. Stomping was too good for him. He wanted to find a big rat, one about dog size, and let old Mr. Rat chew on the cop's dick until there was nothing left but a bloody stub. He'd sit back and laugh at the cop's missing dick. Piss out of *that*, asshole.

Bobby Radcliff came next. He's the one that started it all. He'd seen the video of the Camden robbery and knew it was Bobby. He should have known all along. That prick. He'd sold the guy a few ounces, done him a real favor, and the next thing he knew, his nephew's on the tube pulling down a liquor store and then some cop comes along and shoves his donkey dick about four feet up his ass. All because of Bobby. He was going to wind that skinny bug-fucker's clock when the time came. And he wasn't going to give him to the cops. That was too good for him. Wayne was going to curb stomp him, stick his teeth right on the edge of his concrete stoop and kick in the back of his head. Let the motherfucker gum his food. Let him suck cock for a living.

Cochran took a few more tokes, feeling the hot smoke

seep into his lungs. Fuck foreign weed, he thought, home-grown was just as good, maybe better. Whatever the guy was doing who grew it, he deserved some kind of award. Cochran's brain floated through space on a big fuzzy cloud until he finally got to Timmy, the last name on his list. That was a tough one. Cochran took another toke to think it through.

He really hoped the little punk was dead.

Tim was in his own neighborhood now, working his way down the alley to his house. The sun was low and out of sight behind the row of houses, an orange haze that settled in front of his eyes and blinded him. He heard the sounds of kids playing in the street somewhere in the distance, the rattle of dishes from a kitchen window. Dinnertime. Mom cooking at the stove. The smell of chicken frying. He hadn't eaten in two days but could no longer think of food. His throat was so swollen that it hurt even when he swallowed his own spit. The thought of trying to eat made him want to cry. But his eyes were hot and dry and he didn't think he could.

He wandered up the alley, stumbling over his own feet, and crashed into a row of battered garbage cans. A door opened and a loud voice told him to scram. He rolled painfully across the concrete, bits of stone digging into his elbow. But he didn't scream. The voice told him again to get lost. He stumbled to his feet and kept moving.

The backs of the houses began to blur. Tim counted them off as best he could. He knew he was close, close enough to reach out and touch the fence by his own backyard. He fumbled with the gate, pushed it open and fell face first on the ground. He saw the back door of the house not more than twenty feet away. But he couldn't move, couldn't do anything.

Tim gathered his strength and called out. He thought he was calling for his mother to come and help him.

But nothing came out of his mouth. He closed his eyes and let the pain take his last hopes away.

When he opened his eyes again, he was still on the ground and his uncle was standing over him, a joint dangling from his mouth. He swayed back and forth and Tim couldn't hold the image straight. His uncle took a deep drag on the joint and blew the smoke out over his shoulder. He kicked Tim with the toe of his boot.

"You'd have been better off dead," his uncle said.

He dragged the boy to the house, a busted little sack of bones that hardly weighed anything.

24

The FBI took over the case that afternoon. Two cars pulled up in front of the house, and half a dozen agents walked through the crowd of reporters to the front door. They wore dark suits and wingtip shoes. They didn't knock.

Agent Jeffers—the Agent in Charge—made the announcement. Jeffers spoke with a Texas accent and made eye contact with everyone when he talked. He promised to work in cooperation with the local authorities. They were coordinating their efforts directly with Washington, he explained, and he promised to pass on any meaningful data that came his way. Then he motioned for Glover and the two of them went into the study.

Minutes later, Glover stuck his head out the door and asked Paige to join them.

Jeffers was a tall man, well built, with short black hair. He looked like the kind of man who did sit-ups every morning and kept a daily record. He reminded Paige of some staff sergeants he'd known in the army.

"Captain Glover says you're in charge of the investigation," Jeffers said.

"That's right."

"I've looked at the file. Is there anything I need to know that isn't in it?"

He told him about Susan.

"I know about that," Jeffers said. "Have you done a preliminary?"

"Not yet. There hasn't been time."

"How soon can you get it done?"

"By the end of the day."

"Not soon enough," Jeffers said. "I'll have one of my men debrief her. I want to get this guy."

"We all want to get him," Paige said.

Jeffers looked skeptically at Paige.

"You ever worked with the Bureau before?"

"Haven't had the pleasure."

"Then you've probably heard that we're all a bunch of humorless pricks with big egos and small brains. We come in late, we take over, and we don't share the credit. That about right?"

"Pretty close," Paige said.

"Well, I'm here to tell you it's all true," Jeffers said. "Except for me. I'm the best apple on the whole damn tree. I don't give a shit who gets him or which one of you gets his kisser on the nightly news. I want the man *got*."

Paige didn't know whether to salute or laugh. So he did both.

Jeffers grinned.

"You an army man, detective?"

"Stateside," Paige said. "Military police."

"Reserves. I was a lawyer in Galveston before this."

"And you joined the Feebs?"

Paige didn't think lawyers did that anymore.

Jeffers smiled.

"Yes, I did. I got tired of sitting on my ass helping people figure out new and exciting ways to screw each other. Since then I've been situated in Seattle, Phoenix, and now Philadelphia.''

"You've moved up."

"Feels mostly like I've been moved," Jeffers said. "You people got any idea where this guy is?"

"He could be anyplace."

"You think he's in the city?"

"Maybe. He told Susan Morbach he'd be in touch. That means he's someplace close."

Jeffers nodded. "Who's the guy with the moustache out there?"

"Which one?"

Jeffers smiled. "The one that looks like he's got a fence post stuck up his ass."

"That's Commander Jackson, state police," Glover said.

"From Harrisburg," Paige added.

Jeffers looked thoughtful. "You know in Russia, they used to have a political officer assigned to everything— factories, soccer teams, even the army. Made sure everybody danced to the same tune. Highly effective system for a while."

The agent scratched at his face. "Well, we all got our jobs to do. Don't let me stop you from doing yours."

Glover went out first. Jeffers told Paige to wait.

"You get a lead on that boy yet?"

"No."

"Cochran? That his name?"

"Tim."

"You think he's still alive?"

"I hope so."

"I do, too. He's the best shot we got of putting a face on this guy. Not the only one but the best. What about his uncle?"

"We had to let him go."

"I know that. Anybody keeping an eye on him?"

"We've got extra patrols in the neighborhood, but nobody's turned up anything yet. We've run the boy's picture and we're checking the shelters and the clinics. The word's out."

"You paid him any more visits?" Jeffers said. "The uncle, I mean."

"The judge suggested that we leave him alone. It was a fairly strong suggestion."

"Did you take it?"

"Not to heart," Paige said.

"Then why don't you spend a little time at his place," Jeffers suggested. "Use your own car. Ditch the suit. Pack a lunch."

"Are you trying to get rid of me?"

"Hell no. But I know all about you. I figure if you hang around here any longer, you're just going to get pissed off and surly. I've got too many assholes to plug up and not enough corks to go around. I don't need yours."

The man's a lot smarter than he looks, Paige thought.

Jeffers must have read his mind.

"It's the accent," Jeffers said. "Everybody hears that Texas twang, they start thinking you're about two weeks away from beating up cows for a living. I figure I'll lay it on thick for the state police, see if I can stop that fool from screwing things up more than he wants to."

Paige laughed. "How come we never met before?"

"I don't know," Jeffers said. "Too busy to shit, too tired to wipe. You know how it is. You watch it out there. Don't go running the show by yourself. Let me know what the hell's going on. And if you find that boy, I want you to hang onto him like he was your momma's own tit. Take him someplace safe and get on the phone. By the way, where the hell's the senator?"

"He's planning a rally."

Jeffers scratched his face again. "I heard about that

but I didn't believe it. I'd like to put a stop to it. Dumbest thing since Congress. Will Cross help?''

"Only if he wants to."

And I'm not sure he wants to, Paige thought. Mostly what he wants right now is to get out from under this mess.

"Well, I'll talk to him," Jeffers said.

"If you do," Paige suggested, "I wouldn't worry a whole lot about the accent."

Paige spent the next hour trying to "coordinate" with Agent Smith. Agent Smith was young, diligent, and very serious. He typed everything Paige said into a laptop computer and didn't smile once.

Susan was off being questioned by another agent, and Cross was in the living room conferring with Commander Jackson. Jeffers spent most of his time on the new phone line to Washington, trying to work out the details.

It was nearly six when Paige finished. He thought he would go home, take a shower, grab some food, and see what Wayne Cochran was up to for the evening. Susan opened the door to the study.

"They told me you were leaving," she said and closed the door behind her.

He wasn't sure he wanted her to do that. On one hand, he was pleased that she did. It implied a great deal. On the other hand, it probably didn't mean anything. Paige closed the door all the time when he wanted to talk to somebody. On the other hand, this was Susan Morbach. On the other hand. Shit. It made him tired just trying to keep all the alternatives in his head. He wondered if he would ever reach a point where he could make sense of them. Probably not.

"I'm going to work."

"I want to come with you," she said. She held up her hand before he had a chance to say no.

Which he wasn't going to say anyway. He wasn't sure

what he was going to say. So he shut his mouth and listened instead.

"Jim's on his way. I just talked to him. Actually, I hardly talked at all. He said he wanted to get to the bottom of things." She paced back and forth in front of the couch where he was sitting, worrying a rut in the carpet. "I don't want to see him. I know how that sounds. I don't care how it sounds. It's the truth. I want to go with you. All right?"

"I'll be working," Paige said. "Most of the night."

"So will I," Susan said, her voice rising. "I've *been* working ever since this happened. I don't want to do it alone anymore. Okay?"

He could think of several reasons to say no. To begin with, taking a civilian with you was seriously dumb. Major dumb. But hell, everybody was dumb once in a while. There was also a reason to say yes. If Cochran was looking for surveillance, he probably wasn't looking for a car with a man and a woman in it.

Paige changed clothes at his house, made some baloney sandwiches, and filled a thermos full of coffee. Susan cornered him by the sink in the kitchen.

"Don't you think you could tell me where we're going?"

"We're going to spy on somebody."

"Who?"

"A guy named Wayne Cochran."

"That's the boy from the first robbery."

"His uncle."

"Is he dangerous?"

"Not unless he breathes on you."

25

Cross was frightened, but just like that first night, it seemed to invigorate him. He saw himself in a brand-new light.

The shotgun lay on the front seat covered by a blanket, six shells loaded, one in the chamber. Racked back. Safety locked. He was going to put as many as he could in Bobby. He was going to reduce Bobby to a small mangled puddle of flesh and blood on the floor of the cabin. He was going to blow Bobby into tiny little bits.

He would leave Bobby's head intact. He wanted to watch his face as he went down. All the way down.

But how precisely?

How was he going to do it?

Not the actual shooting but getting in place for it, setting up the shot. For a while he'd entertained the idea of having a little chat with him, but it was awfully hard to talk to somebody with a shotgun in your hand. He had the feeling Bobby might get suspicious.

Of course if he'd had the Glock it would have been a lot easier. He could have stuck it in his pocket or jammed it in his belt beneath his coat. Then he'd just pull it out and blast away. But now he reconsidered the whole scheme. He didn't want to talk to Bobby, didn't want to hear anything from him except whatever noise people made when they died.

Did they actually rattle? He'd heard that they did. Somewhere he'd read that the sound was a lot like porridge slopping down an open sewer drain. That had a nice grue-some feel to it. He tried to imitate it, catching the saliva in his throat and letting it gurgle around. It was an interesting sensation, like having your nuts tickled.

God, he thought, I'm starting to sound just like Bobby.

"What will they do?" Susan asked. "When they find her?"

"If we can prove she was under duress, they'll prob-ably let her go."

Paige couldn't imagine anybody in the DA's office wanting to prosecute the girl, not unless the DA himself thought it would work with the voters. There was talk about his running for mayor, and South Philly was a major voting bloc.

"Will the district attorney go for that?"

"I don't know."

"You mean if he's running for mayor he might think twice about it."

"That's what I mean."

Paige turned to her in the front seat.

"Look, you can't think about this now. It won't do any good."

"Because she might not be alive."

"No," he said. "Because it hasn't happened yet."

Susan glanced out the window at the small houses and wondered what she would have been like if she'd grown up there. I wouldn't be here right now, she thought.

"Do you ever think about the future?" she asked him.

"No."

He'd spent enough of his life thinking about the past. All he wanted to do now was stay in the present.

"Not ever?"

"Thinking about things you can't control is a waste of time."

"The people I know spend all their time in the future," she said. "I never meet anybody who's satisfied with now. It's always, wait until the next job, the next house, the next whatever. They're always on their way somewhere. I wonder what they'll do if they ever get there."

"Maybe they won't get there at all."

She was thinking of her husband, the terrifying appetite of his ambition, and the price they'd paid for it.

"No," she said, "they'll get there. That's the problem. They always do."

She was getting morbid again and she hated it. The feeling was like a virus lodged deep in her heart, breaking out at unpredictable moments. A word, an image, the notes of a half-forgotten song were enough to set it off and she would plunge into despair. In those moments, she couldn't see her daughter's face, could not bring it back from her memory, and her despair became so great that she thought she might never feel happy again.

Susan wanted to ask Paige if he understood how she felt but knew that he didn't. She couldn't blame him for his failing. His world seemed so clear-cut. Not so much right versus wrong, but something more personal, an invisible line of behavior that only he knew existed. Once you crossed it, you were never allowed back inside.

Still, she couldn't blame him, even though part of her wanted to; she wanted to blame everyone.

She fought this battle silently and then put it aside. He was right about that, it did no good. She changed the subject.

"What do you think he's doing in there?"

"Getting high," Paige said. He poured a cup of coffee and offered it to her. She shook her head. He drank it himself.

"Did you ever do that?"

"Get high? Once or twice. In the army. It was hard to avoid."

"What did you think of it?"

"It was all right," Paige said. "I felt kind of silly." He remembered that everybody smoked dope in the army. Most of the time the guards showed up at the posts so stoned they could barely speak. The commanders didn't know what to do. They closed their eyes, hid in their offices, and prayed for better times. They couldn't court-martial the whole army.

"You don't like feeling silly, do you?"

"I don't like feeling stupid," he said. He didn't mind being dumb. Dumb was different from stupid.

Right.

"Because you're not in control," she said.

"I guess that's it."

Susan moved closer to him and put her hand on his arm. He looked at her, thinking that if she wanted him to kiss her he would, and worry about the consequences later. But that wasn't what she wanted. She had another question.

"How do you control your anger?" she asked. "How do you keep it from tearing you apart?"

It was a good question.

I eat it, he thought, just like everybody else. I make a meal of it every goddamn day.

Paige saw something out of the corner of his eye, a shadow that emerged from the doorway of the house.

Wayne Cochran stuck his head out the door.

Paige moved lower in the seat and pulled Susan down with him.

"Quiet," he said. He looked over the dash as Cochran

went back into the house and came out again quickly, carrying a blanket-wrapped bundle in his arms.

Just the right size for a boy's small body.

Jacob Cross found where Bobby had hidden his car, nestled behind a small cluster of pricker bushes. After deciding not to use the flashlight he carried with him, he had trouble maneuvering around the bush in the dark. One of the vines raked the back of his hands. He yelped with pain and dropped the shotgun. It landed in the bushes, and he fell to his knees to get it, the thorns tearing his skin as he shoved the vines out of the way.

He pulled the shotgun toward him frantically, frightened that Bobby might have heard him, that Bobby was somewhere in the dark, laughing at him, waiting for the right moment to put a bullet in him.

It wasn't supposed to be like this, he thought. It was supposed to go down just the way he'd imagined it.

What if Bobby was inside the car?

He moved closer and crouched beside the door, counting off silently, one, two, three, and wrenched it open, shoving the barrel of the shotgun inside. He squeezed on the trigger, waiting for the explosion that would end the terror racing through his guts.

Nothing happened.

He'd forgotten to release the safety.

He flicked off the safety and swung the barrel over the seat into the back. The car was empty.

Cross sat down on the ground. His hands were slick with sweat and his shirt clung to the skin of his back. He sat there feeling the sweat pour out of him, running over his chest and down his forehead, his heart thumping along at a hard steady gallop.

Christ, it was hot out here. He hadn't realized it until now. He thought he might suffocate just sitting there. He pulled himself to his feet and tried to remember the way to the cabin. For a moment he was frozen in place. But he felt worse standing there, and he plunged ahead, in a hurry to get it done.

He stampeded recklessly through the woods, snapping the flashlight on and off to get a quick snapshot of where he was going. After a few minutes, he found a path that looked familiar. He was in a hurry now, angry at himself for screwing up with the shotgun, angry at Bobby for making everything so damn difficult, angry at everyone who had ever conspired to make him look like a fool.

After he was finished with Bobby, with this whole *mess*, he would take care of the rest of them. How didn't matter. How was easy. Jacob Cross could figure out how in his sleep.

He remembered it all now, the worn-out logging road, the sharp right turn in the middle of nowhere into the dark hole of the path. His feet moved faster and faster and he didn't begin to slow down, didn't even think about caution, until he saw the first flicker of the lanterns through the cabin windows.

Paige waited until Cochran's car was at the far end of the street, stopped across from the wall of the old elevated tracks. He was a block behind, waiting until Cochran made the turn. He left the lights off and sped up, the houses going by in a blur, keeping his eyes on the taillights ahead as they went around the corner and disappeared.

"You're going to miss him," Susan said.

"No, I'm not," Paige said and took the corner without looking, the car swerving slightly as he accelerated through the turn, then slowed down.

Cochran's car was fifty yards ahead of him, stuck behind a pickup truck. A red Toyota pulled out of one of the side streets, and Paige waited for the car, turning on his lights as the car moved in front of him. He stayed behind the Toyota, watching the back of Cochran's car as it surged ahead.

Cochran drove several blocks and then turned right on Aramingo.

"He's turning," Susan said.

"Just watch him," Paige said sharply.

Paige waited until Cochran made the turn and then passed the Toyota on the right, squeezing between it and the curb. The driver pressed his horn. Paige accelerated past him. Cochran's car was stopped at the light a block away. Paige hit the brakes and slowed, pulling over to the side. The light changed and Paige started up again.

Cochran moved left on the overpass and descended to Delaware Avenue, heading south.

"Where's he going?" Susan asked.

"He's going to the river," Paige said.

It was the best place to dump the body.

When he saw the lights, Cross dropped the flashlight. It fell from his fingers and landed softly in the grass. He stood completely still, waiting for his nerves to stop jangling and the feeling of calm purpose to settle around him once again.

He wasn't going to make the same mistake he'd made at the car. This time there would be no hesitation, no fumbling around, no more blind terror. He was going to move in fast and get it over with. He was going to do it just like Bobby would.

Cross checked the safety once more and ran down the path. He kept his eyes fixed on the front door, thinking that any second Bobby was going to come bursting out of it. He raised the shotgun as he ran, aiming at the cabin door. His finger tightened on the trigger.

But Bobby didn't come out, not when he got ten feet from the door, not even when he swerved to the right suddenly and ran for the side window, keeping low to avoid being seen. He knelt in the tall grass just below the window, waited, and then stood up beside it with the shotgun still aimed at the door. Cross took a deep breath and looked inside.

A body hung from the center of the cabin ceiling. Cross saw it all in a single glance, the body, the lanterns, the ropes that looped around the rafters and trailed through the rest of the cabin, the pots and pans on the floor. He saw it all but nothing registered. Only the sight of the body slowly turning his way.

For a moment, he thought it was Kimberly. Then he realized it was the body of a man. He couldn't see the face in the light, but he was sure it wasn't Bobby. Cross ran for the door.

He put his foot against it, stepped back slightly to give himself leverage, and smelled the gasoline. His mind told him to stop, but it was already too late. He kicked the door open and stumbled into the cabin.

There was a crash as the first lantern tumbled off the stove and blue flame erupted across the floor at his feet. The air in the cabin seemed to be on fire. It surged into his lungs. Sparks danced in front of his eyes. Cross turned to run but his foot caught on the rope and he fell. High above him, the body twisted faster in the sudden heat, coming around to watch him die.

He saw the man's face as it turned toward him, and his vision seemed to split in two. It was a stranger's face, bloated and grotesque, the mouth caught in an empty rictus. Smoke swirled around him and he wiped away the tears that flooded his eyes. When he looked again, he saw that the face had changed, transformed into a more familiar illusion.

The face—his father's face—smiled down at him.

Cross screamed and reached for the shotgun.

The second lantern fell and the world around him erupted in white hot light. The light embraced him, lifted him up, and he was soaring up through the light, higher and higher, moving out of its reach.

Then falling, plummeting toward the cold darkness that lay just beyond the light, and finding it.

Paige watched Cochran turn into the Conrail yard and drove another hundred yards before he snapped the wheel sharply and made a hard U-turn. The car bumped over the divider, the rear end spinning out slightly before Paige pulled the wheel hard and straightened it out.

He could see the rows of freight cars just ahead, but he'd lost sight of Cochran. It wasn't where they'd found the other boy's body, but it was close enough. Paige slowed down, cut his headlights, and stopped just before the entrance.

"I want you to stay in the car and keep the doors locked," he told Susan.

"But you said he wasn't dangerous."

"That was before," Paige answered. He drove in slowly, pulled ahead about ten yards, and then cut hard to the right, stopping the car in the middle of the entrance.

"I can help," Susan told him.

Paige unholstered his gun and checked it.

"Not this time," he said.

He ran to the first row of cars and stopped. There were two more rows in front of him, stretching out in a long curve toward a group of small buildings at the other end. He stepped across the tracks and looked around. Cochran's car wasn't there. He ran to the second row, nearly tripping over a pile of railroad ties. When he reached the second row, he stopped and listened. He heard the sound of a car door opening and Cochran's heavy steps.

He scanned the row of freight cars in front of him and saw Cochran emerge from one of the open doors. The biker looked around and then jumped to the ground, heading for his own car. He carried the blanket over one shoulder.

Paige walked down the tracks to cut him off. Cochran saw him and ran for his car.

Paige was thirty feet away. He pressed his back against the side of the freight car and squeezed off two shots. The first slammed into the trunk. The second hit the back window, punching a hole in the glass. Cochran threw open the door and jumped inside.

Paige fired again. The back window exploded. Cochran crawled across the front seat, pushed open the passenger door, and tumbled out on the ground. He got to his feet and disappeared between two freight cars.

Paige hesitated, then doubled back, running beside the tracks. When he came around the end, he looked and saw Cochran scramble over the coupling between two cars in the first row. When he reached the row of freight cars, Cochran was halfway to the entrance, coming up fast on his own car.

The headlights came on suddenly, trapping Cochran in the beams. The biker veered to the left and ran along the fence.

Paige tracked him, aiming for the middle of Cochran's back. At the last second, he lowered the gun and fired three times fast.

Cochran stumbled and fell. He landed hard on his shoulder, rolled over several times, and stopped.

Susan got out of the car.

"Stay there," he yelled. He walked slowly toward the place where the biker had fallen, keeping the gun trained on Cochran's body. It didn't dawn on him until he was next to him that the gun was empty.

He pushed Cochran with the toe of his shoe, and the biker rolled over on his back and groaned. There was blood on both his legs. He could see it pouring out of a wound high up on Cochran's right thigh. The second wound was on the same leg, only lower. Much lower. He knelt down.

The bullet had torn off the heel of Cochran's boot.

The biker clutched at his thigh and groaned again. Paige searched him, but found only a small bag of dope and some matches.

"You shot me, you son of a bitch," Cochran said. His face had gone white and his voice sounded weak.

Paige yelled to Susan.

"Get my jacket."

She brought it quickly. He folded it in a thick bundle and stuffed it underneath Cochran's wounded leg.

"Keep pressing on it," Paige told him. "Maybe you won't bleed to death before an ambulance gets here."

He took her arm. "Let's look for the boy."

They found the blanket Cochran had dropped. Paige picked it up. He looked down the row of freight cars toward the buildings. A guard stood beside the open front door and stared in his direction.

Paige yelled at him.

"Police! Go make a call!"

The guard disappeared inside.

All he had to do now was find the body.

Susan found him. He lay in the back of an empty freight car, his head against the wall. Paige stayed on the ground and watched as she knelt down next to him. He heard sirens. They grew louder, and he saw the headlights as they turned into the entrance. Paige took out his shield and waited.

He didn't want to look at the boy, didn't want to hear the news that he'd been too late again.

"He's alive," Susan said.

Paige tossed the blanket into the freight car.

"Stay with him," he said and made his way back to the front of the railyard, his shield held high so everyone could see it.

26

It reminded Paige of the time he spent waiting for his father to die. The swollen silence of the waiting room, the antiseptic whispers of the staff, the boredom and the dread, and the unspoken yearning for some word, some sign, that the wait was finally over.

The room was both cheerful and plain, sad beige carpeting accented by the blue-and-orange fabric of the furniture, a series of romantically colored travel photographs on the walls as though the hospital meant to suggest several postvigil destinations for the survivors after their ordeal was over.

Susan sat with him on one of the couches. Smoking was not allowed. They had been there a little over an hour, and no one had come to talk to them. He had already called Jeffers at the house to let him know what had happened. Jeffers told him to stay there until he got some news.

"Is Cross with you?" Jeffers had asked.

"No. Isn't he with you?"

"Not hardly. He left right after you did and didn't tell a soul where he was going. I wish he was here right now."

Paige laughed. "The senator driving you nuts?"

"I asked him about the rally and he offered me some shit about the will of the people. I think he actually believes it."

"What about Jackson?"

"Oh, he's around here someplace. Him and his elf. He doesn't know where Cross is either. He's not even a good watchdog."

"If I hear from Cross, I'll let you know."

"Good enough," Jeffers said. "By the way, is the senator's wife there with you?"

"Yes."

"I thought as much. He's been asking about her."

"What'd you tell him?"

"I lied," Jeffers said. "I don't especially like being put in a position where I have to do that."

"Then tell him the truth."

"Oh, that'll be real helpful. He'll enjoy hearing that particular piece of news."

"I don't know what else to tell you."

"You could tell me you're bringing her back here just as soon as you can."

"Sure," Paige said. "As soon as I know something." He didn't like it, but he felt compelled to offer Jeffers an explanation.

"There's nothing between us," he said. "She wanted to go with me tonight, and I didn't see any problem with it. I still don't."

"I never said there was. But I'm not the one you have to worry about."

Paige returned to the waiting room, not entirely certain he knew what Jeffers was thinking or what he would tell Morbach if and when he asked.

The surgeon who operated on Wayne Cochran came out first. He was still in his blood-spattered green suit.

"Detective Paige?" he said and smiled when Paige raised his hand.

"I'm Dr. Rosen. Your patient's doing fine."

"When can I talk to him?"

"Maybe tomorrow."

"What about now?"

Rosen shook his head. He was middle-aged and prosperous looking, and when he spoke, he sounded like a man who'd decided against buying a new suit.

"I don't think that's the best choice. We gave him a spinal and he won't even be coherent for another couple hours. The morning would be the best time. Are you the one who shot him?"

"Yes."

"You missed the artery by about half an inch. That's what saved him from bleeding to death."

"How's the boy?"

"I don't know," Rosen said. "I understand he's in a coma."

"Will he live?" Susan asked. She got up from the couch.

"That's all I know. I'm sorry."

They sat down after the surgeon left. Susan leaned on his shoulder.

"I could pray for him," she said.

"Might help," Paige said. "Couldn't hurt."

"You know any good ones?"

"Not offhand."

Twenty minutes later a nurse appeared and waved them over to the desk.

"Are you the parents?"

Paige took out his shield.

"No. The boy's in my custody."

"Where are his parents?"

"Not here."

The nurse made a face.

"How is he?" Susan asked impatiently.

"The infection is widespread, and he's terribly dehydrated. We have him on antibiotics, but we won't know anything for at least another hour. He may make it, he may not. It's very touch and go at the moment." She tried to sound sympathetic. "His heart's still strong. That's one good thing."

"Can we see him?" Paige asked.

"I'll have to ask the doctor about that."

"Then why don't you?"

"I will," the nurse said, taking a form from beneath the counter. "But there's a few things I have to clear up first. Can you give me his full name?"

"Tim Cochran."

"And his address?"

Paige gave it to her.

"His age?"

"I don't know. Thirteen, maybe fourteen."

"Do you know his parents' names?"

"I know the mother's name and address," he said. "She's in Colorado. I don't know where his father is."

"Does she have insurance?"

"No."

The nurse started to write something on the form.

"I'll take care of the bill," Susan said.

The nurse stopped writing.

"Are you sure about that?" she asked.

"Yes. Quite sure."

"It could be very expensive," she said. "And there's no guarantee."

Susan took a checkbook from her purse and wrote out a check.

"Will a twenty-five-hundred-dollar deposit do?"

"For now."

Susan slid the check across the counter, and the nurse clipped it to the form.

"Put my name down, too," Paige said.

"Pat," Susan said.

"It's okay."

The nurse took his name and address.

"I'll speak to the doctor."

Susan said, "You didn't have to do that."

"I wanted to do it. I've got some money. I'll pay what I can."

He was thinking he would sell the house. Not the one he lived in, but the one in Mount Airy where his wife had died. The same one where he'd killed the burglar Grant. Right after Grant had killed Tom Ferris.

Before he died, Ferris had told him exactly how his wife had been killed, how one of Ferris's snitches had killed her, an act of mistaken revenge for something Ferris had done. Paige's own father had helped cover up the truth, and Paige had kept the house for all these years as a kind of memorial, not just for Connie, but for all of them. He'd been to his wife's grave only once, the day she was buried. When he needed to be with her, to remember his old life, he went to the house.

Now in a matter of seconds, he'd made the decision to get rid of it. I suppose that means I'm cured. He had finally accepted the truth of her death. But the lies had been a whole lot easier to live with.

Until now. Selling it was the right decision. The question was, why didn't it make him feel any better?

He realized Susan was staring at him.

He took hold of her hand.

"It'll be all right," he said.

The nurse came out to tell them that Tim Cochran's condition was deteriorating rapidly and that it looked hopeless.

Susan began to cry.

Paige put his arm around her and decided that the real

problem with the world was that there weren't enough lies to go around.

Half an hour later, Jeffers phoned to tell him that they'd found Jacob Cross. He'd got himself blown up in an abandoned cabin somewhere in the New Jersey Pine Barrens.

"Is he alive?"

"That's what they tell me," Jeffers said. "He got burned but he's conscious. They flew him in by helicopter to the airport and then they said they were taking him where you are. They ought to be there soon. I'm on my way. I'll meet you in emergency."

"What the hell was he doing in New Jersey?"

"Nobody knows. But they found another body in the cabin."

Paige looked at Susan and waited.

"It wasn't the girl. They're not sure who it is. It might be the kidnapper. They're working on his teeth now. From what I understand, wasn't much else left. Two of my men are there, going through the wreckage."

"Are they looking for the girl?"

"For what it's worth. I'll see you in a bit."

When he sat down, Susan asked him what had happened. He told her.

"Could it have been the kidnapper?"

Paige shook his head. "Maybe."

"Then Kimberly must be there."

"If she is, they'll find her."

Susan was silent for a few minutes.

"How did Jacob know where she was?"

That's what we'd all like to know, Paige thought.

The emergency room was crammed with the broken and the bleeding. Children cried and screamed, battered drunks sat in Formica chairs, clutching their stomachs, teenagers clustered around their wounded friends, young women sobbed to themselves in the brightly lit corners.

The air was filled with voices speaking all at once, Spanish, English, the high-pitched chirpings of an Indian family, all the stuttering rhythms of the street, each making a demand, each one asking to be served, helped, saved. The faces of the nurses were grim behind the counter as they fought their way through the noise and the chaos, hoping to find something beyond what they already knew—the world was a singularly bad place.

In the corridors and cubicles where the work got done, there seemed to be more machines than people.

Jeffers was already there, standing outside one of the white-curtained cubicles, while inside what looked like a coven of white-robed witches were trying to raise another one of the dead. They were cutting away pieces of clothing. They smelled of ashes and smoke and charred flesh.

"How is he?" Paige asked.

"He won't win any beauty contests," Jeffers answered.

One of the doctors moved away from the table and Paige saw Jacob Cross.

He looked like a piece of raw meat. On one side of his face and neck, the skin was entirely gone. All that was left was red flesh. The flesh appeared to be weeping blood and drops of clear fluid.

Cross stared at him, his eyes bright with fear. The doctor closed the curtain, shutting him out.

"Couple guys in the Guard got caught in a freak tank fire once," Jeffers said quietly. "I was there when they brought them out. Looked like they'd been skinned. They were still alive. Medic said they couldn't feel a thing. The nerves were burned away. Poor bastards thought they were going to make it."

"What about Cross?"

"Oh, he'll make it. The burns look bad but they're not fatal. I talked to the paramedics on the skyphone. Apparently there was a gasoline explosion in the cabin and it blew him back out through the front door. He was lucky. Few other things—broken arm, cracked ribs, some pretty big splinters stuck in him. He's got a world of pain to look forward to when he starts to heal. But he'll *live*."

"Can he talk now?"

The agent frowned.

"He can do just about everything except dance," Jeffers said. "Let's go outside. You look like a man who needs a cigarette real bad."

Jeffers bought a candy bar from one of the vending machines near the lobby. Paige leaned against the wrought iron fence around the corner from the emergency entrance and watched while he ate it in three bites. Paige lit a cigarette and waited for the bad news. Whenever he took someone outside to talk it was bad news; Jeffers probably worked the same way.

"We can't talk to him now," Jeffers said.

"Why not?"

"I asked him already," Jeffers said. "The doctor, too."

"They said no."

"There you go. Cross shook his head and the doctor said he was too injured to answer any questions and would I please get the hell out of his emergency room. By the time he's okay, Cross'll have talked to his lawyer and they'll have it all figured out and we won't get anything anyway. I don't like working up a lather over something that ain't going to happen."

"You think he knows who the kidnapper is?"

"I think he knows *something*." He took an envelope from his pocket and handed it to Paige. "They found this in his car. One of my men gave it to the paramedics. Special delivery."

It was a Polaroid of the dead boy. One of the agents

had sealed it in cellophane. Paige turned it over and read the back.

"How'd he get this?"

"Don't know. Maybe the kidnapper dropped it off with the tape and he decided to keep it a secret."

"You could ask Jackson."

"He disappeared the minute we got the news. Which makes me think he's looking for a way to cover his own ass. If he knows about it. Which I doubt."

Paige read the back again. The choice of words was odd, friendly or threatening, depending how you read them.

"They found another car near the cabin," Jeffers said. "A green Camaro. Nice piece of machinery."

"You ran a check."

"Like pronto. The car was registered to a Robert Hicks in Bordentown. The address turned out to be a Seven-eleven. He's got a post office box but we haven't been able to look at it yet. They're getting the postmaster out of bed. My guess is nobody's used it in a while."

"A green Camaro?"

"Sound familiar?

"We can go back and talk to the robbery witnesses in the morning. But if he's dead, it won't matter very much."

"I don't think the body in the cabin was his. No proof. Just a feeling."

"Then who's the dead guy?"

"Hiker, maybe."

"Or somebody with a car. He knows his car is hot, so he looks for a new one. That'd be the smart thing to do."

"That's what bothers me. He's too damn smart."

"I know what you're thinking," Paige said.

"You do? I'm impressed."

Paige held up the photograph.

"If Cross knew the kidnapper, then the whole thing was a setup from the beginning. If that's the case, the senator had to be in on it."

"Not bad. Puts you in an awkward position, doesn't it?"

"Susan."

"If it was a setup, they might not let her in on it. Judging from what I've seen of her, I'd say it was more than likely they'd keep her clean. But nobody else will see it that way."

"She's not part of it," Paige said.

"I don't necessarily disagree. I'm just commenting on appearances. The problem is, your whole theory breaks down when you get to the robbery."

"Somebody fucked up," Paige offered.

Jeffers laughed. "That's for sure. I can't see Cross being part of that kind of fiasco, can you?"

"Only if he didn't know his partner that well."

Jeffers cocked his head, thinking it over.

"I'm listening," he said.

"If the kidnapper did it on his own and brought Cross in later, Cross might just decide to go with what he's got, use the kidnapping to work up a big vote for his candidate, and then try to take the bad guy out before the big day."

"The rally?"

"That's right. But something goes wrong. The kidnapper figures out that Cross is going to kill him and sets a trap instead. Did Cross have a gun with him?"

"Shotgun," Jeffers said.

"He asked me to help him get a carrying permit."

"When?"

"A couple days ago. He said he was going to buy a pistol. He thought his life was in danger."

"But he bought a shotgun instead," Jeffers said thoughtfully.

"He probably didn't know about the waiting period for handguns. We can find that out if we find the dealer."

Jeffers nodded.

"That's fine as far as it goes," Jeffers said, "but it still doesn't answer the main question."

"Which is?"

"What Cross was doing with the kidnapper in the first place. Let's say you're right, that Cross is using this wonderful opportunity to stuff a few extra ballot boxes. How does he find this guy? Why'd he even bother looking for him?"

"Ask the senator."

"I could. But I don't think the senator knows a pile of shit from a fudge brownie. He's in his own private area code as far as I can tell."

"Then that leaves us with Jacob Cross. And this." He handed the photograph to Jeffers.

"And this leaves us with nothing but more questions we can't ask."

He looked very tired suddenly.

"Damn," he said. "I knew I should've bought another candy bar."

Tim's doctor was already waiting for him when he got back upstairs, and Susan was in tears. He felt himself rolling toward the edge of despair. One more shot of bad news. He didn't have that far to fall.

The doctor surprised him. He'd already spoken to Susan. Now he explained it to Paige.

"We think the boy's going to live," the doctor said. "But there's been a lot of damage."

"What kind of damage?"

"We don't know. He's not really conscious yet so it's hard to say. I'm worried about his renal functions right at the moment."

"You mean his kidneys?"

"Yes, that's what I mean. I'm sorry. They failed once already. Right now he's on the machine and we're going to keep him there for a while. There may also have been some nerve and muscle damage. We can't assess the extent until he wakes up and I have no idea when that might be. There's still a possibility that he won't.''

"He might stay in the coma?''

"Yes.'' The doctor looked uneasy for the first time. "He's been abused. Are you aware of that?''

"I know he's been living on the street,'' Paige said.

"No, I don't mean that. He's been physically abused. We found burn marks on him—from a cigarette apparently. There were also some lacerations on his back and buttocks. They look like they were made by a belt, but I'm only guessing.''

"Did you document them?''

"Yes. The hospital requires it. Pictures. Everything.'' The doctor shook his head. "I've never seen anything like that before.''

Now he knew why Susan was crying.

"It's just a theory,'' the doctor said, "but the coma may be something of a reaction to the abuse—on top of everything else. In his condition, his brain may have just decided to shut itself down rather than deal with the problem.''

The doctor looked away for a moment, wiping his eyes with a quick sweep of his hand. "I know I wish mine would,'' he said.

Paige took a business card from his wallet and gave it to him.

"When you get your report done,'' he said, "I want you to send a copy to me. Don't worry, I'll clear it with the hospital.''

The doctor fingered the card. "The person who did that—will anything happen to him?''

"I can almost guarantee it,'' Paige said.

Susan had been sitting on the couch and hadn't moved. When the doctor left, she got to her feet.

"Can we go home now?" she asked. Her voice sounded so weak that at first he wasn't sure he understood what she meant.

But he did.

Yes, he thought, let's go home.

27

"Ain't this the life," Bobby said. "I feel just like a goddamn drugstore."

He was high again, high on a whole lot of things, high to the point that he wasn't even sure what he was high on. He'd smoked a little reefer on the way into Center City and then stopped at a drugstore and picked up a bagful of over-the-counter medication—different kinds of cough medicine, the ones with alcohol in them, and some pain pills that he'd used before when he'd been looking for a mild buzz.

He sampled a few, smoked a little more reefer, and then played blindman's luck with the handful of prescription pills he had left. He still had some of the blotter acid, and he tore one of the pieces in half, one piece for himself, the other for Kimberly.

He was driving up North Broad just as it started to kick in. The lights around him began to bend inward, rippling across his eyes, and the windshield bulged and throbbed in time to the music that blasted from the radio. It felt just like he was a shark, cruising the ocean floor and watching the fish.

"You know what shark bait is?"

"Uh uh," Kimberly said.

"All of them," Bobby told her and waved his hand across the dash. "Everyone of these fucking bottom feeders." He laughed out loud. "Oh man, we got to do this more often."

Bobby drove north and made a right into a side street, circled around the block and back out to Broad. He turned left and headed back into Center City with no particular destination in mind. The idea was just to keep moving until he found a good place to hide the car. They were probably out looking for it by now. The thought brought him down immediately.

Kimberly had fallen asleep.

"You dreamin' about your daddy?" Bobby asked. "I've been dreaming about him, too. Maybe we'll go see him together."

But right now he had the car and the cops to worry about. He stayed on Broad all the way back, watching the street front and rear. When he was close to Billy Penn, he saw a sign for a garage at the Bellevue and put on his turn signal to make a left. He waited until the traffic cleared and pulled into the entrance, got his ticket from the machine, and drove in.

It felt like he was in a cave, the white concrete walls like huge slabs of rock ready to fall in on him. Bobby steered the car around the curves, one big fun ride all the way to the roof. He pulled into the first parking space he saw and turned off the car.

In the abrupt silence, spooky thoughts crept into his brain. Everyone he knew was dead and he was the last person on earth. He was trapped in the car and couldn't get out. Kimberly was a corpse waiting to suck him into the dark. Fear was a spider inching up his back. Mr. Death was out there waiting to get him, cold creepy fingers plucking at his heart.

Bobby covered his ears with his hands and waited for the spooky feeling to pass. It took a few minutes.

When it was gone, he got out of the car. In the trunk, he took a screwdriver from his tool kit and removed the license plates. He walked down to the floor below and found a rusted-up minivan with Jersey plates and traded. He figured that anybody who let their ride get that bad wouldn't notice that they were suddenly driving around with a different set of numbers.

His hands felt like they were about ten sizes too big but he managed.

He searched the Taurus thoroughly and came up with a couple more interesting items. A pair of handcuffs. The trooper's hat. A dozen back issues of a swinger's magazine. He flipped through the pages and noticed the cop had circled some of the photographs. One showed a woman with a menacing grin holding a dildo in each hand. She looked like she was all set to draw down on him. Bobby tossed the magazines back and went to wake up Kimberly.

It took a minute or so for her to come around. He led her from the car, making sure to lock it.

"Where are we?" she asked.

"In the belly of the beast," he whispered.

He waited on the roof of the garage until it was dark and then led her down the stairs to the street. From there, he walked up Broad to Walnut and then down two blocks to Sixteenth Street. There was an alley behind the office buildings, high and narrow like a canyon. He found a place between a pair of dumpsters and settled on the concrete, wrapping the blanket around them for cover.

"This is where we're going to spend the night," he said. "You ever slept on the street before?"

"I don't remember," Kimberly said. "I don't think so."

"Then this is your chance to be one of the homeless."

"Won't they see us here?"

"Everybody'll see us but nobody gives a fuck."

Bobby felt something jab his leg. He reached in his pocket. It was the key from Susan Morbach's purse. He shook Kimberly.

"You ever see this before?"

"I don't know. What is it?"

Bobby struck a match.

"Take a good look at it."

"It looks like a key," she said.

"Hell, yes, it's a key. It belongs to your mother."

"My mother?" she said as though she thought it impossible that such a person still existed.

"You got to stop copying everything I say. Now take a good look at it and tell me what it's for."

He handed it to her and she held it up close to her face. He struck another match.

"It won't stop moving."

He grabbed her hand and held it still.

"There. How's that?"

She concentrated very hard, staring at the key.

If she gets any closer, Bobby thought, she's going to get it stuck up her nose.

"I don't think it goes to our house," she said. "Maybe it's for someplace else."

Bobby took it away from her. What other place would they have? Then it hit him.

"Where's the campaign headquarters?"

"The what?"

"Campaign headquarters," he said. "Where your old man runs the election."

Where he keeps all that money.

"In Germantown," she said after a moment.

Bobby smiled and put the key away.

"Was that okay?" Kimberly asked. "Is that what you wanted?"

"Everything and more," Bobby said. "Now go to sleep."

She lay back against the wall and shut her eyes. Bobby watched her. In the darkness, she looked a little like his own mother, all skinny and strung out, the way she looked the night she died.

You see, Bobby thought, you wait long enough and your whole goddamn life comes around again, just like reruns on TV.

"We never did get to see him," Susan said. She was on the couch in the living room. He was in the kitchen opening beers.

"What?"

"We never saw Tim," she said.

Paige brought her one and drank some of his. He was still trying to think of a way to talk to her about Jacob Cross. He thought it would be easy but he was wrong.

"We'll see him when he's better."

Susan sipped her beer. "I feel so useless."

She knew exactly what she was doing. It was a simple equation: Tim equaled Kimberly. If Tim survived, then so would Kimberly. She had to laugh at herself for being so transparent and wondered if Paige could see it, too. If he did, she thought, he wouldn't say anything. He was too polite for that. Or too self-contained. Like a black hole. No light escaped from him.

Or preoccupied. He seemed to be worried about something, and she wanted him to get to it. I used to be so patient, too.

"Pat," she said, "why don't you sit down and tell me what's on your mind."

Paige sat next to her and decided that the simplest way was the best. Nice short declarative sentences.

"I think Jacob Cross knows the kidnapper," he said. "There's a possibility that your husband knows him, too."

It took a moment for her to move beyond the shock of what he said. On the surface, it made no sense. But then doubt crept in and left her dreading what he might say next.

She did a neat sidestep, separating the two in her mind.

"Are you sure about Jacob?"

"I'm pretty sure," Paige said. Even if nobody else is. He told her what he knew about the photograph and the car. As he explained it to her, he became more and more convinced that his theory was right. Cross was involved. The only question was to what degree.

"And Jim?"

"I don't know. You tell me."

She laughed in amazement. "You want to know if my husband would allow his own daughter to be kidnapped just to win an election?"

"Not exactly. If he had no other choice, would he keep his mouth shut and play it out?"

She thought it through. Jim was basically an adolescent, willing to believe anything that fed his own sense of invulnerability. If Cross had convinced him that he could win by a landslide *and* get his daughter back safe, no matter how preposterous that promise might be, Jim would believe it unconditionally and never look back.

What sort of people had they become?

"If Jacob Cross told him it was the best thing to do, yes, I think he would. But you don't know if it's true or not. You're just guessing."

Paige shook his head.

"I'm not guessing about Cross."

"Jim wouldn't tell you, even if it were true. He wouldn't say a word. And there won't be any record of it, either. He'll keep it locked away in his head. So would Jacob."

"Do you know any of Cross's friends, anybody who could handle something like this?"

"He hasn't got any friends. He has alliances. You won't be able to touch him."

"There has to be a way. I just don't know what it is right now."

There was a way, one that Susan was just now beginning to consider. If it turned out to be true.

When the time comes, she thought, I'll take care of Jacob Cross myself.

She woke up on the couch. First there was only darkness, then shadows, then the light from the street, grim and without warmth, as it passed through the window shades. She thought it was morning. She lifted the shade and looked outside. It was the middle of the night.

Susan lay back down and pushed her head deeper in the pillow and tried to pretend that things were somehow different than they were. She was twelve and asleep in her room, visions of poets behind rose-colored curtains keeping her awake. She was in college and had spent the evening in a stranger's bed, and now she was back in her own apartment, the hot rush of excitement fading into soft memory. She was in her house and Kimberly was just down the hall. If she closed her eyes tight, she could still believe her daughter was a little girl who dreamed of poets the way her mother had done.

But that wasn't where she was at all.

She was sleeping on the couch in a cop's house, and she wondered if she would sleep in her own bed with those same feelings of innocence ever again.

The sense of loss was like a blow to the heart, a single sharp jab that left a bruise she was sure everyone could see. How had she lived so long and not known what was right there in front of her? How could she have lied to herself so completely? How could she have been so damned alone and not recognized it?

God, she thought, I'm so tired of being alone.

She sat up, unsure of what she was doing but thinking only that she had to do something, had to move to keep the feeling of defeat from overwhelming her. She kicked the sheet from her legs and walked toward the stairs.

She tripped on the first step and caught herself. It was like something out of a movie. The heroine finally makes her big romantic move and falls flat on her face. She covered her mouth with one hand to keep from laughing out loud.

Is that the kind of move I'm making? She climbed the stairs slowly, thinking that it had nothing to do with romance and everything to do with escape. A few quick steps and the lady's troubles would be gone for a few minutes, an hour, for the time it took for her to pretend that they didn't exist.

More false hope. More lies.

She reached the top of the stairs.

No, she thought, when it comes—if it comes at all— I want it to be real. Not an escape but a destination.

She went quietly back down the stairs to the couch and tried to fall asleep again, wondering what Paige would have thought if she'd stepped into his room.

And Paige, awake in his room, hearing the sound of her footsteps retreating down the stairs, thought that he wouldn't have had the courage to have come even that far and certainly none of the sense to go no farther.

28

They moved Wayne Cochran into a private room for the interrogation. The surgery seemed to have shrunk him. His unshaven face had lost some of its puffiness, and he looked like a dead rat. Jeffers had ordered him handcuffed to the bed. Paige thought it was a bit of FBI overkill but Jeffers insisted.

Cochran wasn't going anywhere. He had two IVs stuck in him, one in each arm. His left leg was swollen from the surgery, and his foot was in a cast. The bullet had shattered his heel. The surgeons had reconstructed the bone and inserted two steel pegs in his foot to hold it together.

Paige was there, so was Glover. Jeffers brought another agent as well as a stenographer. The stenographer took the only chair. Susan sat by herself in the waiting room. She had been quiet that morning, and Paige hadn't pressed her or made any demands beyond asking if she wanted some eggs for breakfast. She didn't.

Wayne Cochran was wide awake. He looked at Paige and then looked hard at Jeffers.

His first words were "Who the fuck are you?"

"FBI."

Cochran grunted. "Suck my dick."

The stenographer, a young man in his early twenties, wearing jeans and a bright yellow sport coat, spoke up.

"Should I take that down?"

"Every word," Jeffers said. "They're priceless."

The stenographer grinned and his fingers danced over his machine.

"Who wants to read him his rights?" Jeffers asked.

When nobody volunteered, Jeffers shrugged and did it himself. When he finished, he asked Cochran once more if he wanted a lawyer present during questioning.

"I got a lawyer," Cochran said.

"Is that Mr. Grossman?"

"That's right."

"He's not coming."

Cochran narrowed his eyes and flapped his tongue over his lower lip before speaking.

"That's a bunch of bullshit," he said. "I called his office this morning."

"And then he called me," Jeffers said. "He says you haven't paid your last bill, and he doesn't want your business. He said to tell you good luck."

"You're lying."

Jeffers took the phone off the nightstand and set it on the bed. "Give him another call. Maybe he's changed his mind."

Cochran glared at the agent. "I can't call him. I got these fucking cuffs." He raised his arm and jangled the cuffs.

"You're in real sorry shape," Jeffers said and started to punch in the number.

"Forget it," Cochran said.

"You mean you don't want a lawyer?"

"You heard me."

Jeffers replaced the phone. "If you want a public defender, I can get you one of those."

Cochran shook his head. "They don't do shit."

"So you don't want one at all?"

"I don't want anything from you assholes. I want you to get the fuck away from me."

"How about I tell you what you're facing and then you make the decision," Jeffers said. He took out a small notebook and began to read. "Let's see, we got possession of a controlled substance, possession of a controlled substance with intent to distribute, assault on a minor, battery of same, wreckless endangerment, accessory to armed robbery, and accessory to murder. Your mother would be proud."

"Fuck you," Cochran said.

Paige leaned across the bed so his face was about a foot from Cochran's.

"Want to know how Tim's doing, Wayne?" Paige asked. "Want to know what they're going to do to you in the joint?"

Cochran whipped his head around, spit flying across the pillow.

"I ain't talking to you!" he screamed at Paige. He shook his head back and forth and rattled the cuffs. "I ain't talking to this asshole! I ain't talking to any of you! Get out of here! All of you get the fuck out of here!"

Jeffers put away his notebook.

"You are one miserable piece of shit," he said to Cochran. "Interview's over. Let's go."

In the waiting room, Jeffers scratched the top of his head and said to no one in particular, "That boy's dumber than a blind cow."

Paige stood beside him. "Did his lawyer really call you this morning?"

"Hell, yes. He was beside himself with remorse. Cochran wasn't his usual type of client. He said he drew the line at child molesting.'' Jeffers smiled. ''The moral high ground.''

Susan was suddenly between them.

''Did he tell you anything?''

''Nothing,'' Paige said. ''We'll have to wait for Tim.''

Susan spoke very deliberately.

''That man in there,'' she said, ''does he know who kidnapped Kimberly?''

''Probably,'' Paige said. ''But if he doesn't want to talk to us, he doesn't have to.''

''Then let me talk to him,'' she said.

Jeffers looked at Paige and then at Susan.

''Why not?'' He motioned for the stenographer.

''No,'' Susan said firmly. ''I want to see him alone.''

''I can't do that,'' Jeffers told her. ''He's in custody and anything he says has to be said for the record. I don't make the rules, Mrs. Morbach, I just play by them.''

''Let her talk to him,'' Paige said. ''If it blows up later, I'll take the responsibility.''

Jeffers took hold of his elbow and led him a few feet away.

''Either you know something I don't,'' he said, ''or you're dumber than that cud chewer in there.''

''Just let her do it. I'll cover you.''

''You know, if I'd even thought about something like this twenty years ago, they'd have had me chasing sheep rustlers in Montana. Do you know what you're doing?''

''More or less.''

''Christ Almighty,'' Jeffers said, ''an honest man.'' He dug at the carpet with the heel of his shoe. ''I'm going to take that stenographer downstairs for a cup of coffee. Maybe I'll ask him where he buys his wardrobe. Mine could use some sprucing up. You get it done in ten minutes and I don't want to hear anything more about it unless you land on Boardwalk.''

Paige grabbed Susan and took her down the hall to Cochran's room.

"You got ten minutes," he said. "I'll wait here."

At first, Susan thought he was asleep. Cochran raised his head a few inches off the pillow and sneered.

"Who the fuck are you?"

"I'm Susan Morbach—Kimberly Morbach's mother. They told me you could help get my daughter back."

"They told you wrong, lady. I don't know shit about your daughter, so why don't you just turn your ass around and get out of my room. And tell those cocksuckers to take these cuffs off of me. I got some calls to make."

Cochran rattled his cuffs at her and the noise made her jump. He laughed and shook them again but she didn't jump the second time. Instead, she moved closer to the bed.

"What the fuck are you gonna do?"

Susan pulled a chair over and sat down. She was just about eye level with him and was surprised at how frightened and weak he looked. Another boogeyman bites the dust, she thought.

"Hey," Cochran yelled. "Somebody get this bitch out of here!"

Susan waited patiently for him to stop yelling, and then she said, "I'm not leaving until you tell me what I want to know."

"Oh yeah? Well, fuck you!"

She inched forward and spoke very quietly. Her eyes never left his.

"I want to hear about the man who kidnapped my daughter," she said. "But first I'm going to explain to you why you should tell me what you know."

Cochran's expression changed. He was suddenly very interested.

"Is this some kind of deal?"

Susan wanted to smile but didn't.

"It's a deal," she said.

Twelve minutes later, she handed Paige a piece of paper. There was a name and address written on it.

"What's this?"

"The kidnapper. It's what you've been looking for, isn't it?"

Paige didn't recognize the name but he knew the address. It was six blocks from his house.

29

"**W**e're going to do this small," Jeffers said.

"No air cover?" Teets asked. "Damn."

The area was cordoned off for a four-block radius, two cars at each intersection. A total of twelve men made up the primary assault team, seven of them from the Bureau, not including a hostage negotiating team that had flown in from Washington. Philadelphia provided crowd control and two Special Patrol Bureau—the department's SWAT team—snipers.

The apartment house was a three-story brick tenement on the corner of Third Street and Carpenter—the black section of Queen Village—flanked on both sides by other tenements. A trash-filled empty lot separated the buildings from the rest of the block. A faded red stucco warehouse sat directly across the street; the other corner belonged to public housing, a complex of one-story apartments that looked like a failing elementary school, redbrick walls separated by graffiti-covered slabs of concrete. There was a small grocery store on the other corner opposite the projects.

There were three apartments in the building, but only the first and third floors were occupied. Using a reverse directory, they called Bobby Radcliff's apartment. No one answered. The tenant on the first floor, an elderly black woman named Chardell, hadn't seen or heard anyone in the apartment for several days. The owner of the grocery store said he knew Bobby but hadn't seen him around, either. The two SWAT team snipers—one on the roof of the warehouse across the street, the other on the apartment roof—reported no activity.

"I don't think he's there," Paige said.

"I don't think he is, either," Jeffers said. "But if he is, I don't want to give him time to react."

What he meant was, he didn't want to give Bobby the opportunity to shoot Kimberly Morbach before they hit the front door.

Four agents were assigned to cover the building—one on the rear fire escape, one at the front door, and one each to cover the first two floors. Paige, Teets, Rudolph, plus Jeffers and two other agents would take the apartment.

The tenant on the first floor supplied them with the basic layout of the apartment—they were all the same. They managed to reach the owner of the building—he lived in Sarasota—but it took another hour to get copies of the blueprints, originally filed in 1953 when the building was converted to apartments.

The owner supplied some extra detail but not much. He owned seventeen other buildings in the area and kept getting them confused.

He kept asking if they were going to bomb the building.

Susan was left in the care of one of the policewomen. The senator was en route but was stuck in the traffic that had backed up around the closed-off streets. The day was hot, the humidity high. Crowds quickly gathered at the police lines, blocking the streets. At first, the police tried to keep them clear but eventually gave up.

Teets took one look at the crowd as the assault team assembled three blocks from the apartment.

"This is better than the Mummers' Parade. They think we're the entertainment."

"Okay," Jeffers said. "I'm going to go over this one more time, and if you got any questions you better ask them now."

Jeffers wore a black flak vest under his FBI windbreaker, which made him appear twice as large as usual. They all wore vests. Paige wanted to rip his off and leave it behind. Instead, he pushed it away from his chest to let some air in behind it. He'd had it on for less than ten minutes, and already his shirt was soaked with sweat.

"You four will move in first," Jeffers said, addressing his agents. "If the old lady pops her head out, move her back inside quickly and quietly. Stay on the stairwells.

"We're going to split the entry sequence down the middle—Paige, you and your men on one side, we'll take the other. I want no shooting outside the apartment unless he starts it."

He looked at Paige. "We're the first ones in. If you see him and you've got a clean shot, I want you to take him out. Don't wait for me or anybody." He turned to his own agents. "You two take the living room. Stay there no matter what else happens." He jabbed a finger at Teets and Rudolph. "You two will follow us down the hall to the bedroom. Your job is backup, and I mean backup. I don't want anybody shooting over my head."

"What if you're on the floor, gut-shot, bleeding all over the place?" Teets asked. "Can I shoot him then?"

Jeffers managed a tight smile. "Yes, detective, you can shoot him then. Any more questions? Thirty seconds to secure the floors. That's it. Then we move in. All right? Let's go."

"How we getting there?" Teets asked.

"We're going to walk."

"Just like the Wild West," Teets said. "Okay, boys and girls. Let's saddle up and move out."

Teets had it right, Paige thought. They walked through the dusty deserted streets, faces peering down at them from windows and doorways, waving, a couple of raised fists, no cheering, a cop standing guard in the middle of each block. It was just like a movie. All they needed was a soundtrack.

Paige hadn't gone more than a block before the dust covered his shoes and slacks and clung to his skin. Mingled with his sweat, it formed miniature rivers of mud on his face and hands. He felt dirty, like he'd been working in a cornfield all day.

But not nervous. *Remote* was the word. Walking as if his brain was about ten feet behind him watching every step, trying not to think about anything except the world right in front of him. A woman reporter once told him she thought it was a very nonnegative energy approach. He'd asked her for an explanation and she said it was really a question of doing rather than trying. Paige didn't get that either. The reporter made a face and told him to look into Scientology sometime.

He didn't need Scientology to tell him what to do. He just wanted to stay alive.

Jeffers stopped them a block from the corner of Carpenter and let the four agents move ahead. He gave the agents one minute to get in place. They stopped for a few brief seconds in front of the entrance to the corner store. The owner looked at Paige, gave him a brief nod, and ducked down behind the counter.

Jeffers checked his watch, raised his fist, and pumped it twice in the air.

Paige went in first, taking the steps two at a time, not running but climbing swiftly and steadily, with Jeffers and the others right behind. Up to the second floor, a short turn on the stairs, and on to the third floor.

Then they were in the hallway, the only light coming from a window at the end, and Paige watched their shadows grow long then shorten suddenly as they passed beyond the reach of the sun. They lined up on either side of the door, and one of the agents tried the door. The handle turned, but the door didn't budge.

The other one held a small squat battering ram, stepped back several feet, and swung it at the door. The door snapped, splinters of wood flying through the air. He hit it again and the door opened with a crash, bouncing off the inside wall and then coming back hard. Jeffers pushed it away with his hand and ran into the apartment, Paige right behind him.

He moves fast for somebody that big, Paige thought, and then he was inside and moving fast, catching only glimpses of the living room as they passed through it, a ten-speed on the couch, free weights in one corner, a denim jacket tossed casually on the floor, a backpack hung on a nail. Down the hall, past one door on his left. He kicked open the door. Bathroom.

A quick scan, no more than a few seconds, and he was running for the last door, telling Jeffers with his eyes to go in, not to wait, raising his gun up high so he could get a clean shot, and then Jeffers pushed open the door and careened to his right, giving Paige a clear field of fire, letting Paige take it if he could, a perfect shot.

Of an empty bed.

A momentary pause, like a deep exhaling of breath; then Jeffers kicked open the closet with his foot. He lowered his gun.

"Tell them to double-check everything. I don't want any surprises."

Paige felt himself slowing down, the rush of adrenaline fading, leaving a feeling of weakness that passed through him as he retraced his route methodically, stepping past Teets on his way to recheck the bathroom, only to find Rudolph there ahead of him, pulling back the shower and shaking his head.

"We're all clear out here," one of the agents yelled, and Paige stuck his gun in his holster and leaned against the wall. Teets ambled by, smiling at him.

"Nice party," he said. "No cake and cookies."

Jeffers walked up behind Teets, just as Rudolph came out of the bathroom. He pointed at Rudolph.

"Go get Mrs. Morbach. Teets, you take the living room and send Wallace back here."

"Which one is he?"

Jeffers grinned. "The one in the white shirt."

"Oh, yeah," Teets said, "the sharp dresser."

"Let's do the bedroom," Jeffers said. Paige followed him back. Jeffers slipped on a pair of plastic gloves. Paige did the same.

They were lifting the mattress off the bed when Agent Wallace appeared in the doorway.

"Get the crime scene people up here," Jeffers ordered. "You work with them, make sure they don't miss anything."

"They won't miss anything," Paige said after the agent had gone.

"I know that. I just said it to give him something to worry about."

A few minutes later, Teets stuck his head in the door.

"She's here."

"She find anything?" Paige asked.

"Looks like."

"Go ahead," Jeffers told him.

Susan was standing in the middle of the room with a grim expression. The policewoman was with her. She looked at Paige.

"The bike," she said. "And the backpack. I think that's all she took with her."

"Any clothes?"

Susan shook her head.

"Why don't you go back down to the car? It's going to be a while."

"I'd rather stay here," she said. "I'll keep out of your way."

"Wait in the kitchen."

"Can I take the backpack? I just want to hold it."

Paige glanced at one of the FBI agents.

"Is that okay?"

"No," the agent said.

Susan went into the kitchen.

Teets spoke up. He was sitting on the floor by the television, a cardboard liquor carton at his feet.

"I got a shitload of videotapes over here," he said. "If anybody's interested."

"Any titles?"

"Not that I can see. Anybody want a look?"

"We'll run them tonight."

"No matinee?"

"Tonight."

"Last time I come to one of your parties," Teets said.

Paige kept looking for papers, anything with a name on it. He was searching randomly, opening drawers, sifting through piles of magazines, opening and closing books almost before he'd had a chance to look through them. He had no plan, only this overwhelming need to find something.

He looked at Susan. She had her arms wrapped around the backpack, staring at the floor.

He stopped what he was doing and went back to the bedroom.

"I got something interesting," Jeffers said. "Take a look."

He was pointing to the edge of the mattress, a small section of cording on one corner that looked like it had been pulled out and then restitched. It was a pretty good job; unless you were really looking for it, you wouldn't notice the difference.

"You got a knife?"

"No."

Jeffers started to laugh.

"I used to carry a knife all the time when I was growing up."

"What happened?"

"Got in too many knife fights. I'll be right back."

Paige tugged at the thread, worrying it with his fingers. It was tough. The son of a bitch knew what he was doing. Maybe he was a surgeon.

Jeffers came in carrying an eight-inch butcher knife.

"The smallest I could find." He hooked the blade under the first two loops and popped them open. Paige tried to rip the rest, but they wouldn't budge. Jeffers sawed through them and the corner of the mattress burst open. Paige stuck his hand inside and worked it around.

"I knew a bad guy once, chopped up his wife and stuffed his mattress with her," Jeffers offered. "Said he slept like a baby knowing she was next to him."

Paige found a fat envelope. His fingers closed around the edge and dragged it out.

The envelope was thick with papers and carried no address on the outside. Paige undid the clasp and dumped the contents on the mattress. It was all a jumble at first. Photographs of a woman and a dark-skinned man thrusting a beer bottle at the camera. Another picture of the same woman with a young boy under one arm, the other hand pulling down the top of her dress to expose what looked like a tattoo. It was so small that Paige couldn't tell what it was. He pushed the pictures aside.

Underneath he found a pair of driver's licenses, one

from Florida, the other from Michigan, a handful of faded newspaper clippings and more papers held together with a big paper clip. They looked like court documents. Jeffers picked up the papers while Paige looked at the licenses.

The face was what he had imagined. Thin, bony, longish hair, bright animated eyes and a hard little mouth. He wore a tie and a sport coat in both pictures, the knot a little too big and the collar a little too wide. The one from Florida said his name was Robert Purdue; for the Michigan license, he was Robert Penn.

Paige read the names again. He had trouble believing it at first but then he realized he was right.

The guy named himself after colleges.

Jeffers skimmed the papers quickly and pulled one document out of the bunch and read it carefully. When he was done, he handed it to Paige. It was from the Child Welfare Department of Broward County, Florida.

"Looks like we got ourselves the original bad seed," Jeffers said and handed him the report.

Paige was just getting to the part where it described how Robert Beauchamp, age thirteen, killed his mother and four men by injecting them with rat poison when he heard Senator Morbach in the living room demanding to know just what in the hell was going on.

"You let me handle this," Jeffers said.

"Go ahead. You're the one who invited him."

"Mea culpa," Jeffers said.

Paige thought he could stay away. Then he heard Susan's voice and he got up slowly from the floor, telling himself that it wasn't his fight, that his fight was here, in this room, with the man whose life was now spread out before him on the bed, and then he heard her voice again and he walked down the hall to the living room and stopped at the doorway, as far as he thought he ought to go.

The senator stood in the middle of the room, the finger

of one hand punching holes in the air. Everything came to
a stop.

Susan glanced at him and Morbach turned at the same
time, his face twitching with disgust. Jackson stood guard
behind him.

"What are you doing here?"

"I work here," Paige said.

"Jim," Susan said to her husband, "I think we should
leave and let these men do their job."

"Is that what you think?" Morbach said, turning on
her. "Since when did screwing you get to be part of his
job?"

Susan slapped him. The blow came so quickly that
Paige saw only a blur of motion. Morbach raised his hand,
and Paige came off the doorway fast, taking the distance
between them in two long steps, his own hand closing
around the senator's wrist, pulling his arm down and bringing them within inches of each other, close enough for him
to see the hatred in Morbach's eyes and the bright pink
mark on his cheek, the outline of her fingers clearly visible.

"Don't," Paige said, and held onto his arm until he
felt the tension ease away.

He let go and stepped back, rocking slightly on his
heels, waiting, waiting.

Morbach brought his other hand around in a long overhead swing. Paige blocked it with his left and then swung
his right up from the floor, putting his weight behind it,
and punched Morbach just below his ear, aiming for an
imaginary spot on the other side of his skull, following
through, the pain of the impact reverberating down the
length of his arm.

Morbach fell against Jackson and then slid to the floor.

The room erupted into motion and noise. Teets pushed
Paige back, holding his arms down, and then Rudolph was
there and they were leading him away. He fought them at
first, but not very hard. He soon gave up, his anger gone.

"Outstanding," Teets said. "You on a real roll today." He grinned when he said it, and it made Paige feel a little better but not much.

Jeffers just looked depressed. He pointed at Paige and then at Susan.

"You two. Out of here. Now."

Jackson made a move as if to stop him but thought better of it and stepped aside. Susan followed right behind him. Paige hurried down the stairs and out onto the sidewalk, where he paused to light a cigarette. Susan walked right past him. He called to her, but she didn't stop. He noticed that she had Kimberly's knapsack. He didn't know how she'd managed to steal it from the FBI, but he was definitely impressed.

He caught up with her and put his hand on her arm. She shook it off violently, swinging the knapsack at him.

"Don't touch me," she said. "Just . . . don't."

"Look, I'm sorry. He didn't give me much choice."

Susan glared at him.

"That's a lot of crap. You had a choice. You could've stayed out of it. It wasn't your fight."

"I guess I thought it was."

Susan dropped the knapsack. She waved her fists at him, pounding at the space between them.

"You guessed wrong!" she shouted. "You're not my husband! *He's* my husband, and what happened back there was between us and nobody else! I don't know who I'm madder at—you or him! Or me! For letting things get this far!"

She picked up the knapsack and started walking.

"Where are you going?"

"Home," she yelled.

"Which one?"

Susan stopped.

"Home," she said, turning to face him so he could

see clearly what he'd done. "Where I used to live before all of *this*."

Susan kept the knapsack between them on the way home and didn't say anything more. Not that he expected it. More than once, he thought she might ask him to stop the car so she could walk or catch a taxi or maybe even flag down a passing motorist, anything just to get away from him. She punished him with silence instead.

He pulled into the driveway and stopped behind the FBI car parked in front of the house. Paige saw the curtains move in one of the downstairs windows. The door opened and an agent stepped outside. Susan made no effort to get out of the car. She seemed to be waiting for him to say something.

"We're here."

"I can see that." She looked at the backpack. "I probably owe you an apology for what I said back there."

"You don't owe me anything," he said stubbornly. It was petulant and stupid, but he couldn't think of any other way to be at the moment.

"Right," she said and opened the door.

Paige grabbed the knapsack and wouldn't let go.

"Wait a minute."

"For what? So you can keep acting like a jerk? No thanks."

"I'll stop being a jerk," he said and let go. "How's that?"

Susan didn't smile.

"I think you're going to need a little more practice."

She pushed the door open with her foot but didn't get out.

"I know why you hit him," she said. "At least I think I know. You were trying to protect me. Maybe it was a little more than that, but that was a big part of it. What you have to understand is I don't need protecting right now.

What I need now is a friend. Do you want to be my friend, Pat? Can you live with that?''

"I don't know."

"Try."

"How many tries do I get?"

"Not that many."

She pulled the knapsack to her and stared at the house.

"I want to tell you something, so maybe you'll understand."

"Okay."

"You never asked me how I got the address."

He'd forgotten all about it.

"I figured you'd tell me when you wanted to."

Susan didn't respond.

"You want to tell me now?"

The truth was he wasn't sure he wanted to know. The possibilities went into areas that might be better left alone. Did she bribe him? Did she promise him something she couldn't or wouldn't deliver?

"I told him I'd have him killed," Susan said. "I said that if he knew anything that would help get my daughter back and he didn't tell me, he'd go to prison. And I'd find somebody there to do it. I work with prisoners all the time. I know what goes on. It wouldn't be that hard. I gave him a couple names. He believed me. I made him believe me.

"I just wanted you to know who you're dealing with." She got out and closed the door. He watched her enter the house and sat in the car, thinking he was glad she left before he had the chance to say anything. Out of all the responses that came to mind, he knew the one that was closest to the truth, the one that would have surprised her the most. Or perhaps not.

He thought it was a great idea. He wished he'd come up with it first.

Paige ate a late lunch at Bob's Big Boy and drove back to the Roundhouse. It was more prudent than going to the apartment or to Cross's house. He didn't expect to find anybody at headquarters, but Teets was there with one of Jeffers's agents watching the videotapes.

"How's the arm, champ?" Teets asked.

"I think I broke a knuckle," Paige said. He wasn't joking. The third knuckle of his hand was red and swollen, and it hurt like crazy. Teets glanced at it and clicked his tongue.

"It's a proven fact. Politicians got harder heads than most normal people. You might want to write that down."

"I'll remember it. What have you got?"

Teets pushed a cassette into the VCR and turned it on.

"It's a po-lice drama," he said, exaggerating the word. "Our boy's the star."

The film was only fifteen minutes long, and it wasn't half bad. The acting was amateurish, and the sets looked like they were put together in somebody's garage, but it held his interest more than he thought it would. He wasn't sure he liked it, but that really wasn't the point. He was a cop and cops weren't supposed to like movies where they hung innocent civilians in their jail cells.

"I wouldn't have done anything like that," Teets said when it was over.

"No honest cop would," the FBI agent offered.

"Hell, no," Teets said. "I'd have shot the son of a bitch in the alley, told everybody he had a knife. Couple days off for the hearing board and I'd be rollin' again."

"He's only joking," Paige said, but the agent didn't look like he believed him.

"What else is in there?"

"Don't know. We just got here."

They ran through the tapes. There were newscasts of the first robbery, some television shows, and a couple of bootlegged feature films. Teets popped in the last tape, waited for it to start, and then laughed out loud.

"Goddamn," he said. "Dirty movies. I just knew we'd find something good in here."

It was better than good.

It was Cheryl Silverman.

30

They spent the day by the river. In the morning they hung around Penn's Landing, where Bobby dug through trash cans looking for leftovers. He thought the whole thing was funny; he had four grand in his back pocket and he was scrounging for food. Kimberly ate very little, picking at some fried chicken that he'd pulled from one of the cans.

"Eat," he told her. "You might not get any more today."

"I don't like it," she said.

"I don't like it, either, but I'm eating it."

"It makes me sick," she said and tossed it on the ground.

Bobby picked up the scraps. She had to eat. Maybe he'd find something else for her later.

When more people began to show up on the Landing, they moved to Independence Hall and found a place where they could stretch out on the grass and sleep for a while. Kimberly wasn't sleepy, so he fed her some more cough medicine and a couple of pills and she mellowed right out. It seemed to help her cough, too.

She still looked like death, though. Hair chopped off and plastered to her skull, no color in her face except for the dirt and the bruises, which had turned a sickly shade of yellow, and eyes so sunken and bloodshot they looked like the bottom of a paint can. Nobody would recognize her now, he thought. He didn't even recognize her.

Bobby looked down at her. "I think you need to eat some more, Butch."

"What?"

"Never mind. Go to sleep."

She moved closer to him and laid her head on her hands and did what she was told.

Bobby tried to think about what he was going to do next, whether he was still going to use the trooper's car or risk stealing another one, when he was going to pay a visit to the senator's campaign headquarters, and how he was going to arrange for the final payoff.

He had a general outline in mind, but trying to set up a timetable and planning for contingencies was something else. The more he tried to work it out, the more jumbled it became. His brain wouldn't work right. Plans and ideas floated around, and every time he tried to grab one, it just seemed to float higher and higher out of his reach. Finally, he gave up and went to sleep. Something would come to him.

He woke with the sun beating down and the hot, sticky feeling of sweat rolling over the corners of his mouth, the salt stinging his cracked lips. Bobby wiped it away with the back of his hand, tasting the remnants of the chicken that was still on his fingers, and sat up. The sun was overhead and he guessed it was early afternoon, one o'clock, maybe two. He wished he'd stolen the trooper's watch as well as his car.

His stomach growled, and he knew he was going to have to get some more food soon. There were times, and this was one of them, that he hated his body, hated its needs and demands. He wished he'd been born a robot, and then he wouldn't have to worry about all this petty shit. He could just cruise along and watch all the humans drive themselves nuts.

But that just ain't the way it is, amigo.

He shook Kimberly's arm.

"Let's go. It's lunchtime."

Bobby decided he could risk a trip to South Street, maybe pick up something from one of the sidewalk windows or maybe even a quick visit to his apartment, change his clothes, get a shower, clean the girl up, stop feeling like something the cat left behind the bed. He pulled Kimberly to her feet. She was still half asleep.

"My stomach hurts," she said.

"We'll take care of it," he told her.

They walked up Front Street. He was doing fine until he saw the crowd and then the cop cars, two of them parked nose-to-nose blocking off the street.

Bobby made a quick turn around and headed back to the river. He knew exactly what the cops were doing, and they weren't waiting for the lunch whistle.

They had found the apartment, and that meant they had found Tim. Or maybe his fat, greasy uncle gave them the address. While he'd been dicking around, lying in the sun, the whole world had been beating down his door.

Well, fuck me, Bobby thought. It put a whole new slant on things. Not that he had to change his plans completely. All he'd have to do was speed them up a bit, shift things around, pull a little razzle-dazzle at the end.

Fuck 'em, he decided, Fuck 'em all.

It was popcorn time.

He'd get the money and the girl and settle this whole thing up in a blaze of glory.

Paige parked beside the little convertible in Cheryl Silverman's driveway just before dark. The front door was open, and he looked in through the screen. For someone who drank as much as she did, the house was remarkably neat and clean. He wondered if she had a maid who followed her around the house, picking up the debris.

He was doing the maid's job now, bringing her the tape, one more thing she'd dropped.

Paige knocked several times and waited. He knocked again and heard her call.

"Back here," she yelled. "On the patio."

Paige found his way to the back of the house.

Cheryl Silverman was sitting on a chaise next to the pool, a drink in one hand and a green glass pitcher on a glass-topped table beside her. She wore a pink bathrobe, open to her crotch. No underwear. She didn't bother to close the robe.

"Well, if it ain't the Boy Scout leader. Come to get your merit badge? That's too bad. I'm all out. Want a drink?"

She sat facing the pool. The underwater lights tainted her skin. It looked unreal.

"I hear old Jacob got his ass fried," she said. "Couldn't happen to a nicer guy. You want a drink? I make a helluva margarita."

"No thanks."

"I forget. Boy Scouts don't drink. What do Boy Scouts do these days anyway?"

Paige saw that the pitcher was almost empty.

He pulled a chair next to the chaise and dropped the tape on the table. Cheryl ignored it.

"You help old ladies a lot?"

"Sometimes."

"What about young ones? Which would you rather help, an old biddy or me?"

"That's a tough question."

"No it's not. Not unless you're a faggot."

She drained her glass and poured another one, emptying the pitcher.

"Are you a faggot, Mr. Boy Scout leader? My husband's a faggot. A cocksucking, shit-eating, lowlife, ass-biting faggot." She raised her glass. "Cheers. I got my divorce papers this morning. Hand-delivered by some lawyer dink. I told him to kiss my butt. He didn't take me up on it."

Paige reached for the tape. She grabbed his hand and put it on her left breast.

"Go ahead, squeeze it, tell me if you'd divorce a set of tits like this."

She pressed his palm against her breast and pumped his fingers. He gave her an approving smile. She nodded her head in vigorous agreement.

"You're damn right you wouldn't," she said and tossed his hand away. Paige picked up the tape.

Cheryl squinted over the glass.

"Just what the hell are you doing here anyway?"

"We found this tape."

"Well, good for you. Who gives a shit?"

"You're in it."

She put her drink down.

"You don't say. Let me see that."

Paige hesitated, then handed her the tape. She looked at it carefully and then threw it across the patio. She was aiming for the pool but missed. It struck a chair and crashed on the flagstones.

"Oops," she said.

Paige retrieved the tape.

"What can you tell me about it?"

"What's the matter, you never seen people fuck before? That's it, isn't it? The one with me and the lawn doctor? Too bad we don't get our milk delivered anymore, you could've had a hot double feature."

"Do you know who took it?"

"Of course I know."

He took a photograph from his jacket pocket, a blowup they'd made from Bobby's Florida license.

"Is this him?"

Cheryl grabbed the picture and stared at it hard. When she was through, she let it drop. Paige picked it up. I *am* doing the maid's work.

"That's him," she said. She drank some more.

"How'd you meet him?"

"He brought it around one day."

"How long ago?"

"A few months. I don't keep track."

"Did he ask for money?"

"Are you kidding? What do you think he asked for?" Paige nodded.

"I gave it to him, too. He wasn't very good. He kept staring at me. Made me feel like a goddamn bug."

"Did he tell you who he made it for?"

"I figured he did it for my faggot husband."

"Did he tell you that?"

"He didn't tell me shit."

"What about your husband?"

"Al didn't tell me shit, either. He just punched my lights out and called me a whore. I'm surprised he didn't invite the rest of the goddamn neighborhood in to watch. That's about his speed."

"Wait a minute," Paige said. "I'm confused here. When did this happen?"

"You're confused? Join the fucking club." She sat up, sloshing some of her drink on her robe. She brushed the spill away and licked it off her fingers.

"Okay, I'll tell you what happened. It's the middle of the night, I'm asleep, and all of a sudden I hear these screams from downstairs. I kick Al and tell him to go check it out. For all I know, there's a squirrel in the fireplace. Al starts yelling for me to get my ass downstairs. And there I am on the TV. Then Al starts swinging and calling me a whore."

She took another drink. "Probably would have killed me if Jacob Cross hadn't shown up."

"Jacob Cross was here?"

"Yup. Said he heard the screams and came right over. Thought somebody was getting murdered. He was right about that."

"He said he heard the screams?"

"That's what he said. The cops came and everything. He scooted them away." She laughed. "Mr. Diplomat."

"And Bobby came to see you after that?"

"Who?"

Paige held up the photo.

"The man who said he made the tape."

"Is that his name? Bobby? That's a Kennedy name, isn't it? He didn't look like a Kennedy. He looked like a twerp."

"When did your husband find the tape?"

"I told you, I don't remember. March, April, something like that."

"And Bobby came by a few weeks later?"

"That's about right."

"That would make it sometime in May?"

"Yeah, I guess so. All I remember is I still looked like shit." She smiled. "From the beating. He didn't seem to care. He said I had a great ass."

"I'd like to talk to your husband about the tape."

"I'd like to talk to that cocksucker, too, but right now he's incommunicado. Won't talk to me, won't see me. Probably wouldn't piss on me if I was dying of thirst."

"Do you know his lawyer's name?"

"I stuck the papers on the refrigerator. That's rich. My mom used to put my school stuff on the refrigerator. I'd say my work has improved since then, wouldn't you?" Her voice had changed, taking on a mean edge, as though she had suddenly sobered up and was seeing everything clearly for the first time. She pointed to the tape. "You going to leave that here?"

"I can't."

"Have to watch it a few more times, check for clues?"

"Something like that," Paige said and stood up. "I'll look for those papers on the way out."

"Suit yourself. But you're missing the best piece of ass you're ever going to have."

"You're probably right."

"Well, fuck you, too," Cheryl said. "And all the rest of your little troopers."

He found the papers and made a note of the attorney's name. When he got to the front porch, he heard a crash coming from the back of the house. It sounded like the glass. He waited a few seconds and heard the pitcher go. Cheryl started yelling. He caught a few words and pulled the front door shut.

Paige moved down the drive, listening to the sound of her voice. By the time he reached his car, he could barely hear her at all.

31

Bobby waited until dark to get the car. His luck held out right up to the moment when he handed the kid a hundred-dollar bill to pay for the parking. The kid looked at the bill and then at Bobby and leaned down lower to get a better look, and Bobby wrapped his hand around the gun stuck between his legs and smiled like a bad comedian.

"You want to hurry it up," he said.

"This is a pretty big bill," the kid said and looked again. "Is she okay? She doesn't look so good."

"You in premed?"

"No."

"Then get my change and shut the fuck up."

The kid held the bill up to the light.

"I don't know," he said. "Maybe I better call somebody. There's a lot of bad money going around these days."

"Suit yourself," Bobby said and snapped back the hammer on the gun. He glanced over at Kimberly.

"Please," she said.

It was the *please* that stopped him.

"This must be your lucky day," he said and slammed his foot down on the accelerator. The wooden barrier broke in half, pieces of it sailing over the hood into the windshield.

He spun the wheel hard. The car struck the side of the booth, tore through the back quarter panel and popped the taillight. Kimberly flung herself on the seat. Bobby turned right onto Broad and then a quick right again onto Locust.

"It's always the assholes," he yelled. "They always got to fuck with you." He drove up the one-way street, pushing to get the lights, cutting through the yellow, working the Ford hard until he got to Sixteenth and took another right.

If he got through town and onto the River Drive, he had maybe another five minutes before he could start to lose himself in the neighborhoods around Gypsy Lane. From there he could wind his way through the back streets into Germantown.

The question was, if he got spotted, what to do about Kimberly?

It was a question he'd been thinking about off and on ever since they'd left the cabin. He didn't want to give her up. Yeah, she whined a little too much, and she didn't know how to take care of herself, but nobody was perfect. Women, especially. They were like little kids, they caused trouble just by being there. But he finally had to admit that Kimberly was a lot less trouble than most.

And she made him feel good.

But then he'd trained her, hadn't he? That was the key. You set down the rules and whacked 'em if they disobeyed. He couldn't figure out why people had so much trouble getting it. They got all hung up on being sensitive and fair, and they didn't understand that people really wanted to be fenced in. They *wanted* somebody to tell them what to do.

What if he just took off with her? What if he just said

fuck it and went south? Wouldn't that just charm the shit out of everybody?

But he couldn't do it in the car he was driving. He'd have to get another one, and he'd have to buy it so he wouldn't have to worry about running a stolen car across country. And the few bucks he'd have left after that wouldn't take them very far, not when you figured the high cost of basic living when you were on the run. And it wouldn't get 'em where they needed to live. Only the money would do that.

He'd get the money first, and then he could do whatever he wanted.

Hell, when you got right down to it, he had more choices than the goddamn president, and he didn't even have to wear a suit.

He got on the River Drive at the Art Museum and cruised up the river to the Girard Avenue Bridge. He crossed over and drove straight into the neighborhood behind the projects on the other side.

He pulled over on one of the side streets. Kimberly still had her face buried in the seat, so he dug his fingers underneath, caught her chin, and brought her up.

"You know where we are?"

Kimberly looked around.

"No."

"That's okay. Tell me where your old man's headquarters is."

"On the Avenue," she said.

"In town?"

"Near the train station I think."

"Truth?"

"Truth."

"Good girl," he said and patted her cheek. It seemed to make her happy.

He parked the car in the small municipal lot at the

train station. There were a lot of cars there, and nobody
was going to notice it except the meter maid and she'd just
keep flagging tickets on it to make her quota and maybe in
a week somebody would get the bright idea that it was the
car everyone was looking for.

He told her he was only going to be a few minutes.

"But I'll be watching," he said. "Just like I always
do. Nobody will bother you."

"I know. I won't do anything."

"I know you won't."

Bobby got the trooper's clothes out of the trunk and
dressed in the backseat. Nobody was going to mistake him
for a cop for very long, but it might give him a few minutes
lead time if he needed it.

Now all he had to worry about was the key. He made
a bargain with himself. If it didn't work, he was gone. If
it worked, he'd play it out.

Bobby crossed the lot and the narrow street behind it
to the back of the building. There were three doors, two
stuck close together and a third on the end. This is just like
a game show, he thought. Which one has the prize?

Not the third one. Bobby tried that first, but the key
didn't fit the lock. He moved on to the other two and tried
the one on the left. The key slipped right in. He turned it
once, and the door opened up.

Okay, he thought, now what's my prize?

A hallway. Cheap drywall job with bad seams and a
circuit box next to the back door. A light in the ceiling
grown dim from the dirty fixture. Another door at the end
and one more halfway down. He went to the door at the
end. Locked. Okay. Try the other door. It opened into a
bathroom.

Pretty standard: a urinal and a stall, sink with a white
Formica top, and a chrome towel rack stuffed with hand
towels. But there was a lot of other stuff lying around,

too—a big can of men's hair spray, a hair dryer by the sink, combs and brushes, shoe polish and buff rag, toothbrush and toothpaste, mouthwash, a laundry box full of nice clean white shirts, charcoal gray suit hanging on a door rack, half a dozen ties: a regular grooming salon.

Bobby was thinking that he might steal the suit and a couple of shirts when he heard the door at the end of the hall open and close. He hid in the stall, balanced on the flimsy seat.

The door opened and he held his breath. The next thing he heard was a zipper coming down and then the sound of somebody pissing in the urinal. He leaned over the top and stared down at the top of Senator Morbach's head. The senator had a neat little bald spot in back that he hid by combing his hair over it. No wonder he needed all that shit, Bobby thought. He brought the gun over the top and stuck it in Morbach's neck.

Morbach jumped back, the stream of urine spilling across the front of his pants, but Bobby stayed with him, digging the gun into his neck so hard that he thought Morbach's head would snap off. Bobby wondered if he was going to scream, and he was all set to belt him across the back of his head. But Morbach was more worried about zipping up his pants.

"It ain't that big," Bobby said.

"Who are you?" Morbach asked, his hands frozen at his crotch.

"Don't you know? I'm the bad guy."

Morbach blanched.

Bobby ducked down quickly and came out of the stall. Morbach faced the urinal but turned his head to watch while Bobby locked the bathroom door.

"This is very uncomfortable," the senator said.

"I'll bet it is."

Bobby unplugged the hair dryer and pushed it off the

counter and into the sink. Then he closed the drain and filled it with water.

"What are you doing?" Morbach asked.

"Over here," Bobby ordered. Morbach turned without thinking.

"Zip up your pants. You look ridiculous."

Bobby took hold of Morbach's hand and plunged it into the sink. "Get a good hold on that," Bobby said, pressing his fingers around the hair dryer.

"There," Bobby said, picking up the plug and moving it close to the outlet. "Now we have a real solid basis for negotiation."

Morbach yanked his arm out of the water, and Bobby stuck the gun against his cheek, twisting it into his skin.

"Back in the pool." Morbach put his hand in the water, staring wide-eyed at the plug in Bobby's fingers.

"Make you nervous?" Bobby asked playfully. He jerked the plug toward the outlet, and Morbach's hand flew out of the sink.

"Just testing," Bobby said and eased his hand back in the water with the barrel of the gun.

"What do you want?" Morbach asked.

Jesus, this guy is dense, Bobby thought. No wonder the government was so fucked up.

"I want my money."

Morbach wiped away the sweat that had begun to bead on his forehead.

"I want my money," Bobby said again.

"I don't have it."

"Sure you do," Bobby said and stabbed at the outlet with the plug, missing the holes by a quarter of an inch. Morbach yelled and pulled his hand out. He fell against the stall.

"Your wife says you got three hundred fifty thousand dollars. She already gave me some of it. I'd like some more." Bobby grinned. "Pretty please?"

"It belongs to the campaign."

"Then the campaign's going to be a little short this year, Pedro. Where is it?"

"It's not here."

Bobby couldn't believe how absolutely dumb this guy was.

"Not here," Bobby echoed. "That's good. I didn't think you kept it in your socks. Now where the fuck is it?"

He moved the gun from his right hand to his left, bent down, and slapped the senator hard across the side of his face. Morbach's head smacked the wall. Bobby pushed his nose into the tile, rubbing it around, watching the cartilage flop back and forth.

"What I see," Bobby said, "is somebody with a bad attitude. What I see is somebody trying to weasel their way out of a really bad situation. You think you can hand me that cheapass shit and I'll nod my head and say, golly, I guess I better just give up 'cause this guy's too smart for me."

Bobby gave his head one final push and let go. Morbach fell back against the stall, one hand covering his face.

Someone knocked on the bathroom door.

Bobby brought the gun down fast, jamming it in the side of Morbach's throat.

The doorknob rattled.

Bobby put a finger to his lips.

"Jim? Are you in there?"

Bobby took his finger away and nodded, letting up the pressure on the gun, just enough so that Morbach could talk without choking to death.

"Who is it?"

"It's Jerry. We're working on the signs for tomorrow, and I need you to look at them."

"Not now."

"I'll wait."

"Not *now*," Morbach said. "Go back. I'll be there in a few minutes."

Silence.

"You all right in there?"

"I'm fine. I'll be out soon."

"All right. But we need you."

Bobby waited until he heard the other door close and then took the gun away.

"You're not as dumb as you look," Bobby said. "Let's see how you do with the money. Is it here?"

"No. I told you. It's not here."

Bobby punched Morbach in the stomach hard enough to hurt him but not enough to do any real damage. Morbach doubled up, struggling to breathe.

"Good. Now let's try it again. Is that your office in there?"

Morbach nodded through the pain.

"You got a safe in there?"

Morbach straightened up. He clutched his stomach with both arms and nodded again.

"Then let's go take a look." He dragged Morbach to the door.

"You're crazy," Morbach gasped.

"Probably," Bobby said. "But I've got the gun, so who's going to argue with me?"

While Bobby watched, Morbach locked the front door to the office. He knelt in front of the safe, turned the dial, and threw open the door.

"See for yourself."

Bobby looked inside. Stacks of paper. Three fat legal binders.

"What's in there?"

"More paper."

Morbach opened them one at a time, watching Bobby's face.

"Where's the money?"

"Where's my daughter?"

Bobby laughed. "You think you're cute, don't you?" He raised the gun, moving it in a tight little circle a few feet in front of Morbach's face. To his surprise, Morbach didn't flinch.

"If you shoot me, you don't get any money. In fact, you get nothing. They know who you are."

Bobby lowered the gun.

Someone knocked on the door. Bobby moved closer, jamming the gun into Morbach's chest. The senator held up his hand.

"Jim, we need you out here." It was the one from the bathroom.

"I'll come out there when I'm ready," Morbach yelled. "You take care of it. That's what I'm paying you for."

Bobby waited a few seconds and lowered the gun.

Morbach closed the safe.

"Now," he said, "let's talk about a deal."

It was a straightforward arrangement with only one minor problem that Bobby could see. Morbach didn't have the money.

"I don't have three hundred fifty thousand dollars anymore, not all of it anyway."

"How much have you got?"

"Half. Maybe a little more."

"Half? What happened to the rest of it?"

"I spent it."

"You spent it? That's almost two hundred grand. What the hell'd you buy?"

"I didn't *buy* anything. I invested it. I had some big losses. Nobody knows about them. I intend to keep it that way."

"Wait a minute," Bobby said. "You stole your own money?"

"It's not really mine."

"Then whose is it?"

"It came from cash contributions. Do you understand? Cash. There are no records of it."

"Your wife knows about it."

"Susan doesn't know as much as she thinks she does. She believes the money's legitimate."

"You mean it's illegal?"

"Yes. It's illegal."

Bobby had a wonderful thought.

"Then nobody's going to miss it when it's gone."

"Of course they'll miss it."

Bobby started to laugh.

"I bet they will. I bet they'll miss it all to hell."

Morbach sat in one of the chairs and put his feet up on the desk.

"I'll give you half," he said.

"Just half? Is that the best you can do?"

"That's a hundred thousand dollars."

"Is that the going price for daughters these days?"

Morbach smiled for the first time.

"It's the going price for mine," he said, and Bobby believed him.

So they cut the deal.

The exchange was out in the open, simple and clear-cut. Bobby would bring Kimberly to the rally on Saturday night. Morbach's aide would bring the money. Bobby got to pick the place. They'd make the trade and go their separate ways. With the thousands of people expected to attend, it would be easy to do and easy for Bobby to slip away in the crowd.

Bobby still didn't like it.

"I don't trust you."

"We don't trust each other and that's why it works. What would I gain by setting a trap? You've still got my daughter. If you had to, you'd shoot her, wouldn't you?"

"Yes, I would."

"That's your guarantee."

"What is? Pardon me, but I don't think you give a rat's ass about her one way or the other. Maybe you'd *like* me to shoot her." Bobby smiled. "No offense."

Morbach's eyes turned cold. "But I do care. I want her returned to me safe and sound. So at the end of the rally I can bring her up on the platform to join her mother and father in a joyous and spontaneous reunion." He paused. "She obviously can't do that if she's dead."

Bobby saw Morbach in a brand-new light.

"And you end up like Mr. Wonderful."

"Yes."

"And win the election. Big."

"That's the point. I'm a politician."

Bobby laughed.

"And I'll bet that you'll tell everybody that gave you the money in the first place that the ransom was three hundred fifty thousand, too. Makes everything come out real neat, doesn't it?"

Morbach's expression didn't change.

"So we have a deal?"

"Tell me again who's bringing the money."

"One of my aides will deliver it anywhere you like."

"Which one?"

"His name is Jackson," Morbach said. "He's older, gray hair, moustache. You'll know him when you see him."

"I count the money before you get her."

"You can verify that it's there. Counting takes too long. I imagine by that time you'll be in a hurry to leave."

"What about the cops?"

"I'll make sure that the police will be watching the

stage. Why wouldn't they? No one is expecting something like this to happen."

"I'll need a new car," Bobby said.

Morbach reached into his pants pocket and tossed a key on the desk.

"Take one of the campaign cars," he said. "No one will miss it, and it won't stand out at the rally."

"You *do* think of everything," Bobby said. "I can see I've underestimated you."

"A lot of people do," Morbach said.

"Really? Isn't that something. Will Jacob Cross be there tomorrow?"

Morbach shook his head.

"He's in the hospital."

Bobby feigned a shocked expression.

"Sick?"

"Burned."

"Gee, that's too bad. You ought to send him a card, maybe a fruit basket or something."

"I'll pass on your concern," Morbach said. "I'm sure he'll appreciate it."

"He'd probably appreciate a skin graft a whole lot more, don't you think?"

Bobby laughed to himself, and then in one quick move, the laughter was gone and he was leaning over the desk with his hand pressed up against Morbach's chest, right over his heart, feeling the beat against his palm, so close he wanted to reach in and squeeze the blood right out of it.

"You try to fuck me on this and I'll take your daughter and disappear. You won't even know where to look. But I'll come back. I'll be like fucking death. I got in here, I can get in anywhere."

Bobby took his hand away.

"Other than that," he said, "I believe we got a deal."

———

Bobby moved Kimberly from the Taurus to the campaign car, a small Japanese sedan that he hated the minute he saw it. A piece of rolling tin, he thought, all dressed up with Morbach's campaign advertising. He got her in the front bucket seat and then climbed in himself.

"Are we going now?" Kimberly asked.

"Sure," Bobby said. "Where you want to go?"

"I don't care. Away from here."

Bobby thought it was some kind of phony jerk-off response, but she had a sick, disgusted look on her face. She was serious. He shook his head and backed the little Japanese piece of shit out of the lot. They could go to the airport, get a room in one of the cheap motels, take a bath, watch a little television, maybe check out the plane flights just for fun.

Bobby kept thinking about tomorrow's deal, trying to pinpoint the exact spot where Morbach was going to fuck him.

Bobby believed him when he said the cops wouldn't be a problem. After all, Bobby got to pick the spot for the exchange. He also believed that Morbach would deliver the money.

But once the exchange took place, and Kimberly was out of his hands, Bobby became a real liability for the senator. For everybody.

So that was where he had to be careful. Morbach's aide—if he was an aide and that seemed more and more unlikely—would be the one to deliver it. Maybe the money was wired or stained. Maybe the money was fake.

Maybe the aide would just walk up and shoot him dead.

Bobby banged on the steering wheel.

"People are such cocksuckers," he said and looked over at Kimberly.

She was crying again, tears running down her face. He reached over and wiped them off one cheek. She rested her head against the back of his hand, grateful for the attention.

"Man," Bobby said, "I thought my family life was fucked up."

He'd be doing her a big favor just to get her away from her old man.

32

She'd forgotten how empty the house felt when she was there by herself. The FBI agent by the front door didn't count. He seemed not to be there at all; or at best, he became part of the decor—a lamp dressed in a suit. If she were to suddenly sprout gossamer wings and fly past him out the door, he would probably record his observations in his notebook and return to his vigil without a moment's extra thought—*10:42. Mother of kidnapped subject grew wings and flew away. No other activity noted.*

It dawned on her that at last she had no place else to go. It seemed that she had exhausted them all, including Patrick Paige. Now, without him, she was completely cut off from everything. When the phone rang at the house, as it did several times that night, it was never for her but for the young agent downstairs.

His name was Collins. She learned that from eavesdropping on one of his calls. He caught her, of course, and stopped talking immediately.

"Is that you, Mrs. Morbach?" he asked, and she hung up carefully, feeling only slightly embarrassed at being caught. If I keep this up, she thought, pretty soon I'll have no guilt at all and then I can do anything I want.

And what exactly would she do?

Susan Morbach's mind went blank. Tomorrow was a long time and next week an infinity. There was the rally and then there was . . . the rest of her life.

Without her husband, perhaps without Kimberly.

There, I've said it. Despite everything—or perhaps because of it—she'd put her false hope to rest. It was finding the knapsack that did it, seeing it left like that, the way an animal might leave a bit of food behind in its den, abandoned without care or concern. It had affected her more deeply than she realized.

That was why she had been so mad at her husband—and at Paige. Not because they acted like teenagers—she was used to that by now—but because they hadn't *seen* it, had been more interested in their egos than in her daughter.

She still had the knapsack, had placed it in Kimberly's room on her bed. Doing it, she felt strangely like an archeologist collecting artifacts from her daughter's life, one that might very well be over. Or if not over, then changed so utterly that she might not recognize her if she stumbled over her on the street.

She hadn't given up hope of finding her. But she had given up her expectations of it. And neither man had noticed.

Keep busy, she thought. Stop dwelling on it. That had been her mother's remedy whenever life went wrong. Find something to do, doesn't matter what, just keep your mind and hands occupied and it will all work out.

Susan had laughed at her mother's advice in the past —it was too simple, too common for this modern age, the philosophical equivalent of eat your greens and wear your galoshes. But no longer.

Her mother had been right. She went upstairs to get her clothes for the rally. It was not an unimportant decision.

Despite the media coverage of the shooting and the kidnapping, the rally was their first major public appearance together. The whole thing had a hideous kind of aura, like a bad movie that everyone wanted to see. But she would do it and do it well because she had agreed.

The teal dress, she thought, standing in front of her closet. The color would show off well on television and yet not seem too bright or frivolous to offend the public's absurd sense of decency. They really did expect public figures to act like proper little children despite all evidence to the contrary piled up around their ankles.

The teal dress and the gray pumps and a double strand of pearls pulled up close to the neck. Perhaps a hat, something small and discreet. No, forget the hat. Nancy Reagan wore hats and they always made her look like the Queen Mum.

She heard a car drive up and went to the window. Another cop car. Susan found it amazing that she could tell them on sight now. This one was a blue Ford with a pair of miniature antennas sticking from the trunk. She watched while her husband got out of the car and waited for the others—Commander Jackson, his sidekick O'Brien, and Jerry Abelson, forehead split into two unequal parts by a white bandage—to follow him into the house.

Jim always needed an entourage, she thought. The front door slammed shut, and she heard voices and then the sound of his footsteps on the steps. She remained by the window, her back to the door, and waited until he entered to turn around.

"I didn't expect to find you here," he said.

She was surprised at how calm he seemed.

"This is where I live."

Morbach took one of the large suitcases down from his closet, opened it on the bed, and began filling it with clothes.

"It looks like you're planning on a long trip."

"I'm going to Harrisburg right after the rally."

"So you can start counting the votes?"

Morbach stopped packing long enough to look at her.

"Are you planning on coming back anytime soon?"

"I don't think so," he said.

"And what about Kimberly?"

"What about her?"

"Don't you think you ought to stick around here until we find her?"

Morbach ignored the question and resumed packing, working a little faster now, scooping up whole drawers of underwear and socks, grabbing an armful of laundered shirts, folding them directly into the suitcase, sprinkling half a dozen ties from the closet rack over them, stuffing an extra pair of loafers and a new belt into the space along the sides.

He swung the suitcase off the bed onto the floor, hefting it, testing the weight.

"Susan," he said, "do you know why I married you?"

"I tried to figure that out the other day. I suppose you needed a wife and I was the closest thing around."

"No," he said, walking to the bedroom door. "I thought you were smarter than I was. I thought that without you I'd end up like every other second-rate lawyer in this city, padding my hours, getting drunk in the afternoon. I really believed that."

He stopped at the door. "I don't know how the hell I could've been so wrong."

He called to her from the bottom of the stairs. "O'Brien will be spending the night. He'll take you to the rally tomorrow. Just do what he says, and everything will work out. By the way, the dress is perfect."

———

Paige caught the phone on the third ring, just as he was coming in the front door. He sprinted through the living room to the kitchen and snatched it off the wall.

"Yeah."

"Pat?"

It was Susan.

"Hello."

"You sound out of breath."

"I ran to get the phone. What's going on?"

"Nothing," she said. "Jim was just here. And gone. He left O'Brien to guard the door."

"FBI still there?"

"I suppose so. I haven't been downstairs since he left. That was an hour ago. Are you going tomorrow?"

"Of course."

"I want you to be there."

"I'll be there. What time?"

"I don't know. When my keeper lets me know."

"Forget him. I'll pick you up."

"No, no, I don't want to make this worse than it already is. The state police can take me there. When it's over, well, we'll see what happens when it's over, okay? Any news?"

"Nothing so far."

"If you hear anything, call me."

"I will. Good night.

"Good night, Pat."

Paige opened a beer and drank it standing up. Then he called her back.

"It's me," he said when she picked up the phone. "Are you all right?"

She seemed startled by his question.

"I'm fine. Really."

"You sure?"

"As sure as I am of anything around here." She

paused. "Jim moved out tonight. He just stopped by to pick up some clothes."

Paige lit a cigarette and flicked the match in the sink.

"How do you feel about that?"

She laughed.

"I'm sorry," she said. "I couldn't help it. You sounded like Phil Donahue."

"I'm just asking."

"I know," she said. "But don't. I'll be fine." He heard some noise on the line and then Susan said, "I've been expecting something like this. I shouldn't have been so surprised."

"Where's he going?"

"To Harrisburg. Right after the rally."

"What about Kimberly?"

"I asked him that. He said everything would work out." She paused. "Is there something you haven't told me?"

"No."

"Then why would he say that?"

"Maybe he knows more than I do. Where's he now?"

"I haven't the faintest idea. He could be anywhere in the city, a hotel, somebody's house."

"Shit. Let me talk to O'Brien."

Susan called down the stairs. "Pick up the phone. Detective Paige wants to talk to you."

O'Brien's voice came on the line.

"Yes?"

"Where's the senator?"

"I don't know."

"Don't give me that. I want to know where he's staying."

"I told you. I don't know."

"Then where's Jackson?"

"He's gone back to Harrisburg."

"You lying sack of shit."

"Suck on my ass," O'Brien said and hung up.

"That was helpful," Susan said.

"Wasn't it."

"You won't find him. Not tonight anyway. He's very good at hiding."

"He's not that good," Paige said. "I know where he's going to be tomorrow."

Bobby cut his hair while Kimberly watched television. He had forgotten to buy a pair of scissors, so he cut it with the knife, the same one he'd used on Kimberly. He sawed the hair away, pulling it tight and rubbing the blade across the strands. None of the cuts were straight, and when he was done, his head looked like a wheat field that had been harvested by several combines, each one set to a different height. He ran his fingers through the stubble, trying to smooth it out, but finally gave up. If he put enough goo on it, it would stay plastered to his head anyway.

When he finished cutting, he did a quick dye job, coloring his hair a dark brown. He shaved but left three days worth of moustache on his upper lip.

Bobby checked his face in the mirror. Demented was what he looked like now. Like somebody who lived in a cellar.

He washed out her clothes in the sink and strung them over the shower rod to dry. Then he climbed back into bed.

His face was on the screen. He looked at it carefully and realized it was taken from one of his old driver's licenses. He hadn't looked like that for years. He'd worn the cop's uniform when he checked in, the hat pulled down over his face, so he'd looked even less like that. If he hadn't, the motel clerk would have been on the phone to the cops and he'd be in a cell getting his kidneys worked over. The face on television belonged to somebody else, an

actor who sold dope to kids in the schoolyard on cop
shows.

But now, with his new hair and moustache, he looked
just like one of the Pedros that used to come around and
bang his old lady.

Bobby started to laugh. Is that what happened to you
when you got older? You started to look like somebody
from the fucking barrio? If that was true, the good old U.S.
of A. was in for a load of shit in the next few years.

"You think I look like a Pedro?" Bobby asked her.
"Maybe if I had a sombrero and a burro?"

Kimberly turned her face away from the television set
for a second. She looked worried.

"Who's Pedro?"

Bobby patted her cheek to make her feel better. He
was really getting into this sensitive thing. It was like own-
ing a pet. He'd never had one but how hard could it be?

"Just somebody I used to know," Bobby said.

Jacob Cross felt no pain. They had him on a morphine drip,
and the drug wrapped him in a big fuzzy blanket and he
couldn't tell where he was or whether he was awake or
asleep. He was surrounded by the blanket and nothing
much mattered, not even the dream that kept running
through his head.

In the dream, he was tumbling over and over again in
a huge ball of white light. The light was very warm, and it
felt just like sunlight on his skin. Over and over he tumbled,
and just before the dream ended, he would have the same
strange thought.

He knew where he was. He was floating through
heaven and the light that surrounded him was coming from
God. Jacob Cross was glad about that because he had a lot
he wanted to explain to God, so many things, the part about
Bobby and Kimberly, and the things that he'd done in his
life, but mostly—and this was what he really wanted to

explain, really wanted to *talk* about—his father, especially that business about his smile.

Tim Cochran didn't dream. They fed him medications and kept watch on the monitors, checking his readout every half hour.

The infection was still kicking around his system, his renal output was poor, and there were some peculiar blips on the EKG monitor, blips that made the doctors wonder what he was going to be like if and when he finally came around.

The nurses had fallen in love with him. They took turns doing extra time at his bedside to make sure he didn't slip away unnoticed between checks, the way some of them did in the ICU. That was the trouble with critical patients; they paid no attention to the living and went out whenever they felt like it.

The interns ran an informal pool of the ICU patients, betting on which ones would die first. When one intern suggested that Tim was out in front on the list, the unit RN told him that if Tim did die, the first thing she was going to do was ram a big glass catheter up the intern's miserable ass and break it off. And see how long *he* lived.

33

Bobby didn't call Morbach. It was a simple case of self-preservation. The less time they had to prepare for the trade-off, the less time they had to fuck him over. So he wasn't going to give them any. It was very triangular, very mathematical.

The senator was one point of the triangle, the aide was another, where he and the aide met was the third. He wanted to keep the last point a secret. If he told them the spot, he would be operating on blind faith. So he decided to play it another way.

They checked out of the motel at eleven and drove out to Chester County along the Brandywine, just taking in the sights. They bought lunch at a drive-through McDonald's and parked along the river and ate. Kimberly was quiet but he didn't feel much like talking either, so it worked out just fine. He was amazed how little contact he'd had with the world in the last few days, how everything was set up to keep people from having to deal with one another.

He dropped off his room key at a drive-through window and bought his lunch from another. He bought his newspaper from a metal box on the street and slipped some money to the gas station attendant through a thick plastic tray. America was a great place. You could live your whole life in your car and never touch another person if you didn't feel like it.

When they finished their lunch, he helped Kimberly back into the car and turned on the radio for her. That was all she wanted to do these days, listen to the radio or watch the tube. She fit right into the new American dream.

He had a momentary spasm of doubt, or at least that's what he thought it was. She was like a dumb animal that needed to be taken care of all the time, and he truly believed he was the only one left who could do the job. But he wanted to be sure.

"Listen," he asked her suddenly, "you think I'm a bad guy?"

Kimberly smiled.

"I'll do whatever you tell me to do."

It was an okay answer but not to the question he'd asked. It didn't matter because in another few hours, they were going to be miles away from everybody and everything. He was going to take care of her, make sure she was okay, feed her, clothe her, wash her face when it got dirty, and tuck her into bed at night.

It was a new feeling but one that he was pretty sure he could handle. He'd done all right with his mom, hadn't he?

"I don't even know what the hell I'm doing here," Jeffers said to Paige. "Aside from watching the river flow."

They were at Penn's Landing, leaning against the big metal railings that separated the broad landing from the river. A police patrol boat motored back and forth in the dirty brown water halfway out.

"Look at that," Jeffers said. "They're all set for an amphibious asault."

"It's overtime."

"I don't get overtime."

"But you get a company car," Paige offered.

"I'd rather have a horse."

"Did you have a horse when you were a kid?"

"No. I had a bike like everybody else. Then I drove a Chevy."

"I thought all Texans had horses."

"You've been watching too many movies. The only Texans who have horses these days are the ones who move there from Connecticut. They all wear Stetsons and lizard boots because they think it's authentic. Most Texans I know would rather wear loafers."

"You wear wingtips."

"I'm a sentimentalist," Jeffers said. "Did the state police give him a chopper, too?"

"I don't know. I doubt it."

"Then what's that?"

Paige looked south and saw a small white helicopter coming low up the river. It swung out toward Camden and then cut across the water toward the landing. Paige saw the markings.

"News team."

Jeffers grunted and looked away.

"We got a lead last night," Paige said.

"So I heard. The one at the garage. Had it on my desk first thing this morning. The kid couldn't identify him from the photos."

"He said it might have been him. He just wasn't sure."

"You think it was him?"

"I think it was him," Paige said. "Try this. He parks the car in the lot to get it off the street. When he leaves, the attendant recognizes him, and away he goes."

"What does he do with the car?"

"He gets a new one. He's pretty good at that."

Jeffers swept his arm around.

"And you think he's here."

"I don't think he could stay away."

"To do what?"

"Just to bask in the glow," Paige said. "He likes being a star. There's something else."

Paige told him about his conversation with Susan Morbach the night before.

"You hungry?" Jeffers asked when he was finished.

"Some."

"Come on, I'll buy you lunch. You can tell me all about your theory and I can tell you about the conversation I had with Commander Jackson this morning."

They ate hamburgers in a fake English pub at New Market. There was a bakeshop near the entrance, and the whole restaurant smelled like chocolate chip cookies. Jeffers washed his down with a Diet-Coke. Paige ate half of his and drank two cups of coffee.

"Jackson said he had some intelligence that the kidnapper was going to make another ransom demand today."

"How's he know that?"

"Intelligence," Jeffers said and laughed. "He made it sound like God whispered it to him in his sleep."

"He got it from Morbach."

"I asked him that."

"And?"

"And he did a little dance and I did a little dance and we danced all the way around it. He said he'd let me know more about it this afternoon. I haven't seen him since. I *did* call Harrisburg and reamed some poor fool about his lack of cooperation and all that but I don't think it did much good."

"What about Morbach? Can't you nail him on this?"

Jeffers shook his head.

"Not unless he gives me the hammer," he said. "I couldn't even stop this rally."

"And I thought you were in charge."

"It gets complicated."

"I've heard that before."

"So have I."

Paige ordered another coffee.

"They got an ID on the one in the cabin," Jeffers said. "You're not going to believe this. A New Jersey state trooper. They checked his house. His car's gone, too."

"What kind?"

"Guess."

"Black Taurus." The kid at the garage remembered that at least.

"You win the prize. Everybody's out looking for it right now."

Paige lit a cigarette.

"You think our boy's still driving it?"

Jeffers shook his head.

"But you agree that he's here?"

"I have to work on that assumption."

"What are you going to do?"

"In this particular case? Exactly what Washington has instructed me to do."

"Washington?"

Jeffers smiled. "You know the place. The fool factory. Where you send your money every month."

"Oh that place. What do they want?"

"They're worried this is some kind of convoluted assassination plot." Jeffers held up his hand. "Hey, I know, but that's the way they think down there. Ever since Kennedy, it's been—what if?"

"So what does that mean?"

"It means we guard Morbach. I've been told to put my men in the crowd around the stage."

"That include you?"

"Me especially. I'm *on* stage. If a bullet comes, I'm supposed to throw myself in front of it."

Paige laughed. "Hell of a job you got there."

"I've been told that I can use some of your men around the stage, but Washington specifically requested that the rest function only in a 'limited capacity.' "

"Is that Washington-speak for 'Fuck you'?"

"I believe it is." Jeffers leaned forward. "Now, if you had put yourself in this dreary vision, where exactly would that be?"

"Behind the stage but not too close. Maybe on the hillside in front of the Towers. I can keep an eye on things in back of the stage but not get too close."

"Which side of the hill?"

"The left side. Not as many trees. Better sight distance all around."

Jeffers grinned. "That's what I thought, too. There's one more thing. I've been told that Commander Jackson is expecting an important message from Harrisburg and that he may be called away at any time during the senator's speech. Now what do you think of that?"

"I think I'll keep my eye on Jackson."

"Good choice. I'll watch Morbach."

"And Susan."

"And Susan," Jeffers said after a moment. "I'll watch her, Pat. Don't worry."

"Thank you," Paige said. "One thing to remember about Morbach. He leads with his right."

Killing time. That's what she was doing. She woke up late and ate breakfast. Read the *Inquirer*. Cleaned up the kitchen. Did some laundry. Read through the mail. Cut flowers in the garden. Ate lunch. Made a point of not talking to O'Brien, who had slept on the living room couch, taken a shower, and changed his clothes and was back on the couch in a suit and tie looking like a potted plant.

Finally, the waiting got to be too much.

"When are we going?"

"When they call," O'Brien said. He was reading the paper and spoke to her through the sports section.

"When are they going to do that?"

"Soon."

"Thank you for that stimulating news." She went into the kitchen to make herself another cup of coffee.

Afterward, she got undressed and lay down on the bed. She closed her eyes and the tears came again. She didn't fight them but told herself this was the last time she was going to let it happen today. She would save them for tomorrow. Or the day after. Or for the rest of her life.

Bobby split the last piece of blotter acid with Kimberly and drove to the cemetery behind Strawberry Mansion and waited for the rush to come. He could feel the heat of it on his skin, little pinpricks like the first tingle of a sunburn. They walked among the stones, just killing time.

Bobby wished he had the video camera with him so he could record all of it. That way, when they were older, they could watch it anytime they liked. It would be like that Beatles song, the one about when they were sixty-four. A couple old farts. Watching home movies. Sipping piña coladas. Taking it easy.

He lit a joint, letting the smoke damp down the acid rush, watching Kimberly stretched out on the ground, playing with the grass. He wanted to take her in his arms and never let her go. The feeling was so overpowering that he threw back his head and let out a yell. Kimberly looked at him and smiled.

It was just too much.

Here he was, surrounded by a bunch of dead people, and he had never felt more alive in his whole life.

34

From the grassy hill in front of Society Hill Towers, Paige could look down and see the back of the makeshift stage on the other side of the big fountain. The fountain, rising up in a series of gray metal cylinders welded together in a lopsided wedge, spewed clouds of mist into the air and made everything look dreamy.

Through the binoculars he saw the stage and the long open plaza that stretched out in front of it all the way to Delaware Avenue. Beyond that, he saw the Landing and, on the other side of the river, the stunted industrial shoreline of Camden.

Everywhere he looked there were people. They filled the plaza and the Landing and moved back and forth on the walkway over the avenue. Around him, the hillside was crowded with spectators, and when he looked behind him, he could see faces in almost every window. In the small parking lot, in the center of the three high rises, somebody set off a string of firecrackers and he heard shouts of annoyance over the rat-a-tat sound.

In back of the stage, behind the barricades, he saw the

faces of the police, saw them as they looked nervously in his direction. He knew what that felt like, the first seconds when something out of place happened and you wondered if this was it and your eyes went searching for a place to hide and your hand went automatically for your gun. The firecrackers burnt themselves out and the police by the barricade grinned at one another. He could hear their thoughts: Not this time.

Moving along, he saw Jeffers as he leaned against the front of the stage, staring blandly at the crowd. In the back, he saw Morbach talking to Jackson, their heads almost touching. There was a briefcase at Jackson's feet. Morbach had Jackson carrying his books for him now. Susan sat on a folding chair several feet away, legs crossed, hands folded neatly in her lap, looking exactly the way she had looked the first day they met. He couldn't touch her then. Had he tried? Did she rest a hand on his arm? He couldn't remember.

Paige swung the binoculars around to search the crowd. The mist in the air gave their faces a vague and ephemeral look, as though they were angels who might float up to heaven at any moment. He scanned the crowd in front and then down to the cobblestone street in front of the hill where a long line of cars had backed up, inching their way to New Market.

People yelled and waved to one another; a young couple danced by themselves to the sound of a radio in one of the cars. He was looking for Bobby Beauchamp, searching every unsuspecting face, hoping he might still be wearing the sport coat and the oversized necktie. Finally, he let the binoculars dangle from the strap around his neck and lit a cigarette.

The sun was going down. It would be dark soon.

If Bobby was out there, he'd made himself invisible.

———

Bobby bought two tickets to the 8:40 showing of a new French film about Africa. At least that's what Bobby thought it was about. The poster showed a man surrounded by natives who stared fearfully at the gun in his hand and Bobby thought that just about said it all.

He led Kimberly through the lobby to her seat and left her there while he bought a large popcorn, some candy, and a soda. It wasn't exactly nutritious, he thought, but it would help keep her occupied while he was gone.

Bobby found her staring anxiously at the doors like he'd been gone for hours. It was nice to be missed but this was ridiculous. When it was all over, they were definitely going to have to work on her insecurity problem.

Bobby slid into the seat and set the popcorn and soda on the floor.

"You remember this place?"

Kimberly looked around. "Yes," she said and smiled.

"That's right. We met here. This is our anniversary." He gave her the candy, a box of Milk Duds. "And here's a little present for you. Don't eat them all at once. You'll spoil your appetite for the popcorn."

She held the box and looked guilty.

"I don't like it when you go away."

"I don't like it, either. But I always come back for you, don't I?"

She nodded carefully.

"And I keep you safe?"

Another nod.

"And I don't let anybody hurt you?"

She looked up.

"You'll keep him away from me?"

Bobby knew who *he* was. He even had a face. Now that they'd met, Bobby decided Mr. Death looked just like her old man.

"He won't come around anymore," he said. "I guarantee it."

Kimberly smiled and ate a Milk Dud.

"Now listen to me. When the movie starts, I have to go away again." She started to look panicky. He took her hand and gave it a squeeze. "It's only for a little while and I want you to sit here and watch the movie. It's a good movie and you'll like it. Before you know it, I'll be back and everything will be fine. We'll go for a trip in the car."

Kimberly looked worried and excited all at the same time.

"And when we get there," Bobby said, "you can sit on the beach and you won't even have to wear shoes. Nobody wears shoes where we're going."

"You promise?"

"I promise."

The movie started and Bobby watched for a few minutes; then he told her he had to go. She held his hand and pressed her cheek against it for the longest time. He pulled it away very gently.

"Be sure and eat the popcorn. There's some soda here, too. You got everything you need. I'll be back."

"I believe you," Kimberly whispered. "I know you wouldn't lie to me." She smiled and ate another Milk Dud.

Bobby waited for a moment inside the lobby, using the glass door as a mirror to adjust his shirt and tie.

A voice behind him said, "Too bad you have to work today."

Bobby turned around. One of the ushers was smiling at him.

"It's my job," he replied.

He put the trooper's hat on his head, set it on straight so it looked like he meant business.

He was thinking about Kimberly.

She was so sweet she damned near broke his heart.

———

Bobby moved slowly through the crowd, watching every-one, nodding politely to the folks, touching the brim of his hat.

Walking tall. Playing the cop. It was easy. All you had to do was pretend you could eat bricks and shit gravel. That's what they wanted, a hero right off the silver screen. And that's what he gave them.

Maybe when it was all done, he'd write a song about it. Not the music, just the lyrics, and send it off to Waylon or Willie, somebody like that who knew how to do it right. He would write a letter, explaining it to them, show them how he'd saved the girl and done the right thing.

He passed the hotel and cut across the street, one hand out to stop the traffic. From there he could see the lights of the fountain and the stage. A loud electronic squeal came from the PA system. Bobby stood on the corner and watched.

Morbach was at the microphone, his back to the au-dience, speaking to one of the technicians. There was a row of folding chairs on the stage, and he saw Susan Morbach in a blue-green dress sitting at the end. He waited until Morbach began to speak and then made his way through the spectators who crammed the sidewalk and spilled out into the street.

He spoke to a cop at the barricade.

"I'm looking for somebody named Jackson," he said. "One of the senator's aides."

"You mean Commander Jackson?"

"That's the one," Bobby said. "Would you ask him to come over here? I've got a message for him."

Commander Jackson, he thought. They were both in for a treat.

The cop shrugged and approached a tall man with gray hair and a moustache standing behind Susan Morbach on the stage. Jackson leaned over to listen to the cop, glanced briefly at Bobby, and then climbed down from the stage, picking up the large briefcase by his feet. Susan Morbach swung around in her chair to stare at him. Bobby looked down.

"Yes, what is it?"

Bobby touched the brim of his hat, hiding in its shadow.

"Time to do the deed, sport."

Paige watched Jackson as he spoke to the state trooper, saw the same bland arrogance in his expression, then a sudden frown. Jackson moved quickly around the end of the barricade. The two men stepped off the curb. As they did, the trooper reached down and took the briefcase from Jackson.

They crossed the street and went down the sidewalk directly below him. For a few seconds they were obscured by the trees. Paige moved down the hill a few feet, working his way between the spectators to get a better view. He watched until they got to the corner and turned into Society Hill, their features ghostly and indistinct in the light from the street lamp.

Then the trooper did something odd. He stopped and looked back, turning his head slightly, as though he meant to give the crowd a last clear shot of his profile.

Paige dropped the binoculars.

When Susan Morbach saw Jackson pick up the briefcase at his feet and leave the stage, she turned her chair to watch him. Her husband stopped his speech briefly and looked at her sternly, but she ignored him. Jackson walked to the other end of the stage and spoke briefly to a state trooper. Then he moved around the barricade and walked off.

Susan watched as they stepped into the street, and then her eyes traveled upward toward the Towers and Patrick Paige. She'd seen him there earlier and searched for him now, trying to find him again on the crowded hillside.

When she caught sight of him, her breath quickened.

He was following Jackson and the trooper, moving down the hillside to keep them in view. They stopped at the corner and she saw Paige raise the binoculars to his face and then drop them suddenly. The next second, he was running down the hill.

Susan Morbach stood up.

"Susan!"

Her husband had his hand over the microphone, motioning with his head for her to sit down.

"You son of a bitch," she said and kicked her chair out of the way as she moved toward the back of the stage.

Bobby hurried along, taking Jackson's elbow and steering him through the pedestrians that crowded the narrow sidewalk along Second, past the carefully restored redbrick rowhouses, until they were less than a block from New Market.

Bobby stopped next to the car.

"Get in," he said. He opened the door. A campaign sign broke loose and swung like a pendulum back and forth. Bobby tore it off and threw it on the sidewalk. Jackson went around to the passenger side and looked in the front window.

"She's not here."

"I'm taking you to her."

"I'm not going anywhere. That wasn't the arrangement."

Bobby aimed the gun through the interior of the car. A few more inches and he could have stuck it in the cop's stomach.

"Then you'll die right here. I really don't give a shit."

Jackson opened the door and started to climb in.

"Get away from the car!"

Jackson stood and looked up the street.

Paige was at the corner, shielded by the edge of the building, waving his gun at the people on the sidewalk.

Some saw him, some didn't. A woman with a small dog in her arms began to scream, and the people around her scattered, diving between the parked cars, squeezing themselves against the buildings. One man dropped behind a stoop and lay flat on the sidewalk.

Paige ran forward a few feet and stopped. Bobby was already inside the car. Jackson reached behind him, underneath his coat.

Bobby pressed the gun against his stomach and shot him twice. Jackson flew backward into the middle of the cobblestoned street. Paige heard the car start.

People were running now, streaming toward him until they saw the gun in his hand. They veered off, cutting between the cars into the street. A woman jumped over Jackson's body to get away. Paige sprinted across the sidewalk and threw himself between two parked cars.

He stood up just as the car pulled out. He aimed at the driver's silhouette.

A figure raced by him on the street, heading straight for the car. Paige's vision narrowed to the black circle of the driver's head.

Susan Morbach appeared suddenly, running alongside the car, her hands reaching inside to grab the wheel. Paige brought the gun up hard and ran for her.

One minute he was fine, the next all hell broke loose. Jackson was dead in the middle of the street and he was pulling away from the curb, working fast, not worrying about the cop at the end of the block, punching the little Japanese piece of shit into first and holding the accelerator to the floor, thinking he could still make it, still do what he'd said he'd do. The gun was on the other seat, buried beneath the briefcase. He cleared the parking space and reached for it.

Susan Morbach appeared out of nowhere, screaming at him, tearing at his face and hands with her nails, digging in deep, going right for the bone. She pulled at the wheel and the car did a crazy little zigzag in the middle of the street. Bobby let go and punched at her face, trying to push her away.

But she wouldn't go. He pulled one hand from the wheel and twisted it hard, felt something give way. Her other hand dug into the skin of his cheekbone, fingernails clawing toward his eyes.

She was trying to blind him.

He looked at her, their faces inches apart, and what he saw in her eyes scared him. She wasn't trying to blind him. She was trying to kill him.

His foot slipped off the pedal and the car slowed down. He found the accelerator and pressed down. The engine coughed, then roared back. He brought his right hand back and punched her in the face. His hand caught her on the chin and suddenly she wasn't there anymore. He looked in the side mirror and saw her rolling across the cobblestones behind him and the other cop coming up fast, and he pushed his foot to the floor, swearing at it to make it move.

The car fishtailed and slammed into the side of a parked car. Bobby held the wheel straight and kept going, the sound of ruptured metal screaming in his ears, and he screamed with it, howling like a madman. He turned the wheel hard to the left and sailed toward the opposite side of the street, heading straight for another row of cars. At the last moment, he swung right and straightened out, driving fast up Second, just making the right turn on Pine.

He was running free, barreling down Pine, knowing he was going to make it now, feeling the power in his blood, his heart pumping, pumping, sending it soaring through him, and he laughed out loud, banging on the wheel. He turned on Third and ran flat out, the little car zipping along.

He was still laughing when he crossed the intersection at Cypress Street, not caring about anything, when he saw a shape looming on his left. The taxi, pulling out with a new fare, the driver looking back to get directions, hit him full on and tossed the little Japanese piece of shit across the street like so much scrap metal. It struck a parked car, spun halfway around, and slammed into the rear of another before it finally came to a stop.

Paige lifted Susan off the cobblestones, saw her eyes roll back in her head, and pressed his fingers into the side of her neck, searching desperately for a pulse. His fingers felt thick and useless, like so much dead flesh, and he had a sudden flash of the boy on the concrete, blood spread out beneath him like a misshapen rug, and he probed deeper. He felt a tremor beneath his fingers and focused on the spot. Another tremor, then another.

He set her head down and felt something sticky on his hand. When he took it away, all he could see was blood, so dark, almost black, glistening on his skin. He looked up and saw a young couple standing on the other side of the street, staring at him.

"Come here," he said, and when they didn't move, he yelled, "Get the hell over here!"

They came reluctantly, the man looking behind him for someone to help him, maybe to hold him back, the woman pulling the light cotton sweater tighter around her shoulders. They were moving too slowly. Paige grabbed the man and pulled him down to where Susan lay, her own hand now pressed against the back of her skull.

"Stay here and watch her," he said. "Don't leave her."

Paige took off his coat and covered her. He pointed at the man and said, more forcefully this time, "Don't leave her."

The man nodded. The woman knelt down to straighten out his coat. She took off her sweater and tucked it beneath Susan's head.

Paige ran after the car. He could still see it in his mind, taking the corner too fast, getting away from him. He ran in the direction of that memory, a man chasing a ghost.

Bobby crawled from the wreckage and fell face first on the street. His chest hurt and his breath rattled in his lungs. He touched his chest and pain shot through him. It felt soft where his fingers touched, like his bones had turned to rubber, and when he took his hands away, he felt the first drops of blood run down his face.

Bobby wiped his eyes and his fingers turned bloody and he moved them a little higher, up along his scalp. He peeled back a long flap of skin, loose and slippery in his fingers, and felt his skull underneath.

He leaned over and threw up, wiping away the last string of bile with the back of his hand. He raised his head and saw people staring at him from the sidewalk. One woman had her face buried in her hands, hiding her eyes. He staggered to his feet, took a few steps along the car, and collapsed, falling over the trunk. The pain in his chest tore through him and he retched again.

The taxicab sat crossways in the intersection, the front end buckled on one side, radiator spewing hot steam into the night air. The driver's face swelled against the shattered front window, one arm crushed underneath it, the wrist turned out at a strange angle. The back door opened and the passenger climbed out, hung on the open door for a moment, and then fell to his knees.

The gun. He needed the gun. That was the most important thing. The gun first. Then Kimberly. Then. His mind stopped and backtracked. The gun. He worked his way along the car and pulled open the door. The briefcase lay underneath the dash, wedged into the corner. It had broken open in the crash and money had spilled out onto the carpet. Bobby shoved the money away and felt around for the gun, constantly wiping his eyes to keep the blood from blinding him. His hand touched metal and he pulled it out. The money stuck to his bloody hands. He snatched at the bills, stuffing the blood-soaked cash in his pockets.

He held onto the roof of the car and stood. He gagged once and took a step forward, gagged again, took another, and finally he was walking. Someone approached him, a shadow in the corner of his eye, and he swung the gun around, the barrel bouncing up and down while he tried to aim and fire. The shadow disappeared and he heard a shout and the sound of footsteps running away.

He wiped the blood from his eyes, and his vision cleared. He knew where he was, he knew where he was going. Kimberly. The theater. He felt in his pocket for his ticket stub. They won't let you in without a ticket. He crossed to the other side of the street and mounted the sidewalk.

It was like climbing a mountain, the curb an insurmountable height.

He was dying and he knew it, the pain in his chest getting worse. Something was busted in there. He could hear the gurgling sound his lungs made every time he breathed. It didn't matter. He was going to make it.

Keep moving, keep in step, watch where you're going, hit 'em where they ain't.

Bobby staggered forward, passing under the cool shade of trees. He heard a voice. It was close to him, like a surge of wings in the night air, beating into his ears.

Mr. Death coming on strong, Mr. Death getting real close this time. He snarled at the voice, spit in its face. A mouthful of blood.

He was there suddenly, the street right in front of him, cobblestones and trees and a low hill filled with people who pointed and stared and yelled for him to stop. Bobby whirled around, the sudden motion making him dizzy, and he collapsed against the side of the theater and pointed the gun at them, Mr. Death laughing at him from the sidelines.

Coming back, his mind whispered, coming back to get my baby out of jail.

He stopped at the corner to wipe the blood from his face, pushing the skin down tight on the bone, the pain like a knife through the top of his skull.

Got to look sharp. Got to dress the part. Got to *feel* it in your bones.

He marched across the front of the theater, his legs like hard pieces of wood. He snapped them in front of him, one at a time, left, right, left, right, counting off a rhythm with each bloody step, leaving splatters behind him like drops of paint on the concrete.

Bobby pushed open the front doors and stepped into the lobby. The girl behind the counter stared at him, watched him move like a dead man across the carpet toward the theater. He swung the gun at her.

"Get out of here!" The words came out in a cloud of red mist floating across his eyes. The girl fled.

Bobby kicked open the doors and stopped. The image on the screen was huge and menacing, swallowing him up. He ducked down behind one of the seats and covered his eyes, all weakness and pain. When he looked up, a man's hand reached for him from the screen and he pointed the gun at the face and fired.

A voice screamed. Bobby stood up. Phantoms rushed past him, scared faces zooming out of the dark. He fought his way through them to reach Kimberly, lashed out with the gun, felt the metal strike flesh, heard a cry of pain and kept moving, sinking lower and lower, on his way down to her. He fired at the screen again. His legs gave out suddenly, and he screamed as he fell.

"Kimberly!"

He lay in the aisle, blood pooling in the back of his throat, choking him. He tried to roll over but he couldn't move. Suddenly her hands were on his and she pulled him to his knees and then his feet and dragged him to the front of the theater. Bobby pushed himself up the wall beneath the screen and held her close, feeling the warmth of her face against his chest. The pain eased, seemed to vanish in an instant, and he touched her hair, let his hand drift down her neck.

They were alone in the theater. He could see the faces through the door windows. Peering in, trying to get a glimpse. Extras, he thought, fucking extras. He turned his head away and coughed up more blood.

Kimberly sat against the wall and cried. Her sobs sounded distant, like someone wailing in another room. Bobby took her hand. It felt so small, so tiny, almost like a baby's hand. Music swelled from the screen and drifted over them.

"I told you," he said, fighting to get the words out. "I told you I would."

She wouldn't stop crying.

"Okay," he said. "Going to be okay." He felt tired, drunk tired. The blood was a weight on the back of his throat, holding his head down.

He turned her face toward his and patted it gently. His fingers left soft wet trails on her skin.

"Going now."

He pushed himself up the wall. Kimberly helped him, lifting him so he could stand.

"The front," he said. "Both of us. Don't look back."

He couldn't feel anything now. No pain, no fear, everything drained from him but a feeling he hadn't expected. He was as happy as a man could be. They were going now and he was happy and everything would be fine. He leaned down to kiss her and tasted the salt of her tears.

She led him up the aisle, holding his arm to keep him steady. There were no more faces in the windows and Bobby could see the lights of the lobby through the glass. He wanted to be out of there, into the lights, watching the astonished faces of the extras as he walked past them, one last glimpse to send him on his way.

He moved faster and faster, and then he felt like he was flying and Kimberly was somewhere behind him and he couldn't stop. He pushed through the doors and walked straight into the lights.

A man stood in front of him, a gun in both hands, back braced against the wall. Bobby knew who it was, knew he'd been waiting for him all this time. All Bobby had to do was raise his own gun and get him first. Before he got to him. Before he got to the girl.

He thought, Kimberly, Kimberly, and raised the gun.

Paige kicked the gun away from the body, sent it skittering across the carpet, the sound of the shots still booming in his ears. He knew he didn't have to bother, but he knelt down next to Bobby and looked for any signs of life. There weren't going to be any and he knew it but he did it anyway.

Bobby's eyes had gone glassy and he lay in the same position he'd fallen, legs slightly apart, arms straight out at his sides. The way kids make angels in the snow.

The echoes of the gunshots grew smaller and smaller and finally faded away, leaving only a dull ringing in his ears.

Paige picked up Bobby's gun and went into the theater to find Kimberly. He pushed one door open with his foot and peered inside.

Kimberly Morbach sat in the middle of the aisle. She had her head down, staring at something in her lap. For one brief second, he thought she had a gun, but she raised her head and he saw that there was nothing there. He held the door open and kicked down the stop.

Kimberly didn't get up. She looked up at him expectantly, her face streaked with tears and blood, and asked, "Is Bobby coming back?"

He finally had to carry her into the lobby. She tried walking, but her legs gave out after a few feet, and he lifted her into his arms and carried her the rest of the way.

There were already cops in the lobby. Two of them stood over the body, and another one cruised in and out of the front doors, making a path for somebody coming through.

Kimberly began to shake in his arms.

Paige started to put her down, but she held onto him and he shifted her thin body to get a better hold.

"It's okay," he said. "You're safe now."

She wouldn't stop shaking.

Jeffers came through the front door first. Then Morbach followed, a few steps behind, running a hand through his hair to straighten it out.

"Your father's here." Paige nudged her head gently with his shoulder. "It's all right. Your father's come to take you home."

Kimberly turned her head slowly and saw her father's face, a look of terror spreading across her own.

Morbach smiled and said, "Kimberly."

Kimberly Morbach began to scream.

35

Early November. Another warm evening. The fifth in a row when the temperature had risen above the seventy-degree mark during the day. The heat lingered after sunset, and Paige kept his window down and let the smoke from his cigarette drift into the warm night air.

The lights came on in Jacob Cross's house and Paige watched while the nurse pulled the living room drapes closed. She no longer bothered to stare at him anymore. He'd been there a week now, ever since Cross had come home from the hospital, and she had gotten used to him, especially when he told her he was there for her protection.

Which was a lie. He was there because Jacob Cross was there and he wanted him to know it. Not that it would make much of a difference.

The case was closed and no one would reopen it even if he got down on his knees and begged.

Kimberly Morbach had not been called before the grand jury. Several doctors had testified to her condition, including two prominent psychologists, and the grand jury had refused to indict Kimberly Morbach for murder. The

DA had handled the testimony himself, steering them toward the conclusion that an indictment would be a clear disservice to the girl and the community.

Paige had heard through Kate Evans that the DA was thinking about a gross negligence charge against her father because of what had happened at the rally but finally decided against it. The DA had to make do with some veiled criticism of the senator's actions when he announced the grand jury's decision.

Morbach had won the election but not by anything close to the landslide he needed. The rumor was that his chances of going to Washington were all but gone. Several challengers were already lining up support to run against him in the next one. The newspapers were calling for an investigation into the origins of the ransom money as well as some of Morbach's investments.

Morbach stayed in Harrisburg and refused all interviews.

There was no one left who could connect Jacob Cross to Bobby Beauchamp. Cross had been questioned about it and claimed that he learned about the cabin from Commander Jackson, who hadn't said where he had gotten the information. He had no idea how the photograph of the dead boy had gotten in his car. Jackson was dead, so who could contradict him? Not O'Brien. O'Brien pleaded ignorance of everything and was now acting in Jackson's place until a permanent replacement could be found.

So Paige started spending a few hours each night in front of Cross's house, just to let him know that it wasn't over.

There was a small moving van in Cheryl Silverman's driveway that night. He watched the men as they hauled furniture and boxes out the front door to the van. Cheryl stood on the front porch and he could hear the sound of her laughter as she joked with the movers.

She had a six-pack of beer in one hand and peeled off

a can at a time, tossing them to each of the men as they came up on the porch. It reminded him of something out of Tennessee Williams, the young sexy divorcée drinking beer with the workmen.

She kept one can for herself and walked down the street toward his car. She wore a white pantsuit and carried a large leather purse on her shoulder. It bounced off her hip as she walked. She took her time, offering him one last good look.

"I'm leaving and you're still here," she said when she got to his car. "I thought it'd be the other way around."

She dropped her purse and leaned over the window, resting the beer can on the roof.

"I'm just making sure nothing happens," Paige said.

"You're a little late for that. It already happened."

"You never know."

"That's right," she said. "You never do." She took a sip of beer and offered him some. He took a long drink and started to hand it back.

"You keep it," she said. "How's old Jake the snake doing?"

"Fine, I guess."

She looked at the house and shook her head.

"The whole world turns to shit and he's doing fine. Doesn't that piss you off?"

Paige shrugged. "Where're you going?"

"Florida. I got a girlfriend in Pompano who needs a roommate. She's got a place on the intercoastal. She lies out in the nude and watches the boats go by. Sounds like something I can relate to, doesn't it?"

Paige laughed.

"You know," she said, "I'm real glad you stopped by that time. I mean, when you asked me about the tape. I've been doing a lot of thinking about it—since the divorce and everything."

"I've still got it. You want it back?"

"Nah. You keep it. Take it out once in a while, remind yourself what you missed when you had the chance."

Cheryl reached into the window and took the beer from him and raised the can to her mouth. When she was finished, she handed it back and wiped her mouth with the tip of her finger. A small smudge of lipstick stuck to her finger and she smeared it away with her thumb, smiling to herself.

"How's the girl doing?"

"It'll take a while but she's going to be okay. A lot of bad things happened to her."

"Men happened to her. That's one of the things I've been thinking about. Why is it that men always turn out to be such complete assholes?"

"Is that a rhetorical question?"

"I guess it is. Since you don't seem to know the answer."

She picked up her purse and looped the straps over her shoulder.

"Think he'll see me? Just for old times' sake?"

"I don't know. I doubt it."

"Well, we'll see. You never know. This is my last chance to say fuck you." She shifted the straps of the purse and smoothed out her suit.

"So long, Boy Scout," she said. "It's been real and it's been fun, I just can't say it's been real fun."

She went up the driveway to the front door. Before she knocked, she looked back and waved good-bye. He raised his hand but the door opened and she turned away. Paige saw the nurse shake her head. Cheryl moved in front of her, blocking his view. The nurse started to close the door.

Cheryl pushed the door open just as the nurse raised both hands in the air. Paige bolted from the car.

He was only a few feet from the house when he heard the first shot. It came from the rear. He threw open the door and ran inside. There was a second shot, then four more in quick succession. He ran for the study.

Cheryl Silverman sat on the leather sofa, the gun on the table in front of her. Paige picked it up by the barrel. She didn't seem to realize he was there.

Cross lay on the portable hospital bed in front of the glass doors, the sheets slick with blood. A circle of small holes, darker than the rest of the sheet, clustered around his heart. His face was turned away, as if he was too embarrassed to face them.

Paige sat down next to her.

"Where's the nurse?"

"In the closet. I locked her in there." She looked at him. "Have you got a cigarette? I forgot mine."

Paige lit one and handed it to her. She took a long drag and blew the smoke toward the bed.

"Dumb fucker never even woke up," she said.

36

Tim Cochran was ready to go an hour early. He wore a sport coat and a tie, the first one he'd had on in years. The coat was a little small but he didn't mind. It was the brace on his leg and the crutches he had to use to get around that bothered him. He still wasn't comfortable with them. Sometimes, when he tried to move too fast, he'd trip over them and fall. The therapist told him it would be like that for a while. Tim figured that it was going to be like that for the rest of his life.

His foster parents were okay but they didn't really understand. The man kept trying to give him little pep talks about how he had to be strong and keep fighting it, but at least he didn't tell him to take it like a man. He seemed more embarrassed by what he said than anything else. The woman smiled a lot and called him Timmy and that was okay, too. He didn't really know how long he was going to be with them and he tried not to think about it.

The cop was there on time. He was tall and friendly looking and wore a suit and tie and brought him a gift. It was a book about pirates. Tim didn't care about pirates and thought it was a little kid's gift. What he really wanted was some comic books, maybe the Punisher or one of the other superheroes, but he figured the cop wouldn't know too much about those.

The cop waited while he hobbled to the car and helped him into the front seat. He tossed the crutches in the back.

"You better put on your seatbelt," the cop told him.

Tim noticed that the cop wasn't wearing his. He pointed to it.

The cop laughed.

"Okay, I'll wear mine, too."

They drove in silence for a while, neither one saying anything. Tim didn't know what to say. He'd never really talked to a cop before. But he wanted to say something, just so the cop wouldn't think he was a complete jerk. He just didn't know how.

He had trouble talking these days. The therapist said that his brain had been hurt because of the sickness and that he should take his time when he wanted to say something. Form the words in your head, the therapist said, and when you're sure, just say them. Tim tried it now.

"Where are we going to eat, Officer?" The words seemed to come out of his mouth in a single sound, all fast and jumbled up, the way he felt when he tripped on his crutches. Tim squeezed his eyes shut and wanted to scream. He couldn't even talk right, he couldn't do anything right, he wanted to get out of the car and run and just keep running until he was far away from everybody.

"We're going to a diner," the cop said. "You like diners?"

Tim opened his eyes. The cop had heard him. Maybe it wasn't as bad as he'd thought.

"Sure." He could always say that right.

"Good," the cop said. "One thing. Don't call me officer, okay?"

Tim nodded. No, it wasn't any good. He'd already

done something wrong and they hadn't been together for more than five minutes.

"Just call me Pat," the cop said. "That's my name. I'm Pat. You're Tim. Let's try it."

"Pat."

"Tim."

The cop grinned at him and Tim thought that maybe he'd done okay after all.

The cop helped him out of the car at the diner. It was a big place in New Jersey, and they had to park a long way from the entrance. Tim leaned against the side of the car and waited for the cop to get his crutches. Tim fitted them under each arm and they started walking. It was cold and there were patches of ice everywhere. Tim maneuvered around them carefully, taking his time so he wouldn't trip or fall down. The cop kept his hands in his pockets and walked beside him, letting him set the pace. Tim took it slow, just like his therapist had told him, and didn't fall once.

When they got inside, the cop told him to wait by the counter and disappeared into the big dining room. He was smiling when he came back.

"We're going to eat dinner with some friends of mine. Is that okay with you?"

"Sure," Tim said, and then what seemed like hours later, he added, "Pat."

A woman and a girl sat at the table, and he thought the woman was pretty but the girl looked a little scared. Like she might run away at any moment. If she was that scared, he thought, maybe they could run away together. He wanted to tell her that but was afraid he wouldn't be able to say it right, so he smiled and nodded his head and tried to make her understand that it was okay even if she didn't smile back because he understood.

He handed the cop his crutches and the woman held the chair out for him and he worked his way into the seat.

"Tim, this is Susan, and this is her daughter, Kimberly. This is Tim."

"Hi, Tim," the woman said. "I'm glad to meet you."

Tim nodded again. Then he looked at the girl and fought to get the words out.

"Hi, Kimberly."

The girl nodded and tried to smile. It looked like she was going to start crying. But she didn't. He was glad about that. He wouldn't know what to do if the girl started crying.

The woman looked at the cop and reached her hand across the table to take his.

"How are you, Pat?" she asked.

"I'm fine. How about you?"

"Working on it," she said.

The waitress brought their menus and gave them to the cop. He held them in his lap. He seemed very happy.

"Okay," he said. "Who wants a hamburger?"

By the year 2000, 2 out of 3 Americans could be illiterate.

It's true.

Today, 75 million adults...about one American in three, can't read adequately. And by the year 2000, U.S. News & World Report envisions an America with a literacy rate of only 30%.

Before that America comes to be, you can stop it...by joining the fight against illiteracy today.

Call the Coalition for Literacy at toll-free **1-800-228-8813** and volunteer.

Volunteer Against Illiteracy. The only degree you need is a degree of caring.